Praise for Martin Walker's

Bruno, Chief of Police series

"The delights of [Walker's Dordogne]—from the châteaus along the rivers to the prehistoric cave paintings to the food on the tables—are very real."
—*The New York Times Book Review*

"A satisfying and surprisingly intimate tour through a modern French village, full of character and charm."
—*The Arizona Republic*

"Sure to appeal to readers with a palate for mysteries with social nuance and understated charm."
—*The Wall Street Journal*

"Walker continues to write a series that remains inventive and yet retains its initial seductive charms."
—Popular Culture Association

"In Martin Walker's delightful series . . . the charm of rural France is regularly disrupted—but not too much."
—*The Seattle Times*

Martin Walker

Fatal Pursuit

Martin Walker is a senior fellow of the Global Business Policy Council, a private think tank based in Washington, D.C. He is also editor in chief emeritus and international affairs columnist at United Press International. His previous novels in the Bruno series are *Bruno, Chief of Police*; *The Dark Vineyard*; *Black Diamond*; *The Crowded Grave*; *The Devil's Cave*; *The Resistance Man*; *The Children Return*; and *The Patriarch*, all international bestsellers. He lives in Washington, D.C., and the Dordogne.

www.brunochiefofpolice.com

Fatal Pursuit

Fatal Pursuit

A MYSTERY OF THE FRENCH COUNTRYSIDE

Martin Walker

VINTAGE BOOKS
A Division of Penguin Random House LLC
New York

FIRST VINTAGE BOOKS EDITION, MAY 2017

Copyright © 2015 by Walker and Watson, Ltd.

All rights reserved. Published in the United States by Vintage Books, a division of Penguin Random House LLC, New York, and distributed in Canada by Random House of Canada, a division of Penguin Random House Canada Limited, Toronto. Originally published in hardcover, in slightly different form, in Great Britain as *The Dying Season* by Quercus Publishing PLC, London, in 2015, and subsequently published in hardcover in the United States by Alfred A. Knopf, a division of Penguin Random House LLC, New York, in 2016.

Vintage and colophon are registered trademarks of Penguin Random House LLC.

This is a work of fiction. Names, characters, places, and incidents either are the product of the author's imagination or are used fictitiously. Any resemblance to actual persons, living or dead, events or locales is entirely coincidental.

The Library of Congress has cataloged the Knopf edition as follows:
Walker, Martin.
Fatal Pursuit : a Bruno, chief of police novel /
by Martin Walker. — First United States Edition.
pages ; cm
I. Title.
PR6073.A413F38   2016   823'.914—dc23   2015030924

Vintage Books Trade Paperback ISBN: 978-1-101-97075-1
eBook ISBN: 978-1-101-94679-4

Map copyright © 2012 by Jamie Whyte

www.vintagebooks.com

Printed in the United States of America
10 9 8 7 6 5 4 3

To my fellow grand consuls of the Consulat de la Vinée de Bergerac, a body established in 1254 by King Henry III of England to ensure and uphold the quality of the wines of Bergerac, and later established under French law by King Charles IV in 1322, and by the National Assembly of the French Republic in 1954

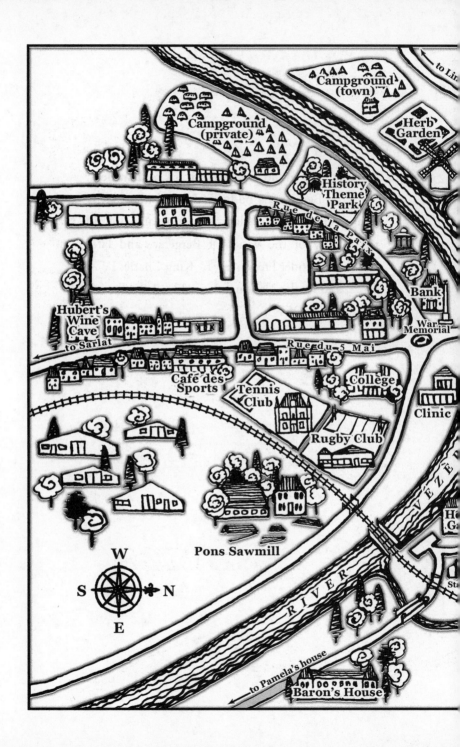

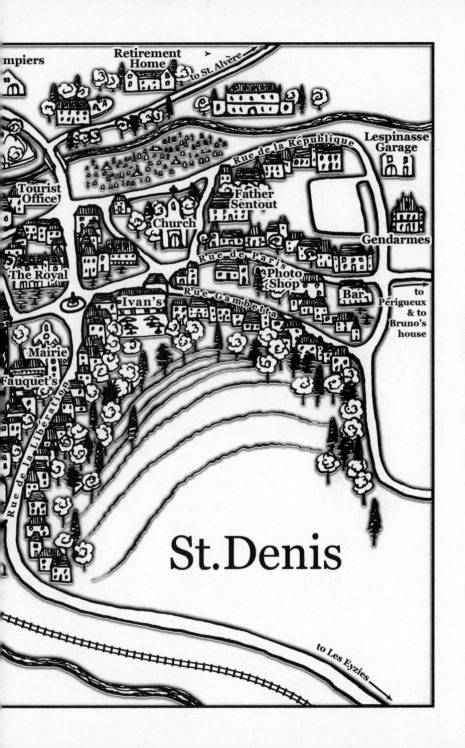

St.Denis

Fatal Pursuit

1

The lunar calendar said that the new moon made this a good day to plant broad beans, arugula and spinach, just as the previous days of a waning crescent moon were said to be the time to weed and to start a new compost heap. As Bruno Courrèges, chief of police of the small French town of St. Denis, planted the seeds he'd brought from his greenhouse, he wondered if this was some old wives' tale. Other gardeners he knew and trusted, prime among them the mayor of St. Denis, swore that the traditional ways of the lunar calendar worked for them, and there was no arguing with the quality of the generous crops they harvested. So when the mayor had given him a copy of the lunar almanac and advised him to try following its advice, Bruno thought he'd make the experiment. At the far side of his vegetable patch, his basset hound, Balzac, gazed at Bruno curiously, probably wondering why he was not allowed to play in this part of the garden.

"There is some science behind it," the mayor had insisted. "It's like the tides of the sea. The moon's gravity draws up the moisture in the soil when it's waxing and lets it down again when it's waning. So plant your aboveground vegetables when it's a waxing moon and your belowground ones when it's waning. It works for me."

The last of the seeds planted, Bruno used his watering can to sprinkle the ground and then stretched to ease his back, turning his face to the early morning sun. He'd picked the last of his vegetables when the moon had said the time was ripe, and some of them were already in the big stockpot he kept atop his wood-burning stove. Cooking a couple of quartered chickens with the carrots, onions and potatoes had made a plain but filling meal for his friends the previous evening. Now with some more vegetables and garlic and a pack of green lentils added, it would provide him and his dog with a hearty stew throughout the week.

Back in the house, Bruno heard his guests moving around upstairs in the new bedroom he'd built under the roof. He added some logs from his woodpile to the stove, closed the damper and then reopened it a notch. It would keep the place warm all day and let the stockpot cook slowly, the way he liked it. He poured the last of the previous evening's wine into the stew and added some hot water.

He wanted to clean his Land Rover and get to the tennis club early for the meeting and subsequent parade of classic cars, a new event in the calendar of St. Denis. His houseguests would get there on their own. Despite the work he had put into organizing the event, Bruno had never thought of himself as a car enthusiast. He did not read car magazines, and he seldom recognized the make of a new car until he saw its insignia. He put fuel in one end of his own vehicles and water in the other and expected them to function; they were merely tools to take people or goods from one place to another. He entrusted their repair and maintenance to experts and assumed they would be more or less efficient. He had driven many different vehicles, military and civilian. These days he mostly drove the utility police vans supplied to him by his employer, the mayor and council of St. Denis, or the aged Land

Rover he had inherited from a hunting friend and for which he had developed a surprising affection.

The Land Rover was not a comfortable vehicle to drive, built before the modern conveniences of adjustable seats, power steering and antilock brakes. Indeed, it was nearly twenty years older than Bruno. He had been surprised to learn this qualified it as a classic car. But it could go just about anywhere—cross rivers, climb the steepest and most muddy slopes and negotiate the most-rock-strewn trails through the woods where he hunted the region's abundant game. And it had never let him down. This was more than he could say for some of the fancy cars his friends drove, which seemed to require the skills of a computer expert as much as a traditional car mechanic. In his days in the French army, Bruno had driven jeeps, trucks, motorcycles and even the occasional armored car. He had a painful memory of the deafening and bone-shaking experience of driving an AMX-30, France's main battle tank, on the testing grounds at Saumur and had vowed never to repeat it. Forty tons was more than Bruno felt he could handle, particularly when the instructor had closed the driver's hatch so that Bruno's vision was limited to two narrow slits and a blurry periscope. Driving held little appeal for him ever since.

Bruno took little pleasure in driving fast and had been called to the scene of too many road accidents to push his limited skills. He had once been taken frighteningly fast around a course by a skilled rally driver, his friend Annette, a magistrate in Sarlat. She had skidded around bends, missed trees by inches and accelerated over the crests of hills in a way that Bruno's head repeatedly slammed against the roof of her specially equipped Peugeot. Bruno thought he had been saved from unconsciousness only by the helmet she had supplied. Such driving was not for him. Bruno's sole ambitions as a driver were to be competent and safe.

This morning Bruno skipped his usual morning run so that he could wash and polish the Land Rover. He had scrubbed the mud from the wheel wells and used a touch-up pen to cover the deeper scratches in the faded-green paint. He had wiped clean the canvas-covered seats and washed the windows, inside and out. He had swept out the dust and gravel from the interior. He had tidied up the rear, putting his tennis gear in one bag, his rugby boots and tracksuit in another and his all-weather garments and hunting clothes in a third.

He had washed the dog blanket that now nestled between the bags, where Balzac could rest while waiting for his master. A newly washed bowl and fresh water bottle stood ready for Balzac's refreshment. When Bruno drove, Balzac preferred to ride on the passenger seat where he could watch the road and landscape and, in the absence of a car radio, listen to Bruno sing. Other than his occasional attendance at church or on convivial evenings at the rugby club, Bruno had sufficient regard for the comfort of his fellow humans to reserve his singing for his Land Rover and his shower.

As Bruno, freshly showered and changed, drove into town, Balzac seemed to appreciate his owner's version of "Que Reste-t-il de Nos Amours?" Bruno tried to catch the breathy, almost-playful tones of the Charles Trenet 1943 original. For Bruno, no other version would do, although most French singers had made their own recordings, singing it too slowly or making it too sad, Bruno thought. His own mood when he thought of his past love affairs was of fond nostalgia rather than tragic loss. The memories made him grateful rather than despondent, so as Bruno pulled his unusually clean and gleaming car into the parking lot by the tennis club, he was pleased to see a familiar ancient Citroën *deux-chevaux.*

Pamela, its owner and the woman who had recently ended

their affair, was standing nearby and admiring the baron's venerable 1958 Citroën DS, which still looked more modern than most of the vehicles on the road. The baron was leaning with one elbow on the roof of his car as he chatted with Pamela and gestured proudly at his second car, the old French military jeep that he used for hunting. It was being driven today by Sergeant Jules from the gendarmerie. Pamela waved and beckoned Bruno to join them as he let Balzac jump out of the car and scamper across to her. He waved back but went to greet his two houseguests, who had followed in their own car, and led them across the parking lot to meet his friends.

It was a fine turnout for the classic-car meeting, thought Bruno proudly, and a very international gathering. His English friend Jack Crimson was at the wheel of his white Jaguar Mark 2, his daughter, Miranda, beside him. Horst, a German archaeologist, was dressed for the part, wearing white gloves and a flat cap as he helped Clothilde, curator of the local prehistory museum, from the seat of her Porsche Speedster. A retired Dutch architect had brought his boxy DAF Variomatic, and someone else had an elderly Saab. Lespinasse from the garage was dusting his perfectly restored Citroën *traction-avant* from 1938, which was the oldest car of the gathering. To Bruno's eye the most striking vehicle was a white E-type Jaguar. From its passenger seat Annette was waving at him, a good-looking and fair-haired stranger at the wheel beside her.

"Meet George Young, an English friend," Annette said to Bruno as he approached, her hand on the young man's arm. "He's from London, where he runs a company bringing British drivers over to take part in French rallies and races. I met him at the Rallye des Remparts in Angoulême, and I persuaded him to bring his Jaguar to St. Denis for our parade. He's going to navigate for me at the rally tomorrow."

Her voice was animated, almost giddy, and she turned back with a shyly affectionate look at her companion as the two men shook hands, and then Bruno introduced his two guests from Alsace. It was about time Annette found herself a boyfriend, thought Bruno. The Englishman looked very suitable. He was about Bruno's height, slim but with powerful shoulders and a friendly smile. His French was fluent as he chatted to the couple from Alsace about his visit—he called it a pilgrimage—to the Bugatti collection at the Musée National de l'Automobile in Mulhouse, near their home.

From the corner of his eye, Bruno saw movement in the woods behind the tennis club and recognized a sullen, skinny teenager named Félix lurking in the trees. Félix was a truant who shunned the tennis and rugby lessons Bruno offered to the other students in the town's *collège*. He was the youngest child of two parents now well into in their fifties. The older siblings had long since left home, and the father had been unemployed for years. His mother, from a French island in the Caribbean, was a cleaning woman at the school. She had bequeathed to her son a skin just a shade or two darker than café au lait, which meant some cruel schoolmates sneered at him as a *métis,* a "half-caste." Félix had suffered a number of brushes with the law for shoplifting, petty vandalism and one case of joyriding in a stolen car. Bruno reminded himself to check on the boy's age; once he was sixteen, his next offense could mean juvenile detention. Bruno was disappointed that he'd never been able to straighten the boy out; he thought of Félix as one of his failures.

"Him again," said Yveline, commandant of the small gendarmerie in St. Denis, who had suddenly appeared at Bruno's side. She was in uniform. "You know we're going to have a lot of trouble with that kid."

"We already have," said Bruno. He gave Félix a stern stare, so the boy would know Bruno had his eye on him, before leading his friends to join a group congregating at a long trestle table set up in front of the club. One of the waitresses from Fauquet's café was serving croissants and *pains au chocolat* and dispensing coffee from two large thermoses to the gathering of drivers.

Bruno had chosen this spot for the cars to assemble, away from the main road and out of sight of the crowds who were expected to line the main streets for the parade. He had almost finished his coffee when two strikingly modern cars arrived. Fabiola was at the wheel of her new Renault Zoe electric car, and behind her came Alphonse, the town's only councillor from the Green Party, in his electric Kangoo van. Alphonse had persuaded the mayor to make a nod to the environment by welcoming electric cars into St. Denis's first Concours d'Élégance. That was the title Annette had dreamed up for what Bruno thought of simply as a vintage-car parade, one of the events marking the name day of St. Denis on October 9.

The idea had come from the baron over a rugby club dinner at the start of the year when the mayor had been thinking aloud about ways to extend the local tourist season beyond the summer months. The first idea had been a visitors' day at the town vineyard, then Stéphane had suggested a special rugby match, and Lespinasse had proposed a sports-car rally. That might usefully be combined with a vintage-car parade, suggested the baron, always keen to show off his splendid Citroën. Bruno had remained silent, knowing that whatever plans were made he'd be the one assigned by the mayor to turn them into reality.

It had been Xavier, the efficient deputy mayor, who had opened his diary and reminded his companions that the date fell on the weekend when the delegation from St. Denis's twin town in Alsace came for its annual visit. They came each year to commemorate the welcome the refugees from Alsace had been given in 1939 and 1940. The first came just after war had been declared in September 1939, when the French government evacuated to the Périgord the civilians from the regions near the German frontier. The following year, after the German reoccupation of Alsace and Lorraine, German settlers were moved in, and Alsatians of French stock were deported. Most of them came to the Périgord. Inevitably, in the four years before France's liberation, friendships were forged and marriages took place, and after the war towns throughout Alsace twinned with those where they had been welcomed.

So the weekend of the town's name day now included a special market with stalls and vendors from Alsace, a rugby match with a team from Marckolsheim and a visitors' day at the vineyard followed by a feast. Lespinasse had arranged that St. Denis would at the same time host the regional heats for the French rally drivers' championship. Father Sentout had arranged a choral service for two choirs with his counterpart from Alsace, and Antoine the boatman had organized a fishing competition. Bruno had been assigned to coordinate it all and to arrange a fireworks display to round off the celebration. It was not what he had been trained to do in his course at the police academy, but this role as impresario of civic events gave Bruno great pleasure. It had also established a firm friendship with his Alsatian counterpart, Thomas, who with his wife was staying at Bruno's home for the weekend, just as Bruno had been their guest during his visits to Alsace for the twin-town reunions.

"I don't see Sylvestre," said Thomas, a worried look on his weather-beaten face. "He's a friend from Marckolsheim, and we're counting on him to bring something very special for the parade. I hope he hasn't lost his way."

Thomas and his wife were devoted hikers, striding across the Vosges near their home most weekends and spending their summer vacations walking in the Alps. Bruno recalled with respect the pace they had set on a long day's hike from Colmar to Mulhouse on his last visit to Alsace. A few years older than Bruno, Thomas was trim and fit, a few centimeters taller than Bruno. His wife, Ingrid, looked equally healthy, despite the bottles of Alsace wine they had brought and downed at Bruno's dinner table the previous evening.

"I'd better give the drivers their briefing," said Bruno, looking at his watch. "It's almost time to begin."

Thomas pulled out his cell phone to call Sylvestre as Ingrid turned to embrace Fabiola and Pamela, whom she had met at Bruno's dinner the previous evening. Bruno took from his shoulder bag a sheaf of photocopies he'd made of the route the drivers would take through St. Denis and began handing them out. Each photocopy carried a number, indicating the order in which the cars would start.

"If I could have your attention," he began, using his parade-ground voice. "The route of our motorcade is clearly marked on your maps. Please set off in order of the number on your map. We'll go through the main streets before turning onto the quayside, where we'll park on the long stretch before the bridge. Please park as I do, facing the stone wall and with your back to the river. Leave enough space for people to walk all around the cars, and keep an eye on your vehicles in case kids try to climb in. I'll lead the way, so nobody should get lost. The baron will bring up the rear in his Citroën DS. And I'd like you to keep at least two car lengths' distance from the vehicle ahead."

As he finished, what looked like a furniture truck turned the corner, sounded its horn and pulled up on the street, too big to fit into the already crowded parking lot. Two young men in white overalls, white skullcaps and goggles jumped from the driving compartment, waved at the crowd and went to the rear of the truck. One opened the big double doors while the other pulled out a long ramp, lowered it to the ground and then clambered inside. Bruno heard the sound of a powerful engine being started, dying with a ragged cough and then starting again. A large cloud of exhaust smoke drifted from the rear of the truck, and then a bright blue, open-topped racing car from another era backed down the ramp.

The windshield was no more than four inches in height and the hood took up two-thirds of the car's length. The front wheels and axle were at the very front of the vehicle, ahead of the curved, flat radiator. Leading back from the driver's seat, the sides of the car curved in to form a pointed rear that looked as sharp as an ax blade. There were no mudguards above the wheels, and a spare tire was attached to the car's side with thick leather straps. The driver revved the engine and unleashed a harsh and potent roar before turning and driving slowly to face the crowd that had been stunned into silence. Bruno could read the red badge on the arch-shaped radiator: BUGATTI.

"Sylvestre always likes to make an entrance," Ingrid said drily once the throaty roar of the engine had quieted. "That's the one he bought last year. He paid seven hundred thousand euros, and he says it's worth a lot more now."

"A Type 35 from 1928, the car that made Bugatti's name," said Thomas, something close to reverence in his voice. "It was the only car of its day that could be driven both on the road and in Grand Prix races. And despite the name, it's a French car, designed and built in Alsace."

"It won every race going," said Young, Annette's friend, in a worshipful tone. "It took the world championship in 1926 and the Targa Florio five years in a row." He moved forward to help the driver from the cockpit and, as if suddenly released from bondage, the rest of the crowd surged forward to cluster around the small Bugatti.

"Welcome," said Bruno, introducing himself and handing the driver his photocopied map. "We're honored to have your car here. You're number nineteen, next to last in the parade. You'll follow the *traction-avant* and be just ahead of the DS."

"Thank you, and please call me Sylvestre," said the man in white, pushing his goggles back onto his brow. He looked to be in his thirties. He had bright blue eyes, a prominent nose and a firm jaw. The grip of his handshake was unnecessarily strong but his smile was affable.

"This is my friend, Freddy, he's from India," Sylvestre said, beckoning forward his companion, also in white overalls. "We're both glad to be here. My grandmother told me a lot about this place. She was born just outside St. Denis, and I thought this was a good opportunity to take a look at some property she left me." His expression was arrogant, almost haughty, as he gazed around at the crowd, before raising his voice to ask, "And which of these charming ladies would like to ride in the Bugatti with me?"

Sylvestre's eyes settled briefly on Fabiola, standing alone. "How about you, mademoiselle?"

"Thanks, but I'm driving my own car, the new Renault," she replied coolly. "We have electric cars in the parade."

"Excellent," said Sylvestre, and looked at Bruno. "In that case, would you have room for one more? I've got a Tesla in the back of the truck, and Freddy can drive it."

Suddenly he seemed aware of Félix, who had somehow pushed himself forward to stand at the side of the Bugatti and gaze reverently into the driving compartment.

"What about you, young man. Would you like to take a spin?" Sylvestre asked. And with what Bruno thought was an understandable glance of triumph at him, Félix clambered inside and seemed to glow with pride as he took his seat. He looked up at Sylvestre in awe.

Bruno had heard of the Tesla, an American-made electric

sports car that ran on some revolutionary new battery, but he'd never seen one. Freddy clambered into the back of the big truck and backed out a sleek gray car. When Sylvestre turned off the Bugatti's engine, Bruno realized that the Tesla was utterly, eerily silent.

2

Shortly after the motorcade had ended and the cars were parked along the quayside, the crowds that had been cheering were now thronging noisily down the steps to the riverbank, when Bruno felt his phone vibrate. He could barely make out that Dr. Gelletreau was reporting a death. Bruno found his way clear of the crowds so he could hear more clearly.

The doctor told him that an elderly man in Savignac-de-Miremont had been found dead by his wife when she returned from visiting her sister. She had immediately called him. The doctor said the cause of death appeared to be a heart attack. The town wasn't in the commune of St. Denis, but, as a courtesy, Bruno took care of birth and death registration for the small neighboring communes, hence the call. He went in search of the mayor to explain why he had to leave and found him admiring the Bugatti with the wide-eyed look of a little boy. Bruno entrusted his dog to Thomas and Ingrid and headed for the gendarmerie, where he had parked his official police van.

The commune of Savignac was composed mostly of farms, woods and meadows, its village tiny. There were barely a hundred people in the whole commune, so at some point almost every adult had to take his or her turn in being a member of the local council. Henri-Pierre Hugon, the dead man, had been serving his third term. That was why Bruno found his house easily. In rural areas, friends and neighbors erect at the home of each new council member a tall pole, bedecked with French flags and laurel wreaths and a sign saying HONOR TO THOSE WE ELECT. Bruno followed Dr. Gelletreau's directions until he saw the pole, its flags now somewhat faded, and turned in to see the doctor's elderly Citroën. The plump old man came to the door as Bruno pulled in.

"How goes the old-car parade?" Gelletreau asked, shaking hands. "I'm hoping I'll be in time to see them all. Somebody at the clinic told me there's one of those lovely E-type Jaguars. This shouldn't take long. Madame Hugon is bearing up very well. In fact she's making us some coffee. As soon as you've finished, I'll call the undertakers."

"Has he been dead long?" Bruno asked.

"He died in his study, and the light was on, so I think it was sometime yesterday evening," the doctor replied. "The central heating was on, which means the body temperature doesn't tell us much. I've been treating him for heart trouble for several years, since he was working in Périgueux. I've had him on beta-blockers, and he'd been very overweight as long as I've known him, even more than me. You knew him, didn't you?"

"Only to say hello to, mainly through SHAP, and I have a copy of his book at home," Bruno said. "He made his living as a researcher. I don't think I know his wife."

SHAP was the Society for the History and Archaeology of the Périgord, a body of local enthusiasts and scholars who held monthly meetings and organized lectures in a splendid sixteenth-century townhouse in the heart of Périgueux. The mayor had been a member for years and had encouraged Bruno to join, for which he was grateful. He tried never to miss the sessions and remembered with pleasure lectures he'd heard on the diet of the prehistoric peoples of the region, the development of medieval castle design and on that brief period in the sixteenth century when Bergerac had been the capital of France, or at least of the Protestants rallying to King Henri IV. He'd also heard the dead man give a memorably dry lecture on Périgueux during World War II, during which few in the audience managed to stay awake. SHAP had helped Hugon publish his book, an encyclopedia of the members of the Resistance in the Périgord. Hugon had spent his life working as an archivist for the *département* and since his retirement had continued to visit the archives regularly in his new role as freelance historian and researcher. He was invariably neatly dressed, and Bruno had heard he was a meticulous worker with a good reputation among local lawyers and notaries.

"How old was he?" Bruno asked.

"He'd have been seventy-five next month. But he never exercised, always down in those gloomy archives. He lived a very sedentary life, and he was a smoker."

Once indoors, Bruno gave his condolences to Madame Hugon, accepted a cup of coffee and asked when she had found her husband.

"About an hour ago, when I got back, maybe it was a bit more than that," she said. Madame Hugon was dry eyed and composed, with no sign of shock or grief. Her hair was white, and she looked to be about the same age as her husband but in much-better health. Short and slim, she wore lace-up flat shoes, a dark skirt and a light blue blouse.

"I'd been at my sister's in Sarlat for a few days. She has a new grandchild. My nephew drove me back because he wanted to see the old-car parade, and Henri had needed the car while I was away. He was working on a big research job and needed to go back and forth to Périgueux and Bordeaux. I'd left meals in the freezer for him."

Her nephew had dropped her at the house, and she'd let herself in. The front door had not been locked. She'd called for her husband, gotten no reply and found him dead on the floor beside the desk in his study. She had touched his cheek, found it cold and called Dr. Gelletreau.

"You didn't call the *urgences*?" Bruno asked. The *pompiers* of the St. Denis fire brigade provided the local emergency service.

"There was no point. He'd obviously been dead for hours. The doctor kept warning him this might happen, but Henri never listened." She shrugged and then looked at Dr. Gelletreau. "He hadn't touched those meals I'd left for him, and from the dishes he'd left in the sink it looks like he'd lived on steaks and fried potatoes, all those things you'd told him not to eat."

"I'm sorry for your loss," Bruno said. "I'd better take a look in the study. What was this big research job he was doing?"

"He'd been at it for a couple of months, five days a week. But he never told me what it was, just something about the war and the Resistance. But he said he'd make enough from it for us to have a nice vacation in the sun this winter. He used to get a hundred and fifty euros a day for his research work. I'd always wanted to see Morocco, and I was looking forward to it."

"Do you know who hired him?" Bruno asked. She shook her head, and Bruno did the math as Gelletreau led the way into the study, where the desk lamp was still lit. If Hugon had been working on a research project for two months he'd have earned six thousand euros, a tidy sum.

In the study, a chair had been overturned, and Hugon's plump body lay sprawled beside it, one leg partly under the desk. His right hand was clutching at his shirtfront, and his face looked as though he'd died in pain, his lips drawn back from his teeth. On his desk was a lamp, an old-fashioned telephone, a blank message pad with a pencil lined up neatly beside it and a closed laptop computer. The printer was on a small side table, switched off, with no printouts in the out-tray.

There was no sign of a diary or notebook that gave a clue to his research. The drawers of the two filing cabinets against the wall were closed. Bruno slipped on a set of evidence gloves and opened each drawer in turn. Most of the files were organized alphabetically and seemed to reflect the names of the people included in his encyclopedia. One file marked "Current Projects" was empty. His bank statements showed no unusual activity, just his pension payments, reimbursements from medical insurance and some modest bank transfers from lawyers, presumably research fees. There was no sign of the six thousand euros. So where was the account book he would have to keep for tax records?

In the bookcase, filled with well-thumbed works of reference, there were two shelves filled with hardback notebooks, covered in black leather and much too big to fit into a pocket. Bruno leafed through them. Hugon's handwriting was neat and precise, and every entry was dated. They were filed in order. The last one on the bookshelf ended with an entry for July 30 of that year. There was no sign of any current notebook, just two virgin notebooks, ready for use.

The only item in the wastepaper basket was an empty envelope from France Télécom. It was postmarked two days earlier, so it had probably been delivered the previous day. Bruno found a file for phone bills. In the past two months there had been far more calls than usual, including daily calls to and from a mobile number that did not feature in earlier bills. Bruno took out his own phone and dialed the number, but an automated reply said the number was no longer available. That was odd. He called the security line for France Télécom and was told the number belonged to an unregistered pay-as-you-go phone.

Bruno went back to Madame Hugon to ask if she knew the

password for the laptop. She shook her head: nor did she recognize the phone number. She added that her husband had kept his diary and account books in his desk, unless he was going to the archives, when they'd be in his briefcase.

"They aren't there now," said Bruno. "And there's no sign of the briefcase."

"Maybe he left them in the car," she said with a shrug, not seeming much concerned.

The briefcase was in the car, but it contained only blank notepads, pens, a copy of the previous day's *Sud Ouest* and a half-empty pack of Royale cigarettes. Bruno went back to the body and found a wallet in the hip pocket. Inside were the usual identity, health and credit cards, along with five crisp, new two-hundred-euro banknotes. Bruno asked where Hugon had kept his clothes and was shown to a wardrobe in the marital bedroom. He checked the pockets of the jackets and the bedside tables but found nothing.

"Was there any sign that anybody else might have been in the house while you were away?" Bruno asked Madame Hugon.

She shook her head. "Not that I noticed. We never had many visitors, except for my sister."

"Did you have any unusual visitors in recent days?" She shook her head. "Did he seem worried by anything?"

"Far from it. He was pleased to have this new research project. Henri liked it when he was busy. He was never one to hang around the house, and he didn't watch much television. There was nothing he liked more than poking around old archives, and getting paid for it was even better."

"Was he working very hard?" Gelletreau asked.

"More than usual. He was in his study until all hours, night after night. But that wasn't so unusual when he had his teeth into something. It was like when he was writing that book. But it didn't seem like it was a strain. It was work, but the kind of work he liked. It always cheered him up to be on the trail of something."

"Did he always work on the laptop, or did he work with documents?"

"Both. He had a big file of papers he'd collected, but he always had one of those black notebooks going as well."

"There's a file marked 'Current Projects' in the filing cabinet, but it's empty and the last entry in the latest black notebook was for sometime in July. So where's the one for August and September?"

"I don't know. Maybe he left it at the archives in Périgueux. They'd always let him leave stuff in a desk."

Bruno went into the kitchen and looked at the dirty dishes in the sink and piled up on the draining board, as if Hugon planned to leave them for his wife to wash on her return. There were four or five dinner plates, smeared with grease, some wineglasses and bowls that might have held soup or breakfast cereal.

"He used the good coffee cups; that's not like him," she said, sounding surprised for the first time since Bruno's arrival. There were three dirty coffee cups beside the sink, all piled together as if they had been used at the same time.

"Did he drink much?" Bruno asked, eyeing three empty bottles of Bergerac red wine, an undistinguished brand that Bruno recognized from the local supermarket.

"He liked his glass of Ricard before dinner and red wine with his meals, just a glass or two. Dr. Gelletreau had told him to cut back on his drinking."

"How long were you away?" Bruno asked.

"Just the three nights."

"So he got through three bottles in three days. That seems like quite a lot for a man on his own."

She frowned, something like distaste in her expression. "I

think he usually drank more when I wasn't here, just like he'd go back to his steaks rather than defrost those nice meals I made."

Gelletreau nodded sagely. "He was never what I'd call a good patient. You can give them all the advice in the world but if they don't want to take it . . ."

Bruno thanked Madame Hugon and asked her if she wanted him to call anybody, perhaps her sister or a priest? She shook her head, saying she'd already called her sister in Sarlat to tell her of the death, and her husband had never been a churchgoer. Once the undertaker had taken the body to the funeral home, she'd drive back to Sarlat and stay there.

"I might put the house on the market," she added.

In the garden, Bruno asked Dr. Gelletreau if he'd signed the death certificate yet.

"No, I was waiting for you to arrive," the doctor said, a little stiffly. Sometime earlier he'd been embarrassed after putting down "Natural Causes" on a death certificate when Bruno had later discovered that the victim had been murdered.

"I don't like this," Bruno said. "All that cash in his wallet, the disappearance of his diary and account book, those phone calls . . ."

"And the three coffee cups," said Gelletreau. "Still, I'm pretty sure it was a heart attack. You saw the way he was clutching his chest. It doesn't look much like a murder to me. Hugon was a heart attack waiting to happen. And he certainly died yesterday."

"So if his wife has an alibi from her family in Sarlat . . . ," said Bruno, thinking aloud.

"If that's the case you've got a real mystery on your hands, unless you've got another one of your hunches."

Bruno looked back at the house, pulled out his phone and called his friend Jean-Jacques, the chief detective for the *département,* to explain his suspicions.

"What does the doc say?" J-J replied.

"Heart attack, looks natural enough."

"And the wife? Does she think it was a natural death?"

"Yes. She found the body after staying with family in Sarlat for a few days, and she doesn't seem concerned. It's just me who thinks there's more to this than meets the eye."

"*Merde,* there's no sign of any struggle, the doctor and the widow aren't worried, and you know the state of my budget and what we have to pay to get an autopsy done. If it wasn't you saying this, Bruno . . ." J-J's voice trailed off. "Who's the doctor present? Is it Fabiola?"

"Dr. Gelletreau seems ready to sign the death certificate, citing cardiac arrest."

J-J grunted. "Well, we can always ask for a second opinion. See if you can persuade Fabiola to take a look at the body when the undertaker comes for it. If she thinks it's worth having an autopsy, I'll go along. By the way, have you heard anything from Isabelle?"

"Not lately," Bruno replied cautiously. In his own paternal way, J-J was almost as devoted as Bruno to Isabelle and claimed she was the best detective he'd ever trained. He'd never abandoned hope that Isabelle might one day give up her meteoric career, first in Paris and then with Eurojust in The Hague, and return to the Périgord to be his successor as chief detective.

"Word from Paris is that she's had some trouble in some big operation in Luxembourg, ruffling a lot of diplomatic feathers."

"That's news to me," said Bruno, making an effort to keep his voice neutral. He knew he would never stop caring about her. "But you know Isabelle, she'll find some way to turn it to her advantage."

"I thought maybe the brigadier might have said something," J-J said. "I know he's more in touch with you than with me, for which on the whole I'm very grateful. It always means trouble when he's around."

"I haven't heard from him for a while," Bruno replied. The brigadier, a senior figure in the Ministry of the Interior with wide-ranging responsibilities in security matters, had been Isabelle's boss before she transferred to Eurojust. "And diplomatic trouble sounds way above my pay grade."

"Probably above mine, too. Still, Isabelle always trusted your hunches, and I've learned there's usually something to them," J-J said.

3

"This event has been a great success," said the mayor, leaning back in his chair with a glass of wine and staring contentedly at the crowded tables that filled the winery. "Our vintage cars made the TV news, thanks to that old Bugatti, and Fauquet's café was packed all day. And just look at this turnout tonight! We'll have to start doing this every year."

He raised his glass in thanks to his companions at the table, the same group that had devised the idea at the rugby club dinner. That means more work for me again next year, thought Bruno, clinking his glass against the mayor's, but he was pleased that the car show had brought in a crowd. Mauricette had told him her hotel had never before been full so early in the season. She'd devised a special offer for the weekend that had attracted the tourists who liked the idea of a winery dinner without the risk of being Breathalyzed on a long drive home. And after the TV and radio publicity for the *concours,* a lot more people were expected the next day to watch the rally. Bruno had spent most of Friday checking on the safety barriers along the route, and once the rally was over he'd have to help the farmers pick up the hay bales they had placed at every corner.

At a sign from Julien, who ran the town vineyard, the mayor

rose to his feet and went to the dais that stood in front of the stacked wine barrels at the end of the winery. There wasn't much space, with the drums, guitars and keyboard for that evening's music and dancing already in place. More barrels stood against the wall, and between them were long rows of tables and chairs, all filled with people who had paid twenty euros a head for the vineyard dinner of soup, pâté, roast duck, cheese with salad and a piece of walnut tart. As much wine as they wanted was included in the price of their meal, all of it from the town vineyard. Most of the diners had also bought tickets for the raffle, five euros for six chances to win. Tapping an empty bottle with a fork, the mayor called for silence and announced that the drawing was about to take place. The first prize was a case of a dozen bottles of the local wine, the second prize was six bottles, and there were three third prizes of two bottles each.

"Would our lovely ladies come forward, please, to draw the winning tickets?" the mayor said, and Fabiola, Annette and Florence joined him on the dais, Fabiola shaking her head in mock despair at the mayor's old-fashioned way of introducing them. He identified each of them as they joined him on the dais: Fabiola as one of the town's doctors, Annette as the local magistrate and star rally driver, and Florence as the science teacher at the *collège*.

"We didn't have teachers or doctors or magistrates like these when I was a boy," the mayor said. "But because we all want to wish Annette the best of luck in tomorrow's rally, I'll ask her to wait a little so she can draw the ticket for the first prize. Florence, please draw three tickets for the third prizes. And Fabiola will draw the ticket for the second prize."

The third and second prizes went to strangers, which was as it should be, thought Bruno, hoping that a tourist would also win the first prize. Each winner had been cheered by his and her neighbors at the various tables, but then a silence fell as Annette reached into the bucket to draw out the winning ticket. She read out the number.

"That's me," called out a male voice, and Bruno saw the Bugatti owner, Sylvestre, rise in his place and clasp his hands above his head in victory. Then he raised his voice to call across the tables to the mayor.

"Have another drawing. I donate my prize back to you." He paused and grinned around the winery. "I can't drink, I'm driving."

He sat down to a round of applause. Annette drew again, and this time Bruno cheered when his friend Ingrid rose to claim the prize. The mayor made a point of saying how pleased he was that the prize went to someone from their twin town in Alsace, adding that the visiting delegation would be at the St. Denis market the next morning, offering their wines and crafts and special foodstuffs.

"And then our local restaurants and producers will offer a food market in the main square after the end of the race, just as we do each Tuesday evening in July and August," the mayor went on. "There'll be roast chicken from rotisseries, hams grilled over open fires, snails, *moules frites,* along with salads, pizzas and apple pies, and wine from the town vineyard. So we'll hope to see you again tomorrow. Now it's time to dance."

He stepped down, and St. Denis's own rock band took its place on the dais. Lespinasse from the garage started with a drum roll. His son Édouard was on bass, Robert the singing architect on rhythm, and Patrick from the Maison de la Presse played lead guitar. Jean-Paul, the church organist, who was also the local piano teacher, climbed up to join them with his accordion around his neck and began with the theme from "Mon Amant de St. Jean." A classic from the bal musette dance halls of the 1930s and recently revived on one of the best-selling CDs in France, it was a song known to all present. Bruno led Florence to the dance floor and saw Fabiola and Gilles, Thomas and Ingrid, Annette and her Englishman, come to join them, and suddenly the floor was full. A cheer went up when the mayor joined them with his friend Jacqueline just as Robert was singing the line about how the girl knew the young man was lying to her, but she liked him anyway.

The music went on with the band's usual mix of Édith Piaf, sixties classics, Johnny Cash and Francis Cabrel numbers until Florence and Annette said they were thirsty and hauled the two men back to their table for more wine. Annette kept her hand in Young's as they sat, and Bruno wondered if Young knew that Annette was the daughter of an extremely rich and controversial financier.

"I'm so glad Sylvestre brought his Bugatti. It was the star of the show," said Annette, over the sound of the music. She gave Young a fond look. "How did you persuade him to come?"

"He didn't need much persuading," Young replied. "He told me he'd been planning to come down here to see some family property, and the chance of winning a Concours d'Élégance was too tempting to pass up. Even if nobody outside the Périgord has heard of the St. Denis *concours,* he reckons the title will raise the price of the Bugatti when he wants to sell it."

"If I had a car like that, I'd never let it go," said Florence so firmly that Bruno and the others turned to look at her. "I'm not really a car person, and I can't say I think of it as good to look at in a conventional way. It was too brutal, too arrogant, in the way it seemed to embody raw power, but it still struck me as extraordinarily beautiful." She paused, and then tossed her head and laughed, trying to shift the mood that she had suddenly made serious. "Anyway, I'd be far too terrified even to think about driving some mechanical beast like that. But there was something very special about the way it sounded."

"A mere seven hundred thousand and it's yours," said Bruno, grinning. "I heard that was what he paid for it. I had no idea they were worth so much. How about that E-type of yours?" he asked Young. "What's that worth?"

"I got it years ago as a wreck for the equivalent of eight thousand euros, restored it myself, and now it's probably worth a hundred grand," Young replied. "I put years of work into it because that's the only way I was able to afford it. The old Porsche that was in the parade will probably be worth about the same. If you cleaned up that Land Rover, you'd get a pretty good price. What year was it built?"

"Nineteen fifty-four," said Bruno. He remembered Hercule, the friend who had bequeathed it to him, saying that he'd been in the French army, fighting in Vietnam, the year his Land Rover was made. Bruno knew that 1954 was a year of special significance for his friend, the year of the French defeat at Dien Bien Phu. Hercule had bought the vehicle decades later, when he'd taken his pension and settled down in the Périgord to hunt and raise truffles.

"Fully restored, you might get fifty or sixty thousand," said Young. "It's a booming market, now that the Arabs and Chinese are getting into classic cars. They want them as investments. Driving the cars is just the icing on the cake. That's how Sylvestre does so well with his auctions. He's already got a showroom in Dubai, and he's planning to open another one in Shanghai. I know he's expecting to get at least a million for his Bugatti, and I presume that's how he plans to finance his Chinese operation."

Florence rolled her eyes, and Bruno shook his head, stunned by the figures he was hearing.

"Is that how you got to know Sylvestre, through these classic-car sales?" Florence asked Young.

"In a way; I first met him at an auction in England a couple of years ago, but we've met since at several rallies. He's a very good driver, and unlike me he's got the money to pursue his hobby seriously."

Young explained that he'd first noticed Sylvestre bidding for a Ferrari Modena Spider. He himself had dropped out when the price reached a hundred thousand pounds, about a hundred and thirty thousand euros. The auction was held at the old Goodwood racetrack, and it had gone down in history because a 1954 Mercedes Formula 1 racing car went for just under thirty million dollars, still the record for a public auction.

"The real money tends to be restricted to private auctions," Young added. "A Ferrari 250 GTO is supposed to have gone for over thirty million at a private auction in Italy, though it may just be rumor. Those private events are by invitation only, and I'm not on the list for any of those. Sylvestre gets invited to them, probably because of his Dubai connections."

"It makes my Land Rover seem cheap," Bruno said. "Are these classic-car sales the way Sylvestre made his money?"

"No, you have to start with a lot of money to get into the game. His family in Alsace is into property, and I gather they're very rich and own shopping malls and office blocks, but I don't know the details. We're quite friendly and usually have a drink or a meal together when we meet up or when Sylvestre comes to London, but I couldn't claim that we're close friends. He's a prickly type, a bit arrogant, but he certainly knows his way around cars."

"Talking about our neighbor Sylvestre?" came the voice of Bruno's friend Thomas, Ingrid on his arm.

"We were just hearing about Sylvestre's car sales business," said Bruno, shifting his chair to give them room to sit down and reaching for the bottle. "Have another glass of wine."

"His family was very lucky," Thomas explained. "They were farmers, with land between Marckolsheim and Strasbourg, and just before war broke out in 1939 the French government bought some of the land to turn it into a military airfield. There was a court case because it was a compulsory purchase, and Sylvestre's grandfather had sued because the government offered too little money. After the war the air force still wanted the airbase and offered a deal by which it paid rent and promised that if it ever gave up the airfield Sylvestre's family could buy it back for the price that had originally been offered before the war. In the 1960s, when de Gaulle thought French security would depend on nuclear weapons, France began cutting back on conventional forces. Sylvestre's family got the land back cheaply, with a runway, hangars, underground fuel bunkers, offices and barracks.

"Strasbourg was then becoming one of the centers of the new European community and wanted a civilian airport," Thomas went on. "Sylvestre's father sold the airfield for many times more than he'd paid to buy it back. But he kept the rest of the land, thinking it was bound to increase in value."

"And it certainly did," Ingrid chimed in. "His heirs became one of the wealthiest families in Alsace. That's how Sylvestre can afford to spend seven hundred thousand on that Bugatti of his."

"That's nothing," said Young, taking out a smart phone from his shirt pocket. He tapped a few buttons and then held up the screen to show an extraordinary, gleaming black car with a hood that seemed to stretch out forever and the sweeping aerodynamic lines of the 1930s.

"*Mon Dieu,* it's beautiful," said Florence.

"This is the most expensive car of all time. What do you think it might be worth?" Young asked.

"Three million," Bruno suggested, plucking a figure from the air. Ingrid said five million, and Annette shook her head, saying she knew the price and their estimates would have to go a lot higher.

"Ten million," Florence suggested, laughing.

"Double that and then double it again," said Young. He suddenly looked solemn, as if this were serious business.

"What is it?" Bruno asked.

"It's another Bugatti, a model known as the Atlantic. Its real name is Type 57C, built in 1936. One of these was bought by the Mullin Automotive Museum in California for an undisclosed sum. The word is that it went for thirty-seven million. It's certainly the most valuable car of all time."

"That's insane," said Bruno, thinking it was almost obscene. "How can any car be worth that?"

"They made only four of them. One is owned by Ralph Lauren, there's the one in the museum, a third was destroyed by a train at a railway crossing, and another was lost somewhere in France during the war. It was being driven from the factory in Alsace to Bordeaux for safekeeping, but it never arrived, and nobody knows what happened to it."

"I agree with Florence," said Bruno, taking Young's phone and looking at the car more closely. "It certainly is beautiful. Is that the one in the museum?"

"No, that's the one owned by Ralph Lauren." He opened another photograph of the same car in silver-blue. "That's the one bought by the museum."

Bruno was about to ask about the one that was lost in the war when Fabiola and Gilles descended to haul them all back to the dance floor.

4

Bruno reined in at the top of the ridge and checked his watch as he waited for Fabiola to catch up on her old horse. He was meeting Thomas and Ingrid at Fauquet's café at nine for breakfast, but there was still time for a decent gallop before taking Hector back to the stables. He looked down at the familiar valley of the Vézère River, still shrouded in the early morning mist. The St. Denis bridge and the quayside where the vintage cars were parked on display were all somewhere beneath that gray cloud. Stray tendrils were rising like wisps of steam as the first, hesitant rays of the sun peeked above the ridge and began to warm the mist away. The spire of the old church and the houses that clambered up the hill seemed to float weightlessly in the sky. His horse and dog were still and silent as their eyes followed his gaze down into the valley until Balzac turned, hearing Victoria's hooves lumbering up the slope toward them.

"What did you think of Annette's young man?" Fabiola asked as she drew alongside and brought her horse to a halt. Victoria gave a curt neigh of gratitude, and Hector turned to rub the side of his head against hers. Sometimes Bruno thought the horses were more socially adept than many of the people he knew.

"Too soon to tell, but I liked him from the little I saw," Bruno replied. "He seemed good-natured and friendly, and he danced well. Apart from his passion for cars, that's about all I can say. But if Annette likes him, that's good enough for me."

"I think it's more than just liking him," Fabiola said. "Did you see how she looked at him? I hope it works out for her. But it won't be easy, her staying here in the Périgord while he's in London most of the time. I'm sure they can have thrilling reunions at rallies and car auctions, but you don't get to know a man that way."

Bruno looked at her with amused affection. "Gilles was in Paris and you were down here, but it worked out for you two."

"Gilles was ready to leave Paris and join me here. I don't think that's the case for Annette and George, and I don't want to see her hurt. Do you think he's ready to make some kind of commitment? Annette will need that."

"He drove all the way down here from London to be with her, so he's obviously more than just interested."

"That's not what I mean by 'commitment,' Bruno. You know what I'm talking about. She seems so much more interested than he is, and that imbalance is not reassuring. And he's not just good-looking, he's seriously handsome, the sort of man who's had lots of girls. Don't you think so?"

Among the many things that baffled Bruno about women was the time and effort they spent analyzing the love affairs of their friends. They seemed to make it all so complicated. Bruno liked to recall a scene from his favorite movie, *Les Enfants du Paradis,* when the actress Arletty turns to the tongue-tied young man who is besotted with her, lets her gown fall and says, *"L'amour, c'est si simple."* Bruno knew it was never quite so easy. There was an old Périgord proverb about love being like food: it changed with the time it spent cooking. But he could never see how it helped for others to pick endlessly over the passions and yearnings of their friends.

"It's early days for them," he said. "They met at the Angoulême rally this summer and again at the car show in Paris, so this is only their third meeting. He isn't even staying at her place."

"They haven't been to bed together yet," Fabiola replied. "She's nervous about that. Annette's not very experienced, and she thinks he is."

"That's for them to work out," said Bruno, and looked at her steadily. "Are you ready to ride on?"

"You aren't over your affair with Pamela," she said, ignoring his question.

"Nor is she, so that makes two of us," he replied, irritated and aware of a childish urge to have the last word. He certainly didn't want to pick over the bones of their parting to talk to Fabiola about his feelings. He touched his heels to Hector's flanks, and his horse sprang forward. Bruno could almost feel Hector's pleasure at being unleashed, bounding almost at once into a canter with Balzac lumbering along behind. Bruno pressed his horse to go faster, galloping to leave Fabiola's probing remarks in his wake and feel nothing but the wind in his face.

Forty minutes later, after stripping off his shirt to wash in the stable sink because there was no time to shower, Bruno walked into Fauquet's café. The clock on the *mairie* tower was striking nine, and the market stalls with the foods from Alsace were already busy. Some in the crowd were eating portions of *flammküchen,* thin slices of pastry covered with onions, bacon and melted cheese. Bruno's mouth began to water as his nostrils caught the aroma. Bruno was also tempted by another stall that was offering bowls of sausage chunks with choucroute and plastic glasses of Riesling. But he could see Thomas and Ingrid were already installed at a window table in the café. Before them were cups of coffee, the local newspaper and a basket of croissants and *pains au chocolat.* Ingrid was glancing through the weekly magazine of *Sud Ouest,* and Thomas handed Bruno the paper. It was already opened to a photograph of Sylvestre's Bugatti on the quayside, surrounded by a throng of people.

"The mayor will be pleased with all the publicity," said Thomas. He tore off a piece of his croissant to give to Balzac.

"I wonder if we'd have done so well if Sylvestre hadn't come with that old Bugatti," Bruno said, swallowing a mouthful of croissant and regretting that he hadn't bought some hot *flammküchen* for them all. But his friends probably got enough of that at home, he told himself as he caught sight of Annette half running through the market to the café.

"Bruno, you've got to help," she said, bursting in. "George has got a terrible migraine, so he can't navigate for me, and I can't be in the rally without a codriver. I asked Yveline, but she's on safety duty with the rest of the gendarmes. Please, please, please, will you take George's place? I won't be able to enter the national rally unless I do well here today, and there's nobody else I can ask."

"I'm not nearly good enough to be a codriver," he said, half choking in surprise and with the effort of swallowing a half-chewed croissant. He drank from his glass of water. "I'm not qualified, Annette. What about Sylvestre?"

"I tried him, and he's competing with that Indian friend of his. And you don't have to drive, just navigate for me."

"Navigate?" he asked. "The rally track is clearly marked. You can't get lost."

"That's not what I mean. You navigate by telling me in advance of every bend and obstacle coming up." From her shoulder bag she took out what looked like two rolls of paper towels on wooden handles and brandished them at him. "I've got your track roll here. You just have to read it out so I know what's coming."

"But I've never done this," said Bruno. "And the last time I drove with you I got carsick."

"You'll be too busy concentrating on the scroll," she said. "Please, Bruno, this really means a lot to me."

He looked at the scroll, realizing that by turning the first wooden handle he could see line-by-line a detailed description of the road ahead. After the start of the rally, he read, there was an eighty-meter straightaway on tarmac, followed by a ninety-degree left turn onto gravel, then a forty-meter straightaway that led into a sixty-degree left turn into a dip with a bad camber . . .

He recognized the descriptions, having driven the track twice and walked parts of it when checking the hay bales that would protect the spectators.

"Did you make this roll with George Young?" he asked.

"I spent days on it before he arrived, driving the route with a tape recorder and then transcribing the tape onto my laptop and finding a printer that could make a continuous roll. All you have to do is read it out."

"I couldn't hear myself think when you drove me around that motor-cross track," he said. "You won't hear me."

"I've got microphones and headphones in the helmets. And I know the track almost by heart. But if I don't have a codriver, I'll be disqualified."

"I never thought of you as a man to turn down a damsel in distress," said Ingrid, grinning at him.

"Why turn down the opportunity for a new experience? You know you'll regret it if you say no," said Thomas, grinning as his wife had.

"And she'll never forgive you," said Ingrid.

"Right, I'll never forgive you," said Annette, laughing as Bruno looked from one face to another and rolled his eyes. She knew he'd have to say yes.

"Do I have time to finish my breakfast?" he asked.

"Five minutes. The rally starts at two, but they'll close the track at noon. Until then we can do test runs. We'll do one slowly so you get used to it, a second one at medium speed and then a third all out. By then you should have learned to handle the roll and judge when I need to hear your instructions."

"So simple," said Ingrid. "What could possibly go wrong?"

"Only the roll can go wrong," said Annette. "If you lose control of the paper, it unravels and piles up all over the car and blocks my vision. I had that happen once, and it's not good. That's why you have to get some practice. I'll wait."

She folded her arms and stood at the end of the table, her jaw set and her eyes fixed on him but smiling at him expectantly. He was reminded of the first time he'd seen her, in the square outside the café in her first week in her new job, showing off out of sheer nervousness by driving too fast. Annette had gotten a parking ticket from him and a speeding ticket from Sergeant Jules. And she was only spared a charge of failing to stop for a pedestrian crossing when Florence realized it was her first job as magistrate and refused to press charges. And now she was a good friend who had learned to temper her own radical views and passion for the environment with a healthy respect for the customs and peculiarities of the Périgord. Bruno had come to respect her professionalism. And in an avuncular kind of way, which was a new sensation for him, Bruno was fond of her.

"This isn't your car," he said in the parking lot, looking at the unfamiliar white Citroën DS3 festooned with advertising stickers for motor oils and car accessories and a big garage in Sarlat. Annette opened the door to reveal internal roll bars forming a protective cage. "Where's your blue Peugeot?"

"This is my race car," she replied. "It's a turbo, borrowed from the Citroën garage in Brive. The owner's son, Fabrice, usually drives it, but he broke his leg waterskiing, so for once I'm being sponsored, which makes it my big chance to get into the national championship. That's why I need you. I can't give up this opportunity."

"What happened to Fabrice's navigator?"

"That would be me. That's why I'm being given his place."

Bruno took the helmet from the passenger's seat and eased himself into the car, feeling the high sides of the special rally seat enclose him. Annette climbed in her side and showed him how the double seat belts worked, straps over each shoulder and two more for the belt, meeting at a circular lock on his belly, like the one he recalled from parachute training in the army. He put on the helmet, and Annette leaned over again to adjust his microphone and plug the trailing wire into a socket between the seats. She did the same for her own audio feed and began a countdown test. He heard her perfectly and then did his own countdown, and she interrupted to say it was good.

"Now try unrolling this while we're parked," she said, putting the first roll into a bracket attached to the glove compartment. Between his feet was a second bracket, and she bent down to insert the main roll.

"Just turn the handles on the top roll to feed the paper and read out the instructions to me as they come," she said. "Keep your feet braced, and whatever you do, don't let your legs tear the paper or we're sunk. Try it."

It was easy enough, sitting in the parking lot, but she kept him practicing for twenty minutes before rewinding the roll, clicking in her own seat belts and then setting off for the start of the course on the road to Les Eyzies. Once on the dirt track, she kept her speed down, and Bruno had little difficulty controlling the paper roll. He even had time to glance up briefly at the route ahead, checking the instructions. The special seats and the double belts kept him securely in place, even when she began to pick up speed. The strain was on his neck, to stop his head from swinging from side to side as she accelerated out of the sharp bends.

"Okay," Annette said. "This time, don't touch the paper, just watch the road and get familiar with the track. I'll go fairly fast but nowhere near full speed."

She got onto the gravel track and shot away, moving slickly through second gear and into third before braking hard for the corner and then skidding as she stepped on the accelerator. Bruno felt stunned by the contrast between his own sense of the sedate pace he would take to drive this route and Annette's suicidal speed. Corners came up far too fast, and bends were whipped through so hard he felt the safety belts cutting into his flesh as they held him in place. Trees loomed before him, and he closed his eyes, sure that a crash was coming. Then somehow they were skidding sideways but still on the track, and he felt the panic rising again, certain that they were about to hit a pile of hay bales, and his neck was aching with the strain of keeping his head from jerking from side to side. He was meant to be learning the route, but his senses were too overwhelmed by fear and tension for anything to sink in.

Bruno gritted his teeth; he would have to get used to this. As the road climbed up into the woods around St. Cirq, he felt his reactions start to adjust to the much-higher speeds and to Annette's mastery of the car. He began to anticipate the corners and brace himself for the car's leap into the air when it crossed even the smallest ridge. He kept telling himself that Annette was completely in control when the rear of the car skidded sharply to one side. It was simply the way that she cornered.

"Let's do that one more time, without using the roll," he said, when she pulled up at the finish. He heard the breathlessness in his own voice. "I'm just starting to get the hang of this."

Without a word, Annette clicked a stopwatch on the dashboard and set off again at speed, but this time he felt ready, his senses catching up with the sheer pace at which the inputs were coming and his body anticipating the lurches as the g-forces tried to hurl him from side to side. Somehow his brain had learned that slamming into a tree was not inevitable and that Annette would hit the accelerator just as she went into the bend rather than wait until she was coming out of it. And he knew he was recognizing bends and corners, the short straightaways and the dips where the car bottomed out. The sense of panic was still there, but diminished. He felt he was back in control of himself.

"Okay," he said when Annette stopped again. "I think I'm ready to try it with the roll."

The next trip was worse. Bruno had almost no time to glance up at the route, and his eyes lost focus as the car bounced over bumps in the road and again when it seemed to take to the air as they went over even modest hillcrests. At one point when Annette braked very hard to go into a sharp right-hand bend, the g-force sent the paper ballooning out between his legs. Then Bruno briefly lost his place on the roll and realized he had to keep his thumb on the paper to mark each line as he read it. Somehow he got through to the end of the ride, and as Annette braked he closed his eyes and waited for his breathing to return to normal. His hands were trembling, and he felt exhausted from the intensity of the concentration.

"Not bad for a beginner, Bruno. That was under seventeen minutes," she said. "Now we'll do it again, only faster. If I'm going to win this thing, we'll have to do it in fifteen."

5

Two laps into the next training session, Annette distracted him by saying, "Someone very good is on our tail, and I think I know who it is. Hang on tight."

Bruno hadn't thought it was possible to go any faster, but Annette raised her pace. Still, he was starting to anticipate each place on the paper roll by the way she shifted gears and braked and by the direction of the g-force upon him at each bend. He learned to start reading out the next instruction as she accelerated out of each bend and to brace his legs to stop the paper from ballooning when the car briefly took flight as she topped each hill.

"He's very good," he heard Annette say as Bruno's tailbone made him wince when she slammed through a dip in the road. "He'll be the one to beat."

Bruno saw her eyes flick to the rearview mirror and was amazed that she could spare time or attention for anything but the road ahead. He felt he had never gone so fast in his life and had never heard anything louder than the roar of the engine as she pushed the tachometer into the red zone. But he kept up his commentary on the road ahead and felt he was beginning to know the route well enough to take the occasional brief glance at the road.

"That was our fastest yet," said Annette, slowing and braking to turn into the assembly area. "I think we'll be fine. How do you feel?"

"I feel very grateful we have air bags," he replied. "As long as they're working, I'll be okay."

She turned to him in surprise as the car drew to a halt. "They aren't working. We have to dismantle all the air bags for serious rally cars. Some of the jolts we take when we land after a hillcrest would trigger them."

Now she tells me, thought Bruno, trying to keep his face from revealing his dismay.

Half-a-dozen rally cars were already gathered, most of them with their hoods up, drivers leaning over their engines. Small knots of spectators were strolling around the cars, and Philippe Delaron, the local *Sud Ouest* correspondent, was taking photos, posing excited small boys against the cars.

"What about that car behind us?" Bruno asked.

"There won't be a car behind us in the rally. We race against the clock, not against one another. That would be too dangerous. Here they are now."

A white Volkswagen pulled up sharply beside them, two figures inside, unidentifiable in their crash helmets. The driver pulled off his helmet, and Sylvestre's face emerged.

"I didn't know you went in for this sport," Sylvestre said to Bruno while waving at Annette. He called across to her, "I bet you'll be the fastest woman on the circuit. But where's George?"

"He's sick," she replied calmly. "Bruno stepped into the breach. He's my secret weapon. Go too fast, and he'll give you a speeding ticket."

As Sylvestre smiled and drove off, Bruno's mobile rang. He had to release his seat belts to get to it and saw it was Fabiola.

"I'm at the funeral parlor, looking at the late Monsieur

Hugon," she said. "I can't see much out of the ordinary. He's been dead at least thirty-six hours, maybe more. And the undertaker washed him down and cleaned him when he arrived, so there's no body waste to examine. There's some interesting irritation around the nose and mouth and in his throat. It could be no more than a cold, and he was certainly a prime candidate for a heart attack."

"Gelletreau was treating him for heart trouble," said Bruno.

"I'm not in the least surprised. In fact, I'd have been surprised if he wasn't being treated for it. He's very overweight and florid, so he must have had high blood pressure. There are nicotine stains on his fingers, so I assume he was a fairly heavy smoker. I found a bit of bruising that could well have happened when he collapsed. Are you sure this is a suspicious death?"

"No, I'm not sure, but there are some circumstantial things that worry me." Bruno explained his doubts about the absent file and notebook.

"I see." She paused and then said, "I presume you asked for an autopsy. What did J-J say?"

"He was reluctant but said to ask if you could take a look to see if you thought an autopsy was justified."

"Not so far, it isn't. But I'll take some swabs and get back to you. Will you be at the rally, watching Annette? I may see you there."

"You certainly will, and you may get a surprise." He laughed, closed the phone and looked at his watch. It was noon; there would be no more time for practice laps.

"Tell me what happens in the real race," he said to Annette.

"They already drew lots, and we go off fifth. That's good because the track and corners won't be too badly roughed up. There are twenty-four contestants, and we start at three-minute intervals. Those who finish first and second in this regional heat qualify for the national championship. Can I buy you some lunch? I need a sandwich."

"No, thank you. I think I'd lose it on the first turn."

"Make sure you drink some water, though. We need to meet up by one-thirty. Regulations require flame-retardant gear, just in case, so you'll need to change. I've got them in the back along with George's overalls, which should fit you. Can I drop you somewhere?"

"Drop me in town. Give me the clothes, and I'll change in the *mairie*. We can meet there later. I ought to show my face at the Alsace market first, just to say hello to the various stallholders. You could get something to eat there."

"Good idea, but stay away from the wine kiosk," she said with a smile. "I want you keeping all your wits about you, so not even a taste of Riesling, please. But I'll buy you a bottle after the race."

The midday sun was warm, and the square in front of the *mairie* was full of people gathered around the dozen or so stalls. Annette paused at one that was offering embroidery and lace, oven gloves and aprons with Alsace motifs. She bought a set of tea towels, murmuring to Bruno that she felt she ought to support them. Bruno leafed through a picture book at a stall run by the Alsace tourist board, recognizing one of the old concrete forts from the Maginot Line that he'd visited with Thomas and Ingrid. He pointed it out to Annette.

"That's just outside the town," Bruno said. "It's a museum now with a good account of the battle that took place there. The French held out for two days. You can see it had two turrets. The Germans knocked out one with artillery and the second with an attack by Stuka dive-bombers."

"I thought it was supposed to be impregnable," she said.

"Nothing is impregnable. The Germans simply went around it and invaded through Belgium, while half of the French army was locked up in the Maginot Line, barely able to get involved in the war."

They walked on, glancing at a stall where Alsace sausages and cheeses were being sold. Bruno greeted his friend Stéphane, the cheese maker, who was tasting the wares while chatting with his visiting counterpart. The busiest stall was the one offering tastings of Riesling, Sylvaner and Pinot Gris. Bruno heard his name called. It was Thomas, who had been called in to help the stallholder cope with the demand.

"A glass for you, Bruno?"

He gestured at Annette behind him and called back, "Not when I'm driving."

Annette bought herself a *flammküchen*. Every table on Fauquet's terrace was taken, but Bruno bought two bottles of water, and he and Annette walked over to the stone balcony overlooking the river. She asked about Fabiola's call, saying it sounded like it could mean work for her or some other magistrate. It was too soon for that, Bruno said, but told her of his concerns over Hugon's death.

"Was that an overweight, elderly man, used to work for the archives in Périgueux?" she asked. Bruno nodded. "I knew him. We hired him from time to time to do research on cases, tax issues mainly. He was a perfectionist and had a very good reputation. I can't imagine him not keeping all his notebooks up to date."

"His wife may have ditched them to try and avoid tax claims," he replied before drinking some water from his bottle. "But she was very open about what he was being paid for the latest job, and there were a thousand euros in his wallet. If she was worried about taxes, I think she'd have pocketed the money before I turned up."

"I hardly think she'd have been thinking about taxes if she walked in to find her husband dead. How long were they married?"

"Over forty years."

"And what was he working on?" asked Annette, finishing her *flammküchen* and pouring some of the water onto her hands before drying them with a paper napkin.

"It's not clear, but it had something to do with the war and the Resistance," Bruno said. "I'll try to find out what he was researching at the archives. Maybe that's where he left the missing file and notebook."

Bruno stood up as he saw the mayor heading toward him, waving to friends right and left as he bustled through the crowd. He began speaking from five meters away.

"I hear you're going to be taking part in the race, so good luck to you both, but a couple of things have come up," he said. He apologized to Annette and then took Bruno's arm and led him a few steps away, his voice dropping to a murmur.

"First, there's Jérôme's amusement park—he wants to buy some land from the town to enlarge the place and put in some new attractions. Could you go see him and get an idea if it's the kind of thing we should approve? He doesn't want to go to the expense of hiring an architect and getting a survey done if it doesn't have much chance of getting past the council.

"Another thing: that fellow with the Bugatti, Sylvestre Wémy, buttonholed me this morning to ask for my help regarding some property his grandmother left him. You know the place, that pretty *chartreuse* on the road to the St. Chamassy cemetery."

The term meant "charterhouse," but in this part of France it was used for a historic building that was larger than a manor house but not quite big enough to be called a château. It was usually a long, low building just one room wide with a single floor, although sometimes there were mansard windows to allow small bedrooms in the roof. Sylvestre wanted to turn the place into several expensive apartments and then sell them, the mayor explained. But the inheritance was divided between him and the

St. Denis side of the family, and some kind of family feud had now developed. Sylvestre was hoping that the mayor might find some way to resolve matters, since St. Denis stood to lose the extra property taxes and the prospect of employment for gardeners and cleaners.

"You know the family, the Oudinots. He's a stubborn old devil. Could you go and see him, Bruno, and find out what the problem is from his side?"

Fernand Oudinot and his wife, Odette, were in their early sixties and still ran their farm raising ducks and geese; they also kept bees and ran a very productive walnut plantation. Bruno knew Fernand through one of the local hunting clubs, and he had a soft spot for Odette. She used her own honey and nuts to make the best *tarte aux noix* in the district; although she had shown Bruno how to make it, he could never get his pastry to turn out like hers.

"I'll find out what the problem is, but I don't want to get involved in a family quarrel," Bruno said. "I'm too attached to Odette's *tarte aux noix.*"

"So am I," said the mayor. "But I had a call from my colleague in Alsace, one mayor to another, asking if I could help. You know how it is."

Bruno nodded and said, "I've got to do this rally first, but I can talk to Sylvestre later and then see the Oudinots tomorrow. They're decent people. And I'll go and see Jérôme, too."

"There's no rush on the amusement park. If you could get us a preliminary report for the next council meeting, that would be fine." Returning to Annette, the mayor kissed her cheeks as he wished her luck in the race. "Just don't damage our town policeman. He's got too much to do."

"I'll do my best," she said, looking at her watch. "And now Bruno and I have to get into our driving clothes." They went into the *mairie* to change, Bruno using his office and Annette the ladies' room. They emerged in white Nomex overalls, all but their hands and faces covered in the material. They got some startled glances as they walked back to the car.

"I'm not sure I can operate that paper roll if I'm wearing gloves," he said.

"I'm the same—I hate driving with gloves. And don't forget to hit the stopwatch when we start because I'll have my hand on the gearstick."

They went through the ritual of shaking hands with the other drivers before getting into the Citroën, donning their helmets and heading for their place in the queue of cars lined up before the start. The lead car took off at the marshal's signal. Bruno felt his heart pounding as they rolled forward to the starting line. He looked across at Annette, wondering if he should wish her good luck, but settled for the all-purpose French word that team members exchanged at the start of a rugby match.

"Merde," he said.

"And *merde* to you," she replied, her voice sounding odd through the headphones. A second later the marshal's arm flashed down to release them. Bruno hit the stopwatch on the dashboard and was then rammed back into his seat by the acceleration, Annette taking off faster than ever before, and began reading from his roll.

"Eighty meters on tarmac then a ninety-degree left turn onto gravel." He remembered the phrases and the sequences as she slammed the car into a skidding turn.

"Forty meters straight to a sixty-degree left turn into a dip. Watch for the bad camber . . ."

And on it went, his body lifting and then slamming back down, jerking from left to right. He tried to brace himself with only his feet, which were pressed hard against the bulkhead.

Annette's hands were braced on the steering wheel, but his were occupied by the roll. He knew when the straightaways were coming and, from time to time, could risk a quick glance at the road.

"Ninety-degree right turn at the bottom of this slope and onto tarmac for two hundred meters . . ."

A blur of faces marked the turn, the people safely sheltered behind hay bales. They were waving, but because of his helmet he could hear nothing except the howl of the motor and the new thrust as the turbo kicked in. Then almost at once she was braking for the next bend, and he was telling her to watch for the tunnel after a thirty-degree right turn.

He almost lost it once when the paper ballooned up and he had to use his knees to hold it down in the well of the car, but he found his place just in time to warn Annette of the next bend.

"Beware of water in the dip at the bottom of this slope, then make an immediate ninety-degree left turn going into the S-bend . . ."

As she hammered the car around the sharp turn, he was aware from the corner of his eye of another car on its side in the ditch along the side of the road.

Then they were through the S-bend and onto gravel, a short straight stretch rose steeply ahead, and then they seemed to sail through the air for a long second before slamming down and into a sixty-degree left turn with a bad camber. There were more faces and hay bales and a short straightaway with a banner over the road and a marshal holding a checkered flag. She went past him at high speed and began braking hard as Bruno hit the stopwatch. It read 15:08. Fifteen minutes and eight seconds. Annette had said they would have to beat fifteen minutes in order to win.

6

"Great job, you're in the lead," said a large, middle-aged man with a beard, opening Annette's door and hauling her out into an embrace. Beside him was a slender youth on crutches, one leg in a cast.

"Bonjour, Marcel . . . Bonjour, Fabrice," said Annette. She removed her helmet and turned to introduce Bruno, who was still trying to sort out the tangle of his paper roll. Finally he rolled it neatly back, took off his helmet, released his safety belts and clambered out. He felt light-headed, and his legs were still trembling from the strain of bracing them throughout the race. He leaned against the car and waved at the two strangers, not quite up to the expected handshakes and polite greetings.

"This is Bruno. He stepped into the breach when my navigator got sick. It's his first rally," Annette said. "Bruno, this is Marcel, the garage owner whose car this is, and this is his son Fabrice, who really should be driving."

"I don't think I could do that course in fifteen-eight," said the young man. "You were great." He looked at Bruno. "Your first ride? *Chapeau.*"

"It was the car," Annette said. "All that power, great brakes and perfectly tuned."

She turned to look at the large blackboard on which the times of each car were marked. They were mostly around 15:15, and one was 15:20. Fifteen-ten was the nearest to their time. Marcel handed Bruno a water bottle, and he drank, gratefully, aware of other drivers and navigators in overalls staring at him curiously. He recognized one of the drivers from a rugby match in Limoges, and another one waved at him, the son of one of the big wine-growers in Bergerac. Bruno waved his hand in return and then saw the slight figure of Félix edging through the crowd and look-ing shifty as he avoided Bruno's eye.

Another car jumped over the hill toward them and raced for the finish line. Fabrice clicked the button on his stopwatch and called across, "Fifteen-thirteen."

"That's Montjoie over there with the blond girl in the red jacket," said Marcel, pointing into the distance. "He made the national championships last year and he did fifteen-ten, so now you and Annette are the team to beat."

"It was all Annette," said Bruno. "I was just a passenger. Jesus, I feel too old for this sport."

"You're the cop in St. Denis," Marcel said. It wasn't a ques-tion. "Was this really your first race?"

"And my last," said Bruno.

"Not if you qualify in this heat," Marcel replied. "If you get into the national finals, it has to be with the same team that qualified."

Damn Annette, thought Bruno. She hadn't told him that. "No exceptions?" he asked, hopefully.

"Death, serious illness with a medical certificate, military orders, that's about it."

"Then I'll just have to hope there are faster cars to come."

"There's one who can beat you, maybe two more, and only two teams qualify."

As Marcel spoke, Annette came around to Bruno's side of the

car to hug him. He knew her well but was momentarily startled as he remembered how small she was, the top of her head barely reaching his chin. Somehow in the course of the last few hours she seemed to have grown in his imagination as she demonstrated her mastery at the wheel.

Another car came across the finish line. This time the marshal at the blackboard wrote down "15:11."

"We're still leading," she said, looking up at him gleefully.

"Does that mean I can go and change?"

"Sorry, no. If there's a dead heat we might have to do it again. That shouldn't happen, though, because the marshals time us to tenths of a second."

Bruno was aware of his name being called and saw a group of his friends—Thomas and Ingrid, Gilles and Fabiola, Crimson and his daughter, Miranda, waving at him from behind the hay bales at the finish line and giving him a thumbs-up. He waved back, and then the mayor was at his side.

"I hear you're in the lead," he said.

"I'm counting on you to get me some military orders to save me from having to do this again," Bruno replied. "Apparently that's the only acceptable excuse, apart from death or serious injury. And shouldn't you be behind those protective hay bales with the others?"

"Rank has its privileges, Bruno. And here's the inevitable Philippe Delaron with his camera."

With the ease of a practiced politician, the mayor insinuated himself into the photo for *Sud Ouest,* Annette between the two men, and then Philippe came forward with his notepad as another car came over the finishing line. The marshal had just finished writing "15:12" when he clutched at his waist and pulled out a mobile phone. He listened briefly and then shouted, "Ambulance," and began clanging a bell.

"Sector seven, the corner by the sawmill at Petit-Paris, a car's gone into a tree," he shouted at Ahmed moments later. Leaning out of the window of the *urgences* vehicle, Ahmed waved acknowledgment, put on his siren and roared off, not quite as fast as the rally cars but at a very impressive speed. Philippe ran to his own car and followed Ahmed, again at a speed that Bruno would have found terrifying before today. Lespinasse followed in his tow truck.

"Don't worry," Annette said to Bruno. "You saw the roll bars and security cages in the car. It's unusual for anyone to be hurt."

"In that case we ought to install them in every car that's built," Bruno said. He'd seen the results of too many car crashes in his years as a policeman.

The marshals halted the remaining cars that were waiting in line for their own runs. There were only half a dozen still to go. Last in line was Sylvestre's Volkswagen. To Bruno's surprise, Sylvestre was the navigator, and his Indian friend Freddy was at the wheel. As he looked, Sylvestre turned, caught his eye and gave a casual wave before rolling down the window and calling for Annette. She strolled across, bent to listen, smiled and backed away with a wave.

"He was just paying us a compliment on our run," she said when she returned.

"I'm surprised he's not driving," said Bruno. "He seemed like the kind of man who'd like to be in the driver's seat. And he seemed pretty quick when he caught up with us this morning."

"Sylvestre is very good, but Freddy's better. He came in second in last year's desert rally in Qatar. That's a big international event with serious prize money. And a team is a team—either one can drive. The navigator is formally known as the codriver. That's why I could race after Fabrice broke his leg."

"And I gather that you're stuck with me if we do qualify," said Bruno.

"I doubt that we will. Fifteen-eight isn't really good enough.

And the best we can hope for is to qualify in second place. Freddy's bound to win. Even if he weren't such a top driver with a big corporate sponsor, he's going to be the last car to race, which means he knows what time he has to beat. That's a real advantage."

"What do you mean 'a big corporate sponsor'? What has that to do with how he races?"

She gestured at a large truck in the parking lot across the road with a big VW logo on its side. "That's his support team with mechanics, spare parts and different sets of tires for the various conditions. There's even a guy with a radio to tell him the times of the drivers who set off just ahead of him. These rally championships are big business, Bruno. Marcel isn't paying for this car himself; he's got Citroën behind him. You must have seen the Citroën advertising after they won the world rally championship. Victories sell cars."

Bruno nodded, understanding that he was involved in something much bigger than he'd assumed when Annette had first appealed to him that morning. There was big business here and serious money, a great deal of organization and a whole subculture built around the rallies.

Suddenly, electronic feedback howled across the assembly area as the marshal at the blackboard started speaking into a bullhorn. He adjusted it, and the howl died. "No injuries," he said. "Driver and codriver are unhurt. The car cannot be driven, so number seventeen is scratched. The race resumes."

"What about the cars that were already on the track before the crash?" Bruno asked Annette.

"They'll have been waved down by the marshals, and now they'll have to come back and run again, once the tow truck has cleared the route."

Marcel came up to them, his mobile phone at his ear. He said "Thanks" into the mouthpiece and then looked solemnly at Annette.

"I'm not sure you're going to qualify," he said. "I have a friend stationed on the course with a stopwatch. Number eighteen, Rostand, from Toulouse, was two seconds ahead of your time at the halfway point. Villeneuve from Cahors, number nineteen, matched your time. They're two good drivers, both in Citroëns like yours, and then there's the VW team."

"And it usually helps to run again," said Annette, looking crestfallen. Marcel shrugged.

"Come on, let's take a stroll, see our friends," said Bruno, taking Annette's arm. "Until all the results are in, there's nothing we can do but wait."

Reluctantly, she followed across the assembly area to the hay bales where their friends were gathered with steaming mugs. Bruno could smell cinnamon and cloves.

"I know it's not cold, but Miranda thought it would be fun to make some mulled wine," said Crimson, holding up a large thermos. "You're in the lead, so you deserve some."

"Thanks, but not yet," said Annette. "If there's a dead heat we may have to race again, and there are some very good drivers to come."

"This is my first time at one of these rallies," said Gilles. "I'd never realized how popular they are. There are hundreds of people here and around the course. We had trouble finding a place to park."

As he spoke, the marshal brought up the next car to the starting line and waved the flag to commence the run. Now Sylvestre and Freddy were no longer last in line; the three cars that had interrupted their runs because of the crash had returned to take their places at the rear. Bruno heard Fabiola and Miranda asking Annette what had happened to her English codriver, the three women drifting away to one side to talk among themselves. Good, thought Bruno, it will distract Annette from watching the clock.

"Do you know your face was absolutely white when Annette pulled up after her race?" Gilles asked. "You looked like you were going to be sick."

"I very nearly was," Bruno replied. With half an ear he could hear the women murmuring. He could pick up only individual words and phrases, like "migraine" and "handsome" and "serious" and "up to him." They were evidently talking about Annette's new boyfriend.

"You've no idea how fast it felt from the passenger seat," Bruno said to Gilles and Crimson. "Make sure Annette doesn't tempt Fabiola into taking up the sport. She drives fast enough already."

The next car started badly, wheels spinning as the driver used too much throttle. He must have lost a second or two.

"That's why it's good to be one of the early ones," Annette called across to Bruno. "The start is getting chewed up. We'll have to watch that if we're told to race again."

"Where did Annette learn to drive like that?" Crimson asked.

"Madagascar, when she was working for Médecins Sans Frontières," said Bruno, thinking that the mulled wine smelled very inviting. "But I think she has a gift; it seems to come naturally to her."

At three-minute intervals, the remaining cars took off, a little slower than the earlier ones, the drivers cautious after seeing the first wheelspin. Then they began to come over the hill to the finish line. The first one was clocked at 15:10, the next one was 15:09, and then Freddy in his VW was just 15:03, beating Annette's time by five seconds. The VW pulled over, and Sylvestre and Freddy clambered out, their fists pumping the air, and ran to embrace each other at the front of their car.

Annette was still in second place, but then the last car passed the finish line, timed at 15:08. The marshals began to confer. Annette had one hand to her mouth, the other hand clutching

Fabiola's arm. Her eyes were opened enormously wide. Bruno felt himself being caught up in her excitement. Would they have to race again?

Sylvestre strolled across to join them. Bruno shook his hand and murmured congratulations. Annette was now bouncing up and down on her toes as she waited for the marshals to do something. Finally one of them turned to the blackboard. Annette's name remained in second place as the marshal filled in the tenths of a second. Annette had been timed at 15:082. Her rival for the vital second place came in at 15:084.

"We did it!" she screamed and turned to jump into Bruno's arms, her small body trembling with emotion as she planted a smacking kiss on his cheek. "We're in the national championship!"

Bruno forced himself to smile as he hugged her and pretended to be delighted, although inside he felt a foreboding that was mixed with dismay. Once had been more than enough. Their friends clustered around slapping them on the back and cheering. Philippe Delaron was taking more photos.

"Thanks," Bruno said to Crimson. "I hope there's enough of that mulled wine left in the thermos for me to have a glass or two. In fact, give me two glasses; there's someone I should talk to."

He took the glasses across to Sylvestre, who was leaning against his VW, eyes closed and head back, enjoying the last of the autumn sun.

"Congratulations again," said Bruno, and handed him a glass. "Where's your partner?"

"Freddy is in the marshals' tent doing the paperwork." He took the wine, sniffed it, sipped and then nodded his thanks.

"I heard from the mayor that you're having some problems with your property here, and he's asked if I could look into it, see if we could help."

"I'd be very grateful," Sylvestre said, his manner suddenly businesslike. "It's because of one of those foolish family feuds that's made worse by jealousy. My grandmother had a brother, and they shared the family property here when their parents died. It's a pleasant little château with about fifteen hectares of land. Since my grandmother moved to Alsace when she married, she couldn't use the farm, and she agreed with her brother to split the estate. She got the *chartreuse* and garden, and her brother, my great-uncle Thibaut, got all the land. She didn't bother to get a formal easement from her brother giving her a right-of-way onto the property."

Bruno nodded sympathetically, thinking he could guess what was coming.

"It was fine as long as Thibaut was alive, but when Thibaut's son Fernand learned that our side of the family was becoming wealthy through property investments, relations cooled a bit. When my grandmother died, it got worse. Fernand asked for the return of some of the family furniture she brought to Alsace when she got married. Naturally we discussed it the next time we came down here one summer to stay at the house. We were very polite and friendly, but we said no. Our grandmother had wanted the furniture to stay with her grandchildren. The family feud began, and pretty soon it started to escalate. You know Fernand keeps geese?"

Bruno nodded. "So do I, just a couple. They're pretty common in the countryside around here."

"Yes, but they're very noisy. When we said no, Fernand moved a couple hundred geese to within about five meters of the back of our house, on land that was his. They started cackling just after dawn, and it went on until nightfall. That was the end of our vacation, and for about ten years we didn't bother coming down here. But on principle we determined to keep the house. We paid the taxes, and then five years ago my mother came down for the twin-town reunion, staying at a hotel. She went to see the house and hired a local company to come and do maintenance, repaint the place, repair the roof and so on. She tried to see Fernand, but he wouldn't let her into his house.

"Two years ago, I came down with her and saw the possibility of converting the house into three really nice residences, selling them and washing our hands of the place and of the other branch of the family. My mother refused. It was her family inheritance. She died last year, and I telephoned Fernand to invite him to the funeral, but he slammed the phone down on me. Then I wrote to him, saying what I proposed and that I'd send the builders in, put a swimming pool where the vegetables used to be and fix up the garden. He wrote back saying he had no objection to any building works I proposed. So I wrote thanking him and went ahead, putting over a hundred thousand euros into the conversion. When I came down this time with Freddy, I parked the car, unpacked and went to see Fernand, hoping that we'd be putting the feud behind us."

"But it didn't work out like that."

"No, he met me on his doorstep, didn't invite me in, and then gave me a nasty smile as if he'd been looking forward to this moment. He asked how I intended to sell any of these conversions when he wouldn't allow any of the new buyers to cross his land to get to the place. That was when I found out there was no right-of-way."

"He can't stop you from getting access to your land."

"He doesn't have to. I can use a small and very narrow dirt track. But I can't sell the residences as luxury holiday homes if that's the only way in. And then this morning, Fernand fired the second barrel. The geese are back."

7

When Annette came back from the caravan the race marshals were using as an office, she was hanging on to the arm of George Young, who was beaming, evidently delighted at her success. He seemed to have recovered from his migraine, if that was what caused him to miss the race, and shook Bruno's hand to congratulate him.

"This calls for a celebration," he said. "My treat—but you'll know better where we can go around here, Bruno."

Bruno scratched his head. On Sunday evenings out of season, Ivan's bistro was closed, and there was not much choice in St. Denis beyond the local pizzeria. But Young was right; Annette was entitled to a celebration. Bruno had planned to make dinner for his guests from Alsace, a simple meal featuring some of his homemade pâté, followed by his vegetable stew, cheese and salad, all accompanied by the big round *tourte* of country bread he'd picked up from the bakery that morning. But Annette's success deserved better than that. Had it been anyone else, Bruno would have called on Maurice, a local duck farmer, and picked up some fresh foie gras to fry very fast in its own fat and serve with a sauce of honey and balsamic vinegar. But although she was no longer a vegetarian, Annette drew the line at foie gras.

Maybe he could call the baron and see if he'd caught any trout that day.

"Didn't the mayor say there was going to be a special *marché nocturne* tonight, in honor of the race?" Annette asked. "I'm sure lots of the other drivers will be there, so I wouldn't mind going."

"I've never been to one," said Young. "Let's do it."

The idea for a night market had started just up the road in the hilltop village of Audrix, where the local farmers were invited on Saturday evenings in summer to sell their produce from stalls erected around the village square, which the *mairie* filled with tables and benches for the public. It had begun modestly with pâtés, salads and strawberries, foie gras and cheeses, a stall that grilled steaks and lamb chops and another selling wine by the bottle. It proved highly popular with the locals as well as tourists and quickly expanded to include *haricots couennes,* beans cooked with pork rind, as well as *pommes frites,* omelettes and soups. Then a local farm began offering snails in their shells with butter and garlic, and the *mairie* rebuilt the village's old stone baking oven in the center of the square to produce fresh bread and pizzas. By the end of the first season, local bands and singers were performing, there was a donkey cart to take children around the village, and it was hard to find a place at the tables. By the second year, half the villages of the Périgord were offering similar events.

St. Denis, never a village to rush into things, watched and waited. Bruno and the mayor and their friends sampled the other markets, observed what worked and what didn't and carefully planned their own version. They didn't want loud rock music, since they had learned that the diners liked to hear themselves talk. They decided to offer folksingers, jazz groups and balladeers until ten o'clock, and then a disco took over so the people could dance. Bruno and the mayor had tasted the cheap plonk sold at inflated prices in other markets, so they insisted on offering only good local wines and kept a close eye on the prices. With the local butcher they set up a proper barbecue that produced steaks, lamb, chicken and fish. Huge cauldrons were brought in to cook *moules marinières* and paella. Bruno persuaded his friend Stéphane to bring his cheese stall, the Vinhs to offer their Asian food, and Fauquet to keep his café open until midnight and to make vast quantities of his own ice cream.

They had brought Florence into their plans from the beginning, since she had persuaded the local education authorities that the best way to teach environmental sciences was to have schoolchildren run their own small farm at the *collège*. It was doing well enough to provide the night market with eggs, chickens, tomatoes, zucchini and lettuces. Florence also insisted on proper plates, glasses and cutlery rather than plastic forks and paper plates and arranged for the use of the *collège*'s industrial dishwashers. The older schoolchildren earned pocket money for setting up the tables and benches in the town square. Since Florence reckoned that there was not much use in the children growing food if they didn't know how to prepare it, she had set up a voluntary cooking class in the *collège* kitchens after school hours. So the children had their own stall offering the pâtés, lemon tarts, apple pies and brownies they had made.

Bruno was proud of the town's night market and happy to agree to Annette's request. "It's a warm enough evening," he said.

"And it's going to be a spectacular sunset," said Young, looking at the scattered low clouds in the west, already touched with pink and gold as the sun began its slow decline.

"We arrange those specially for occasions like this," came a new voice, and Yveline joined them, embracing Annette and adding her own congratulations. She was in her gendarme uniform, with the two white stripes of a lieutenant on her shoulders. "You'll have to show me how to drive like that."

"Please don't," said Bruno. "My nerves couldn't stand it." He introduced her to George Young as Annette's friend, to make it clear he'd be joining them. "Are you on duty this evening, or can you join us at the *marché nocturne* in town?"

"I'm on duty, but I can take a meal break, and I'd probably take a stroll around the market anyway." She glanced at Bruno's fire-retardant driving clothes, smiling as she raised an eyebrow. "Will you change into your uniform, or will you be eating disguised as a snowman?"

"You're right, I've got to change, but first I'd better call my houseguests to tell them where we'll be having dinner. You'll enjoy meeting my friend Thomas, Yveline. He's another *flic*, municipal police like me."

"*Merde*," she said, rolling her eyes in mock horror. "Just what we need, another cop like you."

After calling his friends, Bruno steered Young toward Monique's, the new wine bar on the rue de Paris, to wait while he and Annette changed in the *mairie*. As they came out, they ran into Florence, who was supervising her pupils as they unloaded crockery and cutlery along with some of their pies and pâtés from the back of her car. Annette invited her to join their table for dinner.

"I'd love to. Another of my pupils is babysitting my kids this evening," Florence replied. "But I may have to be up and down a bit, since I'm supposed to keep an eye on the youngsters."

"I may have to take a turn at barbecue duty," said Bruno, glancing across to where Valentin, the town butcher, was manning the grill. The tables in the square were beginning to fill, and Florence and Yveline sat at one to reserve spaces for them all. Annette and Young went to collect plates, glasses and cutlery from the stall run by Florence's pupils. Bruno bought a bottle of white wine and another of red from Raoul at the town vineyard's stall and took them to the table where Thomas and Ingrid had just arrived. He introduced them to Yveline and went to place an order for the meat.

Young joined Bruno at the barbecue, carrying plates and insisting on paying the bill. "I've ordered a small steak and a lamb chop for each of us, but chicken for Annette," Bruno said.

When they returned to the table with the loaded plates, the baron had joined them, bringing a double portion of mussels cooked in white wine for the table to share. Yveline had already bought salad and *pommes frites* for everyone, and Florence had ordered apple pies for dessert. Bruno, who enjoyed the way these night markets always seemed to expand beyond the original guests to create an unexpected fellowship in which all shared the food, poured the wine and offered a toast to Annette. Thomas went for more wine, and Ingrid came back from Stéphane's stall with some goat cheese and Cantal.

"What's it like, being married to a policeman?" Florence asked Ingrid. "Do you worry about what might happen to him?"

"Of course," Ingrid replied. "But it's what he wants to do or, rather, he did, until these new rules and management systems came in with Sarkozy. Now they have targets and quotas for arrests, and Thomas agrees with Bruno that's no way to judge police efficiency. He's thinking of taking early retirement."

"He's not the only one," Yveline chimed in. "They're turning us into not much more than traffic cops. That's not why I joined the gendarmes. It's all right for Bruno; he works for the mayor, who likes the way Bruno operates. He hardly ever has to make an arrest."

"That can work in a small town like St. Denis, where I know everybody," said Bruno. "It wouldn't work in a big city."

On the stage, Arlette, a newcomer to St. Denis who had recently joined the *mairie* as an accountant, was adjusting the microphone as she settled on a stool and began to play some classical guitar music. Yveline was asking Young if there was much theft in the antique-car business, and Florence was telling Annette about the latest efforts of the *collège* computer club to design a video game they hoped to sell. The sun was setting, streaks of rosy pink and red alternating with the scattered lines of cloud, and the old stone of the *mairie* had turned into a rich gold. It was that brief moment of twilight before someone turned on the lamps over the diners, and Bruno murmured to himself one of his favorite words.

"*Crépuscule,*" he said as he looked at the red sheen of the setting sun on the bend of the river, not aware that he had spoken aloud until the baron repeated it back to him.

"*Crépuscule,* one of the loveliest words in our language, for one of the loveliest times of day just as it gives way to night," the baron said softly, gazing at the shifting planes of red and crimson light on the river. "Sitting here, with wine and food and surrounded by friends as generations must have done before us in this very place, makes all the world's troubles seem very far away. Sometimes I imagine the prehistoric people sitting here on the riverbank, sharing their roast mammoth or whatever it was, and watching the sun go down just like us."

He raised his glass. "I drink to them, whoever they were."

"I never thought of you as such a romantic," said Bruno.

"When you get to my age, you'll realize that we men are the real romantics. Women are much more practical; they have to be." The baron paused, turning his head to look at the stage. "Who is that girl playing guitar? She's good."

Bruno explained, and as he spoke, Arlette ended the piece, put down her guitar and picked up a lute. She was a tall, slim young woman but seemed to have a wiry strength. She was shy, usually playing with her head bowed so her face was hidden by long wings of straight, dark hair. She bent to raise the microphone higher and announced she intended to play an old medieval song by one of the troubadours of the region, Bertran de Born, a twelfth-century knight who had been lord of the castle of Hautefort. She began to pick out a delicate but haunting melody on the lute.

Suddenly to the surprise of all at the table, Young rose to his feet and began to sing in a fine tenor voice, in a language that Bruno could not understand although it seemed distantly familiar. He heard the baron mutter that it was Occitan, but then all fell silent as Young sang through to the end, Annette gazing up at him entranced and then bursting into applause, in which other tables joined. Ingrid called out "Bravo," and Valentin the butcher banged his tongs against the grill and demanded an encore.

"Another?" Arlette called down to him from the stage.

"Mon chan fenisc ab dol et ab maltraire," Young called back, and she nodded and began to play again, a slower song that sounded like a lament.

Bruno had applauded politely with the rest, but while he respected the antiquity of the music and the tradition it represented, it was not much to his taste. Young sang well, and it was interesting to come across a man whose main interest was cars who also had this side to his character. Annette clearly delighted in it and in Young, but except for their common interest in motor sports he seemed an unlikely partner for her. Annette was fair-haired, slim and pretty in the way of a little girl. She looked much younger than her years and had a shy, almost-timid manner until you got to know her. Bruno would have thought Young was the type to be attracted to a more dramatic, assertive kind of woman, one of those leggy blondes who liked fast cars and discos. Maybe he was misjudging Young, but again Bruno wondered if Young knew of Annette's father's wealth.

"Where did you learn that?" Annette asked as Young sat down, kissing him on his cheek. "You were brilliant."

"I read Romantic languages at university, and Bertran de Born was required reading," Young said, laughing as he picked up his wineglass. "I'm not a great fan, all that glorifying of wars and battles and how he loved to fight and see men die. One of his poems was about Richard Lionheart, to tell him there was too much peace about and it was time for some more slaughter."

"We have an early start tomorrow to get back to Alsace, so for us it's time for some sleep," said Thomas, rising. "Thank you all for a very fine weekend, and you are always welcome to visit us."

8

After saying good-bye the next morning to Thomas and his wife before they set off on the long drive home to Alsace, Bruno was in his office going through routine paperwork when his desk phone rang. He put aside a circular from the office of the prefect of the *département* on police exceptions to the thirty-five-hour workweek, thinking there were many weeks when he worked twice that much, picked up the phone and recognized the voice of the manager of the local supermarket.

"Another shoplifting case, caught on the security camera," Bruno heard. "You can probably guess the identity of the kid who did it?"

"Félix again?" Bruno asked with a sigh.

"Right, and as you know, it's not his first time. We're holding him here in my office with our security guy, and we'll wait for you."

"I have to contact his father first, then the youth services people. You know the rules for juveniles, whatever your cameras might show."

"I know these damn rules only too well, Bruno. You're never going to straighten these kids out if you baby them."

"Come off it, Simon. You've got the lowest shoplifting rate

in the *département*. I'll be there as soon as I can. What was he stealing?"

"A set of stereo headphones."

To double-check on Félix's age, Bruno first went to the dusty room filled with old files that the mayor called his archives and pulled out the large ledger that recorded the town's births and deaths. He saw that Félix would not be sixteen for another ten days and, as Bruno suspected, he had to be treated as a minor. He returned to his office and called the youth services in Périgueux, but no one was available to talk to him. The receptionist said he should use someone from the social services at his own *mairie* to sit in for the preliminary questioning.

Bruno sat back, considering. The rules on dealing with minors were strict, and on the whole Bruno thought they made sense. If this case was going anywhere, a magistrate would have to be called in, and the magistrate who usually dealt with juvenile cases was Annette, as the most junior in the office. He called her and explained. Her office was in Sarlat, but she was in a meeting with a lawyer in Les Eyzies. She could join him at the supermarket within the hour.

Félix's father wasn't at home, but Bruno knew he could find him in a local café that had offtrack betting and TV sets permanently tuned to horse racing. He rounded him up, and along with Roberte from the *mairie* they headed for the supermarket. A discreet door at the side of the row of checkout counters led to a staircase and the office upstairs.

Félix was slumped on a chair in the corner of the room. He was wearing jeans that were too short for him, an old denim jacket and a T-shirt. The sneakers on his feet had seen better days, one sole repaired with duct tape. The security man, Bertrand, whom Bruno knew from the rugby club, was standing over the boy. He was wearing a single earphone in one ear with a flesh-colored wire leading from it and disappearing under his collar.

That was new, thought Bruno. Simon, the manager, was behind his desk. Four TV screens on the wall showed images from the security cameras. A fifth TV stood on a filing cabinet.

Félix looked up at the new arrivals, his lip curling in a sneer at the sight of his father and Bruno. Bruno tried to remember what it had been like to be almost sixteen and to have no money when prosperous schoolmates were buying CDs and fashionable clothes and seemed to have endless supplies of one-franc pieces to put into pinball machines.

"You should be at school, Félix," he began after the usual greetings. "Would you like to tell me what happened?"

Félix shrugged and turned away to look out of the window.

"Answer the policeman, you little jerk," said Félix's father, stepping forward aggressively. Bruno put a restraining hand on his arm.

"Simon, do you have a statement?" he asked.

"Mine and our security guard's statement are already typed up, signed and witnessed," said Simon, handing the neat sheets of paper across his desk, briskly confident in his familiarity with the procedure. "You realize that I have no latitude in these cases. Company policy is that all shoplifters must be pursued to the limit of the law. And it's not the first time with this kid. I've made a copy of the videotape for you, but let's take a look at it."

The TV screen on the filing cabinet flickered into life, showing a washed-out image of the aisle with CDs, DVDs and electronic equipment.

"We have one fixed camera here and another for the alcohol, since they're the two high-value zones. The other cameras are on swivels so they can monitor different aisles," Simon explained. "The boy came in just as we opened at eight-thirty, when there's always a bit of a rush, as he well knows. He probably thought he could slink out without us spotting him."

"I wanted to get to school," said Félix in a low voice, the first time he had spoken. He was looking out the window at the parked cars as if these proceedings had nothing to do with him. His arms were folded protectively across his chest.

The screen showed a modest throng of shoppers walking along the main aisle and then a thin youngster peeling off and going into the electronics aisle, straight to a section with stereo headphones. He pulls down three or four, examining them in turn. Then he turns his back on the camera while appearing to replace the headphones and walks quickly to the end of the aisle and turns left past the microwaves and coffeemaking machines.

"I was watching the camera, spotted Félix and thought he was behaving suspiciously," said Simon, reading aloud from his copy of his written statement. Bruno recognized the wording. It came straight from the template given to all the store managers by the company's legal office.

"So I used the radio to alert Bertrand, the security guard, who was standing by the entrance. When Félix walked through the checkout without paying, Bertrand stopped him and asked him to come to the office. The boy tried to run out of the store, but Bertrand caught him by his jacket, and these headphones fell from under his arm where he'd hidden them. The retail price is thirty-nine euros and ninety-nine cents. Bertrand then made a citizen's arrest, and we called you at once."

"Anything to say, Félix?" Bruno asked.

"Ask him why I took that brand of headphones," said the boy, still gazing at the world beyond the window.

"Why do you think he took that brand?" Bruno asked.

Simon shrugged. "Maybe he liked the color. I don't know."

"Is it the best brand or the most expensive?"

"No, it's a midprice model. Some are over a hundred euros."

"Why did you take that brand, Félix?" Bruno asked.

"Because that was the brand I used to have, earphones that

I bought here a week ago with money that I earned chopping wood. Ask my mother, she can confirm that."

His father grunted something that might have been agreement. Bruno knew that Félix's mother worked weekends cleaning houses, as well as cleaning at the *collège* during the week. He could imagine that the boy's only pocket money would come from odd jobs he found through his mother.

"So what happened to your old earphones?"

Félix continued to stare out the window. "Tell him to ask his son."

The plot thickens, thought Bruno. Simon's son, Tristan, was the same age as Félix and in the same class at the *collège*. Tristan was big for his age, a forward on the school rugby team and strikingly good-looking with clear skin, curly fair hair and very long eyelashes. When he began playing rugby, his mother had badgered Bruno about the game being too rough and could Bruno guarantee that his handsome features would not get damaged. But Tristan's manners did not match his looks. He was brash, noisy and inclined to throw his weight about. Bruno had warned him several times about dirty play, and he'd noticed that while most of the good young rugby players seemed popular with the local girls, Tristan was an exception. They steered clear of him. Bruno looked quizzically at Simon, who was blushing.

"Let's talk privately," Bruno said, and led Simon out into the corridor and then into the staircase where they would be out of hearing.

"Could Tristan be involved in this in some way?" he asked. "I'm trying to understand why Félix said we should ask him about the earphones."

"I don't see how," Simon replied, but he wouldn't meet Bruno's eyes.

"Has Tristan got earphones of his own?" Bruno pressed.

"Yes, a much-better set, he got them for his birthday." Simon paused and then sighed. "But I confiscated them last week because he wasn't doing his homework." He looked up at Bruno. "When they get to that age, it's not easy to discipline them."

Bruno nodded sympathetically. Simon was a slim man, shorter than Bruno, and about the same height as his wife. She was a burly woman, an aggressive tennis player with a loud voice who seemed to change her hairstyle and color almost every week. Their son took after her, rather than Simon. Tristan was already bigger than his father and probably stronger.

"So if I went to the *collège,* do you think it's possible that I'd find Félix's earphones on Tristan?"

"Look, Bruno, this kid Félix has been in trouble with the law before. My son has never been caught doing anything wrong. You'd have no right to do that, none at all."

"I know your son. I'm his rugby coach, and I've seen him behaving badly on the field too many times. It's not just that Tristan seems to have little idea of fair play; he's cost us more penalties than anyone else on the team. It's very unusual for anyone to be sent off in *collège* games, but it happened to him twice last season. You know I've threatened to drop him from the team unless he starts to control himself?"

"No, I didn't know that," Simon said, sounding tired and sad. Again he wouldn't look at Bruno.

"Do you think your son is a bully?"

"It's just his age, high spirits; he'll settle down."

"Let's hope you're right," Bruno said. "But it looks to me as if your son took Félix's headphones, and Félix came in today to replace them from the store run by Tristan's father. He might even have seen it as a kind of justice. Does that sound plausible to you?"

"It was still shoplifting, and anyway, the procedure has started. We can't drop it now."

"Of course you can. I can take care of Bertrand and Roberte. Even if you go ahead, Félix is still a few days short of sixteen. As far as the law is concerned, he's a juvenile, so nothing is going to happen to him, except that the very word 'justice' will leave a nasty taste in his mouth. But he's not going to get off lightly. I'll go back in there, take him home with his dad, put the fear of God into him and search his room. If there's any more evidence of shoplifting, I'll throw the book at him."

"What about Tristan?"

"You're his dad, that's up to you," said Bruno. "But if you want to go ahead and press charges against Félix, I think I've got reasonable cause to haul your son out of his classroom and, if I find those headphones, that would be a case of theft, probably theft with threats of violence. And your son has passed his sixteenth birthday, so in the eyes of the law he's an adult. Do you really want me to do that?"

Simon closed his eyes, his mouth working. He seemed about to speak but then stopped himself and clenched his jaw.

Bruno decided to use his last weapon. He spoke so quietly that it was almost a whisper. "I don't think your wife would like that."

Simon closed his eyes again and took a deep breath and looked at Bruno and shrugged. "Okay, I'll drop the charges. And I'll pay for the headphones. But if that kid ever comes in this store again, we'll film his every move."

"You're right," said Bruno, knowing it was time to leave Simon with some shred of self-respect. "And I'll make sure Félix knows that. And we both know you're doing the right thing, Simon. You're a good man." Bruno slapped him gently on the shoulder. "I'll take him off now and search his room and make sure he never gives you reason to regret this."

"Regret what?" came a familiar voice and the sound of high

heels on stairs as Annette appeared. She was wearing her usual working uniform of a dark blue suit and a white blouse buttoned to the neck, a black leather briefcase in one hand.

"Bonjour, Bruno," she said, kissing him on both cheeks and holding out her hand to Simon. "Monsieur," she said.

"Congratulations on your success in the rally, mademoiselle," Simon said. "I saw the report in the paper today. But your photo did not do you justice."

"Whereas mine showed me scared to death," said Bruno, smiling. "I think we're almost done here, Annette. Simon here, the store manager, has decided not to proceed with charges against the boy. But I thought you and I should at least visit his home and see if there is any evidence there of other thefts. I can explain the details as we drive."

He led the way back to Simon's office, introduced Annette, thanked Bertrand and Roberte and said he'd drop Roberte back at the *mairie* now that the magistrate was present. No need, she said, she'd take the opportunity to do some shopping. Félix was staring wide eyed at Annette, as if awed to be in her presence. He must know about her success in the rally, Bruno thought. He took Bertrand aside and said the store manager would explain the agreement he'd reached with Bruno. Bertrand nodded his okay. Bruno turned back to inform Félix and his father that he and the magistrate were going to search Félix's room at home. He showed everyone out into the corridor, picking up the set of headphones from Simon's desk and slipping them into his pocket as he said to Simon, "Since you're paying for them . . ."

Bruno took Félix's father in his police van, and Annette followed with Félix. Bruno used the drive to explain that he'd persuaded the store to drop charges on account of Félix's age but on the condition that there was no other evidence of shoplifting.

"He's a handful, that kid," said his father, lighting a cigarette as they drove. He had lit one earlier as soon as they were out of the supermarket. Bruno plucked it from his hand and threw it out of the partly open window. "Not in a police van," he said. The man shrugged, coughed and opened the window fully to spit. "His mother can handle him, but he never listens to me."

"Maybe that's because you don't have a job and you're never at home, always in the café," said Bruno.

"There aren't any damn jobs, not for someone my age, not anymore."

"Your wife finds work to do, and so does Félix. Lots of old people would pay a few euros to get their wood chopped, their gardens taken care of."

"Is this about me or about my son?"

"Both. If your son is getting into trouble, and we both know it's not the first time, it's your job to take an interest. You could steer him back onto the straight and narrow, set him a good example. What was your job when you worked?"

"Storeman at the sawmill, until they closed it. I had that job for nearly thirty years, ever since I came out of military service."

"Which unit were you in?"

"Infantry, One Hundred Tenth Regiment, based in Germany at Baden-Baden."

Bruno had been based there for a few months after finishing basic training, before he went on the course for the combat engineers. There had been over fifty thousand French troops stationed there at the time, including the headquarters of two army corps before the army finally withdrew from German soil in 1999.

"Not a bad posting," said Bruno. "Did they give you conscripts the extra money for being outside of France?"

"Not much, but yes, a few of those deutsche marks. I remember a bar we used to go to, Chez Hannes, it was called, run by a big German guy who'd been in the Foreign Legion, always ready to tell a few war stories. He'd been in Indochina and Algeria."

"I've been there," Bruno said, remembering. "If I remember rightly, Hannes was as bald as a badger, but he had one of those big handlebar mustaches, and he'd sing 'Le Boudin' when he got drunk."

"That's right, the old legionnaires' marching song. *Putain,* I can see the old bastard now with all those tattoos on his arms." He laughed, his eyes lively as he remembered. "Hard as nails, Hannes was. You should have seen him throwing people out when there was a fight. I wouldn't have wanted to be on the wrong end of one of his punches."

They drew up outside Félix's home, an old public-housing block of four stories and no elevator.

"Did you ever tell Félix about those days, what it was like when you were young and in the army? He'd probably be interested."

The old man looked sideways at Bruno, then nodded grudgingly before climbing out of the car and lighting another cigarette. Bruno sighed as Annette parked behind him. He'd talk to the manager of the old folks' home, see if there were any odd jobs that could be found for an old soldier.

Félix had a small room to himself. It contained a single bed, a small chest of drawers, an old card table and a chair. The floor was covered in old linoleum, holes in it patched with duct tape. Two hooks on the back of the door provided the only place to hang clothes. There were no photos of pop groups or pinups on the walls, only an array of photos of sports cars and horses taken from magazines. There was no laptop, no radio, and Bruno knew Félix was one of the few *collège* students with no mobile phone. The room smelled stale with an overlay of dirty socks. Bruno checked the drawers and found T-shirts and threadbare underwear, another pair of jeans. One drawer contained about a dozen apples. There were some cores in the wastepaper basket. On the card table was a pile of schoolbooks and beside them two old issues of *Cheval Magazine,* lacking their covers. Bruno looked up; they had been stuck to the wall with sticky tape.

"Obviously he likes horses and cars," said Annette, looking around. She closed the door behind her. "Are you going to tell me what happened here? I'm called to a shoplifting case with a juvenile, and suddenly it's all dropped when I know that manager is supposed to demand legal action."

Bruno explained and brought out the headphones. "Do you think I should give them back to him?"

"No, I think you should get the bully to return Félix's own phones. In the circumstances, you're pushing your legal rights in searching this boy's room. If the father hadn't allowed you inside, I think I'd have stopped you. And I don't see any evidence of other shoplifting here, except maybe those apples."

"You're right. But this kid is going to get into more trouble unless somebody sets him straight, and pretty soon. The next time he gets into trouble, he'll face juvenile detention," Bruno said. Annette made a face, evidently disapproving of the tougher new laws Sarkozy had brought in.

"I've never been able to get through to the boy, not through rugby or tennis or anything else, and I don't think his dad has much of a relationship with him," Bruno went on. "Félix is a loner, scrawny, not big for his age, with no friends that I know of, a bit of a victim."

"If he'd been arrested, we could have gotten him assigned to community service," Annette said. "That might have helped, gotten him started on something that might lead to a job and a bit of self-respect. But now that the case has been dropped, there's no cause to arrest him."

Bruno nodded thoughtfully. "I'm wondering if these pictures

of horses tell us something. Maybe we could steer him into work that way."

"You mean Pamela's riding school? It's worth a try." She looked around the drab room, sadly. "*Mon Dieu,* how the other half lives."

9

Fernand and Odette Oudinot lived in a cottage that had in the old days belonged to one of the farmworkers employed by the owners of the *chartreuse*. With a lot of hard work they had transformed it into a welcoming and attractive home. They had turned the attic into a large bedroom with its own bathroom, and downstairs they had knocked down walls to make two large rooms, a huge kitchen and a separate dining room, where Bruno had often been a guest. They had also created a large archway into the connecting barn, where in the past tobacco plants had been dried. The lower part of the barn was now a vast living room, twelve meters long and five meters wide. Its large and double-glazed windows gave spectacular views down the slope where Fernand kept a small herd of cows. Fernand had done most of the conversion work himself. Upstairs were three guest rooms, each with its own bathroom.

At the other side of the large vegetable garden and far enough removed to be almost out of earshot was another barn, where the geese, ducks and chickens were kept at night. Beyond them stood a *pigeonnier,* a tall tower that still housed pigeons for the family pot, a large pond and then two hectares of land where the birds roamed free. Then came the orchards and the walnut plantation, and just over the brow of the slope was the *chartreuse* that belonged to Sylvestre.

The whole place was a tribute to the ability of the farmers of the Périgord to adapt. It was hard to make a living from ducks and geese alone, so Fernand's dairy cows brought in a little extra money, and the calves he raised were known to produce the best veal in the district. And in the summer, the three guest rooms were rented out by the week for farm vacations. The guests ate with Fernand and Odette, roamed the farm and enjoyed the countryside. Odette cared for her bees and cooked endlessly, making jams and her splendid pies and tarts to sell in the market along with her honey. From her vegetable garden came strawberries and zucchini, tomatoes and eggplants, peppers and every other vegetable Bruno could think of. What wasn't eaten by the paying guests was pickled, preserved and put into jars to be sold in the market in winter. And with all of this, Odette still found time to cultivate the daffodils that made the hillside dance in spring and the roses that she'd trained to wind prettily around the doors and windows of her cottage. It made a splendid palette of colors in summer with the sunflowers that flanked the guests' barn and a lower meadow filled with wildflowers where her bees and hosts of butterflies dallied and feasted.

Fernand and Odette had made their home and their farm into one of the better-known places in the Périgord. Hardly a tourist brochure was printed without a photo of their ducks and geese in the shadow of the *pigeonnier* or their garden with the rose-covered cottage behind. It was every city dweller's fantasy of the French countryside and the rural heritage that most French people still held dear and to which every French politician paid homage. The mayor's own campaign brochures featured him smiling as he picked tomatoes in Odette's garden or sat on the terrace helping Fernand shell walnuts. This was the image of La

Belle France and a promise that some core of that grand tradition was still to be seen and enjoyed.

"Bonjour, Bruno," Odette said, wiping her hands on an apron and advancing to kiss him on both cheeks. A plump and motherly woman, Odette had rosy cheeks as round as two little apples. She smelled of flour and jam and good cooking. Behind her on the giant stove were four large copper pots, each bubbling with black currants, and on the kitchen table an army of empty jam jars waited to be filled. *"Tu as mangé?"*

Bruno grinned at the traditional farm welcome, the eternal question "Have you eaten?" It was an invitation as much as a welcome, and Bruno loved to eat in this friendly home, staring down at the grazing cows and the ducks and geese waddling among them.

"I'm on duty today, so I can't stay, Odette, much as I'd like to," he said. "Is Fernand around?"

She directed him to the workshop, a lean-to attached to the barn for the ducks and geese. Fernand was using a small circular saw to cut logs for the winter and stacking them neatly under the eaves of the barn. When he saw Bruno, he pushed his protective goggles up onto his bald head, shook hands and said with his bright blue eyes glinting, "Time for a *p'tit apéro*? I keep a bottle here that Odette's not supposed to know about. You can tell me about the race you were in. I saw it in the paper."

"Not this time, Fernand. It's business, although very unofficial. The mayor got a call from a mayor in Alsace about this trouble with your cousins over the *chartreuse*. He's tied up today with the regional council meeting or he'd have come himself, but he asked me if there's anything we can do to help."

"It's a family thing," Fernand said. "I can't say I'm happy about the way it's built up, but I don't want to see the big old family house turned into some fancy place for rich tourists."

"You have a few tourists here yourself."

"Yes, but what we do is tourism on the farm; ecotourism, they call it these days. The kids get to play with the ducks and chickens, see the cows and calves, pick vegetables for their lunch—it's educational. The Alsace part of the family wants to do something very different, make a fortune by selling off these luxury apartments. It's crazy; this is the countryside, not the heart of Paris. Besides, there's some bad blood built up between us over the years."

"How do you mean? I thought you and your aunt, Sylvestre's grandmother, agreed to divide it, she got the *chartreuse* and you got the land."

"Yes, but we had a verbal agreement that we'd try to keep it all together in the family, not start selling it off. The Alsace family used to come down here every year, and we'd light the fires, air the beds, take care of the garden, get a meal ready to welcome them."

"What went wrong?"

"It was money, of course. When our parents died—they died within three weeks of each other—there was this land and there was a fair bit of money saved up. I was underage, but I wanted to stay with the farm, so my aunt agreed to let Jeannot, our neighbor, take me on as an apprentice, and he and I farmed this land together. The idea was that I'd take over the farm when I came of age. That was fine, just what I wanted, but then she came to me and asked if she could use the money to invest in some business project that she and her husband had back in Alsace. She promised to pay me back, with interest, and got a *notaire* to make it all legal."

"And did she pay you back?"

"Oh yes, in cash and right on time, but she paid me only three percent interest a year at a time when inflation was roaring away. And she used our money, my money, to help her new family buy back the aerodrome, which eventually made them millionaires.

I'd just married Odette, and I had a fight with my aunt at the wedding when I said I wanted to be paid what the money was worth before the inflation, as well as the interest. That was when it started. She said a deal is a deal, and there was nothing in the contract about inflation. Anyway, it went on from there, me and Odette struggling to build this farm up and make ends meet, while she and her family up in Alsace were buying fast cars and fancy clothes. And she took all the family furniture, although half of it was mine."

"What would it take to settle this?"

"They've got all the money in the world. It wouldn't hurt them to let me have the *chartreuse,* as compensation for all the money I lost through inflation, and the interest I lost along with it. I sat down one night and worked it all out, using the government's own inflation figures. Last time I looked, it was close to half a million euros they owe me. And I'm not asking for anything that's not mine by right. So if they think they can make some more money from this place, they'll have me and my rights to reckon with. And it's not just me; it's our Martine. All this will be hers when Odette and I are gone, and I'd like her to have the *chartreuse.*"

Bruno nodded. Martine was a late child, probably now in her thirties, who'd gone to the lycée in Périgueux and then to university in Bordeaux and got some high-powered job in Paris.

"Is she still in Paris?" Bruno asked, thinking she might be prepared to reach some sensible settlement with Sylvestre.

"She's based in England now, got her own business helping French companies get established in London. She's doing very well, employs three or four people," Fernand said proudly. "She was always good with languages."

"Didn't she get married, must be ten years ago or more, just about the time I got here and took this job?"

"She married a colleague from Paris, but it didn't last. I never took to him. She's divorced now, no kids, more's the pity. Odette can't wait to be a grandmother. And I'm not getting any younger. I'd love to have a grandson take this place over one day."

"Do you see much of her?"

"She's here now, just came for the week on one of those discount flights from London that come into Bergerac. Only cost her fifty euros, there and back. She's off seeing friends in Périgueux, but she'll be back for dinner. Come and join us. You'll like her."

Bruno had to decline, citing a previous engagement. He left his car outside the cottage, and Fernand led the way through the walnut plantation.

"I saw the parade of old cars the other day, but I was sorry we missed your race. We were having lunch with friends in Rouffignac. But I saw that white Jaguar again as we were driving there. It raced right past me."

"The E-type?" Bruno asked. "Are you sure?" That was Young's car. Why was he driving around when he was supposed to have been laid low by a migraine? Maybe he wasn't as attached to Annette as she seemed to think.

"Oh yes, and it was the same driver, the fair-haired young man."

They walked on over the brow of the hill. Strolling through the geese to the wire fence Fernand had erected just a few meters from the rear of the *chartreuse,* Bruno saw the building had two wings enclosing a large courtyard with a handsome old tree in its center. About thirty meters beyond the archway that led into the courtyard was a separate gatehouse. The main house was about fifty meters in length, with mansard windows in the roof.

"Sylvestre turned each wing into a separate house, and he plans to keep the gatehouse for himself," said Fernand, over the noise of the geese. "I've fenced off his land from mine, so you'll have to walk around from here and get to his house by the dirt path that leads off from the road." He opened a small gate in his fence to let Bruno out of the enclosure for the geese and back into the walnut plantation.

"Any message for him?" Bruno asked.

"Tell him to restore to me what his family owes, and I'll remove the geese and sell him an easement for an access road. I'll even put up with him living in the gatehouse."

Bruno continued alone on a pleasant stroll through the trees and out to the single-lane road of tarmac. The potholes in the road suggested heavy use by trucks coming with building materials for Sylvestre's conversion. The path that led off to the *chartreuse* was muddy and narrow, marked by ruts that had been filled in with gravel. Trees and bushes on each side had been battered by the truck traffic. Nobody interested in a luxury home would want to arrive this way. And the closer Bruno approached, the louder the cackling of the geese.

Once past the path, Bruno whistled in admiration and pulled out his mobile phone to take some photos. To his left was the two-story gatehouse with a four-by-four vehicle outside. It was about the size of Bruno's own cottage, big enough for at least two generous bedrooms upstairs. Straight ahead was the stone archway leading into the courtyard with another four-by-four vehicle parked in the shade of the central tree. The *chartreuse* itself was a fine building, with two white pillars supporting a porch above the main door, tall French windows to either side and mansard windows on the floor above. The barns to each side of the courtyard had also been given tall French windows, and the walls of local stone had been cleaned and repainted.

As he advanced he saw to his right an all-weather swimming pool with a sliding glass roof where somebody was swimming laps. Behind the pool stood a handsome stone *pigeonnier* just beyond a terrace. A long stone building, evidently newly built and topped with solar panels, seemed to be the pool house. Expensive deck chairs lined the length of the pool. On a terrace between the pool and the house stood a large wooden table and chairs where Sylvestre was sitting with a dark-haired woman in jeans, an off-white cotton sweater and very large sunglasses. As he approached, Bruno saw a tall, slim bottle that signaled an Alsace wine on the table, along with green-stemmed glasses and a large ashtray.

"Bonjour, Bruno, this is an unexpected pleasure," said Sylvestre, rising and speaking loudly above the geese. "Do you know my cousin, Martine? Will you join us in a glass of Riesling?"

"I'm glad to see at least two members of the family are talking," he said and turned to Martine. "I've just been to see your mother and father. He's very proud of you and your career in London."

"Did he add that he can't wait for me to drop it all and start giving him grandchildren?" she replied, an edge to her voice as she stretched out a lazy hand to be shaken.

She took off the sunglasses and gave him a lopsided smile. Her voice was lower than he'd expected and her accent pure Parisian. Her dark hair fell gracefully to her shoulders from a side parting. Bruno guessed it had been expensively cut. She wore no makeup, except perhaps for something subtle that made her eyes look striking. They were her father's eyes, bright blue and twinkling. She had a wide, full mouth, perfect cheekbones and an imperious nose that some would have found too large for her face. Bruno thought it gave her character. Her legs were long and her shoulders broad. He noticed she was wearing flat shoes of the kind people wore on yachts in glossy magazine ads. She could be a model herself.

"Your father said something about wanting grandchildren to leave the farm to, and he's right to be proud of it and the business he's built with your mother. But I think everybody's inheritance could be improved if the two wings of the family could reach an agreement," Bruno said. "The mayor is hoping that can happen because he likes Sylvestre's project. He thinks it will bring more tourists and maybe a few more jobs for local people."

"The *mairie* is already enjoying the new property taxes I'm paying," said Sylvestre. He gave a short, barking laugh. "If anybody can reach a settlement, it will be me and Martine."

"You've made the place look great," said Bruno. "I wish you luck, and if I can help in any way . . ."

"Thanks, but let's not talk of that now." Sylvestre poured a glass of wine and pushed it across to Bruno. "I don't think you were there the other day after the parade when we got talking with your doctor and that Green council member, Alphonse, about electric cars. He was wondering if I could help organize a special race for them in the Vézère Valley. Martine is in public relations, and she's been sharing some ideas she has about getting sponsorships to make it happen."

"I imagine your Tesla would start as the favorite," said Bruno. "Talking of that car, where is it?" He looked around.

"There's no way I'd bring it up that rutted path. The truck with the Tesla and the Bugatti is in the secure parking lot of that logistics company in Le Buisson. I hired the Range Rover to get into my property and to get around." Sylvestre gestured to the vehicle parked in the courtyard behind him. "Alphonse said he'd talk to the mayor, and he called me this morning to say the mayor is interested in the idea."

"The mayor has become an enthusiast after the *concours* and yesterday's rally," said Bruno as a splash came from the pool and Freddy hauled himself out. He was thin and wiry, a mass of black hair tumbling down from his chest and into his trunks. He grabbed a towel from one of the deck chairs, put on a terry-cloth robe and came to shake hands before excusing himself to go and change.

"You're a brave man," said Bruno. "It's too late in the year for me to go swimming in the open air."

"The pool is heated by those solar panels," said Freddy, in good French but with an accent Bruno didn't recognize.

"How are you enjoying the Périgord?" Bruno asked. "Is this your first visit?"

"I like it a lot, all those old castles. And it's very green, a pleasant change after living in the Emirates. Excuse me, I should go and change."

He nodded courteously and left, and Bruno noticed that he headed for the gatehouse rather than the main building.

"Perhaps I could come and see you about the electric-car-rally idea," said Martine. "My father tells me you're the mayor's right-hand man."

"No, that's his deputy, Xavier, the *maire-adjoint*," said Bruno. "I'm just the municipal policeman, but I'd be happy to make an appointment for you to see the mayor. It's this family feud that I'm here for. You two seem to get on well, and your father seems to be open to some kind of financial settlement—"

"He is," said Martine, smoothly interrupting. "But every time he meets Sylvestre, all the old family resentments come out, and he starts demanding the return of a grandfather clock and some bed of my great-great-grandmother and talking about historic inflation rates. If there's a deal to be made, Sylvestre and I will do our best to reach it, and then it will be up to me to sell it to my father."

"Which way did you come here?" Sylvestre asked, and Bruno explained how he'd walked through the woods from Fernand's home.

"So he didn't steer you the other way around, where you'd

have seen a perfectly good road that goes around his walnut trees and comes out by my swimming pool. That's the logical way to get here, but he's fenced it off."

"The law gives you a minimum right of access to your property," said Bruno. "You could turn that rutted path into a decent gravel road, and it would make for a handsome approach."

" 'Minimum' is the word, not even two meters wide, and since it's not my land I can't make it into a paved or tarmac road. Still, I'm going to put down the gravel. But that doesn't solve the problem of the geese. Even with double glazing and earplugs, they wake me at dawn, and it goes on all day. It's enough to drive me crazy. I'd never be able to sell any of these apartments."

"That reminds me of a tourist who came to the *mairie* to lodge a complaint about the house he'd rented for a week," said Bruno. "It was just on the outskirts of St. Denis, and the people in the houses on each side kept chickens. The tourist wanted me to find some way to silence the cockerels who woke him at dawn every day."

"What did you say?" Martine asked. She'd been raised in the country herself and sounded amused.

"I asked him why he'd come to the French countryside where cockerels were to be expected. And he should count himself lucky that the neighbors didn't raise geese or donkeys."

"Peacocks are the worst of all," she said. "Their screams sound like someone's being murdered." She turned to Sylvestre. "Don't worry, I won't suggest my father get some peacocks—as long as you're prepared to be reasonable. In the meantime, just to show goodwill, I've brought you a peace offering."

Sylvestre sat up when she reached into her shoulder bag and brought out a sheaf of photocopies of handwritten pages that looked as if they came from a private journal or diary.

"It's about that Bugatti you're interested in," she said. "It's the unpublished memoir of an RAF bomber pilot shot down in 1941 and rescued by someone driving a car that sounds like the car that obsesses you. When the airman died, his family sent his unpublished memoir to the Imperial War Museum in London. I'd been working with them on getting French sponsors to help promote a new exhibition about French escape routes for downed pilots, which is how I heard about it."

She handed the pages across to Sylvestre, who took them as if receiving some holy relic and began quickly scanning the pages.

"Is this about the Bugatti that disappeared in the war when being driven to Bordeaux?" Bruno asked.

She looked at him in surprise. "You know about it, too?"

"I just heard about this lost Bugatti at the dinner that followed the Concours d'Élégance. Some people were talking about the most valuable cars in the world. I didn't know it was that famous."

"I'd never heard about it until I was doing some business with the new Bugatti headquarters in London, and Sylvestre let them borrow his old sports car for the launch of their showroom," she said. "Once I heard his name, I realized that we were cousins, even though we were on opposite sides of the family feud, and I introduced myself. We agreed to meet for lunch, and he told me of his interest in the lost Bugatti."

"This airman says he was hit by flak after bombing the Michelin plant in Clermont-Ferrand, lost an engine, and the crew had to bail out," said Sylvestre, lifting his head from the pages, his eyes alight with excitement. "He was picked up by someone in a black Bugatti who didn't give his name but was in his midforties and said he'd been a pilot in the First World War. He drove very fast and dropped the airman at a château where the family spoke English. They got him in touch with some people who had access to an escape route to Spain over the Pyrenees. He says it was called the PAT, after a British naval officer named Pat O'Leary who had helped to start it."

"Any route from Clermont-Ferrand to Bordeaux would probably have come through this region," said Bruno.

"A man in his mid-forties who drove fast, a pilot in the Grande Guerre—that could be Robert Benoist," said Sylvestre. "He won the French, British and Italian Grand Prix, and he went on to win Le Mans and run the Bugatti racing team. Who else would they trust to get the Bugatti to Bordeaux?"

He turned to his cousin, his eyes shining. "This is amazing, Martine. I won't forget this."

10

Back in town, Bruno turned down the rue de la Paix and pulled into the parking lot by the river that served the amusement park. Bruno had long considered it an eyesore. At the far end of the park was a stretch of scrubland, almost a field, between the windmill and the camping site farther downriver. That would be the place to park cars, tucked well back so they didn't spoil the view of the river from the other bank. Whatever Jérôme said about his plans for expansion, changing the parking area was going to be Bruno's first recommendation to the mayor.

Bruno had visited the place twice, once as a new arrival in St. Denis and more recently when he had taken Florence and her young children there as a treat to ride the carousel, to eat sausages smothered in mild mustard and ketchup inside a baguette and to watch him win each of them a stuffed animal at the popgun range. She had ignored the children's pleas to see the burning of Joan of Arc and the guillotine beheading Marie Antoinette, the park's two more renowned attractions, and marched them into the water garden to eat their sausages and paddle in the shallow streams. When Bruno saw the burning at the stake, he had been mildly impressed, thanks mainly to the clothes worn by the figure of Joan. They were fashioned from a special kind of paper that burned furiously with a bright flame, like the blond wig that ignited in a suitably dramatic manner as a bell tolled, black smoke poured out, and the visitors were wheeled out to make room for the next batch.

"They're banning Joan," said Jérôme when Bruno went into his office. "They've been at me for years about it, first for the smoke and then for the asbestos that we used to make the model. And now the new prefect is pro-Green, so I'm sunk. I have to think of something else, and I remembered something my father always wanted to do."

A burly man in his forties with a long, thin nose and a salesman's easy patter, Jérôme was a member of the town council who was usually at odds with the mayor over anything that might increase his taxes. The mayor in return kept an eye on any of Jérôme's more imaginative plans for new exhibits and had memorably vetoed the scheme to reenact a Black Mass being performed on the naked form of one of King Louis XIV's mistresses.

"My dad dreamed it up in the seventies, when I was still a kid, and the small farms around here were closing down or being brought together into bigger units with tractors, and all the old rural life was disappearing. Dad thought people would like to see how it used to be, so he had this idea to re-create a nineteenth-century village with its schoolroom, blacksmith, apothecary and basket weaver, people dressed in period costumes, making knives and spinning wool and weaving cloth on looms."

"I think the mayor would prefer that to the Black Mass," said Bruno as Jérôme unrolled a large blueprint that more than covered his desk.

"I'd put a waterwheel in here in a little cut I'd make in the riverbank and use that to grind corn, then we could sell both the flour and the old-fashioned bread we'd make. At the far end beyond the windmill, I'd have an old-fashioned farm with ducks, geese and chickens, a petting zoo for the kids with some sheep and dwarf goats and a display of traditional farm implements, including horse-drawn ones. My dad had already started collecting some. We'd have a restaurant called the Old Farmhouse Kitchen, and I want to start a brewery. I'd keep the existing amusement park, minus poor old Joan, of course, and build this new village on that land beyond the windmill. We just use it now for storage. What do you think?"

"I think the mayor will like it. I certainly do, and it sounds like it means some new jobs in season."

"About five or six jobs, probably, but if it works well, it could be more. The thing is, Bruno, we can promote it as educational, which would mean school groups coming here and bringing in business outside the school holidays."

"You'll need more parking space. Could you use some of that land beyond your windmill, over by the campsite but on the side near the road rather than the river?"

"That makes sense. Yes, why not?"

"Just two more questions," said Bruno. "How are you going to replace Joan of Arc, and how do you get that effect on Marie Antoinette's neck when her head rolls into the basket?"

"For Joan, I'm going to build an exhibition of nineteenth-century clothes with a small photo studio attached so people can dress up and have their photos taken—singly, couples, the whole family. But Marie Antoinette is a trade secret."

"Come on, Jérôme. I worked out that you have a small pump in there that shoots out the fake blood, but it's the neck that interests me."

"It's spaghetti in tomato sauce behind a sheet of glass, but don't you agree it looks good? I came across it in England when I went over for a rugby international. I saw people eating it on toast in a café and couldn't believe my eyes. Spaghetti and toast—

those English will eat anything. And they sell it in cans. But as I looked, I thought it was just the thing for Marie's neck, so I brought some cans back."

Bruno took his leave, telling Jérôme to drop off a copy of the plans at the *mairie*. His working day was over, his horse needed exercising, and he needed to pick up his dog. And tonight was the regular weekly dinner with his friends. He found himself smiling as he drove up the familiar road, imagining their reaction when he told them of Jérôme's use for tinned spaghetti.

Even though his affair with Pamela was over, Bruno always enjoyed the approach to what he still thought of as Pamela's house, even though she no longer lived there. Gilles and Fabiola had bought it, and Bruno still kept his horse, Hector, in the adjoining stables along with the old mare, Victoria. And his dog, Balzac, often spent the day there with Hector, whom he'd known since he was a puppy. Gilles was waiting for him, the horses already saddled. Hector nuzzled at Bruno, expecting his usual apple. Bruno gave it to him as he stroked Hector's smooth neck. Balzac put his paw on Bruno's foot by way of greeting, and Bruno gave him a biscuit. The basset hound wolfed it down and then darted around the horses' legs, eager for his customary run. Bruno donned his riding boots and hat as Gilles explained that Fabiola would meet them at Pamela's riding school where there was a new horse she might buy. Gilles had just started learning to ride, so Bruno checked the saddle girths and kneed each horse gently in the stomach so he could tighten the straps a notch. They set off side by side at a sedate walk, Balzac trotting ahead.

"Do you remember Annette's English boyfriend talking about the Bugatti the other night, the one that's worth millions?" Bruno asked. "Something has come up that might make a story for you." He explained what he had learned from Sylvestre about the downed British airman and his handwritten memoir.

"Robert Benoist?" Gilles exclaimed. "I've heard of him, a hero in both world wars and a Resistance leader. I'm pretty sure he was arrested and shot. They held a special race in his name in the Bois de Boulogne in Paris after the war. There's a plaque about the race in the Bois. I'd better go and see Sylvestre; it's the kind of story *Paris Match* loves."

Gilles had taken a buyout at the magazine after getting a book contract and deciding to leave Paris to be with Fabiola, but he still wrote articles for them as a freelancer.

"Ready to start riding?" Bruno asked. "We'll start with a trot and then go into an easy canter along the firebreak."

He set off, holding Hector back from the gallop he was expecting and glanced back to see Gilles riding well. Balzac was trotting at Bruno's side, looking up from time to time as if waiting for the pace to pick up. Bruno now loosened the rein and let Hector canter up the shallow slope that led to the forest and the long firebreak that would take them to Pamela's riding school. At the start of the firebreak, he reined in.

"Wait a few seconds after I set off and let Victoria set her own pace. She's too old for gallops, but Hector's impatient for his run." Bruno's horse was tossing his head, eager to go, but Bruno kept him circling until he saw Gilles understood. Balzac was already fifty meters ahead, looking back to see if Bruno was coming. "I'll rein in at the far end and wait for you. We're in no hurry, so there's no need to rush."

He loosened the reins, bent down in the saddle and let Hector bound forward, moving almost at once into a stretching run that swiftly became the gallop he and his rider had been waiting for. The trees blurred away on each side, and Bruno narrowed his eyes against the rush of wind as Hector's hooves drummed on the turf. Within seconds, Balzac was passed and left behind, and Bruno felt the familiar strain in his thighs as he bent far forward, his rump clear of the saddle and his horse moving as if he could run forever. All too soon the end of the firebreak loomed ahead, and he sat back in the saddle, taking deep breaths as Hector slowed. He turned to see Gilles cantering easily in the distance with Balzac bouncing valiantly along beside the horse. As they came closer, Bruno smiled at the way Balzac's ears flapped like some primitive set of wings.

"You're riding well," Bruno said. "You're better than me when I was a beginner. Pamela says you have a natural seat."

"I certainly enjoy it. I just wish I'd started when I was younger."

They walked the horses down the bridle trail that came out on the ridge above Pamela's new place and paused, looking down at the half-dozen children on ponies walking around the sand-floored ring. Miranda sat on her white mare in the middle of the ring as she watched them circle. Pamela was in the paddock, standing by a low hedge over which two older youngsters were taking turns jumping.

"It looks busy," said Gilles. "And Fabiola's here already; there's her car, though I don't see her."

"Probably trying out the new horse," said Bruno, looking down at the freshly painted doors and windows of the office and stables. The old house Pamela had bought along with the riding school still looked down at heel, but Bruno could see men working in the emptied swimming pool repairing the leaks, and the shutters on the *gîtes* gleamed with new paint. There was a lot of work to be done to get the *gîtes* ready for the next tourist season, and for the moment Pamela and Miranda along with her children would all be living in the main house. Bruno admired the courage of the two women, each of them determined that her hard work and energy could make a success of what had been a failing riding school. Pamela had a good track record, having made a success of renting out her *gîtes* at her former house. Miranda had her father's money behind her, which didn't hurt.

As Bruno and Gilles walked their horses past the apple orchard toward the stables, they heard a shout and saw Fabiola cantering toward them on a dappled gray mare with a distinctive, darker mane. The mare was smaller than Victoria, Bruno saw, probably a good size for Fabiola. She reined in alongside them and edged her mare forward alongside Gilles so she could reach over and touch his hand.

"I'd try to kiss you, but I think we both might fall off," she said. "You, too, Bruno, consider yourself kissed. How was your ride?"

"Wonderful, perfect autumn weather, a good gallop, and Gilles is riding well. How's the mare?"

"Perfect, but I'm not sure I can afford the asking price until we pay the mortgage on the new house," Fabiola said. "We might have to wait until next summer when we start getting some money from the rentals. They want four thousand for her. She's six years old, a Spanish horse, Andalusian but bred in France. Pamela thinks she can get the price down a bit, and then I might be able to afford it.

"Enough of that," she went on. "Bruno, I've got some good news, well, maybe not good, but you'll be pleased to know I'm recommending an autopsy on Monsieur Hugon. I've already told J-J."

"That's great. Thanks very much," said Bruno.

"The autopsy might not tell us much because, if it's what I think it is, detection after this amount of time won't be easy," she went on. "I've asked J-J for a forensic check on the room where the body was found."

"What do you think it was? Poison?"

"It's possible, only possible, that cyanide was either put into his drink or sprayed straight into his face. But it's not easy to be sure. Cyanide traces dissipate very fast after death, and then human tissue can produce cyanide gas as part of the decomposition process."

"What kind of drink? Could it have been coffee?" Bruno recalled the three dirty coffee cups beside the sink. Madame Hugon had said they were her favorite cups and had been surprised that her husband had used them. Could he have been killed by his visitors?

"Yes, indeed," Fabiola went on. "Half a gram of potassium cyanide is usually fatal, and in crystallized form, mixed with sugar or artificial sweetener, the victim is unlikely to detect it. You don't need much, less than the amount of salt you'd put on your *pommes frites*. Or it could be delivered by a spray, which could be indicated in this case by the irritation around the victim's nose and mouth."

"Isn't cyanide a controlled substance?" Gilles asked. "You can't just go into a pharmacy and buy it."

"No, but it's used a lot in the metals industry and in electroplating and by some photographers. I can think of several workshops and garages in town that would probably have it. You even find it in some fertilizers," she said. "And it isn't hard to make for anybody with a basic knowledge of chemistry. I could make enough for a fatal dose from heating green almond shells and then running the hydrocyanic gas that's released through a solution of baking soda. It would be even stronger if I excluded air when I heated the shells and replaced it with an inert gas like helium or nitrogen. I could even do it through heating polyurethane. Some fire victims actually die of cyanide poisoning from the polyurethane in a mattress."

Bruno stared at Fabiola, stunned by the contrast between what she was saying and the bucolic scene around him, the autumn countryside and the laughter of children in the riding ring, the snorting of the horses and Balzac's busy foraging beneath the apple trees.

Fabiola followed his glance and added, "You could even make cyanide from apple seeds, if you had enough of them. One of my teachers in medical school had a grisly sense of humor and used to talk of ways to commit the perfect murder. Cyanide was his top choice, especially for anyone with heart or respiratory problems. It works by stopping the body from processing oxygen."

"Why is it hard to detect?" Bruno asked.

"It breaks down so fast. The usual toxicology tests don't work too well just one day after death, and they're almost useless after two days. If Hugon drank it in coffee, we might get an indication from signs of burning in the esophagus or stomach. If he was killed by a spray, then we'll have to use a new technique, by looking at his liver cells with a biomarker called ACTA, which stands for 'aminothiazole and carboxylic acid.' We don't have that capability in the Bergerac lab, so the body would have to be shipped to Bordeaux."

"What made you think of cyanide?" he asked.

"I found a trace of potassium on the nasal hairs and something else that I think might be DMSO, dimethyl sulfoxide. DMSO is a terrifyingly efficient way of carrying cyanide into the body, so efficient that it's known in chemistry labs as liquid death. That's why I recommended an autopsy and a full forensic check of the room where the man died."

Bruno's mind was racing. Who had a motive to kill Hugon? His wife was in the clear; her alibi in Sarlat had been confirmed. Bruno had spent part of the afternoon on the phone with the Périgueux archives and the Resistance archives at the Centre Jean Moulin in Bordeaux, trying to trace the subjects of Hugon's

research. In Périgueux, it turned out, Hugon had been working on property tax records and files for registered foreigners in
the *département* in the prewar years. In Bordeaux, he'd called up
files covering the earliest years of the Resistance, from 1940 until
the end of 1942, when German forced-labor requirements sent
floods of young Frenchmen fleeing into the Maquis, hiding in
the woods. In both places, Hugon was well known enough that
he was allowed to roam at will through the stacks, so not all his
searches could be traced.

"So are you going to buy the horse or not?" Gilles asked, jerking Bruno from his thoughts.

"Yes, if Pamela can get the right price, or if we can reach
an agreement that we buy her jointly, put her to a stallion, and
then I get the mare, and Pamela gets the foal." Fabiola turned
to Bruno. "Pamela plans to buy mares so she can grow the herd
more cheaply than by buying new horses."

They rode down to the stables to greet Pamela and Miranda,
and by the time they had unsaddled and brushed down the
horses, Crimson had arrived in his old Jaguar with the baron.
They carried the half case of wine they had brought into the old
house and put it on the kitchen table next to the baron's old iron
cooking pot, which was sitting in a box of hay to keep it warm.
Beside it were stacked two cans of the baron's homemade pâté, a
large apple pie and a wooden platter crammed with small round
cabécous of goat cheese, a wedge of Stéphane's Tomme d'Audrix
and a cylinder of English Stilton that Crimson had bought on his
last trip to London.

The dinner to be prepared was a new ritual that had begun
when Pamela and Miranda had first moved to the riding school,
and Bruno, Florence, Fabiola and the baron had taken turns
bringing dinner for the two women. The evenings had been so
enjoyable that now each week they held a similar dinner, with

each of the friends taking turns to provide the food and wine. This evening was the baron's turn to feed all eight of them, and since Crimson claimed to be a hopeless cook, he provided the wines from his well-stocked cellar.

They were now so accustomed to preparing the meal that they fell automatically into their usual roles. Fabiola polished the wineglasses and set the table, and Miranda's father decanted the wines he'd brought before starting to slice the big, circular *tourte* of fresh bread. The baron opened his cans of pâté, explaining that he'd brought one of venison and one of rabbit. Pamela went to the vegetable garden to pick lettuce for the salad while Bruno and Gilles took the big plastic *bidons* to the spring that burbled from the hillside to bring back some water. Meanwhile Florence and Miranda bathed their children and prepared them for bed, but they would eat with the adults before heading upstairs to snuggle into the old feather beds that had come with the house.

It was the kind of evening that Bruno most enjoyed. It felt like being part of a family, with friends and good food, the presence of children, even when they squabbled, and the comforting knowledge that this had taken place last week and the week before that. Above all, he could expect to be with these same people the following week and uncounted weeks ahead. Strange, he thought, that they never ran out of things to talk about: local politics, the economics of riding schools, the merits of local vineyards and the best way to prepare various dishes.

As he and Gilles staggered back with the now-heavy *bidons,* Bruno thinking how to run a pipe system down to the house from the hillside, they ran into Pamela with her lettuces. He asked her to wait a moment when they reached the house and explained his concern for young Félix and his interest in horses. Could she find a use for the youngster around the stables, perhaps in return for riding lessons?

"If he's prepared to muck out the stables, I certainly could, but he doesn't sound like an attractive youth or even particularly trustworthy," she replied. "Still, bring him round, and I'll take a look at him. How's he going to get here?"

"I'll take care of that," Bruno said. He'd taken some garden waste to the *déchetterie* that weekend and seen an old bicycle that Jacquot, the custodian of the recycling center, had salvaged. He'd found it to be in working order and put it to one side. Bruno had already called Jacquot to say he had a use for it.

Inside the large kitchen, where Crimson had lit a fire in the elderly wood-burning iron range that stood against one wall, the baron was explaining to the freshly bathed children the art of making a cassoulet *périgourdin*.

"Down in Toulouse they think they know about cassoulet, but we know better," he was saying as he lifted the lid on the pot to let them smell the rich aroma. Four pairs of young eyes hung on his every word. "A real cassoulet has to contain stuffed neck of duck and some duck sausage, and I like to add some *manchons* of duck as well because my grandmother always put those small pieces of duck into hers. A cassoulet is always based on white beans with onions and tomatoes. It's fine to add some ordinary pork sausage as well, as long as it's been made with plenty of garlic, but without the duck it's just a pale shadow of a true cassoulet. It also needs to cook very slowly, which is why I made it this morning and left it cooking in the haybox all day."

"Time to eat," called Pamela, putting out a bowl of cornichons to go with the pâté. Bruno stared at her with affection and admiration as they took their places. Crimson poured them each a glass of white Bergerac from Château Montdoyen, and Miranda gave the children water from the spring. Pamela picked up the large serving spoon, and Florence began passing her the children's plates.

"This cassoulet smells magnificent, Baron," Pamela said. "Bon appétit, everyone."

11

The next morning, after an early ride with Hector, Bruno picked up the elderly bicycle from the *déchetterie* and arrived shortly after eight at the project where Félix lived. He walked up the stairs with Balzac at his heels and tried the bell. He heard no sound of ringing, and no one came to the door, so he began knocking. After a moment Félix's mother opened it, wearing a wraparound apron over her working clothes, and invited him in for coffee.

"I heard you sorted things out for Félix at the supermarket," she said, leading him into a cramped kitchen before putting the kettle on and washing a bowl at the sink. Even after all the years in St. Denis, she still spoke with a West Indian accent. "Thank you, we don't seem able to do much with him."

"Unless you do, he's going to get into real trouble," Bruno said as she spooned a coffee-chicory mixture into the bowl from a jar and poured in boiled water, followed by a splash of milk. "I saw from the pictures in his room that he seems to like horses."

"Horses and cars, anything mechanical, but it's mainly cars he likes. I sometimes think he only likes the horses because it gives him something to talk about with his dad, but he's always liked animals. He's one of those boys who collects stray dogs. They always follow him home, but we could never afford to keep one." She looked down at Balzac and smiled. "Would your dog like a bowl of water?"

"Yes, please," he said, knowing that people with little money took pride in offering something to others. "That would be very kind."

She washed another bowl at the sink, filled it with water and bent to give it to Balzac, who gave her hand a tentative lick. She fondled his ears as Balzac drank. "We used to have a dog when Jacques was working."

"Is Félix up yet? He's got to get to school."

"I get him up about now, so he comes with me when I go to work."

"Perhaps you could get him up now. Tell him I'm here and want a word with him before school."

When she left, he took a sip from the mixture Félix's mother called coffee and grimaced. Rather than offend her, he poured most if it down the sink. After a couple of minutes Félix appeared, his face washed and his hair wetted down, wearing the same clothes as the previous day.

"Bonjour, Félix. You like horses?" Bruno asked.

"Don't mind them." His mother gave him a bowl of the chicory mixture and the heel of what looked like the previous day's baguette. The boy looked down at Balzac and tore off a piece of the stale bread to give to the dog. He dunked the rest of it in the muddy-brown liquid and began his breakfast. His mother gave him a nudge, and he said a grudging "Thank you for helping yesterday."

"How would you like to learn to ride?"

"What?" His head jerked up, and he swallowed some food the wrong way, choked and coughed his throat clear. He swallowed and then looked up. "Ride a horse, me?"

"You'd have to work hard instead of paying for it, but do a good job and there might even be some pocket money in it for you. But if you do a bad job, or don't turn up for work, it's over."

"How d'you mean? Where are you talking about?"

"The riding school near Meyrals is looking for a part-time stableboy. They're willing to give you a trial. You'll spend Saturday mornings and some evenings cleaning out the stables and putting hay in the horses' mangers, and they'll get you started, learning to ride."

"That'd be great." His eyes lit up, but then they dulled again. "How'd I get to Meyrals? It takes two hours to walk there. What time would I have to start?"

"You'd have to be there by eight on the dot."

"I'd have to leave before six." He looked down at his shoes. "I could run part of the way."

"Can you ride a bike?"

"Yes, but I haven't got one."

"Your mother says you like mechanical things. Could you fix up an old bike, repair punctures, keep it oiled and the brakes working?"

"Yeah, Édouard used to let me help him sometimes on his bike at his dad's garage. That's where I learned to ride one."

Bruno nodded. That was interesting; he hadn't known that Félix was friendly with the garage owner's son. Édouard was a good kid and a fine rugby player. He'd flattened Bruno with a hard tackle in the last juniors' match against the old men. Bruno suppressed a smile at the memory and led Félix and his mother downstairs, where he pulled the old bike from the back of his van. "Could you fix this one up?"

Félix lifted the front wheel, squeezed a tire with his fingers and then spun it. He tugged at the loose chain, lifted the rear wheel, spun it and tested the brakes. His movements were deft and confident. He put the bike down and used his hand to wipe dust from the seat.

"It's working already, but I could probably clean it up and tighten that chain. It could use a good going-over."

"You fix it up as best you can, and I'll lend it to you," Bruno said. "Then after school today, we'll go to the riding school in my car, and if they like the look of you, they'll give you a chance. You'd better shower and get into some clean clothes before you go. I'll pick you up here at five, and you'd better be ready because there's a catch. If you aren't ready and looking presentable, the deal's off. If the school decides after they try you out that they don't want you or if you don't turn up on time, I take the bike back. So rather than leave it out here at night, you might want to keep it in your room."

"Can I take it up now?"

Bruno nodded and held the door open as the boy shouldered the heavy old bike and staggered up the stairs. When Félix had gone, he looked at the boy's mother. "I'll need you and Jacques to make sure the boy gets up on time every Saturday and that he takes care of that bike."

"I understand," she said, squaring her shoulders before she went on. "He was always little for his age; that's why he gets bullied a bit. It was fine while Édouard was in the same class, they got on well together, but Félix failed his exams and was kept behind for a year."

Félix trotted out through the door of the apartment house, shaking his hands as if he'd just washed them and grinning at Bruno and giving Balzac a pat before he set off beside his mother to the *collège*. Bruno watched them go and then led Balzac into his Land Rover and set off for Fauquet's café for a real cup of coffee and a croissant before he started work.

From his office in the *mairie,* Bruno called Annette to tell her that Pamela was prepared to give Félix a chance at the stables and then asked if her English boyfriend had been serenading her with his troubadour songs. His name is George, she said, chiding him. She reported he'd been in good form the previous evening when they'd gone for dinner in Sarlat. She sounded happy about it, so Bruno didn't mention that George had been seen driving his E-type when he was supposed to be too sick to be in the rally.

He also briefed her on Fabiola's decision to call for an autopsy on Hugon. She might want to warn the *procureur* that there could be a murder investigation to organize, and certainly an inquest into Hugon's death. He promised to send her a report later that morning. Then he began to check his e-mails and found one from the mayor, attaching a copy of a memo from Alphonse suggesting that the *mairie* look into the possible benefits of organizing a rally for electric cars. The mayor asked for Bruno's views.

He raced through the rest of the e-mails, at least half of them from garages trying to sell him a rally car. He supposed they'd seen Philippe Delaron's race report. Another one came from the Périgord rally club saying that he'd omitted to sign up for membership before competing, which meant they could annul the result unless he paid them a retroactive registration fee of fifty euros. He forwarded that one to Annette. He was just finishing his report on Hugon's death when the mayor's secretary, Claire, slinked into the room in a new dress that was too tight for her generous frame.

"A Mademoiselle Oudinot to see you," she said, batting her eyelashes and somehow putting salacious meaning into the words. That would be Fernand's daughter, Martine, obviously reverting to her maiden name since her divorce. He asked Claire to show her in and to make two coffees from the mayor's own blend, not the usual sludge from the communal pot.

"This is business, Claire," he said briskly, hitting the SAVE key on his report. "The mayor has become a rally enthusiast after the weekend, and we're counting on my visitor to help."

Martine was dressed for business in a dark skirt and blue pin-striped blazer over a white blouse. Her hair was severely pulled back into a tight bun in a way that did little for her looks, but Bruno still found her remarkably attractive. She was wearing lipstick and a little more eye makeup than the previous day and was carrying a slim briefcase in black leather. He stood up to receive her, shook hands across his desk and sat down gingerly, trying to avert the usual squeak from his elderly chair. As always he failed.

"I've put some thoughts down on paper about this electric-car rally we mentioned yesterday," she said, pulling some papers from her briefcase.

"Obviously we will need sponsors to finance this, and I've listed those I think most likely to be receptive to the idea. We'll need the mayor's influence to get the other communes up and down the Vézère Valley to cooperate, along with the regional council. I propose we call it the Lascaux Green Grand Prix, since that combines the most famous name in the region with an emphasis on the environmental aspect of electric cars. That should also guarantee support from the tourist board, and it gives media a second reason to cover the race. The combination of the most modern form of transportation with the prehistoric art of Lascaux makes a neat juxtaposition, too."

Bruno sat forward, resting his arms on the desk, trying not to show that he was impressed.

"This is my list of what needs to be done by the mayor, by the Périgord rally club whose backing we will also need and by the gendarmes, who will have to submit a report on the feasibility of the race route I have proposed. It will be my job to recruit the sponsors. I know several of the key figures in the various firms I've listed, and it's an area where I have a lot of experience. Here's my CV with a list of references from companies I've worked with."

Martine then handed him a map that showed the route she suggested for the race, starting at the parking lot by the Lascaux exhibition center, going through the heart of Montignac and across the narrow stone bridge leading out of the village. The route then turned off through the picturesque village of St. Léon-sur-Vézère, past the Château de Losse and up around the prehistoric park of Le Thot. It took the curving hill road after Tursac and turned off to swing around the Château de Marzac and then returned to the main road through a long, narrow street in Les Eyzies. From there it took the long straightaway to the turn that led to the Grotte du Sorcier and through the woods to come down through St. Denis with the finishing line at the far side of the bridge.

"You'll see that I've tried to include as many tourist sites as I could," she said. "But I'm sure we can adapt the route if there are any I have left out or any that we need to add for political reasons." She smiled at him, a sudden hint of playfulness in her eyes. "We certainly don't want any of the mayors to feel left out.

"I'm proposing three different kinds of sponsor, starting with the various car companies themselves along with Électricité de France and all the renewable energy companies we can recruit," she went on. "The second tier would be governmental, the European Union's energy commission, its environmental commission, its commission for tourism and equivalent bodies from France. The advantage of that is that the EU commissions only provide matching funds, so if they offer money the French authorities are under real pressure to provide funds of their own. The third tier would be the international public, starting of course with every school in the Périgord, since we will promote this race as being about their future. We challenge every schoolchild to donate five cents toward the cash prize we offer to the winner of the race—the publicity value will far outweigh the money we raise that way."

She handed over another sheet of paper. "Here's my marketing plan for targeting these different tiers. You can see that my preliminary calculations suggest that with my estimated income target of three million euros the race should cover its costs and make a reasonable profit, which will naturally go to financing green energy at all the other tourist sites in the region, starting with the Lascaux Cave itself."

He sat back, blinking partly in admiration, partly in surprise, at the figures in her proposal. "This is admirable, Martine. You must have put a lot of work into this, and you didn't have much time. I'm really impressed."

"Good," she said coolly. "Here's a note on my proposed terms. We will need to establish a nonprofit foundation to administer and run the overall project as well as the race itself. The foundation will contract with my company for the exclusive marketing rights, from which I will take an agreed percentage of all the outside funds that we raise under my plan. Fifteen percent is the usual rate in the public relations industry. I will also organize and commission all the advertising, to include press, broadcasting and electronic media, and take the standard ad agency rates."

Bruno scribbled down notes as she talked and did the math. He looked up. "Your fifteen percent of three million euros would net you four hundred and fifty thousand. We could never sell that to the council. Once the press got hold of that they'd all be thrown out at the next election. The average income per head in this commune is less than twenty thousand a year. The mayor would reject the whole idea. I wouldn't even take it to him."

"But I don't get a penny unless I make this work by raising the money," Martine snapped. She sat back, her eyes blazing at him. For a moment he thought she was going to walk out. Instead, she sipped at her coffee and then gave him a crisp smile.

"You said you were impressed by my proposals. These aren't just ideas, Bruno, it's a serious marketing plan. I'm experienced at this. What's more, I'm a woman from a local family, and I want this to work."

"Yes, I said I was impressed and I am." He knew he was dealing with an experienced businesswoman who must have gone through many negotiations such as this. She would have presented and sold many marketing plans and met similar hesitation when prospective clients saw the bill. Bruno was out of his depth, but he knew his local politicians.

"I was impressed first of all by your understanding that we'd need to get the enthusiastic support of all the local communes, which means their mayors and councils," he said. "I know you were born and raised here, but you don't live here. I do and I know these people, their concerns and the kinds of budgets and payrolls they are accustomed to dealing with. They simply won't understand these fees you're proposing. They'll be shocked. They'll dig their heels in, which means this goes nowhere."

She was looking at him thoughtfully.

"I'm sure you have a plan B," he said. "And you probably have it in your briefcase ready to show me because the one thing I'm missing here is what happens after the race. This can't be just a one-off event, because if it works half the regions in France will be fighting to stage their own race. We need a long-term plan for another race next year and every year after that. If this is going to work, it will be because the Vézère Valley becomes a household word for racing, like Le Mans or Silverstone or the Nürburgring."

"Of course I envisage that," she said. "There's a note on the list of prospective sponsors that says we're looking for a five-year commitment. That means it will be the biggest boost to the tourism industry this region has ever had," she said firmly. She was still full of self-confidence and showed no sign of backing down from her fees. After a moment, she smiled at him. "Your mayors and council members will all see that, or they will when we explain it to them. You can sell this project, Bruno. They trust you."

Bruno smiled inwardly. She was changing her approach from combative one moment to appeasing the next. Didn't she know that every policeman in France had learned to play good cop/bad cop within months of starting the job? Bruno might not know much about business negotiations, but he knew how to get what he wanted from interrogations, and this meeting wasn't so different. He returned her smile and sat forward. His hands were relaxed on the desk, and he opened them, spreading his arms so that his body language suggested agreement and understanding.

"Yes, Martine, you may be right about that. And I recognize that you're an expert in your field and you're probably worth every centime. But you don't want these people whose support we need to think you're being greedy. You have to make this about them and their valley and their local businesses. Right now, I'm worried that they'll take one look at your proposed terms, and they'll think it's all about you."

She raised her eyebrows and leaned forward, resting her chin on her hands and gazing at him with interest. "So, as the local expert, what do you suggest?"

"Don't try to take all the money up front. Delay the payments. Cut your fee to three percent the first year, and raise it in stages for subsequent years. That gives you a stake in the project's long-term success."

"I'll then have skin in the game," she said. "That's the current business school jargon for sharing the risk."

"I wouldn't know," he said. "Around here we'd say bread today, jam tomorrow."

"Okay," she said, stretching out her hand. "Three percent the first year, five percent the second year, seven percent the third and then ten percent thereafter."

He held up a hand. "You mentioned you would expect the standard agency rate for all advertising. I don't know what that is, but we'd better have it on the same sliding scale."

She withdrew her hand a little and eyed him, considering. Ah, he thought, she's playing the silence trick, putting pressure on me to fill it. But he knew how to do that.

"Of course, all of this is speculative until I take you in to convince the mayor and then introduce you to all the councils in the valley to make your presentation. But on that basis, a sliding scale for both fees and advertising commissions, you'll have my full support."

He held out his own hand. "Do we have a deal?"

She remained still, but she did something with her eyes that made them unreadable. "What about you?"

Bruno raised his eyebrows. Could she possibly be thinking he would take a bribe? He stared at her levelly and said nothing.

"What's in this for you?" she said, cocking her head as though simply curious. "Would you want to be hired as security consultant?"

"I'm the chief of police for St. Denis, so I'll do that anyway as part of my normal work," he said. "I believe we can make this work for the good of my town and the whole valley. That's enough for me." He paused. "There is just one more thing."

She arched her eyebrows. "And what is that?"

"If we shake hands on this, I'll take you to lunch, then we go to see the mayor."

Without a smile or any other visible expression on her face, she reached forward, took his hand and shook it once. "Agreed."

Then she smiled, and suddenly she looked like a different woman, still entirely professional and businesslike but very much more human.

12

Even though Martine had relaxed sufficiently to loosen her hair from its bun so it floated free, the lunch had been a mistake. Bruno was too well known to be permitted an undisturbed meal with an attractive stranger. Ivan himself came from the kitchen to hover and to be introduced. He was followed by Bruno's hunting partner, Stéphane, a local cheese maker; Julien, from the town vineyard, and Rollo, the headmaster at the local *collège.* Then Dr. Gelletreau arrived, declaring proudly that Martine had been one of the first babies he had brought into the world after opening his practice in St. Denis. He promptly sat down at their table.

Once they had finished Ivan's plat du jour of steak-*frites* and returned to Bruno's office, Martine took from her briefcase the thinnest laptop he'd ever seen to amend the papers outlining her terms and printed them out at Bruno's desk. After a brisk and businesslike hour of discussion with the mayor, Bruno excused himself when his mobile rang with the special tone that signaled someone from the brigadier's secure network was trying to reach him. With the sense of foreboding that always came when he heard from this powerful official from the interior ministry, Bruno took the call in his office.

"Bonjour, Bruno," came the brigadier's crisp voice, sounding suspiciously affable. "I'm calling to let you know this is official, and we're giving full support to a multinational operation that's being led by Eurojust. It has to do with money laundering, possibly with a terrorist connection, and it's being led by an old friend of yours, Commissaire Perrault. It seems you parted on difficult terms, so she asked me to smooth the way."

"Would this be the operation in Luxembourg that went wrong?" Bruno asked.

"Where did you hear about that?"

"Just a rumor among cops. Commissaire Perrault used to serve down here, you'll recall. She has a lot of friends in the region."

"Sounds like our friend Jean-Jacques has been indiscreet again. It wasn't serious, just a bureaucratic dispute. It just delayed things a bit, but it's all being straightened out now." The brigadier's tone changed, becoming brisk again. "I'm sure you'll be entirely professional and give her your complete cooperation. I'll fax the usual letter to your mayor. And remember, Perrault is in charge, and she'll call you shortly."

It had been a long time since Bruno had thought of Isabelle as Commissaire Perrault. Even after the passing of time and the pain she had caused him, his heart still skipped a beat at the thought of her. The brigadier's "usual letter" attached Bruno temporarily to the minister's staff. The letter to the mayor, Bruno's nominal boss, was simply a formality. If the brigadier chose, he could activate Bruno's reserve status in the French army and place him under military discipline. That would be disagreeable, but coming under Isabelle's command would be disagreeable in a different and deeply personal way.

During the passionate summer months of their affair he would have called her the love of his life, and the intensity of the attraction and the physical passion remained. But for Isabelle, her career in Paris and now at Eurojust in The Hague took a higher priority than the love of a simple country policeman in the Périgord. If she had stayed as a detective in the Police Nationale in Périgueux, she would by now be the heir apparent to Bruno's friend Jean-Jacques, and they might have stayed together and fulfilled Bruno's dream of a family of his own. He had resigned himself to losing her. But during one of those occasional reunions when they had not been able to resist each other, she had become pregnant and had chosen to abort the child without telling him until the deed was done.

Biting his lip, Bruno went down the old stone steps of the *mairie* into the fresh air and walked to the center of the bridge to stare at the river and tell himself he was no longer in Isabelle's thrall. He had just enjoyed a delightful lunch with an attractive woman, although there had been no time or privacy to navigate that deliciously treacherous terrain that two unattached strangers could explore as they got to know each other. And now Isabelle was coming back into his life. He let out a long sigh and headed across the bridge to the open parkland behind the medical center, waiting for her call and wishing Balzac were with him. Balzac, who had been Isabelle's gift to him after the death of Bruno's first dog, was just as attached to her as his master. His phone vibrated, and he braced himself before answering.

"Bonjour, Bruno, I hope you're well," came the familiar voice, dear but disturbing. "Are we secure?"

"The button on my phone is green. We're secure. The brigadier said you're running a multinational operation. What's up?"

"Money laundering with some Arab connections and links to terrorist financial networks. The Brits, Germans and Belgians are involved, and the Americans are in the loop. There's now a Périgord connection, so I'll be coming down to maintain the surveillance. We've been monitoring two principals, and their cell phones show them moving around St. Denis."

Bruno felt he knew what was coming. There were not many people newly arrived in St. Denis with international financial connections. Was it Sylvestre and Freddy?

"The names are Sylvestre Wémy, a French citizen, and Farid Iqbal, born in India but traveling on a Portuguese passport after buying his citizenship with a million-euro investment. Do you know anything about them?"

"I was sitting by their pool yesterday, and I was racing against them in a rally the day before that," he replied, enjoying the gasp of surprise he heard down the phone. "Sylvestre owns property here, and Farid, who calls himself Freddy, won the rally. Apparently he also won some big race in the Middle East. Sylvestre is from a rich Alsace family and owns a showroom in Abu Dhabi selling classic cars. He had a grandmother who was born in St. Denis. How can I help?"

"You already have. We didn't know Farid was a racing driver. The car business is how they manipulate the money. I'll be arriving tomorrow or the day after with a surveillance team—if the brigadier and I can clear the paperwork in time. Plotting their phone locations on a map, we think they're in a large three-sided building with a farm nearby but no real access road and no other neighbors."

"That's the house Sylvestre inherited from his grandmother. The nearby farm belongs to another wing of the family, and they're at loggerheads over the inheritance. Audio surveillance won't be easy because the farmer is trying to drive them out with hundreds of cackling geese."

She laughed, a sound that touched his heart. "We usually use bailiffs; driving people out with geese sounds very Périgord. Do they have any other visitors?"

"Not at the moment, except for another family member who's trying to settle the feud. Martine Oudinot is her maiden name.

She's in her thirties, married and divorced, so she might have a different name. She runs a PR company in London. I can e-mail you her cell-phone number. She was there at the house when I called on them yesterday."

"Thanks. It's good to be working with you again. I'll call to say when I'm arriving. And be careful not to do anything that might alert them. So far we're just monitoring them." She paused, as if about to hang up, and then in a different tone of voice, she asked, "How's Balzac?"

Bruno smiled at the question; they would always have Balzac. "He's in great form. He runs after me when I'm riding, and he's learning to hunt. But there's a lot of puppy left in him—he still rolls onto his back for a tummy scratch whenever you stroke his ears."

"I'll look forward to that—and remember that some of the truffles he finds will be mine," she replied, chuckling, and he thought he could imagine the grin on her face. "Take care." She closed the connection.

He smiled as he closed his phone, and there was a spring in his step as he returned across the bridge to pick up his van. He had time to stop at Lespinasse's garage before picking up Félix for his interview at the riding school. Jean-Louis's son, Édouard, who had protected the boy from the bullies, was probably the nearest thing Félix had to a friend. That made him a potential ally to steer Félix into a better life.

The garage was, for Bruno, one of the symbols of the way St. Denis was being forced to change. Just like Delaron's photography shop, which had been rendered obsolete by the ubiquitous camera phone and gone out of business, Lespinasse's garage had closed its gas pumps, unable to compete with the cheaper prices at the supermarket. Even the *mairie,* which had long used the garage to refill its various vehicles, including Bruno's police van, had worked out it could save nearly a thousand euros a year by using the discount pumps. And the traditional work of local mechanics had been eroded by the new generations of cars that needed less servicing and more the skills of a computer technician. So Lespinasse had reinvented his business as a place to restore old cars, and Édouard had developed a useful sideline in tuning motor-cross racing bikes and restoring old motorbikes. Spending two days a week at the technical school in Périgueux and four days a week at the garage, Édouard was becoming as good a mechanic as his father and would get formal qualifications when he completed his technical course. But Bruno still felt a pang as he pulled into the garage and saw the gaps where the pumps used to be.

"*Salut,* Bruno," said Jean-Louis, emerging from beneath the hood of the Jaguar E-type that Annette's boyfriend had been driving. He extended his forearm to be shaken, sparing Bruno his oily hand. "You did well at the rally. If you want to take up the sport, I've got a useful little Peugeot for you."

"One rally with Annette was enough for me," he replied. "What's wrong with the E-type?"

"Nothing, but I offered to give it a tune-up just for the pleasure of working on the car. It's a bit different from Jack Crimson's old model. The owner is coming back to pick it up tonight at about seven. I'll have it purring by then."

"Is Édouard around?" Bruno asked. Jean-Louis gestured to the rear garage where the motorbikes were kept, and Bruno found Édouard and Félix working together on the old bicycle rescued from the dump. The bike had been transformed, cleaned and polished, the chrome on the handlebars sparkling and the chain tautened.

"I'm impressed," said Bruno after greeting them. "You guys have done a good job."

"Félix did most of it," said Édouard. "He just needed to borrow some of my tools."

Bruno checked his watch and looked at Félix. "If you leave now, you'll be at the stables in half an hour or so. I'll see you there. I need to talk with Édouard about something first."

Félix set off, pedaling hard, and as they looked after him, Édouard said, "He told me what you did at the supermarket."

"I remember doing something of the kind for you a few years back, when the head teacher caught you pinching his prize tulips."

"I remember," Édouard said, grinning. "It was Mother's Day."

"It turned into father's day pretty fast when I took you back to your dad," said Bruno. "I could hear your howls as I drove off."

Édouard laughed. "Dad always had a strong arm. The spanking probably did me good. Listen, Félix is a good kid at heart, but he's always been too scrawny to play any sports, and he never really fit in. That's why he always got bullied."

"I gather you helped protect him from the worst of it."

"There was not much I could do, being in different classes. And you know how kids can be. His mother being a cleaning woman at the school made it worse. Even the girls would ask him when he'd be washing the windows, teasing him. I tried telling him to make a joke of it, but he didn't really know how to handle it."

"Has he got the makings of a mechanic?"

"He knows his way around an engine, and he's helped me strip a gearbox. But he's not what I'd call a natural, you know, like some people can just listen to an engine and know what's wrong."

"Like you and your dad," said Bruno. "It must be in the blood."

"He'll do well with the horses," said Édouard. "He always got on well with animals, and I know he likes being at that little farm the new teacher started at the *collège*."

"We'll see," said Bruno. "I'm glad he's got a friend in you, even though I know you're busy with tech school. Are you enjoying it?"

Édouard nodded. "There are a couple of teachers there who really know what they're doing. One of them was a merchant seaman, working on engines on the Corsica ferries. He's great on diesels and technical drawing, and the electrics guy is brilliant. We do a lot on car computers because he says that's the future."

He paused, evidently with something else to say but choosing his words with care. "I'll keep an eye out for Félix, but it's not like there's any work for him here. So far my dad is just making ends meet. Maybe if this classic-car business picks up after this weekend . . ."

"I understand," said Bruno. He'd never assumed that the small garage could afford another employee. "I'd better get along and see how Félix does with the horses."

At the riding school, Pamela told Bruno that Félix was doing well enough to be invited back to work on Saturday. They left Félix loading hay into the stable mangers with a pitchfork, and Pamela took Bruno for a stroll around the paddock where Miranda was teaching three little girls to trot on their plump ponies.

"The boy's not frightened of the horses, they seem to know he's comfortable around them, and he's a willing worker. That new Andalusian that Fabiola is interested in can get a bit lively, and he did well to calm her. What do you think I should pay him? I can't afford minimum wage."

"Pay him in riding lessons, and maybe after a while you might want to give him some pocket money. But don't give him too much. I'd say ten euros for a Saturday should do it."

"You'll have me arrested for exploiting child labor," she said with a laugh. "The occasional ten euros won't break me. And what if I paid him in kit? I've got an old pair of riding boots that should fit him, and the last owners left an assortment of riding caps and jodhpurs in the tack room."

"I think he'd be delighted. But don't give it all at once. Dole it out, make him know he's got to work for his rewards."

"Like I did with you, you mean?" she said, turning to him and smiling as she took his arm. "You were very patient with me. It's one of the reasons I always knew you'd be good with horses."

"You said once that I was the first man you'd been with since your marriage broke up."

"It's true, and I'm glad it was you, Bruno. I just hope Miranda finds someone as kind. She's the kind of woman who really needs a man in her life, and it's been hard on her, being left with the children."

Bruno looked at her, startled. Surely she couldn't be hinting that he should take the role. Pamela knew him well enough to read his thoughts.

"*Mon Dieu,* not you, Bruno!" she said, laughing. "Miranda would be quite wrong for you, although I can see many a man would find that plump, pink innocence rather enticing. She'd try to domesticate you and bring you carpet slippers. You'd be driven to drink within weeks."

Bruno paused, wondering what to say in response, and finally came out with something that sounded lame, even to him. "She has a new life now, new friends, the riding school to run."

"That's the problem. The riding school takes all her time in the days, and the children fill the evenings and weekends. It doesn't leave much time to be out and about and meeting new people. Maybe you could talk to her father, tell him to start throwing some more of his parties."

"I have enough on my plate without getting involved in matchmaking," said Bruno, although mentally he was running through the list of the unattached men in the district. There was a new vet in St. Cyprien whom he'd played rugby with and a new teacher at the lycée in Sarlat whom he'd met at one of the junior tennis matches in the summer.

They turned back to the stables, where Félix was whistling as he hosed down the yard in a pair of rubber boots that looked much too big for him. He looked up as they approached, and his face turned solemn as he addressed Pamela.

"I've given them all hay and water, but I thought I'd stay to help the girls unsaddle the ponies," he said. "Is that okay?"

Pamela nodded. "That would be fine, Félix. I'm pleased to see you making yourself useful. Will we see you on Saturday morning? We start at eight to get ready for the first lessons at nine."

"Oh, yes, I'll be here, but could I also come back tomorrow after school?"

13

Bruno pulled in at Lespinasse's garage just after seven and heard the deep and potent roar of a perfectly tuned engine. Young was in the driver's seat, and Jean-Louis stood proudly alongside as Young smiled his appreciation at the work that had been done.

"Would you like to come for a spin?" Young asked Bruno.

"Very much." He climbed inside, surprised at the size of the steering wheel and the old-fashioned knobs and switches on the dashboard. He enjoyed the deep leather seats and the wood trim. He felt very low to the road.

"The only new element is the safety belts," said Young. "They weren't required when this was built. Where shall we take her?"

Bruno took him up the long and winding hill road that led to Boutenègre and then through the woods to the long, straight stretch of road between St. Cirq and Les Eyzies. As soon as they reached the straightaway, Young dropped into second gear, and the acceleration hit Bruno like a punch in the back. He glanced at the speedometer, and it seemed to indicate a much-slower speed than he would have imagined, and he suddenly realized it must be marked in miles per hour. By the time he had calculated they were doing a hundred and eighty, Young was slowing for the tight bends that led to the bridge over the river and the narrow main street of Les Eyzies.

"I was glad to hear your migraine cleared up so fast," Bruno said as the sound of the engine diminished to a throaty murmur. "I had to stand in for you at the rally, and Annette scared the wits out of me. And now it seems I'll have to do it all over again."

Young apologized, saying some vital business had come up.

"To do with Sylvestre?" Bruno asked, thinking of Isabelle's call.

"In a way," Young replied, glancing at him sideways. "How did you know?"

"Pull in here on the right," Bruno said. "We'll never hear each other once we're on the road. You and Sylvestre both seem to be interested in the same car, the one whose picture you showed me from your phone."

"Did he tell you about the Bugatti?" Young asked. "Damn him, he may have all the money, but it's my family."

"I don't understand. How do you mean, your family? Did they own it? I thought you said it was lost in the war."

"It wasn't lost. It disappeared," Young replied. "Anyone who finds it will make a fortune, and my family was very much involved in that car."

Young explained that his great-grandmother's brother had been William Grover-Williams, a British racing driver who lived in France, married a Frenchwoman and worked and raced for Bugatti in the 1930s. He'd been born in France in 1903, where his father had been a horse breeder. At the age of sixteen, he talked his way into a job as chauffeur of a Rolls-Royce that belonged to William Orpen, a British artist who had been commissioned to come to Paris at the end of the First World War to do portraits of the participants at the Versailles peace conference. Grover-Williams fell in love with Orpen's mistress, a Frenchwoman named Yvonne Aupicq, and later married her. In 1928, he won the French Grand Prix and the following year, in a Bugatti 35B like the one owned by Sylvestre, Grover-Williams won the first Monaco Grand Prix. Bugatti hired him as a regular driver, along with his friend Robert Benoist, who went on to win the first twenty-four-hour race at Le Mans. Grover-Williams also acted as a salesman for Bugatti among his fashionable friends and was allowed to drive the now-missing Atlantic model around Paris.

"One of the few remaining photos of the car from the period shows Yvonne standing by the car with her dogs, Scottish terriers," Young said.

"So driving is in your blood," said Bruno. "Is that why you're so passionate about cars and about this one?"

"Grover-Williams was a hero in our household. My mother was his great-niece, although she was born after the war and never met him. And he was a real hero in the Resistance with Benoist."

During the war, Grover-Williams had volunteered to join the SOE, Britain's Special Operations Executive, an underground organization that sought to build, arm and train Resistance fighters in occupied Europe. He and Benoist built the Chestnut network in and around Paris, using their racing connections to arrange parachute drops of arms.

"That's where things become murky," Young said. "The official record says Grover-Williams wasn't parachuted in from England until early 1942, by which time the famous Bugatti had disappeared."

As Hitler planned the German invasion of Russia in June 1941, a crash program to build more weapons took over the Bugatti factory in Alsace, Young explained. The cars and some of the machine tools the Nazis did not need were evacuated to Bordeaux. In February 1941, the factory records show that the famous Bugatti Atlantic left for Bordeaux. But it never got there.

"Was Grover-Williams driving it?" Bruno asked.

"It's not clear. The official records suggest that he was undergoing training in England until early 1942, but we have family letters that say he went to France in early 1941 on some secret mission, and some of his French friends remember seeing him in Paris with Benoist around that time."

Somewhere between Alsace and Bordeaux, the car had disappeared. Both Grover-Williams and Benoist were later arrested by the Gestapo and died in concentration camps. Nobody ever knew what happened to the car nor whether either of the two racing drivers was at the wheel.

"So you are here looking for the car?" Bruno asked. "I imagine you're not the first to try to track it down, if it still exists."

"I found something interesting in the family papers, a reference to friends Grover-Williams trusted, a British family living in a château in the Périgord, at Rastignac. I've managed to track down an old woman who worked at the château as a maid during the war, and I've been trying to see her for weeks. I finally got the call that she would see me on the morning of the rally. That's why I had to let Annette down and leave you in the hot seat. I'm sorry."

Bruno wondered why he hadn't told Annette the truth, but instead he asked, "And did the maid know anything about the car?"

"Not a thing. She seemed baffled by my question. She said everybody else who had wanted to talk to her asked only about the valuable paintings that had been in the château. Apparently the Nazis took them during the war and burned the place down. It looks pretty good now, though."

"Did the château seem familiar?"

"Yes, but I couldn't place it."

"We call it the French White House. The design was copied by the architect who did the one in Washington. Ours is the original, although I wonder if the Americans believe that."

"Well, it was a wasted day. And I'm sure Sylvestre will be miles ahead of me. He's got the money to hire professional researchers."

"So you're competing?" Bruno asked, noting that reference to professional researchers. There were not many of them in the region, other than the late Monsieur Hugon. Could Sylvestre be his mysterious client?

"Absolutely, we're competing," said Young. "I had suggested we join forces, but Sylvestre just shook his head and smiled in that infuriatingly superior way of his. I thought my bit of family knowledge might give me an edge."

"What do you know about Sylvestre and his friend Freddy?"

"That he's rich, does well in his classic-car business, particularly since he and Freddy launched the new showroom in Abu Dhabi. And Freddy is a hell of a driver. I don't know Sylvestre that well. When we meet, usually for a meal or a drink when he comes to London, we talk about cars. But he's never asked about my personal life."

"Does he know of your link to Grover-Williams?"

"Not from me. It's about the only advantage I have, so I've kept it to myself. But that Rastignac connection doesn't seem to be getting me very far."

"There's somebody else in on the hunt now," said Bruno. "A journalist friend of mine who sometimes works for *Paris Match*. His interest is the story rather than the car, but he picked up something that seemed to interest Sylvestre."

Bruno told Young of the downed bomber pilot's memoir, how he was picked up and helped to escape in the Bugatti by someone who sounded like Benoist, though it may have been Grover-Williams.

"Does Sylvestre know what's in this memoir?" Young asked excitedly.

"Yes, and he seemed excited by it, which makes me think he hasn't found any sign of the car itself. He's still looking for clues."

"Just like me," said Young, looking wan. "But from his manner when he last spoke, he seemed a lot closer to it than me."

"There's one thing that intrigues me," said Bruno. "This all happened some seventy years ago. Even if you find the car hidden in some abandoned barn, it will probably be rusted away by now."

"That depends on how carefully it was stored. It was made of a special alloy, part magnesium, so rust wouldn't have been a problem. Magnesium has a low ignition point, which explains why they couldn't weld the car and had to use rivets instead. There's a long ridge running along the roof where the rivets held the bodywork together."

"Still, the chances of finding it must be pretty slim," said Bruno. "And it's even less likely that it would be in a fit state to restore to a point where you might be able to sell it for the kind of money you were talking about."

"There are five key parts," said Young, ticking them off on his fingers as he spoke. "The engine, the chassis, the transmission and the front and rear axles. If someone finds three of those, it counts as a restoration. And with that car's legend, it's worth thirty or forty million, maybe more."

"Maybe you should talk to my reporter friend," said Bruno. "I don't think you're going to get very far on your own."

Bruno drove in front of Young toward Gilles's home. Careful of his car's suspension, Young went slowly up the long approach on the dirt road. As they topped a gentle rise, they could see the old farmhouse in the gentle hollow below. It was flanked by two barns that Pamela had converted into self-contained *gîtes,* the stables and the pigeon tower. The buildings formed a natural courtyard, dominated by an old ash tree in the center, and a vine-covered terrace made a charming spot for dining in summer. Two embracing wings of poplars were set back from the house, and something about the way the farm blended into the landscape made it seem both peaceful and welcoming.

They found Gilles at work in the spare bedroom of the main house, which he had turned into his study, lining the walls with bookcases and filing cabinets and with a big old dining table as a desk. It stood by the window with a fine view over the grass tennis court and swimming pool at the rear of the house. To Young's surprise, on a bulletin board where Gilles had pinned notes, photos of Fabiola and various business cards and reminders to himself was attached a printout of the car Bruno had first seen on Young's mobile phone.

Bruno introduced the two men and, over a glass of wine, Young explained what he knew of the lost Bugatti and his family connection. Gilles had already been researching on the Internet and had downloaded from the Imperial War Museum in London a copy of the memoir by the downed RAF pilot. Young scanned it quickly, asked for an atlas and asked if the Michelin factory at Clermont-Ferrand was inside the border of the territory administered by the Vichy regime. Bruno confirmed that it was.

"So if the car picked him up near Clermont-Ferrand, the direct route to Bordeaux would come through the Périgord," said Young.

"The best road would go through Terrasson and Périgueux," said Bruno. "That would take him right past the Château de Rastignac." Young explained his fruitless visit to interview the former maid.

"Let's be frank about this: my interest is the story, which is a pretty good yarn even if we don't find the car. People always like reading about mysteries," Gilles said, looking at Young. "But what about you? Is your real interest the car or the money it might make?"

"The money would be fine, but I probably wouldn't get much more than a finder's fee," Young replied. "Ownership will be a legal mess. I imagine Bugatti would have a claim, but it was wound up decades ago, and I don't know who would have the rights to the old assets. The heirs of the driver might have some claim, depending on the contract he had with Bugatti to deliver it. The owner of whatever place it might be hidden would have some claim, if only for decades of storage fees. And even if it is found and can be restored, full restoration costs would run into the millions."

"In that case, why not broaden the search by publicizing it?" Bruno asked. "We could bring in Jack Crimson, whose contacts might find something in the SOE archives—the Special Operations Executive did all kinds of espionage during the war. You might consider asking Florence and her computer club to trawl the Internet for any links to any of the people or places linked to Grover-Williams. And why not get *Sud Ouest* to run a story and see if any new information turns up? It might mean you'll have to share any finder's fee."

"Let's not bring *Sud Ouest* into this; they're competition," said Gilles. "At least wait until I run the story of the search for the lost Bugatti in *Paris Match*."

Young looked uncertainly from Bruno to Gilles, obviously unsure how much to trust them and wondering whether he'd have any chance of success on his own. Bruno and Gilles exchanged glances. They didn't know much about Young, but if Annette liked him, Bruno was prepared to give him the benefit of the doubt. What Bruno couldn't say was that most of his interest in this affair was professional. Sylvestre and Freddy were the targets of Isabelle's operation, which made them serious suspects. And if Sylvestre had indeed been in the market for a professional researcher, there was even a possibility that they might be linked to Hugon's death.

"If we go this route, making the search public through the

press, how might the money be shared out?" Young asked. "Please bear in mind that I've lived with this story since I was a boy. I can't tell you how many times I sat at my mother's knee, hearing about this amazing ancestor of ours, one of the great racing drivers as well as a Resistance hero. What I'm trying to say is that this is very personal for me, and I've put a lot of time and effort into it. So however the money gets shared out, I think I should get half."

"That's not just greedy; it's premature," said Gilles. "We don't know what else we'll find out or who might contribute crucial new information."

"I'll be frank," Young said. "The money is quite important to me, but it's not the only thing. If I get credit as the man who played a key role in finding the lost Bugatti, that would be wonderful for my business. It would really make my name and also allow me to give old Grover-Williams his due. It's tragic that a man like that could be almost forgotten."

"I can see that," said Gilles. "He and Benoist both deserve to be better known, and that's one thing I can contribute."

"Yes, but as you said, it doesn't matter to you whether the car is found or not. You still have your story." Young was looking grimly at Gilles as he said it.

"It's a much-better story if it is found," said Bruno, trying to still the sudden note of hostility that was developing between the two men. "Why don't we simply ask Annette to adjudicate anything to do with money? We each know her and trust her."

Young grimaced and gave a long sigh. "Okay, but I have real doubts about doing anything that might bring Sylvestre into this. I don't trust him, and I'm sure he'll have thought through all these questions about ownership, and he can afford the best legal advice. He might even have found some way of buying the rights to any Bugatti lost in transit during the war."

"I understand that," said Bruno. "But once this search goes public, you and he are on an equal footing. And you say your company will benefit from the credit you'll get in *Paris Match* as the man who launched this search. You're also the relative of Grover-Williams. It will be your story, not his."

Young sipped at his wine, looking solemnly at each of them in turn. Then he put out his hand toward Gilles and said, "In that case, I think we have a deal."

14

Bruno drove home to change, check his ducks and chickens and take Balzac for a brisk walk through the woods. It was in the stillness of the trees that Bruno did his best thinking. He liked this time of year when the first leaves had begun to fall, but the canopy above him was still golden brown, tinged with red where it caught the last rays of the setting sun. The birdsong was changing as the summer migrants moved south. The hunting season had opened, but he had not been out yet, preferring to wait until the weather grew colder and Balzac's training had progressed. Bruno whistled, and the dog came to heel at once, but he was still learning the whistled notes that sent him skirting right or left before driving Bruno's much-desired *bécasses* back to his master. Young as he was, Balzac seemed fearless, ready to chase away even a big fox. Feeling a sudden burst of affection, Bruno knelt down to stroke him and tell him what a fine hunting dog he would be.

As he walked back, he thought of his next steps. He would need to ask Sylvestre about Hugon. Even if he denied knowing the man, Sylvestre's face might show some reaction. He should ask Madame Hugon if she'd ever heard the name and whether any new mail had arrived for her husband since his death. He needed to ask other members of the history society whether Hugon had talked about his latest research job. The euro notes in Hugon's wallet were new; the numbers might be traced back to the bank where they were first issued.

As for Isabelle, her investigation into terrorist finance was beyond his skills, though he could help with some modest surveillance. When he reached his home, he went to a locked cupboard in his barn and took out two battery-operated surveillance cameras that he'd salvaged from one of the brigadier's earlier surveillance operations at a local château. He thought they might come in handy someday. Then he called Isabelle.

"Where are our two suspects now?" he asked.

"Their phones show Sylvestre in Trémolat and Farid in central Sarlat, each in a fixed location, so I assume they're having dinner. It might be another day or two before I can get down. This is turning into a real mess," she replied. "Since we've been using the Americans' TFTP, we have to go through all kinds of hoops to abide by European rules on data sharing with the U.S."

"What's the TFTP?" Bruno asked.

"Terrorist Finance Tracking Program. They've got the best data. But in order to use it Europol is required to verify each individual case and ensure every request we make is necessary and tailored as narrowly as possible to minimize the amount of data collected. It's crazy—we're all fighting the same people—but we have to live with it. In the meantime, whatever surveillance we can mount depends on you and Jean-Jacques."

"Leave it with me and let me know when you can get here," he said. "But if you can monitor their movements by their phones, what else do you need?"

"We need to know about any visitors or meetings they have, that's the priority, along with the license plates and registration numbers of whatever vehicles they're using. We want to know if they're visiting Internet cafés to use an e-mail address we don't know about."

"Okay. I might be able to help with the vehicle numbers. I took some photos of the place where they're staying on my phone and their rental cars were parked there. Your technicians should be able to blow up the images. I'll e-mail them to you right away. Is Jean-Jacques providing any support?"

"He's trying but he's short staffed. I know you'll do your best, and thanks, Bruno. Give Balzac a hug for me."

She hung up, and before setting off Bruno mentally reviewed the map of the region that he carried in his head. He couldn't use the direct road that led to Sylvestre's place in case he or Freddy returned early and saw his car. Nor did he want to alert Fernand by using the access through the Oudinot farm. There was a hunting trail he knew that went close enough, so Bruno loaded Balzac into the passenger seat of his Land Rover and headed down the lane, through St. Denis and out on the road to Le Buisson. When he got to the distinctive bend in the hunting path, he pulled out his map and a compass to check the bearing to Sylvestre's house. Ten minutes later, Balzac snuffling at his heels, he reached the road and saw the loom of the *chartreuse,* helped by a porch light that had been left on.

He took one of the cameras from his rucksack, checked the new batteries and the data stick he'd installed to record the images and used black masking tape to fix it in the fork of a tree where it had a clear view of the muddied track that led to the lodge and courtyard. He put the second camera in a spot where it had a view of both the pool area and the path that Oudinot had sealed off. That would have to do. He checked that neither camera was visible from the road or the house, led Balzac back to the Land Rover and returned to St. Denis. Back in town, his phone was showing four bars of reception so he sent the photos of Sylvestre's place to Isabelle.

There were only two customers left in Ivan's bistro, strangers who seemed to be speaking English. Ivan looked at his watch when Bruno came in with Balzac, gestured him to a seat at the bar and poured out a generous glass of scotch. "I've got some tuna salad left and some apple pie, and you can share the *nasi goreng* that Mandy's making for our dinner. That suit you? And what about your dog?"

"*Santé,*" said Bruno, taking a sip of the scotch. "That all sounds good, and just a bowl of water for Balzac, please. I fed him before I left home, and it's been a long day. How's Mandy?"

Ivan invariably returned from vacation with a girl he'd met, usually one whose cooking skills could enlarge his own repertoire. There had been a Belgian girl who broke his heart but left him with half-a-dozen ways of preparing mussels and the recipe for a thick chicken stew called *waterzooi*. A Spanish girl had introduced St. Denis to gazpacho and paella, and the departure of the German girl with her Wiener schnitzel was sincerely mourned by Ivan's customers. He could never get the breadcrumb coating quite right without her expert assistance. His last vacation to Southeast Asia had raised hopes among the townsfolk that he'd return with a Thai woman who would broaden his menu yet further. Instead, he'd fallen for a breezy Australian who could wipe the floor with Bruno at tennis and was working with Ivan while waiting for her application to study at the wine school in Bordeaux to be approved. Having spent a year in Indonesia before meeting Ivan on the beach at Kota Bharu in Malaysia, she knew how to prepare a range of Asian foods.

One memorable evening she had produced for Ivan's regulars a *rijsttafel* of a dozen different dishes: chicken in peanut sauce, caramelized beef *rendang* braised in coconut milk and chilies, duck roasted in banana leaves and pork braised in sweet soy sauce. There had been different kinds of noodles, rice and spring rolls, and while the names of the various dishes escaped Bruno, the meal had lasted for hours, and he had never forgotten it. Tonight's *nasi goreng*, which Mandy translated as "fried rice," was rice with salted dried fish, prawns, hard-boiled eggs and shallots, all generously flavored with garlic and tamarind. Bruno had enjoyed it before.

"Mandy's fine, but what about you? Tell me about this stylish new girlfriend of yours, Martine."

"Not a girlfriend, just a local woman back for a brief visit to her folks," Bruno replied. "She's going to be helping us set up a new rally for next year, so it was a business lunch, at least until Gelletreau decided he wanted to join us and tell stories about her childhood measles and whooping cough."

Balzac padded across to greet the middle-aged couple who had finished their meal. They made much of him before calling across to Ivan for the bill in broken French, and Mandy came out from the kitchen to say good-bye to them. But first she introduced them to Bruno, saying they were Americans from California on vacation. Bruno's English had been improved by his time with Pamela, and it was fluent enough if full of mistakes. He was able to ask where they had been so far, and they enthused about their visit to the Lascaux Cave earlier that day. Like most local restaurateurs, Ivan kept a stand by the door filled with tourist brochures, and Bruno pulled out one for them that listed the main attractions. They left, promising to return for another of Ivan's meals, and Ivan steered Bruno to a table set for four and went into the kitchen to fetch the tuna salad.

The *nasi goreng* was delicious, and the apple pie came with a generous scoop of vanilla ice cream. The three of them were chatting over coffee when the door opened and a very late customer came in. Bruno turned to see it was Martine, looking dressed to kill in a little black dress beneath her stylish raincoat, and her eyes blazing.

"I'm glad to see you here because it's you I'm looking for, Bruno," she began. "You only gave me your office phone number or I'd have called your mobile. I came here because I thought after lunch the people here would know where to find you. Sorry if I'm interrupting, but I need to talk about Sylvestre."

"Sit down, join us," he said, pouring her a glass of wine and then helping her take off her coat. "This is Ivan and Mandy, and my dog is called Balzac. Have you eaten?"

"Yes, thanks," she said, leaning down to fondle Balzac, who always had a soft spot for women. Maybe it was something about their scent, Bruno thought, as he caught a hint of Martine's vaguely familiar perfume.

"A dog like this is just what I need to calm me down," she said as Balzac licked enthusiastically at her hand. "Sylvestre took me to the Vieux Logis in Trémolat, but other than the food it was a wretched evening. That bastard said he wanted a settlement, but what he wants is just outrageous. And now I know why my dad can't stand the man. He had the nerve to tell me that if he doesn't get his way he'll bankrupt my parents with lawsuits. He said he's already filed a complaint that my father's ill treating his geese."

"He won't get far with that," said Bruno. "Your dad runs a model farm, and he's well respected. But if this gets serious, I can recommend a good local lawyer, a retired magistrate who probably knows your father and would certainly know his reputation. His fee would be very modest."

Briefly he explained the family dispute to Ivan and Mandy, who wanted to know what Martine had eaten at the Vieux Logis, a famed local hotel whose restaurant was said to be on the verge of winning a second Michelin star.

"The food was great—foie gras, *coquilles St. Jacques,* roast veal with truffles—but it nearly turned to ashes in my mouth," Martine said. "He even tried to buy me. Would you believe that he promised me fifty thousand euros in cash if I could persuade my parents to sell the surrounding land to him at ten percent above market price? We were waiting for the dessert, but at that I threw my napkin in his face and walked out. I would have thrown my wine after it, but the glass was empty."

"I wish I'd seen that," said Mandy, laughing. "I always enjoy a good scene in a restaurant."

Martine turned to Bruno. "Remember that Indian friend of his at the *chartreuse*, Freddy? Do you think they're gay?"

"I have no idea, but it seems the more I hear about Sylvestre the less I like him," Bruno replied. "If he's being aggressive with you, it's time to counterattack. We can check in the morning, but I'm pretty sure the land around his *chartreuse* will be zoned for residential use, since there are already buildings there. Your dad can apply for a construction permit to build half-a-dozen very cheap bungalows for social housing all around the *chartreuse*. He doesn't have to build them, just get the permit. It's his land. He could use it as a threat. The cottages would destroy Sylvestre's views and his setting, and when he hears the term 'social housing,' he'll fear the worst."

"You mean he'll imagine being surrounded by unemployed families and immigrants with lots of noisy children who'd sneak into his swimming pool and puncture the tires on his car?" asked Martine, her face lighting up with a mischievous grin that Bruno enjoyed as much as it surprised him. She might sound like a Parisian businesswoman, but he was beginning to recognize the depth of her Périgord roots.

"Yes, that's the idea," Bruno replied. "You said he gave you his proposal. Did you have an alternative plan to make to him?"

"Yes, I spent a lot of time talking my dad into it, as a deal that could work for both sides of the family. But it would mean we'd all have to cooperate, and Dad is reluctant to have any dealings with Sylvestre. I put the plan to Sylvestre over dinner. I suggested that we all cooperate to develop the *chartreuse* and our farm for ecotourism as a unit. Sylvestre would contribute the house, and we'd contribute the farm. We'd create a new company in which we held equal shares, and the company would pay my parents a salary for running the farm. There wouldn't be a cost because the farm makes a good income as it is, but my parents aren't getting any younger, and this way we could run the whole thing as a commercial enterprise."

"It sounds very reasonable, and when your parents retire you could hire a young couple to take over the farm," Bruno said.

"Exactly, and the deal would give them the prospect of getting some equity in the company or the right to buy one of the houses. I thought it was a decent compromise, but Sylvestre turned me down flat and said the only deal he'd accept was one that let him buy the land around the *chartreuse.* That was when he tried to bribe me, with a nasty smile that said he thought anybody could be bought, including me. Frankly, I don't think I could bear to work with him at all."

She turned to Mandy and Ivan, who had been following the exchange with interest. "Sorry to inflict my family feud on all of you. I must be spoiling your dinner, but thanks for letting me get it off my chest."

"Not at all, it's been interesting," said Ivan. "We'd better think about closing up for the night, and we'll look forward to seeing you again and hearing the next episode in the family saga."

"Maybe the best plan is to bring your cousin to eat here, and I'll put some ground glass or something in his food," said Mandy. They all erupted in laughter.

"If Bruno hadn't heard that, I might have taken you up on it," said Martine before rising to her feet. "Maybe it would be better to sprinkle a heavy dose of laxatives over it, preferably just before he goes off to race one of those fancy cars of his."

Ivan waved aside Bruno's attempt to pay for his meal. Bruno

thanked him and left a ten-euro note as a tip. He helped Martine back into her coat as they said good night to Mandy. Escorting them to the door, Ivan noticed that a light rain was falling and handed Bruno an umbrella.

"Where's your car parked?" Bruno asked her, opening the umbrella and holding it over their heads. Balzac was looking up at them, wondering what these humans planned to do. Bruno was asking himself the same question.

Martine gestured down the street. Then she looked at him, flashing that mischievous grin again. "Good thing I rented a car—otherwise I wouldn't have been able to walk out on Sylvestre."

Bruno laughed, took her in the arm that wasn't holding the umbrella and leaned forward to kiss her good night on both cheeks. To his surprise, as he drew back she leaned forward and kissed him firmly on the mouth, her lips surprisingly soft and a sound like a purr coming from deep in her throat. It lasted only a moment, but it touched him.

"That was a lovely surprise," he said. "Just as lovely as the sight of you when you walked into the bistro. You took my breath away."

"Play your cards right, and it might not be the last of my surprises," she said, taking his hand. "Come on, you and Balzac can walk me to my car. Unless, that is, you want your friend Ivan to keep on watching."

Bruno turned to see Ivan locking up while giving Bruno a wink, Mandy standing beside him grinning widely as she made the thumbs-up sign.

"Our shameless behavior will be all over St. Denis by lunchtime tomorrow," said Martine.

"Sooner than that," said Bruno, smiling as they walked on, huddling together beneath the umbrella. "They'll talk about your loose Parisian ways, taking time off from Michelin-starred restaurants to lead the innocent town policeman astray."

"Innocent, hah! You forget I was born here. They're more likely to talk about the wicked policeman and the helpless maiden." She stopped as they reached her car.

"If this rally project goes ahead, you'll be spending quite a lot of time here," he said, not letting go of her hand. "There'll be plenty of time to get to know you. I'd like that."

"And I'd like to get to know you," she replied, turning into his arm. In her high heels, she was as tall as Bruno, but somehow she found a way to nestle into his chest. She raised her face to be kissed before sliding from his grip and opening the door of her car. Once installed, she gave Balzac a last pat and blew a kiss to Bruno as he closed the car door, and he and his basset hound watched her drive off into the wet night. As he walked back to his own vehicle, he remembered that he'd again forgotten to give her his mobile number.

15

The next morning Bruno took Hector on an unusual route, a bridle trail that ran past the village of Audrix and then through the woods that led to St. Chamassy. From there it was an easy canter to the ridge above the Oudinot farm. He dismounted to go through an old-fashioned wooden gate whose catch was too low to reach from the saddle and walked Hector the rest of the way. He put Balzac on a leash, knowing that otherwise the ducks and geese would be too great a temptation. He hitched Hector to the fence around the sheltered vegetable garden and loosened his saddle, casting an envious eye on Odette's still-healthy crop of lettuces and tomatoes, and knocked on the kitchen door. Martine opened it, and her face lit up with pleasure before she glanced down at her dressing gown and carpet slippers, put her hands to her hair and said, "Oh no, Bruno, you could have given a girl notice."

"You look wonderful to me," he said, but she was already bending down to welcome Balzac, who was clearly delighted to renew the acquaintance.

"Come in, Bruno, come in, we're just having breakfast, and there are lots of brioches left for you," called Fernand as Martine darted through the archway to the living room and up the stairs to the guest rooms. Bruno took a seat, and Odette poured him coffee and pushed toward him a plate of brioches, still warm from the oven.

"I always make them for Martine," she said. "They're her favorite, ever since she was a little girl." Alongside the brioches was a bowl of fresh butter, probably churned by Odette, and pots of homemade jams.

"She never eats all the ones I make, so maybe your dog would like one." Without waiting for his reply, she handed Balzac a brioche, probably the first he'd ever tasted, and he took to it gladly, wolfing it down in two bites and looking up hopefully for more.

"Sorry to call so early, but I heard that your compromise offer to Sylvestre went nowhere, and I thought I'd better ask what you plan on doing next," Bruno said. "I have to report back to the mayor—you know he's taking an interest."

On the ride over, Bruno had wondered how to advise the Oudinots, now that Sylvestre was heading into such serious legal trouble. But that was not something he could reveal to them.

"Martine talked me into making that compromise offer, but it doesn't surprise me that Sylvestre turned it down flat," said Fernand as Odette brought a pot of fresh coffee. "And would you believe he tried to offer Martine a bribe of fifty thousand euros to reach a deal she could get me to swallow? It's shameful, trying to turn her against her own parents."

"I gather he's trying to buy some of the land from you, which would at least mean you need have nothing more to do with him," said Bruno. "How much is he after?"

"He wants all the land up to the ridge, about three hectares in all, which would give him that land where I've put the geese, the woodland all the way down to the road and about a hectare on each side of his buildings."

"Construction land is going for about eight euros a square

meter these days," said Bruno. "But most of the land you'd be selling is too hilly to build on. And forest land is barely a thousand a hectare. You could squeeze three or four units of social housing onto the flatter bits but that's all. So the market price for your three hectares would be around twenty-five thousand. And if he's prepared to pay another fifty thousand on top, that would add up to a decent offer."

"That's just what I was saying when you arrived," said Odette, looking crossly at her husband. "But he won't have it. And it's not as though you were using that land for anything. It's just patchy woodland."

"I grant you that a direct sale would mean we never have to deal with him again but it leaves out all the other matters I was telling you about," said Fernand stubbornly. "There's the loan to his grandmother, the interest they never paid, the family furniture they took. And since he really needs that land I won't sell it for market price. He'll make money from the timber alone. No, I'd want a fifty percent share of the timber sale."

"Say you ask him for forty thousand euros for the land plus the fifty he offered Martine," said Bruno. "Add it up, throw in ten thousand for the timber and you're getting to a nice, round number, a hundred thousand."

"That's exactly what I told him this morning," said Martine, making an entrance in jeans and a black turtleneck sweater, her hair brushed. Bruno's glance lingered on her, remembering how soft her lips had been the previous evening.

"I'll have to talk to him, but I'm pretty sure the mayor would support that," Bruno said. "It's a very good price and would settle the feud. What's more it would spare you those lawsuits he's been threatening. That's an aggravation and an expense you don't need. Shall I tell the mayor you're thinking about it?"

Fernand looked unhappily at his wife and daughter and then back at Bruno. "You can say I'm thinking about it, but I'm not making any promises. And this is my decision to make, not for the womenfolk." He rose and headed for the door, taking a jacket from a row of coat hooks. "I'd better go and see about the geese."

Bruno rose as well, but as the door closed, Odette said, "He'll come around. I know him, he just said that to save face."

Bruno nodded and said to Martine, "You've met my dog. Do you want to say hello to my horse before I head back?"

"Love to," Martine said and plucked a carrot from the vegetable basket as Bruno kissed her mother good-bye and thanked her for the delicious brioches. "I've never met a horse yet that didn't like carrots."

"Do you ride?" he asked, as they left the house.

"Not for years, but if I'm coming back here more often I'd like to take it up again," she said, and then stopped in her tracks as they turned the corner and saw Hector gazing calmly as they approached. "He looks magnificent. What's his name?"

"He's called Hector, and he's got his eyes on that carrot."

Without a trace of hesitation Martine advanced on the horse and began stroking his neck as she fed him the carrot. He joined her, patting his horse's neck but keeping his eyes on Martine's profile. She might have changed out of her dressing gown, he thought, but she hadn't bothered with any makeup. Her complexion didn't need it. Hector had finished his carrot and was enjoying Martine's gentle scratching of the soft flesh under his jaw.

"Would you be free to join me for dinner this evening?" he asked.

"Yes, so long as it's not a fancy restaurant. I had enough of that last night." She turned from Hector to look at him, that cheerful mischief in her eyes again. "And if we go back to Ivan's the gossips will never stop. I'm surprised some busybody hasn't already called my mother."

"I thought I'd cook for you, and you could see my place," he said, and held his breath as he waited for her reply.

"I'd like that," she said, serious now. "But I'd better be back early, otherwise my mother would probably start planning a wedding and naming her first grandchild. And you should know that's definitely not in my plans. I love my mom and dad, but they drive me crazy sometimes. You heard that stubborn father of mine—not a decision for 'womenfolk.'"

Another independent woman intent on her own career, Bruno thought. Why is it they're always the ones to whom I'm most attracted?

"In that case we should start early, about seven, so you can be home by ten or so. Do you know where I live, or should I pick you up?"

"It's out on the Rouffignac road, one of the turnoffs after that prehistoric burial site at La Ferrassie, isn't it?"

"That's right," he said, wondering how she knew that. She must have been making inquiries. "There's a stone tower for electricity just opposite the turnoff. Drive up the road and turn left, and you'll see my home."

"That will be something to look forward to," she said. "I'm spending the day calling on all the mayors from here to Montignac to try to persuade them to back the electric-car rally. Your mayor set it up. I'll tell you how it went when I see you at seven." She leaned forward to give him a quick kiss on the lips and then bent to stroke Balzac as Bruno tightened the saddle and swung himself onto Hector.

"You look very dashing on horseback," she said and waved good-bye. He resisted the temptation to rear Hector up onto his hind legs and leap into a gallop and trotted sedately off with Balzac jogging along behind.

When Bruno got to the *mairie,* the mayor called him in to

show him the fax from the brigadier requesting Bruno be given a temporary assignment to his staff. He signed it with his fountain pen and handed the fax to Bruno, telling him to file it with the earlier ones.

"What can you tell me about this operation he wants you for, Bruno?"

Bruno explained briefly and then described the failure of his efforts to help Sylvestre and Oudinot reach a settlement over the *chartreuse*.

"That wouldn't be because you seem to have developed a friendship with Martine, would it?" the mayor said, a twinkle in his eye.

"News travels fast," said Bruno.

"Madame Lespinasse was putting the cat out last night and saw your fond farewells. She told Fauquet at the café, and now it's all over town."

"Between you and me, Sylvestre is one of the targets of this money-laundering operation I've been hauled into. Not that I'll be doing much, just helping with the surveillance. I think we're still a long way from making any arrests. Knowing the brigadier, he'd rather monitor them and track down all their contacts as opposed to locking them up right away."

"Is he coming down himself to run this show?"

"No, it's a Eurojust operation, so Inspector Perrault will be taking charge."

"You mean Isabelle? I hope that doesn't cramp your style with Martine, whom I very much liked when she explained her plans for this electric-car rally. She's a smart woman, probably another highflier like Isabelle. You do like to live dangerously, Bruno, when we've got all these fine young farmers' daughters yearning to settle down with a solid man with a good job like you."

"That's why you are now happily settled down with a Franco-

American historian with a professorship at the Sorbonne," Bruno replied. "Jacqueline is hardly a farmer's daughter."

"Touché." The mayor smiled. "But unlike you, I'm too old to interest them. What about Hugon? Any progress there?"

"An autopsy is being done with an eye on possible cyanide poisoning," Bruno said. "We haven't had the results yet, but Jean-Jacques is now involved. I've made the usual inquiries, but I'm having trouble identifying Hugon's last big research job. Jean-Jacques is getting one of his experts to crack Hugon's password and get into his computer."

"Have you asked any of his friends at SHAP? You remember Doumergues, the retired history teacher from Sarlat, the one who gave us that monograph about the lost artworks of Rastignac? It might have been before your time. He was probably Hugon's closest friend, and he called me the other day asking about the funeral. I suppose the autopsy will delay that. But you might want to give him a call and see if he knows what Hugon was up to. I must say Hugon being poisoned sounds very unlikely, unless it was his wife, of course."

He gave Bruno the telephone number, and Bruno went back to his office to make the call. He explained that the police were still investigating whether Hugon's death had been suspicious.

"Goodness, that doesn't sound like Henri. And he was in fine form when I last saw him, like a dog on the trail of a good scent. He wouldn't say much about the job he was doing, but he certainly picked my brains clean about Rastignac."

"What did he want to know?" Bruno asked, aware that Young's research about Rastignac had drawn a blank.

"You know about the paintings that disappeared: seven Cézannes, five Renoirs, four Manets, three Toulouse-Lautrecs, a Matisse and one of Van Gogh's Arles paintings?"

"I thought they were destroyed when the Nazis burned the place?"

"Not according to the maid, who says she saw German soldiers loading tubes wrapped in tapestries into some trucks. She thought they were wrapping the paintings, the entire collection of the Bernheim family, who had a famous art gallery in Paris. The Bernheims thought the paintings would be safe with their friends the Lauwicks, the Anglo-American family who owned the château. But it wasn't the paintings that Henri was interested in; it was their friends, particularly any English friends. The widow Lauwick's daughter had married an Englishman named Fairweather, and they had lots of English friends, one of them a famous racing driver."

"Would that have been Grover-Williams?" Bruno asked, sitting up in his chair in excitement.

"Yes, how on earth did you know that? And Henri asked me the same question. Young Jacques Lauwick, the son, worked at *Vogue* magazine and knew all the fashionable people of Paris, and Grover-Williams was part of that beau monde. He and his wife stayed at Rastignac before the war."

"Did the Lauwicks have any connection to the Resistance or to any escape networks to help Allied pilots who'd been shot down?"

"Not that I know of, but if you have any names I can look up the copy I made of the château's guest book."

"A British naval officer named Pat O'Leary," said Bruno, looking in his notebook. He heard a jolt as the phone on the other end of the line was placed on a desk or table, and he heard the squeak of a filing cabinet drawer and then the rustling of paper.

"No, nobody of that name," Doumergues said when he returned to the phone.

"What about Robert Benoist?"

"The racing driver? Yes, he was there before the war with Grover-Williams."

"Did you ever hear anything about a car being hidden at or near the château?"

"That's what Henri asked me. No, I heard nothing about that, and I interviewed all the surviving people who had worked there during the war, before the Nazis burned the place down. They used phosphorus, you know, and the fire burned for five days. A terrible thing."

Bruno carried on with his questions, but Doumergues knew no more. Bruno thanked him, promised to let him know when the date for Henri's funeral was set and called the curator at the Centre Jean Moulin, the Resistance archives in Bordeaux, an expert whom he had consulted before. He asked what was known about an escape route known as PAT.

"It was named after Lieutenant Commander Pat O'Leary of the Royal Navy, but that was a ruse to disguise the founder's real name," the curator replied. "He was a Belgian army doctor named Albert Guérisse, and he got more than six hundred out across the Pyrenees before being arrested by the Gestapo. He was sent to the Natzweiler concentration camp in Alsace, but he survived the war. It was a dreadful place, where they gassed over eighty Jews just so they could obtain their skeletons for some awful anthropological museum that Himmler set up in Strasbourg to demonstrate the alleged inferiority of the Jewish race."

Bruno shuddered but pressed on with his inquiry. "Do you know of any connection the Belgian doctor might have had to the château of Rastignac?"

"Not offhand, but if I look it up will you tell me the whole story next time you're in Bordeaux?"

"Yes, and I'll buy you lunch while I relate it," Bruno replied. He put the phone down and called Jean-Jacques.

"I'm on my way to Hugon's place now with my forensics team," came the familiar cheery tones. "The widow is driving from Sarlat and will meet us there. If you join us, we could have a walk in the garden and talk about this surveillance job."

"There's more than that to discuss," said Bruno. "We may have a suspect, or at least someone we need to question. I've worked out who was Hugon's mysterious last client, and he also happens to be the subject of our surveillance job."

"I should be there in about half an hour," said J-J and closed his phone.

Bruno had a few minutes before he would have to leave. As he was about to call his police friend Thomas in Alsace, he remembered something. He called up the photo of the famous Bugatti that Young had sent him and printed out two copies. One was for him, the other for the collection on Félix's wall. Then he called Thomas, who started to thank him for a pleasant stay in St. Denis. Bruno interrupted him.

"Hang on, Thomas. This is urgent. We're on a murder investigation, involving that researcher whose death took me away from the vintage-car show after the parade. You remember? It seems his last mystery client for a big research job was Sylvestre, which makes him our top suspect. We'll be bringing him in for questioning. I need to know everything you can tell me about him—the gossip, the rumors, everything."

"*Mon Dieu,* are you sure about this, Bruno? Sylvestre's a big man around here, wealthiest family in town, a big employer at that garage of his."

"If you want confirmation, I can get the head of detectives for our *département* to call you if you like. He's leading the inquiry."

"*Merde,* where do I begin? Well, I told you about the airfield, so you know where his family money came from. It must be twelve, thirteen years ago as a young man straight out of business school that he started this classic-car business. I think it began as a hobby, but he saw the possibilities and then opened his garage and began hiring top mechanics and buying up old cars to restore them."

The boom in old cars hadn't really taken off then, Thomas explained. Sylvestre's big breakthrough came with two Mercedes from the 1930s that he found at an estate sale of some French general who had died. The cars were probably loot from the war. He got them cheap, fixed them up and the local paper reported that he got over a million for the pair of them at an auction in Germany. He went on from there, specializing in old Mercedes. He went all over Europe looking for them in Italy, Spain, Scandinavia and then eastern Europe—places where the classic-car business was in its infancy. Then he opened his showroom in Abu Dhabi.

That had been in 2007, just before the financial crash. The next year, the rumor was that Sylvestre was in real trouble, all his money tied up in stock he couldn't sell. He had to lay off some of his mechanics. The banks wouldn't lend him any cash to tide him over. He tried to sell some of the family's property holdings, but there were no buyers. Then Sylvestre suddenly obtained some financing, waited out the recession and when the oil price went up his Abu Dhabi business turned into a gold mine.

"He's the last of his line, which makes him the most eligible bachelor in Alsace," Thomas went on. "He lost his parents when he was in university. They were both on board that Concorde that crashed at Charles de Gaulle Airport. So now he owns all the land and property and the car business. He's got thirty mechanics working for him, and his collection of old cars is said to be worth more than the shopping malls."

"Any idea where he found the money when he needed it?" Bruno asked.

"Not for sure, but there were rumors about some big Arab investors he'd gotten to know in Abu Dhabi. I don't know if it's true or if he found a bank to bail him out. Sylvestre had a lot of contacts in the financial world from his time at business school, INSEAD, outside Paris."

"What do you know about that Indian friend of his, Freddy? How long has he been around?"

"I think he was involved in the Abu Dhabi venture from the beginning. He's here in Alsace from time to time, and some people think that he and Sylvestre are a couple, but Sylvestre's always been a man for the ladies. A couple of years ago there was a story that he was getting married to one of those titled German girls, a *gräfin* or something with a 'von' in her name. One of those glossy celebrity magazines had some paparazzi photos of them together on a yacht in Monaco during the Grand Prix. I don't know if anything came of it. I'll ask Ingrid, she knows more about those things."

"Thanks, Thomas. That's very helpful, and I'll be sure to keep you informed of where we're going with this."

"Please do; the mayor will need to know if it looks like our town's leading citizen is about to get arrested. Meanwhile I'll keep this under my hat. And I'll call you after I talk to Ingrid."

"Right, give her my best."

Madame Hugon was standing in the front garden when Bruno pulled up in his car. J-J had not yet arrived. He got out to greet her, and she said, "I'll miss this garden. I planted those roses and laid out the flower beds. But I can't stay here after this. Suspicious circumstances! It's the last thing I ever expected to hear about Henri, such a gentle man. We had our differences, but we were married a long time and got very used to one another."

"I know, I'm sorry to cause you this extra trouble," he said. "There may be nothing to it. You know how the police like to be sure."

She nodded solemnly, and then J-J's car arrived, the forensic van close behind, and J-J clambered out shouting, "We've driven past this damn place twice already, and if I hadn't seen your police van we'd have gone past again."

"Commissaire Jalipeau, this is Madame Hugon," said Bruno.

"My apologies, madame, and my condolences. Forgive my little burst of temper. May we come in? We'd better dress up first."

He handed Bruno a snowman, police slang for the white paper overalls that forensics rules required, and pulled one from the back of his car to squeeze into it, grumbling about its inadequate size. Bruno and the rest of the team put them on and donned hairnets.

"Do I have to wear one of those ridiculous things?" Madame Hugon asked. J-J replied that so long as she wasn't going into the room they were interested in, she needn't bother. Her own traces would be all over the house, anyway. Yves, the head of the forensics unit, led her to his van to get an oral swipe for DNA and to take her fingerprints.

She finally led them in, and Bruno noticed at once that the place had been cleaned, or at least the dirty crockery in the kitchen had been washed and put away, and there was a smell of cleaning fluid in the sitting room.

"Have you cleaned the study as well?" he asked.

"No, I couldn't bring myself to go in there again," she said. "It's as he left it, or, rather, as you left it. I cleaned the rest of the place the other day after you were here."

"Did you touch his clothes?"

"Yes, I bundled them all up into a couple of suitcases and took them to Action Catholique. I checked there was nothing in the pockets, of course. There were just some papers, a supermarket bill and some receipt from the post office."

"What kind of receipt? Do you remember? It could be important," J-J asked sharply.

"I'm not sure, but it looked like the kind of thing you get when you send something by registered post. Henri was always careful to do that when sending reports or papers to his clients."

"What did you do with it?"

"I must have thrown it away, maybe threw it into the fireplace or the bin. I really don't know. Do you need me anymore, or may I go back to the garden? It's painful for me to be here."

"Of course, madame," J-J said. "Could you let us have your birth and wedding dates, please? We'll try those for the computer password, otherwise we'll have to resort to special measures."

She wrote them down for him on a pad, added her husband's army number from his military service and went back to the garden to sit on a wooden bench, a balled-up handkerchief in her hand.

"Poor woman," said J-J. He stood in the doorway after Yves opened the study, put the laptop into a plastic bag and handed it to one of his colleagues, who returned with it to the van. Bruno leafed through the mail that Madame Hugon had piled onto a hall table. There was an electricity bill, a couple of catalogs and a history magazine wrapped in clear plastic with Monsieur Hugon's name in the address box.

"I'll check the fireplace, you check the garbage," J-J ordered, and Bruno took a large plastic sheet from the pile of evidence bags that Yves had put by the door and emptied the contents of the kitchen bin onto it. Mercifully, there was little but orange peel and a banana skin, coffee grounds and some screwed-up papers: a supermarket bill; a bill from a coffee shop in Sarlat; and a post office receipt for registered mail, sent by Monsieur Hugon to a Monsieur F. Iqbal, *poste restante,* Strasbourg central post office.

"Bingo," Bruno called to Jean-Jacques, and the chief detective hurried into the kitchen at a speed that belied his bulk.

"What have you found?"

"Sylvestre's business partner, Freddy, the Indian racing driver, was Hugon's client, sure enough," said Bruno, showing him the postal receipt. "I'm sure he and Sylvestre are in this together, and they hired Hugon to find out about the lost Bugatti. Who but Hugon's client would take away all the research notes and notebooks about the job? And who but the killer would have come here to Hugon's house to take them?"

"I thought you were supposed to have searched this place when you first came here," said J-J.

"I just had suspicions at the time," Bruno said defensively. But the suspicions had been his, so it was Bruno's responsibility to make sure all the evidence was gathered. "You're right, I'm sorry. I should have looked more carefully at the time. No excuses."

"So now you want to arrest them?" J-J asked.

"We have to question them. This makes them our prime suspects."

"Okay, I accept that. But we're not sure it's a murder yet, not until the Bordeaux lab confirms Fabiola's theory about cyanide poisoning. I'm hoping to get something from them by the end of the day, but I'm told it's a complex process, so it might be tomorrow."

"So then do we bring them in?"

"Maybe so, but let's think this through," said J-J. "Consider the relative importance of a case of local murder here in your little commune against a case of international terrorist finance. What is the brigadier going to say if you derail the whole investigation by arresting Sylvestre tonight? What's Isabelle going to say when you torpedo the first big investigation she has led?"

Bruno bit his lip in frustration, understanding that again J-J was right, even though holding back went against all his instincts.

"And if you are convinced this is a murder, what do we do then?"

"Then we tell Isabelle and the brigadier, and you know as well as I do what they'll say. They'll tell us that we can always bring the murder charge once their operation is complete, but, for now, terrorism trumps murder. And both the minister of justice and the minister of the interior will agree with them, and so will ninety-nine French citizens out of every hundred, me included."

16

He might not be able to arrest Sylvestre, Bruno reflected, but the fact that Oudinot was now considering a sale of some land to his estranged relative gave him the perfect excuse to call at the *chartreuse*. But first he went home to clean and tidy the place for Martine's visit, to put some more wood into his stove and to set the table for dinner. Most important, he had to decide on the meal he would prepare.

Martine was born and raised in the region, so truffles and foie gras would be too routine. Her mother would certainly have prepared a classic series of dishes to welcome Martine's return, and the farm produced ducks and geese and raised some of the best calves in France. Fernand had been the man who had taught him how to recognize a classic veal calf, raised only on its mother's milk. First, he said, peel back the calf's eyelid, and if you see any red veins in the eyeball, it is no longer being raised *sous la mère*. To be sure, Fernand had continued, he steered Bruno to the back of the calf and asked him to raise its tail. Fernand had then leaned forward and used his thumbs to prize open the calf's bottom. "Look at that," he said. "Not a single red vein to be seen. That's the kind of calf you want."

He didn't want to serve a heavy meal, so that excluded beef and lamb. That left fish. Bruno called the baron, a devoted fisherman who was an infallible source of fresh trout, and asked if he planned to fish that day.

"I was in the boat with Antoine this morning, and we got some lovely young trout," came the reply. "Better than that, we went afterward to that little stream that comes down near St. Cirq and got enough *écrevisses* to feed half a dozen. Do you want to join us for dinner?"

Bruno savored the idea of cooking the wonderful local crayfish. "I can't, Baron. I've got a big date tonight, but I'd love to buy enough for two from you."

"Who's the lucky girl? I heard you'd been seeing Oudinot's daughter, the one who went to Paris."

Bruno laughed, shaking his head. "There's no way to keep secrets in St. Denis. Yes, that's the one. I was going to grill some trout, but now I'm thinking of *écrevisses à la nage*. When can I drop by and pick them up?"

"Anytime this afternoon. I'll be working in the garden. I'll save you a dozen. What do you plan to drink with them?"

"I was thinking of a bottle of Pierre Desmartis's cuvée Quercus."

"A fine choice, but what do you plan for the rest of the meal?"

"A zabaglione for dessert, with my own goose eggs. And to begin, you remember that Dordogne food fair we went to in Périgueux, when Pascal, that friend of mine from Neuvic, gave us each a can of the caviar they're making there? I haven't used it yet, so I thought I'd make some blinis and serve that as a first course."

"Don't forget a glass of ice-cold vodka to go with the caviar. That should do the trick. And you might try using Monbazillac instead of Marsala for the zabaglione; it works very well. Are you going to serve it on its own?"

"No, I was going to poach a couple of pears and throw in some fresh blackberries. There're still lots of them in the hedge."

"Excellent. Well, you certainly can't buy the *écrevisses* from me, but next time I catch some you can make that meal for the two of us, or a few more of us if I catch enough."

"Done, even if I have to save up to buy the caviar."

"Wait for when your truffles are ripe this winter, and you can exchange some of them for more caviar from Pascal."

Bruno put a bottle of vodka in his freezer and sat down at his laptop to search for something on the web about Freddy. He knew a fair amount about *Sylvestre* but nothing about Freddy. Isabelle had given his real name as Farid Iqbal so he entered that name, along with "Abu Dhabi" and "car race." Most of the sites that came up were in Arabic, but there were a couple from an English-language paper, *Gulf News.* He clicked on the first and found a photo of a beaming Freddy on the winner's podium at a racetrack in Dubai that described him as a well-known sports enthusiast and businessman, running the classic-car auctions in the region.

The second article was an interview with Iqbal when he and Sylvestre had opened their showroom in Abu Dhabi and staged the first of their auctions. Freddy described being born and brought up in Ahmedabad, in Gujarat state in India, the son of a successful businessman who had sent him to school in Switzerland, where he had been introduced to go-kart racing. He began to win races and placed third in a European championship race when he was just fifteen. But then his parents were killed in a Hindu-Muslim riot that lasted three days and resulted in over a thousand deaths in Gujarat in 2002.

"My parents were martyred in a Hindu pogrom, and it was then I understood the great responsibility of being a Muslim," Freddy said in the interview. "That is why I am so at home here in Abu Dhabi among the faithful."

Bruno sat back, thinking that Isabelle's connection of the car auctions to terrorist financing suddenly made sense. He could see how it might work. Sylvestre sold cars to wealthy Arabs who then registered the cars in the Emirates. They could transfer legal ownership of a valuable car to someone with terrorist connections who then exported the cars back to Europe to be sold at another of Freddy's auctions. The proceeds would be legal, and the money whitewashed. Bruno scrolled down through more websites but learned only that the total sales at Freddy's most recent car auction had topped ten million dollars.

He put Balzac in the van before setting off for Sylvestre's *chartreuse*. He'd found that people tended to be more friendly and talkative when his dog was present and pondered how far he should go with his questioning. Should he ask Freddy what was in the envelope Hugon had sent to him and whether he knew of Hugon's death? Should he ask Sylvestre if he and Freddy had been the clients for Hugon's search for clues about the lost Bugatti, or would that alert them too soon? He decided to play it by ear.

There was nobody in sight when he arrived, but one Range Rover was parked in the courtyard and another by the gatehouse. He knocked there first, and after a moment heard an answering shout. A few seconds later Freddy opened the door, wearing shorts and a sweat-drenched T-shirt.

"Sorry, I was working out on the rowing machine," he said, and glanced briefly down at Balzac, who was wagging his tail in that friendly way that he greeted strangers. Freddy didn't react to Balzac's overtures and looked back at Bruno. "You need to be fit to be a racing driver. What can I do for you?"

"Is Sylvestre around?"

"He's in the main house, but he's on the phone to China. It's about opening the Shanghai showroom next month." He was standing in the doorway, one hand on the door as if impatient to get back inside and close it.

"Will you be going, too?"

"No, I have business in the Gulf to get back to."

"I can wait until Sylvestre is free," Bruno said. "Is he likely to be long?"

Freddy shrugged. "Who knows? He's been on that call half an hour already."

Trying to find a way to prolong the conversation, Bruno said, "You told me the other day you liked the castles that you'd seen here in the Périgord. Which ones have you visited?"

"I haven't really visited them, just seen them while driving around. There was one on the cliff overlooking the big river; I think it's the Dordogne. I remember Sylvestre saying the English had it, and the French built another castle on the other side of the river. And I saw one by the road on the way to Sarlat and another one from the autoroute on the way down here."

"Do you have castles like that in India? I remember Sylvestre saying that was where you were from."

"Yes, of course."

"I wanted to ask you about that Tesla you were driving," Bruno said, trying a new line of conversation. "What sort of range do you get from it?"

"It's got different settings for whether you want to race or cruise or drive in town, but for normal driving about two hundred kilometers."

"And is it fast?"

"Very."

"How do you find the Range Rover?"

"It's okay around here. I prefer the Porsche Cayenne; it gets better traction in the desert."

"Is that what you were driving in that race you won? I remember Sylvestre telling us about it."

"I've won several, but the one he was talking about was a rally through the desert when I came in second. If there's nothing else . . ." His voice trailed off, and he looked across the courtyard where Sylvestre was coming out of the main house.

"There he is, and now excuse me," said Freddy as he stepped back inside and closed the door.

That didn't go well, Bruno said to himself as he strolled through the courtyard to greet Sylvestre. This time Balzac got a better welcome as Sylvestre bent down to pat him.

"Do you have a moment?" Bruno asked. "It's about the problem you have with Oudinot. I notice that I can't hear the geese today."

"They were there at dawn, but he rang the bell about an hour ago for feeding time. He'll probably have them back here later. Can I offer you a coffee?"

"Thanks, that would be good, and maybe some water for the dog."

Sylvestre led the way back to the main house, saying, "I made the family what I thought was a very decent offer. I just want to buy three hectares that would give me the land up to the top of the ridge. Then Oudinot and I need never have anything to do with one another again."

"There's a saying that good fences make for good neighbors," said Bruno. He paused in admiration as he entered the main hall, paved in checkered-black-and-white stone with a handsome wooden staircase curving up to the next floor. A door to the left led to a sitting room and Bruno saw a couple of chrome and leather armchairs. Sylvestre turned right, through a dining room with a long and heavy table that looked antique and into a very modern kitchen, where an iPad mounted on a speaker system was quietly playing classical music. Bruno sat on a high-backed stool at the raised counter overlooking the cooking area where Sylvestre filled an electric kettle and began loading coffee into a *cafetière.* He put a jug of milk and some sugar on a tray with two cups and filled a stainless-steel bowl with water for Balzac, who lapped at it eagerly.

Bruno turned to look out of the French windows to the court-yard. Between him and the windows was a sofa facing a giant TV screen and flanked by two armchairs. There was a second dining table in bleached pine on which stood an open laptop and note-book and a mobile phone that had a headset attached. The table was large enough for eight chairs and for a very futuristic chair in black mesh and chrome that faced the open laptop.

"That looks like a very pleasant place to work. You've done a great job with the remodeling," Bruno said. "I can see how frus-trating the situation with your cousins must be for you."

"I'll win in the end," said Sylvestre casually, pouring the hot water into the coffee. "I can afford lawsuits, and he can't."

"Oudinot is aware of that, and I understand he's considering the offer you made to Martine, but he's worried about losing out on the sale of the timber."

"That's a new one. I hadn't heard of any concern about tim-ber, and anyway, I've got no plans to cut these woods down." He poured Bruno some coffee. "In fact I'd rather keep them. They add to the rural atmosphere."

"He's also got some good cards to play," Bruno said. "You may know that all the communes are supposed to provide a certain proportion of social housing for low-income people, the disabled, and so on. We're desperately short of such places, and if Oudinot applies to build some very cheap social housing all around your buildings, he'll get instant approval. The mayor would have no choice. It's Fernand's land, and it's already zoned for residential use. You'd find that just as much of a problem as the geese, maybe more so."

"I see." Sylvestre stared at Bruno for a long moment. "I pre-sume you have a solution to put to me."

"He'll want a high price per hectare, plus the fifty thousand you suggested to Martine and a half share of any eventual timber sale, for a total sum of a hundred thousand euros. You get your peace and quiet, no geese and a good access road. And I'll propose to the mayor that he put the road leading here on the list for upgrading. I think he'll do it because he wants this business settled and your tourists to start coming here and spending money. Of course, he would also like to have the social housing."

"A hundred thousand is a lot more than the land is worth."

"I know that, but it buys you the certainty of the access and the calm you need to make this place a profitable business. Otherwise all the money you put into it could be wasted."

"A hundred thousand also buys a lot of lawyers," said Sylvestre.

"And not one of them would be able to stop Oudinot surrounding you with social housing."

Sylvestre nodded, looking beyond Bruno to the French windows and the garden. He seemed to reach a decision and looked back at Bruno.

"Fine, you can tell him I'll go with that." He stretched out his hand, and Bruno shook it, saying, "You won't regret this."

"And I want the transfer done fast, with a contract of sale signed before I have to leave for China in two weeks. More coffee?"

"Just a quick cup, I've got to get back for a meeting with the Police Nationale," Bruno said, wondering how far to push Sylvestre. "They're investigating what looks like a suspicious death, maybe a murder."

Sylvestre raised his eyebrows. "Really? You don't expect a murder here in the sleepy Périgord?"

"It was the day of the vintage-car parade, the day before the rally," Bruno said. "You might remember I had to leave to go and register the death of a named Hugon. He was a retired archivist who still did some freelance researching on the side, mainly for local lawyers. It looked like natural causes to me, and the local doctor said it was a heart attack. But one of Hugon's lawyer clients was trying to find some research Hugon was supposed to have finished and found his recent files had all disappeared. So he called the *préfecture,* and they sent detectives. Hugon should have been buried today, but it looks like they're doing an autopsy. His wife is very upset. She was the one who found his body."

"That's understandable." Sylvestre had shown no reaction that Bruno could discern.

"As soon as I've seen the Police Nationale, I'll talk to the mayor and get him to talk to Oudinot and recommend the deal," Bruno said. "We'll try to get this wrapped up quickly. What number can I call you on?"

Sylvestre pulled out his wallet and gave Bruno a business card with his e-mail address and various phone numbers.

"By the way," Bruno said as he turned to leave. "How's your search for that Bugatti going, the one you and Martine were talking about?"

Sylvestre shrugged. "Nothing new to report, but thanks for coming by and for bringing your basset hound. He's the kind of dog that makes me smile."

17

Bruno checked his watch and headed for Pamela's riding stables. He'd have to take Hector out early if he were to be back in time to prepare dinner. But he also wanted to have a word with Félix. After he pulled in, Balzac went off to paw at Hector's stable door while Bruno went in search of Pamela. She was in the office, looking tired but going through her accounts.

"The good news is that we're no longer operating at a loss," she said, looking up at him cheerfully. "The bad news is that it's only because Miranda and I aren't taking any wages out of the school yet. But in terms of utility bills, taxes, fodder and running costs, our heads are above water. One bad vet's bill, however, and we drown."

"You've only just started, and you haven't started renting the *gîtes* yet," Bruno replied. "They'll provide a good income next summer."

"Yes, but in the meantime we have to pay money to get them repainted, repaired and have the plumbing fixed. Sometimes I wonder why I ever let myself in for this."

"You enjoy the challenge and you're good at it," Bruno said. "How's Félix doing? Is he still turning up on time?"

"Every day, and he's doing well. He's out with Miranda now,

helping her escort the pony trekkers. I thought it was time to put him on horseback, and they're only walking along. He's on the Andalusian; she seems to like him. She also seems to like Hector; it's a pity he's a gelding. That might have saved me the stud fees we'll have to pay to get her with foal."

"If Félix is not back soon, can I ask you to give him this with my compliments?" He handed her the printout he'd made of the photo of the lost Bugatti that Young had sent him. "Tell him it's a gift for his wall collection."

"You might find it fighting for space. He found a set of very out-of-date *Cheval Magazine*s in a stable loft and asked if he could take some home to put the pictures up in his room. I got the impression that the cars were now taking second place. It's a bit like you, Bruno. Once you got close to horses and began to enjoy them, you wondered where they'd been all your life."

"Thanks to you," he said. "I hope the boy gets as much pleasure from horses as they've given me."

"I know he's been in trouble, but he's a sweet boy, Bruno. The horses like having him around, and so do Miranda and I. He's even started having an afternoon cup of tea with us when he gets here from school."

Ah, the British, thought Bruno, smiling to himself. It's just as we were taught in school: they believe everything can be resolved with a nice, hot cup of tea.

"I'm happy to hear that he's doing well, and I'm grateful you've taken him on," he said. "I understand you can't pay him yet, but could he be useful in the long term? I mean, maybe you could get him to paint the *gîtes* and do some maintenance? I think his dad might be ready to do some odd jobs like that, and it would be good for them to work together."

"Let's wait and see. In the meantime, I've had a couple of phone calls about your new romantic interest. I'm told she's called Martine, is that right? Daughter of a local family who's briefly back from a high-powered career in the big city?"

"I only had an after-dinner drink with her at Ivan's last night," he said. "You know how people talk."

"Passionate embraces in the rain is what I heard," she said, arching an eyebrow and giving him one of those ominously cool smiles that she did so well. "That sounds rather serious. And now you're blushing."

"A good-night kiss in the rain is hardly a passionate embrace," he said, irritated with himself as so often before that he could never control his blushes. "I'm a bit pressed for time, so I'd better take Hector out before I have to go and see J-J about a case he's on. Fabiola probably told you there's an investigation into Hugon's death."

"She said there would be an autopsy, but you know how discreet she is about her work. But if you're pressed for time, I'll take Hector out with the others when Miranda gets back. I always enjoy riding him."

"Thanks so much for that. See you tomorrow." He blew her a kiss and was about to drive back toward town when her mobile rang. Her face went grave as she listened, and she put out a hand to keep him close.

"Bruno's standing right here beside me," she said, after a while in English. "Hold on while I brief him."

"It's Miranda," she said, reverting to French for Bruno's sake. "One of the girls has fallen off her horse and been injured. It could be serious. Some boy was throwing stones at the horses, and one of them hit Denise in the eye. There's a lot of blood, and the other girls are panicking. Miranda fears the girl could lose her eye."

"Find out where Miranda is exactly and tell her I'll get there as soon as I can," he replied. "In the meantime I'll call the *urgences.*"

He pulled out his phone and punched in his speed-dial number for the *pompiers*.

When Pamela gave Miranda's location, Bruno knew the *pompiers* could never get there in a vehicle. It was at a ford across a small stream, deep in the woods behind Audrix. He told Albert, the chief fireman, to get to a hunter's cabin known as La Mique, after a local specialty, a dumpling that one of the hunters always made there. From there the *pompiers* would have to proceed on foot with a stretcher, following the trail to St. Chamassy.

"I'll take a horse, it will be faster," he told Pamela. "Is Hector saddled?"

"No, but my Primrose is, I was about to take her out. I can exercise Hector for you later."

"You stay here and start phoning," he said as they strode toward Primrose's stall. "Alert Fabiola and then call the injured girl's parents and tell them to meet us at the clinic. Then you'd better call the other girls' parents and reassure them. Does Miranda know who this boy was?"

"I didn't ask."

"No matter," he said, swinging himself into the saddle. "I'll find out. I'll leave Balzac with you."

Bruno set off at a trot and then into a canter. Both he and the horse knew these trails, and they were mostly too narrow and tangled for any faster pace. He picked up his pace when they came to a firebreak in the woods, Primrose seeming to understand the need for urgency, but then they had to slow again as he descended the narrow trail that led to the stream and then walked the horse upstream to the ford where he found the girls. La Mique was another three or four hundred meters down the path.

"Thank God you're here," said Miranda. She was sitting on the bank, the injured girl on her lap. Someone had tied a rough and bloodstained bandage around the girl's head, but the rest of her face was as white as snow and she was shivering.

The other girls were huddled together on the bank, watching and silent. One of them was crying, and Félix was trying to comfort her. He was wearing an old shirt from which the sleeve was missing. That had probably been the source of the makeshift bandage, Bruno thought. Someone, probably the boy, had sensibly looped the horses' reins together and tied them to a branch.

"Bruno's here," one of the girls shouted, and the injured one moved her head when she heard it. Bruno went across and knelt beside her, recognizing her from his tennis classes. She was ten years old, the daughter of one of the bank managers in St. Denis.

"Hello, Denise, everything is going to be fine," he said, taking her hand and leaning down to kiss the part of her brow that wasn't covered by the bandage. Her clothes were soaked from the stream and from her own blood. Head wounds always bled badly, he remembered. He took off his jacket to cover her and give her some warmth, noting that Félix's old denim jacket was already covering her chest. "And you're being very brave, Denise. The *pompiers* are on their way, and Dr. Stern is waiting at the clinic to fix you up, and your parents will be there, too. Just lie still in Miranda's arms, and you'll be fine. I need to learn what happened, but if you want me, just call, okay?" He felt her hand squeeze his by way of answer.

"It was a big boy, a young man, waiting in the trees until we were mostly across the stream, and then he came out and started throwing stones," Miranda said. "Denise was last in line, just ahead of Félix. He's been great, taking care of the horses and calming the other girls down and then tearing his shirt for the bandage. And he tied up the horses without being told. I don't know what we'd have done without him."

"Will you know the young man again?" Bruno asked.

"Certainly, I'd know him anywhere."

"How many stones did he throw?"

"Three," came Félix's voice. "The first one missed, the second one hit me, and the third one hit Denise. I know who it was, and I think he was aiming at me."

"Tristan?" Bruno asked, and Félix nodded. Some of the other girls confirmed it. Tristan was well known among the school-children.

"Where were you hit?" Bruno asked the boy.

"Here." He pointed to his thigh. "I'm going to have a big bruise. It's lucky, really. If it had hit the horse, she might have shied, and I'd have come off into the stream like Denise did. She screamed as she hit the water. Besides that wound, I think she hurt her shoulder badly when she fell."

"You've done very well, Félix," Bruno said, clapping him on the shoulder. "I'm proud of you, and I'll make sure Pamela and your parents know what a fine job you did here. Do you know the way back to the riding school from here? Pamela is waiting there, and we've asked the parents of these other girls to meet them there."

The boy nodded again, then said, "Yes, Bruno, I know the way."

"And do you think you could lead the rest of the girls back to the riding school while I wait here with Denise for the *pompiers*?"

"If you take over Denise, I can lead them back," said Miranda before Félix could answer. "We really need Félix to bring up the rear just in case any of the girls fall behind. But I need to get the rest of these girls home. Their parents will be waiting and going frantic. I doubt if they'll want their daughters to come out riding again and we've got that damn mortgage to pay. Oh, God, why did this have to happen?"

Bruno put his hand on her shoulder to calm her. "Denise is what's important now." He knelt down to talk to the girl.

"Will you be okay waiting here with me while Miranda takes

the other girls home?" he asked, and heard a faint "Yes." Gently he took her from Miranda, and as he enfolded her in his arms he saw that one shoulder was hanging low. It looked like she'd broken her collarbone in the fall. Bruno's face set hard as he thought of what this meant. Tristan was sixteen, old enough to be judged as an adult.

When Miranda had the remaining girls in their saddles, Bruno asked her to take Primrose back on a leading rein. He'd travel with Denise to the clinic. Shortly after the others had gone, Félix turning in the saddle from his post at the rear to wave a good-bye, Bruno heard noises from the undergrowth at the far side of the stream, and Ahmed and Alain appeared carrying a folded stretcher. Ahmed had done the paramedic course required for the *urgences* service, and after splashing and stumbling through the ford he quickly examined Denise.

"The bleeding's stopped," he said. "Whoever applied that bandage did a good job. But her collarbone is broken." He took off his shoulder bag and found a sling and long bandage that he used to strap Denise's arm in place. They strapped Denise into the stretcher for the hike back to the ambulance and the fast drive to the clinic. Bruno was able to put his jacket back on, still slightly damp and with some smears of blood on the collar. From inside the vehicle, Bruno could hear the siren howling, and he had to brace himself as Alain made fast turns. It reminded him of driving with Annette. Then they were at the clinic, Alain pushing his way through a small crowd gathered on the steps so Bruno and Ahmed could get the girl inside and into Fabiola's examining room. She was waiting there with Denise's parents. She had changed from her usual white coat into scrubs and operating gloves, her hair tucked into a skullcap and a surgical mask hanging around her neck. Bruno had been aware of a camera flashing as they carried Denise in. That meant Philippe was taking pictures for the paper. This was getting more and more serious for Tristan.

"Don't go yet," Fabiola said to Ahmed as they put Denise down. "You may have to drive her to the hospital in Périgueux. But let's get her out of those wet clothes and take a look."

Denise's mother fought back tears as she bent down to kiss her child and take her hand. Her father wrung Ahmed and Bruno by the hand with a muttered "Thanks," and Bruno told him the one to thank would be young Félix.

Fabiola cut the girl's clothes off with scissors, strapped her arm back into place and wrapped her in blankets. Then she removed the bandage and wiped Denise's face and neck and shoulder clean of blood, though more of it had clotted in Denise's hair. "I don't think it's as bad as it looks," Fabiola said, for the parents' benefit as much as for Denise. "The main cut seems to be in the eyebrow, and there's a tough bone there that took some of the force. The cheekbone is also cut but not as deeply. It's strange that there is no mark on the brow."

"She was wearing a riding helmet," said Bruno, remembering seeing it on the bank beside Miranda. "They must have taken it off to apply the bandage."

Fabiola took a small flashlight from the cabinet at her side, gently opened the swollen eye and shone the light inside.

"The flesh around the eye is bruised and scratched, but the cuts aren't too deep," she said after a careful examination. "The pupil is reacting to the light but not as normally as I would like, and I think she's got a concussion. Do you know if she lost consciousness?"

"No, but we can ask Miranda or Félix," Bruno said.

"Do you remember everything that happened, Denise?" Fabiola asked.

"I remember a pain and falling and being in Miranda's arms and then Bruno came," the girl said, sounding sleepy.

"Good girl," Fabiola said and continued her examination. Finally she looked up at Denise's parents. "I can't be sure and I'm hoping there's no damage to the eyeball, but I'm worried about a possible detached retina. I don't think her sight will be affected, but I'd like to be sure, so the ambulance will take her to Périgueux, and I'll arrange for an eye specialist to be waiting. Depending on what he says, we may have to send her on to Bordeaux. In the meantime I'd better give Denise a local anesthetic and stitch that cut on the eyebrow and then make sure the collarbone is properly set."

Bruno excused himself, and seeing that the hall outside was full, he let himself into Fabiola's surgery to make some calls. The first was to Yveline, to brief her and ask her to meet him at the supermarket where Tristan's father worked before heading to Tristan's home. Then he alerted Annette, as the magistrate in charge of prosecuting juveniles. Bruno was determined to leave nothing to chance. He rang social services in Périgueux, but as soon as they heard Tristan was over sixteen, they said it was no longer a matter for them. Then he went outside to find Philippe, who was on the phone to one of the other girls' parents who was at Pamela's riding school, just having been reunited with his daughter.

"You're sure the youngster throwing the stones was Tristan, the son of the guy at the supermarket?" Philippe was saying into the phone, his eyes on Bruno. "Your daughter is certain of it, and the other girls say the same? Can I quote you on that?" He listened for a moment, nodded and then closed the phone and asked Bruno, "You going to arrest the little bastard?"

Bruno nodded and said, "But there's something else, a good part to this nasty story. The hero of the hour was Félix. Apparently the stones were aimed at him, and one of them hit him. Tristan has been bullying him for years. But when Denise was hit and fell into the stream, Félix took charge." He described what

Félix had done and told Philippe he could find the boy at the riding school. "St. Denis should be proud of a youngster like that, who kept his head, bandaged Denise and did all the right things. You can quote me on it."

"I can't use Tristan's name; he's a juvenile."

"Not anymore, he isn't," said Bruno, walking away. "He's turned sixteen."

By the time Bruno reached the supermarket, Yveline was just pulling into the parking lot in a gendarmerie van. As they mounted the stairs to Simon's office, Bruno told her Denise was being taken to an eye specialist in Périgueux. He wanted Yveline to make the arrest. Bruno was not under the same pressure as the gendarmes to meet arrest quotas. They strode together into Simon's office without knocking.

"I'm here only as a courtesy to you, Simon, since your son is now officially old enough to be arrested as an adult," Bruno began. "His bullying has gotten out of hand. He was throwing stones at Félix this afternoon, and one of Tristan's stones hit a ten-year-old girl in the eye, and she may lose it."

Startled and rising to his feet, Simon began to interrupt.

"Shut your mouth and just listen," Bruno snapped. "The girl's on her way to an eye specialist in Périgueux right now. And I'm going to your house with the gendarmes to arrest your boy on a charge of aggravated bodily harm. It's aggravated because that's what the law says if a weapon or a missile is used. And I think I should warn you that Tristan very probably faces a custodial sentence in a youth detention center. You may follow us to your home if you want and arrange for a lawyer."

"But don't use your phone to do so while driving or I'll arrest you for that," said Yveline. "And on no account call your home or your son or try borrowing anybody else's phone to do so. I'll be checking your phone records to make sure of that."

They turned and marched out, leaving Simon to scramble

from behind his desk to follow them, firing off questions. Were they absolutely certain it was Tristan? Who were the witnesses? Wasn't the boy still a juvenile? Had he not been provoked by Félix? Was it not some form of accident, perhaps a silly prank that had gone wrong?

Bruno and Yveline ignored the questions. As they got to her van, Bruno saw Simon fishing his own car keys from a pocket and heading for his car. Bruno suddenly became angry, thinking that there was one important question Simon had not bothered to ask.

"You haven't asked the name of the little girl who was the victim," he shouted. "She's Denise, the daughter of Paul-Michel, the bank manager. I imagine that as soon as he stops sitting vigil outside the operating room he'll call his lawyer. You might want to prepare for a lawsuit, and also for some questions from the press. Philippe Delaron was at the clinic when I brought Denise in, her face covered in her own blood."

As Yveline drove onto the Limeuil road, where Simon had one of the expensive houses overlooking the valley, Bruno adjusted the rearview mirror to see Simon following behind in his Mercedes, both hands on the wheel but his mouth opening as if he were talking. Of course he'd have a hands-free phone in his car! He should have thought of that. Bruno told Yveline to be sure to check whom Simon had been calling.

Simon lived in a modern house designed to look like a traditional Périgord building, but the tiles and the color of the stone were wrong and the garden contained some unusual decorations, including a fountain disguised as a miniature stone windmill and an old bicycle that had been deliberately overgrown with plants. The shutters were painted a bright blue that might have been more suitable in St. Tropez, and the flower beds looked as if they had been planted by a drill sergeant with an obsession for absolute symmetry. Yveline rolled her eyes at Bruno as they rang the doorbell and heard it chime the opening notes of "The Marseillaise."

"Bonjour, Bruno," said Amandine, Simon's wife, looking startled to see him with Yveline and holding up her hands in a way that Bruno knew meant she was letting her nail polish dry. Then she saw her husband's car drawing up behind the gendarmes' van. "What's this about?"

"We need to see Tristan. Is he in?" Bruno asked.

"Yes, he's upstairs in his room. Why?"

"We need to question him about an assault on a little girl this afternoon," said Yveline, trying to move past Amandine who had taken a startled step backward, her jaw dropping, but trying to stop Yveline from entering.

"It's Denise, the bank manager's daughter, and she might lose an eye," said Bruno, trying to distract Amandine long enough for Yveline to get past her bulk. "Several witnesses have identified Tristan as the boy who threw the stone that hurt her."

Amandine's mouth opened and closed, but she stayed immobile and then shouted, "Simon, stop them."

"Madame," said Yveline coldly, "either you let me past or, as well as your son, I'll have no choice but to arrest you for obstructing the police in the course of their duty."

"It's not true, Tristan was with me here all afternoon," Amandine said, grudgingly allowing Yveline to pass. "He's not well, he's delicate . . ."

"That's fine, Amandine," said Bruno. "If you say he was with you all afternoon and hasn't left the house, we'll just take your statement to that effect. Why not show me where I can sit down to take your statement?"

"Don't say a word, Amandine," Simon called from over Bruno's shoulder. "I've got a lawyer coming, and he said none of us should say a word until he arrives."

"Don't be a fool, spending good money on lawyers when I can clear this up right now," she told her husband, throwing him a contemptuous look. "Follow me into the kitchen, Bruno."

By the time he heard footsteps coming down the stairs, Bruno had Amandine's brief statement, signed and made official by the stamp Bruno kept in his shoulder case with other forms, evidence bags and gloves, dog biscuits and carrots for the horses, along with keys to the various municipal buildings. Her statement included the key phrase that it had been made "freely and voluntarily and under pain of perjury."

Yveline pushed Tristan into the room, looking stunned as he stared down at his hands handcuffed before him. A pair of earphones that looked familiar to Bruno were still hanging from the mobile phone tucked into the breast pocket of his shirt. Some tinny music was still playing. Bruno donned a pair of evidence gloves, plucked out the phone and put it in an evidence bag with the earphones.

"Madame Vaudon has just given me a statement asserting that her son was with her in the house all afternoon," he told Yveline, keeping a straight face. "Tristan's phone should therefore bear out what she says. If not, she's in trouble for making a false statement."

"He's under arrest anyway, even without the assault charge," said Yveline, holding up an evidence bag with a half-filled plastic bag inside it. "Almost half a kilo of marijuana. Were you aware, madame, that your son used illegal drugs?"

Amandine rose to move to her son, and Yveline said firmly "Stand back" and then "Stand aside, monsieur," as Simon hovered helplessly in the doorway. She pushed the boy out, Bruno following behind, and heard Amandine berating her husband as "an utterly useless apology for a man."

At the front door, Bruno turned and said, "Your son will be

at the gendarmerie until the magistrate comes to press charges. Your lawyer is free to join us there, but it would be a good idea to telephone the gendarmerie first and see when the magistrate will be available. Thank you for your cooperation, and, Simon, you might want to make your peace with Denise's parents while you can."

Sitting in the backseat with a white-faced Tristan while Yveline drove, Bruno pulled out his phone to call Pamela. He needed his van and Balzac, and he still had to collect the *écrevisses* from the baron before Martine arrived for dinner.

18

As he left the baron's place with his bag of crayfish, Balzac sitting up beside him, Bruno pulled off the road to answer his phone. He always did that now, ever since being called to a fatal road accident that had been caused by a woman texting as she drove. The screen told him the call was from J-J.

"The forensics guys have everything they need from the house, but Yves is still trying to get into Hugon's computer," J-J said. "And there's no word yet on the autopsy from the lab in Bordeaux, so we're heading home. There's just one thing: one of my detectives who was watching the rally on Sunday and saw Freddy win swears it was Freddy he saw on the station platform in Le Buisson yesterday evening getting on the train for Agen. But you said you'd heard from Isabelle that he was having dinner in Sarlat."

"Not quite," Bruno replied. "She said his phone was at a fixed location in Sarlat."

"Maybe he's playing games with his phones, leaving the one we know about in one place while he goes off to do business elsewhere, probably with a phone we don't know about. I've assigned someone to check the surveillance cameras at the station in Agen, but if he's being careful about surveillance, they aren't difficult to avoid."

"Have you heard anything from Isabelle about when we should expect her?" Bruno asked.

"No, she must still be held up by paperwork. You wouldn't believe the number of forms I've had to fill in, defining the limits of the surveillance we're supposed to mount. I've still got to get a magistrate to countersign them and witness my guarantee to destroy any film or tapes not needed in court."

Bruno felt a twinge of alarm as J-J ended the call. He'd filled out no forms and asked no permission for his own amateurish attempts to keep watch on the two targets. Perhaps he'd better keep that knowledge to himself or even dismantle his cameras. He'd have to change the batteries by the next evening, he told himself, even if he took the risk of leaving them in place. But perhaps Isabelle and her team would have arrived by then.

He raced home, stopping only to buy bread just before the bakery closed. He had thirty minutes at the most before Martine was supposed to arrive. That left him no time to shower if he was going to pick some fresh lettuce and feed Balzac and his chickens.

He dealt with the animals first, then picked the lettuce and put another log into the wood-burning stove. He checked that he'd put the vodka into the freezer. He always kept a couple of bottles of white wine and champagne in the fridge. He knew that he didn't have the two hours he needed for the dough to rise to make proper blinis to go with the caviar, so he'd have to offer toast instead. But then he remembered how Pascal at the food show had made what he'd called his instant blinis using egg whites. It was not the best time for an experiment with a new dish, he thought, but what the hell? Bruno washed his hands and face, ran his wet fingers through his hair and then gargled quickly with mouthwash to wash away the taste of the day.

In the kitchen, he began making the court bouillon for the crayfish, pouring into a large saucepan half a bottle of Thomas's

Riesling with the same amount of water. He peeled four shallots and sliced them thin and did the same with two carrots. He diced three stalks of celery and a thin leek and put all the vegetables into the saucepan with a couple of chopped cloves of garlic, one whole clove and some coriander and fennel seeds. He ground in some salt and pepper and then took a small *piment d'espelette,* the red pepper grown in the Basque country, from the bunch that hung from the beam in his kitchen, and added it to the broth as it heated. He looked at his vegetable basket, where he kept apples mixed with the potatoes to stop them from sprouting. No, potatoes would make the meal too heavy. Perhaps rice? No, he'd serve it just with the vegetables in the bouillon.

He opened the jar of caviar and put it on the table with a tiny silver coffee spoon for each of them. He'd found them in a *vide-greniers,* one of the town's regular jumble sales where people emptied their attics of stuff they no longer needed. Now for the blinis. He measured a hundred grams of buckwheat flour into a bowl, mixed in a little salt and pepper and made a well in the center of the flour. He took an egg from the bowl by the stove and was about to crack it and separate the white from the yolk when he heard the sound of a car coming up the road and turning into his driveway. Balzac was already at the door, bounding out as soon as Bruno opened it to investigate the new arrival.

Balzac liked new people, and he liked women, so he was squeaking with excitement when he reached Martine's car just as she opened the door. Bruno thought for a moment Balzac was going to leap into the car, but instead the dog put his front paws onto the sill of the car door and gave her a happy bark of greeting and an amiable sniff at her black jeans as she swung her long legs from the car and stood up. Bruno came forward to give her the *bise* on each cheek, but she kissed him firmly on the lips and then bent to caress Balzac. She was wearing a T-shirt of black silk beneath a short tweed jacket of dark blue, white and black checks that had been nipped in tightly at the waist. It had been beautifully cut to work as casual clothing or something more formal. It was somehow businesslike and playful at the same time and made Bruno regret that with the pressure of time he had decided against changing.

"Horses, basset hounds, country dinners and a man in uniform—are there no limits to the props you use to seduce a woman, Bruno?"

He looked down at his uniform, suddenly realizing he had not cleaned Denise's blood from his collar.

"I'm sorry, I just got back. It was one of those days, dramas, injuries, arrests . . ."

"Not that awful attack on the little girl that was on the radio just now?"

"Yes, that was part of it. But when I had to choose between starting the dinner and having a shower and changing my clothes, the dinner won."

"A true Périgourdin in your priorities, and quite right, too," she said. Suddenly her eyes widened in surprise. "Is that blood on the collar of your jacket? You should soak it in cold water right away." She handed him the bottle she had brought.

"I asked Claire what wine you liked, and she checked with Ivan who said your favorite was Château de Tiregand. But that's what my dad usually serves when I come home, so I thought I'd bring you something different that I came across when I was skiing in Gstaad. I was amazed to see a Bergerac wine, this one, Château Monestier La Tour. I loved it."

From the look in her eye and the way she was speaking quickly, Bruno realized that Martine was probably just as nervous as he about the evening ahead and where it might lead. They were in that enticing but dangerous moment when each of them knew that all was possible between them but feared that a single false step could send the edifice of fantasy they were constructing tumbling down into embarrassment and disappointment.

"What a generous and inventive thought," he said. It was a wine he recalled drinking years ago and not being overly impressed. But he'd heard that the vineyard had come under new ownership, and its wines were now spoken of with deep respect by people whose judgment he trusted. "I always think a wine is better when it comes with a little story attached like that. So now I'll always think of you in the Alps, swooping downhill and dancing with the mountain whenever I see this wine."

She took his arm companionably and asked him to show her his garden. He pointed out the white oaks where his truffles were growing underground, introduced her to Napoléon and Joséphine, his two geese, and to Blanco the cockerel.

"Named for the rugby player," she said, rising even higher in his esteem when she recognized the name. She cast the experienced eye of a country girl over his vegetable garden, noting the well and nodding in approval at the three compost heaps, each at a different stage of fermentation.

"Are those woods yours?" she asked.

"All the way up to the ridge. That's where I get my mushrooms, and there are a couple of spots where I can usually count on truffles. The meadow down below is mine as far as that lower hedge. The stream on the right is the boundary."

"Does your well work?"

"Yes, I used to depend on it for water and still use it in summer for the garden. It's good to drink; somehow it tastes better than the stuff from the water tower. We'll be drinking it tonight with our meal."

"Where do you keep your horse? Is there a barn behind the house?"

"Hector stays at a friend's house to keep her horse company, and so she can take him out for exercise when I'm tied up with police work. I do the same for her when she's busy. It's Fabiola, Dr. Stern, at the clinic." After a moment he thought it politic to add, "She and her boyfriend, Gilles, are good friends of mine."

"Now tell me what you're planning for us to eat."

"*Écrevisses à la nage,* the crayfish caught by a friend this morning about three kilometers from here," he said. "So we're drinking white wine."

"Lovely, I haven't had those for ages." Martine squeezed his arm in glee. "Mandy says you're known in St. Denis as a good cook."

"I wish I could cook Asian food like she does," he said. "Before the *écrevisses* there's champagne and then some vodka to go with the caviar and the blinis that I'm making, and as soon as Balzac comes back from his security patrol of the chicken run we'll go into the kitchen and I'll cook. Meanwhile, I hope you appreciate this sunset I've arranged for you."

"It will last another few minutes. Why not go and put your jacket in cold water and come back with some champagne. Meanwhile I'll enjoy your view."

"It's hardly as good as the view from your folks' house, with the valley and the river."

"That's why I like it, all these ridges, one after the other, and not another house in sight," she said, almost dreamily, as Bruno left. He put his jacket in to soak and donned a black leather jacket over his uniform shirt. Fetching the glasses of champagne, he cast an eye on the court bouillon, which was just about to start simmering. He turned down the gas and added another splash of Riesling. Back on the terrace he and Martine toasted each other, and then Balzac returned, perhaps at hearing the familiar sound of glasses being clinked. She took his hand as they strolled back into the house, and he showed her the sitting room with its dining table set for two and the wood crackling warmly in the stove. He took off his jacket and draped it over the back of a chair.

She did the same, looking briefly around and noticing the absence of a TV before glancing at his collection of CDs. She picked out Francis Cabrel's *Hors-Saison* and said, "I remember falling in love to that song when I was twenty. I'm in a mood to hear the album again, but softly."

In the kitchen, she perched on the high stool at the counter, topped up their champagne glasses from the half bottle he'd opened and then poured herself a glass of his water from the well. She sipped at it, considering, and then said she liked it. She watched as he washed his hands again before going back to the blinis. He cracked the egg he'd put aside when she arrived and poured the contents back and forth over the bowl to separate the white from the yolk. He put the yolk into the flour, added a wineglass of milk and began whisking, pausing only to add, little by little, a second wineglass of milk, some chives and then a tablespoon of butter. When the mixture was well mixed, he began to whisk the egg white until it began to stiffen, then folded it into the batter and put the gas on high under a frying pan he greased lightly with butter.

"One of the few times I don't use duck fat," he said. "This isn't the proper way to make blinis, but I didn't have time for the yeast to rise. I hope this works well enough."

He put a tablespoon into the batter, filled it and poured it into the pan. He did this four times. As the batter spread out and began to sizzle, he reached into the fridge, pulled out a bottle of the cuvée Quercus, opened it and put it in an ice bucket. After a couple of minutes, he used a spatula to turn the blinis over and took the vodka from the freezer.

"How hungry are you?" he asked.

"Two blinis will do for me. Are you serving them with crème fraîche, or do you have some other devious recipe?"

He flipped the blinis one more time, took the bowl of crème fraîche from the fridge and showed it to her and then put the blinis onto a warmed plate with a knob of butter. He then poured the *écrevisses* into the simmering bouillon and invited Martine to the dining room. She brought the vodka, so frozen that it poured sluggishly into their small glasses, and then she divided the caviar into two portions. She spread some cream onto her first blini, covered it thickly with caviar, ate, and her eyes widened.

"That's good," she said, and finished the blini before raising her vodka glass and draining half of it. *"Naz dorovya,"* she said, or that was how it sounded to Bruno. "I think that's what Russians say. There were a lot of them in Gstaad this year, and they seemed to say it all the time when they drank. Another blini for you, too?"

"Yes, please. I can make more if you change your mind," he said, thinking a fashionable ski resort like Gstaad was way out of his financial league. Martine's business probably made her a wealthy young woman, he assumed, remembering the amount of money she seemed to assume was customary for the work she did.

"Where did you get the caviar?" she asked. "Is it Russian?"

"No, it's French, from around here. Now that we have sturgeon in the river again, a friend of mine has started a business. We used to get Russian caviar sometimes when I was stationed in Bosnia with the UN, though I can't imagine how the quartermasters got hold of it. Our Dordogne caviar tastes as I remember it."

"This tastes as good to me as any I've eaten. If our electric-car rally comes off, we can proudly serve our homegrown caviar to the winners. *Vive la France!*" She finished her second blini and downed the rest of her vodka. "And now do we go back to the kitchen to watch the master at work again?"

"No, we go back to watch me fumble to peel the *écrevisses* and get the veins out and then we wait for them to cool a little as we enjoy the white wine and toss the salad."

"You don't peel them before you put them in the bouillon?" she asked.

"I find it easier this way, and it helps me get the tails out without tearing the flesh. Getting my fingers a bit burned seems a modest price to pay."

"Somebody once said that laziness is the origin of genius because smart people look for easier ways of doing things."

He smiled. "I don't think I'm that smart to begin with." And then stopped as he heard the opening notes of the title song on that album. "Here's the song you fell in love to."

"I remember the song better than I remember the guy," she said. "I had a lot of growing up to do."

"We always do," he said. "Malraux in his *Antimémoires* says he asked an old priest what he'd learned after a lifetime of hearing confessions. And the priest thought for a moment and then said, 'There are no grown-ups.' "

"Thank heavens for that," she said, smiling, taking his hand and giving Bruno that dangerous feeling that their eyes were saying much more than their mouths. "Time for the *écrevisses*?"

He nodded, took the empty plates and returned to the kitchen, opened the white wine and poured each of them a glass before fishing out the crayfish. He filled a bowl with iced water from the fridge and took a set of evidence gloves from his bag and donned them before twisting off the heads and squeezing out the flesh from the tails and taking out the long veins. Between each one, he dipped his fingers into the iced water to cool them.

"The ice water is a clever trick; the laziness of genius again," she said. "This wine is terrific, and this is the best evening I've had for quite a while."

"I'm glad," he said, putting the crayfish back into the bouillon and turning off the gas before turning to look at her. "I feel the same."

"What now?" she asked, her eyes teasing.

"Now we wait until the bouillon cools to the point at which we want to eat," he said, peeling off the gloves and taking a sip from his wine.

"In that case . . ." She eased herself from the stool and came around to stand close to him and began to unbutton his shirt. She dipped a finger into the bowl of iced water and left it there while looking into his eyes. Then she brought up her chilled finger, rested it lightly against his bared nipple and leaned forward to kiss him as he shivered from the sensation. Her tongue teased at his lips, and she murmured, "You haven't yet shown me your bedroom."

Later, in front of the stove in the sitting room, Balzac was dozing with his head on Bruno's thigh as Martine caressed the dog's silky long ears. She was wearing Bruno's white terry-cloth robe, and he had slipped on a rugby shirt and the trousers of a tracksuit. The emptied bowls of crayfish and salad plates were beside them on the floor. She had declined the zabaglione, insisting she'd eaten too much already. Now she put down her wineglass, looked at him fondly and said, "I'd like to stay, but my mother will be wondering where I am."

"I'd like you to stay, too, but I understand. Can we meet again tomorrow?"

"Will you let me do the cooking?"

He laughed. "You mean the meal was as bad as that?"

She gave him a gentle slap on the thigh. "No, don't be silly. It was perfect. But I'd like to cook for you, and you seem to have everything I might need in your kitchen. Can you get away a bit earlier tomorrow to give us some more time together?"

"I'll try. Coffee before you go?"

"That would be great. You can make it while I dress."

Bruno put the kettle on as she went back to his bathroom. He spooned coffee grounds into his *cafetière,* readied the cups and sugar and then glanced at his phone, which was giving the gentle beep that said he had text messages waiting. The first one was from Fabiola, to say that the specialist had diagnosed Denise with a slightly torn retina, relatively easy to repair, and she would stay in the hospital in Périgueux.

The second was from Yveline, telling him that Tristan had been released into the custody of his parents but would be charged with aggravated assault and illegal possession of cannabis tomorrow at the *procureur*'s office in Sarlat.

The third was from Isabelle, and read: "Paperwork fixed. Arrive this evening. Propose to drop by for briefing unless inconvenient."

He typed back "Not tonight. Breakfast at Fauquet's café at 8 tomorrow," and was just clicking SEND when he heard a car coming up the road and then saw the glare of headlights turning as it headed for his driveway.

The car stopped, its headlights illuminating Martine's vehicle. Then it reversed back down the driveway and turned to head off toward the road. It must have been Isabelle, realizing when she saw the other car that he was not alone. She had no right to expect that he would be, he told himself, but felt embarrassed just the same. She would probably tease him tomorrow about having a new friend, but there would be an edge to it.

The kettle was boiling. He closed the phone and made the coffee, letting it rest before he pushed down the plunger. He went into the living room to clear away the bowls, plates and glasses, and then Martine was back fully dressed and looking terrific, eyes shining, skin glowing.

"Did I hear a car?" she asked.

"Probably someone who took a wrong turn. But there's good news from the hospital. That little girl, Denise, her sight will be fine, though they'll keep her in for a few more days. I'll try to get to Périgueux to visit her. Maybe you'd like to come, too, and we can have dinner there."

"Sure, but not tomorrow, that's my evening to cook for you." She leaned forward and kissed him. "The cold water has got the blood out of your jacket. I hung it up to dry, but it will still need cleaning."

She looked at her watch, drank her coffee quickly and said, "Do you think I'll pass my mother's inspection, or will she detect that I've been disporting myself with a louche bachelor all evening?"

I don't know, he thought, since I never had a mother. But he said, "You can complain about the boring local official you had to dine with while persuading him to support your plan for the rally."

"The one who told me that his wife didn't understand him just before he made a clumsy pass at me over the dessert," she countered. "Bad breath, overweight and with hairs growing out of his nose."

"That's the one, but don't pile it on too thick."

She came into his arms and kissed him good night, then bent to stroke Balzac. At the door she stopped, turned toward him and said, "I'm glad about that little girl, Bruno, and thank you for a wonderful evening. Your food more than lived up to my expectations, and so did you. I'll look forward to tomorrow, at about six, unless you call me."

"About six should be fine," he said. "We can walk Balzac together before dinner."

He stood at the doorway to watch the taillights of her car disappear, knowing himself to be a very lucky man but wondering how long it would last and how much time they might have to deepen the relationship before her work took her away again. Independent and wealthy, she had her own business to run in London; he could see her coming back to the Périgord only for visits even if the rally project worked out. And even then she'd feel obliged to stay with her parents. He sighed, thinking that his love life seemed to run in a predictable but ultimately unsatisfying pattern, driven by his attraction for women who were determined to forge their own lives without the conventional constraints of a family and children. He shook his head and went back indoors to slip on some shoes and a jacket and take Balzac out for the last stroll of the night.

19

Refreshed by his morning ride on Hector, Bruno entered the café a few minutes before eight and glanced at Fauquet's copy of *Sud Ouest* as the owner put a still-warm croissant on his plate and began making his espresso. Bruno shook hands with the regulars and explained that he was meeting someone and took his croissant and the paper to a table by the window. Some new horror in the Middle East took up most of the front page, but there was a small headline saying "Horseback Girl Blinded in St. Denis?" Below it was a passport-sized photo of Denise's bloodstained and bandaged face that steered him to an inside page, where he found a much-bigger photo of Tristan in rugby clothes, probably blown up from a team photo, with the caption "Teen vandal arrested." A smaller photo of Félix had the caption "Young hero saves the day—Police."

"Specialist eye doctors in Périgueux were battling last night to save the sight of a ten-year-old girl from St. Denis as a local schoolboy rugby star was arrested for throwing the stone that may blind her," the story began. It must have been printed before the good news came from the hospital. Farther down the page there was Bruno's official police photo. He was quoted as saying the town should be proud of Félix. Tristan's lawyer was quoted as saying he would appeal to the public prosecutor for his client, just a few weeks beyond his sixteenth birthday, to be treated as a juvenile for "a foolish schoolboy prank that had ended in tragedy."

Fauquet brought Bruno's coffee, muttering, "Terrible business, that poor little girl. You won't catch me using Simon's supermarket anytime soon. You know there's talk of a boycott?"

"It wasn't Simon's fault," Bruno said. "His son's sixteen, old enough to be responsible for his own behavior. A lot of local people work at the supermarket, so I hope that idea goes nowhere." He handed the paper back to Fauquet as he saw Isabelle heading across the town square toward the café with that unmistakable stride of hers, a long black coat floating out behind her. "Would you bring an extra croissant and some more coffee for my guest?"

Fauquet turned, looked through the window at Isabelle and back at Bruno. "It's her again, is it? The one who broke your heart."

"Just get the croissant," Bruno replied, shaking his head in mock despair. The one disadvantage of the close-knit community of St. Denis was that his love life seemed to be everybody's business.

"I hope you know what you're doing, just when you've started seeing Oudinot's daughter," Fauquet went on.

Bruno rolled his eyes and then stood as Isabelle came into the café, eyed him grimly and presented her cheeks for the usual *bise* in a way that signaled she wished that courtesy did not require such a greeting.

"Bonjour, Bruno, I'm sorry you weren't able to brief me yesterday," she said coolly. "It means we have all the more work to do today. I see you're in the local paper again."

"Never a dull moment in St. Denis," he said.

"That's not quite how I recall it," she shot back, and then flashed a smile at Fauquet as he served her breakfast and said how pleased he was to see her in his café again. She murmured a polite reply about how much she missed his croissants and turned back to Bruno.

"You can't brief me here," she went on. "I've arranged a room at the gendarmerie. We'll go there as soon as we've finished our coffee. So, tell me, how is that poor little girl?"

"Doing better, she won't lose an eye. But it won't do the riding school any good, and it's a tough enough business venture in times like these without clients having stones thrown at them."

"J-J told me the place is now being run by your mad Englishwoman in partnership with that spy's daughter. I can see why you're concerned."

"That's really not worthy of you," he said mildly. "You know perfectly well that her name is Pamela and that she's Scottish and that Crimson is not just retired but a good friend to the brigadier as well as to me. You'll have me thinking you're getting prejudiced against our friends across the Channel."

Isabelle was the only one who still referred to Pamela as "the mad Englishwoman," the nickname she had been given by the locals when she first arrived in St. Denis. Pamela had long since been affectionately absorbed into the community, but it was one of Isabelle's few unpleasant traits that she would never accept any woman she saw as a rival, even though she had long since left Bruno to focus on her career. He'd have to make sure he steered Martine out of Isabelle's way.

"Are you and Pamela still an item?" Isabelle asked casually, sitting back in her chair as if she couldn't care less either way. "J-J wasn't sure. I'd have thought she was a little old for you."

"I hope J-J said it wasn't any business of yours," he said, irritated, and instantly regretted letting Isabelle see how easily she could provoke him. She'd always known how to get under his skin. He took the final bite of his croissant, washed it down with his coffee and then smiled at her, most of his memories still precious and fond.

"Shall we start again, without any point scoring?" he asked, leaning forward. "You're looking great. From the way you strode across the square it seems like your leg has fully recovered, which is also great. And congratulations on your new job. I'm sorry I wasn't available at such short notice yesterday, but as you know from the newspaper it was a difficult day."

"Okay," she said coolly, as if acknowledging a brief truce rather than a peace treaty. Then she smiled, with what seemed like a trace of an old affection. Perhaps she was mollified that he had made the gesture of reconciliation. "I hope I'll get to see Balzac."

"You can come with me to pick him up. He's having a regular checkup at the vet and getting his nails clipped. I'm always worried about hurting him if I clip them myself. He can come with us to the gendarmerie; they know him well."

As Bruno paid for their breakfasts, Fauquet came across and handed him an envelope.

"I almost forgot," he said. "That kid you called a hero in the paper today came in about seven-thirty and asked me to give this to you. He said he didn't have a phone. Then he rode off on a bike."

Bruno quickly scanned the note, neatly written in individual letters that were not joined up. Félix thanked him for the photo of the car and said he'd seen another photo just like it and, if Bruno was interested, could they meet at the seniors' home at 12:30?

Bruno put the note away, wondering what Félix meant. He thanked Fauquet, and he and Isabelle took his van to the vet's office, where Balzac was declared to be in excellent shape. As the vet brought the dog out, Balzac saw Isabelle and galloped toward her, ears flapping like the wings of some mythical creature, half dog and half bird, before he leaped into Isabelle's arms, licking passionately at her throat.

"That's what I call a welcome," said the vet, staring admiringly at Isabelle as much as at the dog. "I wish I got them like that."

At the gendarmerie, Sergeant Jules gave her a welcome just as warm and enfolded Isabelle into an embrace in which she was almost hidden by his vast bulk. She was delighted to see he was still passing his annual fitness tests, she told him.

"Oh, we don't bother about those around here," he said cheerfully. "How long are you with us for?"

"Not sure yet," she said, and went in to pay her courtesy call on Yveline as post commander and to thank her for offering a work space.

"She hasn't changed a bit," said Sergeant Jules, fondly. "You should never have let that one get away, Bruno."

"If only it had been up to me," he replied.

Isabelle came out with Yveline, who greeted Bruno formally and showed them into the room set aside for Isabelle's team.

"We'll need a statement from you on what you found at the scene of Denise's injury, Bruno," Yveline said. "Can we do that sometime this morning before the *procureur*'s meeting this afternoon?"

"As soon as I've briefed Commissaire Perrault," he said, and followed Isabelle into the modest room with two desks, two chairs, a phone and an empty bookcase.

"I see the facilities here haven't changed, but it's certainly a warmer welcome than we used to get with Capitaine Duroc," Isabelle said, putting her computer case on a desk and handing Bruno her coat as she took a chair. He found a hook on the back of the door. "So what can you tell me?"

He described what he had learned of Sylvestre and Freddy since meeting them at the Concours d'Élégance, from the family row with Oudinot to Sylvestre's hunt for the lost Bugatti.

"I mentioned that the Police Nationale were planning an autopsy of Hugon, but he showed no reaction," Bruno went on. "I also talked to a policeman in Alsace, a friend of mine, who said there was a rumor that Sylvestre came close to bankruptcy in 2008 with the financial crisis and was bailed out by Arab contacts. Certainly his operation in the Gulf seems to be very lucrative, and he's planning a new showroom in Shanghai."

"What's your impression of him?"

"Very smart and determined, probably ruthless when he has to be, but also ready to cut his losses and strike a deal, which is what he's doing with the family feud."

"You mean you think he might be open to working with us if he knew the alternative was a prison term?"

"I think it's very likely, unless he is a lot more frightened of his Arab friends than of going into a French prison." He paused and added, "There's a complication. J-J and I think Sylvestre and Freddy might be involved in a murder. They were working with a local researcher, a retired archivist who died in suspicious circumstances. There's an autopsy under way in Bordeaux as we speak, and we're waiting for the report."

"How was this man killed?"

"We suspect cyanide poisoning. That's what the lab is testing for. The dead man had recently sent off some papers to Freddy at a *poste restante* in Strasbourg."

"Researching what?" she asked. Bruno explained about the lost Bugatti, its history and the fact that one just like it had sold for thirty-seven million dollars.

She shook her head in disbelief. "That much money may well be worth killing for. But let's wait and see if the lab confirms the cyanide before I discuss the implications with J-J. I'm sure he'll agree to wait until my operation is complete. He'd better."

"He and I already talked about it," said Bruno. "I think you'll find him sympathetic, but as soon as the lab confirms it, he'll have to bring in the *procureur,* who might not be so ready to cooperate."

"We'll see. What can you tell me about Farid, the one you call Freddy?" she asked. "Have you met him?"

"He's not at all forthcoming, and I've met him only briefly. I tried to start a conversation but was politely rebuffed. He's a fitness freak and a very good driver. And he seems to be living in a separate house from Sylvestre, so I don't think they're gay. Can you tell me where you're going with this operation?"

"We're trying to draw a map of what we think is a very sophisticated financial network," she said. "Sylvestre and Farid are the middlemen, taking the money at the auctions from the buyers and then distributing it to the supposed sellers. And from what we can see, Farid is the one in charge, the one making the connections. Sylvestre is just the facilitator. Some of the business is legitimate; we're trying to identify the part that isn't. So far we've found five people involved in different European countries, each of them with known terrorist connections. We're also tracking the bank accounts, the routes and companies through which the money is moved. Once we've mapped the whole network, we'll pounce."

"How close are you?"

"Pretty close, but we might not have mapped the whole thing."

"You know Sylvestre is heading for China in a couple of weeks? That's the deadline he's set for the deal with Oudinot to go through."

"Thanks, I didn't know that. It means we might be facing a

deadline when he'll be out of our jurisdiction." She made a note to herself on a pad and then looked up. "Anything else."

"Yes. When you asked me to conduct discreet surveillance I installed a couple of cameras left over from a previous case, the one your American friend Nancy was involved in. I'll need to change the batteries tonight, but I imagine you have much-better equipment."

"You know that's illegal." She raised an eyebrow.

"No, it's not. I'm a licensed hunter and known to be a wild-life enthusiast. Monitoring wildlife movements on a friend's land with cameras is perfectly legal. And I'm not responsible if the wildlife has moved them so they unfortunately cover the entrance to a house rather than the undergrowth."

"You might just get away with that here in the Périgord," she said. "What's the recording system? I hope it's not transmitting on Wi-Fi. If their computers are good enough, they might pick that up."

"No Wi-Fi. It's on a small data card, and Sylvestre was work-ing on what looked like a top-end Apple laptop. I don't know what Freddy was using, or rather Farid, as you call him."

"How friendly are you with Oudinot, the man whose land borders Sylvestre's house?"

"Very friendly, and he often asks after you. We met him a couple of times at *marchés nocturnes* that summer when we were together."

"I can't say I recall him, but I suppose I might remember him if I saw him again. Would he let us use his property for proper surveillance?"

"He'd be delighted. He hates Sylvestre, or at least he did, but who knows, now that they're getting close to a deal? The problem is that I don't know how discreet Oudinot would be. But there's a small hut on his land less than ten meters from Sylvestre's house that would be good for surveillance except for the noise of the geese. I told you about them."

"Could you arrange for the geese to be withdrawn once we're installed?"

"Probably. We could say it's a goodwill gesture to help the deal go through. I can do that today. What about Freddy's trip to Agen when his phone was in Sarlat? J-J was worried that he might know his phone's being monitored."

"We're cool on that. We got him on the security camera at Agen station, meeting someone of interest to us from Toulouse. It helped that you sent us the photos with the license plates."

"I'm glad. Other than Oudinot, how else can I help?"

"Get me those data cards from your cameras tonight."

"Do you want me to remove the cameras at the same time?" he asked.

"Why would I want to interfere in the perfectly legal wildlife-monitoring techniques of a law-abiding citizen?" She smiled, a wicked twinkle in her eye that touched Bruno's heart. He'd never really get over her. He rose to go.

"Just one more thing," she said, a little hesitantly. "Would you mind leaving Balzac here with me for the day?"

"Of course," he said. The dog had been her gift to him when his previous hound had been killed in another operation in which they worked together. "Balzac would like that."

He left, walked back to his van and then stopped at the wine cave of Hubert de Montignac, whose extraordinary collection of vintages of Château Pétrus and of Château Angélus going back fifty years and more had made it one of the great tourist attractions of St. Denis. For the locals, it was also the place to take their *bidons* of glass or plastic to the huge vats at the back of the shop and fill them from the tap with good Bergerac white and red for a couple of euros a liter. Bruno was looking for something between those two extremes of wine for Martine's dinner that evening. He spent a pleasant twenty minutes gossiping with Nathalie, the saleswoman, and tasting a couple of wines he did not know, before leaving with a bottle of Anthologia, a white wine of sauvignon from Château Tour des Gendres that he could seldom afford. Then he set off to see Oudinot at his farm, wondering if he might be fortunate enough to catch Martine before she set off again to woo the local mayors and councillors into supporting her plan.

20

Bruno was waiting on the bench in the pleasant garden of the *maison de retraite,* a grandiose modern building that the *département* architects thought suitable as a seniors' home, texting Isabelle that Oudinot would be delighted to allow her team to use his hut for a police operation. Bruno had been evasive about the purpose when he'd gone to Oudinot's farm to seek permission. Oudinot had at once assumed that it was to investigate Sylvestre for tax evasion. When Bruno had shrugged his shoulders and refused to deny it, Oudinot had rubbed his hands gleefully together and pronounced himself eager to cooperate. He would withdraw his geese that very day and call on Sylvestre to shake hands on the deal and announce that the geese were gone as a gesture of goodwill. With any luck, Oudinot had added, he'd get Sylvestre's signature on a contract and a check before the taxman took all the money away.

"Bonjour, Bruno," said Félix, suddenly appearing, slightly out of breath after running all the way from school, and holding out his hand to be shaken. "The science teacher showed me what you'd said about me in the paper and read it out in class. And then the headmaster called in my mom to show it to her. It made her cry, and she said I had to be sure to thank you."

Of course, Bruno thought, his parents wouldn't get *Sud Ouest* at home. "It was no more than the truth, Félix. We're all proud of you. And did you hear the good news that Denise will be fine?"

"Yes, Madame Pantowsky told me she heard it on the radio."

That was the science teacher Bruno knew as Florence. "Well, what is this mysterious photo that made you write me that note?" he asked.

"I know of a photo of the same car, that's why we're here. It belongs to my grandfather, so I thought I'd take you to see him, and he'll show it to you and tell you the story about my great-uncle."

"Do you visit your grandpa often?"

"Two or three times a week. I like him. They eat early here, so he brings out a sandwich for me from the dining room when he knows I'm coming. He's over eighty, but he's in pretty good shape."

The St. Denis retirement home was close to the town cemetery, which Bruno had considered unfortunate until he'd learned that most of the inhabitants enjoyed the convenience of being able to attend funerals without having to walk too far. Some even claimed to take comfort from being able to gaze out over their eventual resting place. The home was a curious mixture, a few rows of single-story buildings that contained one-room apartments all surrounding an aggressively modern structure that contained the offices, recreation and dining rooms and wards for those too enfeebled to continue living in the single-room dwellings where they could be surrounded by their own furniture and belongings. The gardens were a pleasant mix of ornamental flower beds and small allotments, where the residents were encouraged to grow vegetables for their family or for the communal kitchen.

Félix's grandfather lived in one of the studios, as the single rooms were called. He came to the door and welcomed his visitors, kissing his grandson on both cheeks and shaking Bruno's hand. Bruno recognized him as one of the group of old cronies who sat around a table in the cheapest of the town's cafés, drinking their glasses of *petit blanc* and watching horse racing as they grumbled that St. Denis and the whole country were not what they'd been in their day.

"I didn't expect you so I didn't bring a sandwich," the old man said, then ruffled Félix's hair. "How's my little nut-brown grandson?" He glanced up at Bruno. "That's what I call him because he's the color of a walnut, best-looking man in the family. I was very proud when I saw what you said about Félix in the paper."

"I brought Bruno to look at your photo album, Grandpa," Félix said. "He's interested in the photo you have with this car." He showed him the printout of the Bugatti that Bruno had given him.

"You know that album by heart," the old man said affectionately as he moved slowly to the bedside table, sat down on the neatly made bed and gestured to the others to join him. He began leafing through to a familiar page that displayed four small, square photos in black and white, each one about twice the size of a passport photo. The images of young Resistance fighters with rifles and Sten guns and armbands that carried the letters FFI, for Forces Françaises de l'Intérieur, were instantly recognizable as dating from World War II.

He put a wavering finger on a snapshot of two men standing by a car that looked to be the very image of the Bugatti on the printout. One was wearing flying gear, the fur-lined jacket open to reveal a uniform. He was hatless, his hair smoothed back glossily. He was standing beside a young man in farming clothes whom Félix's grandfather identified as his older brother, Henri, a member of the Resistance who had been killed later in the war.

Beside this photo was another of the same young man in farming clothes carrying a Sten gun with his hand on the shoulder of a young boy who looked to be about twelve.

"That's me with Henri, the family hero," the old man said. "That was in the summer of 'forty-four, just before he went off to fight. He went from the Resistance straight into the French army and was killed that winter in the fighting around Strasbourg. I never saw him again after the photo was taken. It broke my mother's heart. She died not long after the war, and my dad followed soon after, when I was away doing military service."

He asked Félix to pass him the magnifying glass, and the boy darted across to snatch it from the windowsill beside the room's sole easy chair, clearly its usual location.

"You can see the family resemblance—me, my brother and young Félix here," the old man said, his voice quavering and his hand trembling as he held the glass over the little photo.

"What's that ruin in the background?" Bruno asked.

"Rastignac, after the Nazis burned it. It was springtime, and I remember watching it burn for days."

"The one that was supposed to have all those paintings that disappeared?" Bruno asked.

"That's it, just the other side of Thénon. They were nice people, the owners, even the English ones in the family. My dad worked for them in a way, he was a *métayer*, but every Christmas they'd have all of us *métayer* families up to the château for a party and give the children presents. Not all the landlords were like that, I can tell you."

The *métayer* system was a form of sharecropping that had been common in the region until it was finally regulated almost out of existence by President François Mitterrand's Socialist government in 1983. The tenant farmed the land, and in return the landowner took a half share of everything that was produced—crops, livestock and wine, everything except the family's chickens and their eggs. In the reforms after the war, the landlord's share was reduced to a third, but it was still widely blamed for rural poverty, and the system's existence helped explain the remarkable number of Communist Party members among the rural population.

"How near was your farm to the château?" Bruno asked.

"You can see from the photo, which was taken in our farmyard; it's about a kilometer away. The land we farmed stretched out the other way, toward Labouret, all the way down to the River Cern. We had cattle, wheat and tobacco, an apple orchard and a woods full of walnuts. We spent every winter's night around the stove, shelling them."

"Did you ever see the car that's in the photo?" Bruno asked.

"Only from a distance. The driver wanted to hide it, I don't know why. He was supposed to be a famous racing driver, but I forget the name, maybe never knew it. My brother said he'd hidden the car in one of the old tobacco-drying barns that belonged to a friend of his. The government didn't trust us to dry the tobacco ourselves because it was rationed, so a lot of the old barns were disused."

"Was this friend also a *métayer* for the château?" Bruno asked.

"No, I think the barn belonged to the family of a girl he was sweet on. They'd been at school together in La Bachellerie, where I went to school."

"Do you remember the name of the family?"

"No, but her name was Marie-France. She got married to somebody else after my brother was killed, and they moved away. One thing I do know is that they didn't just hide the car; they dismantled it. My brother said he helped take the body off and the seats out, and they put it in with some other old farm equipment, broken plows and the like. I don't know what they did with the bodywork."

"Did you come back home when your father died?"

"Yes, they gave me a week's leave from the army. I was stationed at Montauban, down near Toulouse, so it wasn't too far to come back for the funeral. It was lucky, in a way; the rest of my unit was sent off to Indochina. A lot of Henri's old Resistance pals turned up for the funeral, and one of them said he'd give me a job when I got out. I'd been a driver in the army, and that was what I did when I came out, drove a truck for the logistics firm in Le Buisson. That's why I settled here."

"You never went back to look for the barn or the car?"

The old man shook his head. "Nothing to go back for, not for me. After my dad died, I still had a year to go in the army, so the landlord found a new tenant. I hadn't really thought about that car until today." He picked up the magnifying glass to examine the photo more closely. "Fine-looking vehicle, isn't it? I bet it would go like the wind."

"What about that pilot in the photo, did you ever meet him?"

"No, but Henri told me he was English, from the RAF. Somebody in the château had connections to another Resistance group that organized escape routes across the Pyrenees into Spain. Henri said he often wondered what had happened to that fur-lined flying jacket. He'd have liked to have it for himself."

He moved the magnifying glass to a photo of half-a-dozen young men, all armed and wearing FFI armbands, standing around an old Citroën. "That's my brother and there beside him is Jean-Pierre, the one who gave me the job. He'd dead now, of course." He looked up at Bruno. "Why are you interested in all this?"

"That car, it's famous, and probably pretty valuable if anybody could find it. I know some people who are looking for it, and there may even be a murder involved. That's why I'm investigating. Is there anything else you remember about it?"

"I can't say I do." The old man put down the magnifying glass and stared at Bruno. "Murder? Who was it got killed?"

"Sorry, I'd better not say anything until we get the results from an autopsy. It's still a matter of suspicion at this stage. When the investigation is over, I'll come back and tell you all about it. Can you tell me if anyone else has asked you any questions about this car recently, or has the topic come up in any way?"

"No, the only one who's ever asked me about it is Félix, when we look through the album together. It's mainly his great-uncle Henri who interests him, but he's always liked cars. I'm only sorry the photo is so small."

"If you like, I could get it blown up for you and also the one of you and Henri," Bruno said, thinking that Philippe Delaron could easily do it; he owed Bruno several favors.

"I'd like that. Do I have to take them out?"

"I'll do it, Grandpa." Félix took the album and gently prized the two photos out of the little triangular pouches at each corner and handed them to Bruno. He carefully put them inside his notebook, shook the old man's hand and thanked him. At the door he asked if Félix was going back to school.

"In a few minutes, then I'm going to the riding school again."

"Thanks for this, Félix. Take care."

Félix didn't move but looked up shyly at Bruno. "Could you do me another favor? I'd like to give Grandpa a photo of me on a horse. Could you take one for me, please?"

"No problem, we'll do it next time I see you at the stables."

Bruno went back to his office and texted Philippe, asking him to come to Bruno's office in the *mairie*. Then he called Florence at home, knowing that she'd be there with her children during lunchtime. Rollo, the headmaster, had excused her from the usual roster of supervising the school lunches because her children were still so little.

"I'm calling to thank you for letting Félix know about the story in the paper today," he said when she answered. "I gather his mother was very touched."

"It was good of you to say what you did," she replied. "I've been worried about that boy, and at the way Tristan bullies him, but he usually makes sure to do it in ways and places so we can never catch him at it. And if we do catch him, there's not much we can do beyond telling him off, so despite what happened to poor Denise I'm glad you managed to nail him. What happens to him now?"

"It's up to the magistrate, which in this case is probably Annette, and as you know she always tries to avoid putting anyone into a detention center. It depends on whether the *procureur* decides to intervene. Given the publicity and the prospect of some political pressure, I suspect that he'll probably feel that he should. He may decide to take it out of Annette's hands and give the case to a more experienced magistrate."

Even as he spoke, Bruno realized that he hadn't followed up on this case as he should have. If he hadn't been in such a rush to get back to Martine he'd have gone to the mayor and asked his advice. The mayor would probably have called the subprefect in Sarlat, who in turn would have had a quiet word with the *procureur* about this being the kind of assault that stirred public opinion. But did Bruno think juvenile detention was really the right treatment for Tristan?

"What do you think should happen to Tristan?" Florence asked. "I know the boy deserves to get punished, and he probably needs a real shock. But I'm with Annette; I never like the idea of putting young people in prison, even a special detention center. If the girl had been blinded, I might think differently, but since they saved her eyesight . . ."

"I was so angry with him when it happened," said Bruno. "All

I could think of was making Tristan pay for it. He's been a bully for years, spoiled rotten by his parents and so cocksure that he could get away with anything. And now there's the drug charge as well. The *procureur* can't ignore that after all the fuss he's made about drugs in the past."

"You know possessing drugs triggers automatic suspension from the *collège,* so that means Tristan will not be going to the lycée as he expected."

"What sort of student is he?"

"Lazy and arrogant, doing just enough to get by, and he's intelligent enough to get away with it. He's from a good home with educated parents, books in the house, his own laptop at home. I've caught him plagiarizing his homework a couple of times, just copying stuff straight from some website or other, usually Wikipedia. And he's done the same in other classes. His parents have been warned that it could mean holding him back a year, but they said they'd hire a private tutor to make sure he caught up. They want him in a good lycée and then in a good university. Juvenile detention would probably wreck his life."

"He very nearly wrecked Denise's life and did his best to do the same to Félix, so how do we treat a nasty young thug like Tristan?"

"We get you and me and his parents together and we try to hammer out some agreed course of action," Florence said. "I don't see what else we can do. If Tristan doesn't go to prison, what's likely to happen to him?"

"Two years of community service, probably with a hefty fine that his parents can easily afford to pay. Part of the problem is with them. The husband is henpecked by Tristan's mother, who thinks her little darling is perfect. She swore out a false statement saying Tristan was with her when we know from witnesses and from his phone that he was throwing rocks at Denise at the time."

"Can't you use that to make her see some sense?"

"I don't think the *procureur* would want to charge her with perjury, not for a mother trying to protect her child. She'd get no more than a slap on the wrist."

"She doesn't know that."

"They have already hired a good lawyer for Tristan, who will probably tell the mother she's unlikely to face any trouble. But maybe you're right. Let me discuss this with Yveline. We can't let this drop here."

"I've got to get the children back to school before I start teaching again. Meanwhile I'll have a word with Rollo and see what he thinks. And thank you for calling."

"My love to your children," he said. "And I'll consult the mayor."

Bruno called Claire to ask if the mayor was free, to be told he was in a meeting. She would let him know when it ended. He used the time to call the *mairie* at La Bachellerie to ask if they had any school attendance records for the late 1930s and the 1940s. No, he was told, they would all be somewhere in the archives of the *département* in Périgueux. He looked up the number, called and asked for Madame Tronquet, the same helpful person to whom he'd spoken about Hugon's searches. Yes, she said when he was put through, they kept their school registers, organized by commune.

"Could someone look up the records of La Bachellerie for 1935 and 1938? I'm looking for any other details about a girl called Marie-France who was in the same class as a boy named Henri Boulier. It's very urgent and it's important, part of what we think is turning out to be a murder investigation. If you want to check with Commissaire Jalipeau of the Police Nationale . . ."

"No, no, it's all right, Monsieur Bruno. I was reading about you in the paper today, about that poor little girl who got hit in the eye. I'll do it myself and call you back."

Bruno began going through his e-mails, deleting or acknowledging as he went, when his mobile phone rang. It was J-J, saying that the Bordeaux lab had confirmed Fabiola's theory. Hugon had been murdered with cyanide, sprayed into his face. J-J had a meeting scheduled with Isabelle at the St. Denis gendarmerie in an hour's time to discuss the implications of the murder for Isabelle's operation. The *procureur* would send someone and could Bruno attend? He checked his watch and said yes, telling J-J that he'd already briefed Isabelle on the matter.

There came a knock on his door, and the mayor came in, sat down and said, "I presume you want to know about Tristan? I already had Simon calling me last night, asking if I could use my influence with the *procureur* to go easy on his son. As you know, that supermarket is now the biggest taxpayer in the commune."

Bruno said nothing.

"I know you're not a great fan of putting teenage kids in prison. Nor am I. But you understand the politics of this, particularly with the drugs as a second charge. Rollo tells me that Tristan had so much cannabis he suspects the boy may have been dealing it to others in the school. Have you heard anything about that?"

"No, which makes me feel guilty. I had no idea that amount of stuff was available around here, and I ought to have known, or at least kept more of an eye on the *collège*."

The mayor nodded. "Rollo also said Tristan will now be suspended, but I can't see how that will help. Is there anything we can do that would keep the boy out of jail and also get him back on track? Isn't there some early engagement system for the army?"

"There used to be," said Bruno. "That's what I did. But seventeen is the minimum age now, and the army probably wouldn't have him after this. We'll need to find him a useful and preferably tough job for the rest of the school year, then if he stays out of trouble and Rollo agrees, Tristan can retake his final year and go on to the lycée a year late."

"Any ideas? Remember, we can't give him the kind of job that some unemployed person could fill, which rules out most community service work."

"That means an internship, and it would have to be with someone he could look up to, someone to set an example."

"You mean the way you seem to have taken Félix in hand?" the mayor asked, smiling for the first time since he'd come in.

"No, I couldn't give Tristan full-time attention," Bruno said. "I'd been thinking about a farm, but it would take too long to make him useful. You're on the *conseil régional,* and we've got the state forests. Do you know any foresters who might fit the bill? Get him doing something like that, and the *procureur* might give him conditional probation."

"You mean if he doesn't shape up he goes straight to jail?"

"Exactly."

"I'll talk to the chief forester." The mayor rose.

A few minutes after he'd gone, Madame Tronquet called Bruno back and asked for his fax number. She would send him a copy of the school register. Henri Boulier had been a classmate of Marie-France Perdigat, whose address was listed as Perdigat; the coincidence of names suggested a farm that had been in the same family for generations. Bruno thanked Madame Tronquet profusely and hung up just as his fax machine began to whir. Then came a knock on the door, and Philippe Delaron arrived.

"I was doing some shopping at the supermarket when I got your text," he said. "What's up?"

Bruno gave Philippe the two photos and asked him to blow them up and give him two copies and suggested Philippe keep copies for himself, since it could well turn into a story.

"You know Gilles, the guy who used to be at *Paris Match*?"

"Yes, Fabiola's boyfriend, the lucky guy."

"He's been working on the background to this, and I'm sure he'll do the usual deal with you—he gets the story nationally, and you break it in *Sud Ouest* at the same time. One look at that photo of the car, and Gilles will know what it's all about. These were taken in wartime. The kid in the second photo is now a sweet old guy called Boulier who's in the *maison de retraite*. The guy with him holding the gun is his big brother, Henri, a Resistance fighter who was killed later in the war, and the man in uniform is a downed RAF pilot whom Henri helped to escape over the Pyrenees."

"That's a pretty nice story as it stands, but what about the car?" Philippe asked. "It's a beauty."

"Gilles can tell you all about it," Bruno said. "I'll call him now if you can start working on those blowups. I've got a meeting at the gendarmerie on a separate matter that will also be a big story, and I'll make sure you get it first."

He called Gilles to brief him and told him to expect a visit from Philippe with photographic evidence that the Bugatti had been in the region at the time of its disappearance. He briefly related what Boulier had said and added that the car had been dismantled and hidden in a barn somewhere on a farm called Perdigat, near La Bachellerie.

"Jesus," said Gilles. "This is starting to get real. As soon as Philippe gets here, we can go over to La Bachellerie and take a look."

"That's exactly what I hoped you'd say," said Bruno. "If you're still at the house at about four, I may see you. I want to pick up Hector for an early ride."

He ended the call, put on his kepi, checked his appearance in the mirror and strolled down the rue de Paris toward the gendarmerie, thinking it was convenient to have a couple of inquisitive and friendly journalists around. They could save him a great deal of legwork.

21

As he passed the office of Brosseil, the *notaire,* the door opened and Oudinot emerged looking extremely pleased with himself.

"Ah, Bruno," Oudinot greeted him. "The deed is done, the land is sold, and the feud is settled. Sylvestre has signed the contract pledging the sale and paid a fat deposit to ensure that the deal goes through as quickly as possible. You must come to dinner at the farm so I can thank you for all your help, and I still want you to meet my daughter, Martine, properly, over dinner."

"Congratulations," Bruno said, startled, but thinking quickly. "You know, I met your daughter when she came to the *mairie* to explain her proposals for the electric-car rally. She's a charming woman and obviously very good at business; you must be very proud of her."

"Very much so, I just wish her business let us see a little more of her or at least to get started on making me a grandpa. Then again, my wife tells me she suspects there may some new romantic interest in Martine's life."

Trying to forestall his blushes, Bruno glanced at the door of the notary's office behind Oudinot, which remained closed.

"Wasn't Sylvestre in there with you to sign the deal?"

"Yes, of course, but he's staying. Apparently he has some other property deal he's arranging, so he stayed behind to discuss it with Brosseil. I have to get back to the farm. So you'll come to dinner and get to know Martine a little less formally. Shall we say Sunday evening at seven?"

"I'll be delighted to come, and I'll look forward to it, but now you must excuse me; I have to get to a meeting at the gendarmerie."

"Of course, but I'm so pleased it all worked out with Sylvestre. I really made him pay through the nose for the land." Oudinot looked around with a conspiratorial air and whispered, "When should I expect those colleagues of yours to come about Sylvestre's taxes?"

"As soon as they get here, I'll let you know, and not a word to a soul. I know I can count on you, Fernand."

"Indeed you can. Au revoir, Bruno."

Oudinot headed to his car, parked immediately behind a Range Rover that Bruno recognized as Sylvestre's. With a glance at the still-closed door of the *notaire,* Bruno walked on, wondering if the sale to Sylvestre would still go through if he were arrested before the final contract was signed. If not, he'd forfeit his deposit, so Oudinot would at least have that. As he trotted up the gendarmerie steps, noting J-J's official car parked down the street with Annette's blue Peugeot behind it, Bruno wondered what other deal Sylvestre might be negotiating.

The meeting was being held in Isabelle's temporary office. J-J was in the visitor's chair, beaming paternally at Isabelle, who rose with a smile to let Bruno kiss her cheeks. Balzac jumped out from beneath her desk to greet his master.

"Thank you for letting me have some time with him," she said, bending to stroke the dog. "Maybe you could bring him again tomorrow? I'd like to keep him with me, but I don't think my hotel would welcome his staying in my room tonight."

"Of course," said Bruno, picking up Balzac's leash from her desk. "I'll buy you croissants again at Fauquet's if you like. I'll be there at eight tomorrow morning."

"If you two dog lovers have finished, our real business is all settled," said J-J. "Isabelle and I have agreed that you and I can continue our investigation into Hugon's murder as far as we can without alerting the two suspects, but once Isabelle's operation is complete, we can move in."

"If Isabelle succeeds in turning Sylvestre into an informant, her operation could last for some time," Bruno said, his tone deliberately neutral. J-J looked surprised, and Isabelle gave Bruno a sour look. "Or didn't she explain that?"

"She didn't have to," said J-J. "Prunier got a call from the minister's office saying that this Eurojust operation was to be given my complete cooperation and top priority." Prunier was J-J's boss, the police commissioner for the *département*.

"I understand," said Bruno. "You'd better make sure nobody from the Bordeaux lab says anything about the autopsy. Murder by cyanide spray is unusual enough for people to start talking. If Sylvestre hears about that, he's smart enough to deduce that the game is up."

"I'll make sure nobody talks," J-J said. "I have to go to Bordeaux anyway. One of the two targets is there today, the Indian fellow, and I have a meeting with the Bordeaux detectives who have been handling the surveillance there."

"I'm told you have another meeting in the post commandant's office over the case with the little girl who was almost blinded," Isabelle interrupted, looking at Bruno. "That young magistrate from Sarlat is going to be there, so you mustn't let us keep you. And don't forget those data cards you promised me."

"Just one thing," Bruno said. "If your surveillance picks up anything about a property deal that Sylvestre is arranging, not the one with Oudinot himself, I'd be grateful to know what it might be."

"So long as it doesn't compromise my operation, of course," she said and fell silent, pointedly waiting for him to leave.

In Yveline's office next door, the mood was grim, and even from the corridor he'd heard their raised voices. Yveline sat stony faced, and Annette's cheeks were flushed and she looked flustered. As if grateful for the distraction, Annette looked at her watch when Bruno entered. He apologized to them both for being late, explaining he'd been called in to see J-J about another matter.

"I was expecting him to be at this meeting as well," Annette said. "The *procureur* said to be sure to get his views on the cannabis aspect of this case."

"I'm sure he'll be here as soon as he can," said Bruno. "Are you both agreed on how to proceed against Tristan?"

"No," said Yveline firmly while at the same moment Annette was saying, "Not exactly."

"The young man has been told he'll be charged with aggravated bodily harm and possession of cannabis in quantities suggesting he's a dealer. It's open and shut," said Yveline. "Annette is trying to get me to recommend a noncustodial sentence, and I won't. Tristan needs locking up. If he just had a couple of joints, maybe, but he had half a kilo, and I don't want that being peddled around to the kids in this town."

"You know as well as I do that juvenile detention centers are like a high school for criminals," said Annette. "They're understaffed, underfunded and probably do more harm than good. This is an intelligent youngster from a stable and comfortable home who made a bad mistake, two bad mistakes. But there's a chance we can set him right. If he goes inside, we're likely to have a very smart criminal on our hands when he gets out."

"I don't think a stable and comfortable home entitles him to escape the penalties the law requires. It doesn't seem to have done him much good so far," Yveline replied.

The two women, usually good friends, glared at each other, and then they both looked at Bruno, each of them obviously expecting him to agree with her. He could lose two friends here if he couldn't find a way to move them beyond their immediate argument.

"I don't know what to say," Bruno began. "I think you're both right. Tristan is a nasty piece of work who deserves to be punished. At the same time, if he goes into a detention center he's probably going to come out as even more of a menace than when he went in; we all know that."

He paused. "As I understand it, we're not taking a decision here. We're simply expected to come up with a recommendation for the *procureur* and, if we can't agree, we send him separate recommendations, and he makes the choice."

Yveline nodded agreement, and Annette said, "He specifically asked us to come up with an agreed recommendation."

"Well, it looks like he's not going to get one from you two, but he will be getting one from the mayor, and since the mayor has been a senator and sits on the *conseil régional,* I think he'd take that one very seriously."

"Where does the mayor come into this?" Yveline asked, suspiciously.

"Tristan is one of his constituents, and Tristan's father is the very competent manager of the supermarket, which is the biggest employer and leading taxpayer in St. Denis." Bruno opened his arms and gave an exaggerated shrug, as if to say matters were now out of his hands.

"You can't have one law for the rich and another for the poor," Annette began, and this time she looked in appeal to Yveline, who was nodding vigorously.

"That's shameful," Yveline said.

Ah, thought Bruno, it worked. They're agreeing with each other.

"Shameful, probably, but it's the reality, it's politics," he said. "The mayor is planning to find Tristan some tightly supervised physical labor in the woods with the forestry department. But what if we three agree to insist on putting some real teeth into that? Tristan is prosecuted and found guilty, sentenced to two or three years, but then the sentence is suspended on the strict condition that the court get a satisfactory weekly report from the forester. One false move, one day playing truant, and he goes straight to jail."

Yveline and Annette exchanged glances. Yveline shrugged. Annette said, "If that's the best you think we can do . . ."

"I think it's important that we come up with a joint recommendation," he said. "Let me draft something and then leave you two to tidy it up and put it into the right terminology." Bruno, disguising his relief, took a notepad from Yveline's desk and began to write.

Ten minutes later, escorting Annette to her car, he asked, "How's George Young? Still looking for that famous Bugatti?"

"Don't talk to me about that damn Bugatti. I get enough of that from George. I don't think he's making much progress, and it's getting him down," she said in a tone that suggested she no longer felt swept off her feet.

"I went to a lot of trouble to get him something I thought was bound to cheer him up," she went on, sounding aggrieved. "I planned it as a kind of consolation present, and he barely even thanked me before setting off again on this wild-goose chase of his."

"It sounds like he's a bit obsessed by it," said Bruno sympathetically, thinking that Annette would naturally prefer Young to devote all his attentions to her. "But I think he has been interested for a long time, through the family connection he has with the English racing driver."

"I suppose so. I just wish he'd talk about something else once in a while." They reached her car, and she stopped, looking appealingly at him. "Am I being unreasonable?"

"No, not at all," he said, an image of Martine unbuttoning his shirt the previous evening suddenly entering his mind and making him think it was sad that Young was wasting that unique and precious time that a kindly Providence reserved for new lovers. "But I suppose you could say that in a way it's flattering that he wants to share with you something that's so important to him."

"It's not just the car, it's also this rivalry he has about the Bugatti with Sylvestre. It gets on my nerves, and I went to such a lot of trouble to get him that damn radiator."

"Radiator?" he asked.

"A real Bugatti radiator, they're very distinctive with a kind of horseshoe shape. You remember Marcel, whose car we drove in the rally? He has one on the wall of his garage, along with ones from a Rolls-Royce and I don't know the names of the other cars. But this one had BUGATTI written on it, and I wheedled and fluttered my eyelashes, and finally Marcel let me buy it from him."

"Young must have been delighted."

"He was, for about thirty seconds, then he asked where I'd found it, and when I told him he said he had to run."

"And that surprised you? You hand him a piece of solid evidence that a Bugatti has been right here in the Périgord, and you don't expect him to go hunting to see which car it might have come from?"

She looked down at her feet, a little abashed. "I suppose so. But he didn't have to rush off right away, did he?"

"No, of course not. And I suppose you never have to rush

away in the mornings to be on time for work? Perhaps he sees this as his work. By the way, did Marcel say where he got the radiator?"

"Years and years ago, he said, when he first opened the garage. He found it in some local junk shop in Sarlat that closed down years ago."

"So as soon as Young realizes the trail has gone cold, he'll come back to you," said Bruno. "And you are young and lovely and alive and loving, all the things that a Bugatti radiator is not. I suspect he's the kind of man to appreciate that. So cheer up, Annette."

"Thanks, Bruno." She rose on tiptoe to her full height and kissed him on the cheek before getting into her car and giving him a smile and a wave as she drove away.

With Balzac at his heels, Bruno walked back to pick up his van, noting that Sylvestre's Range Rover was still parked outside the *notaire's* office. And Freddy was in Bordeaux. That meant the coast was clear. He could pick up the data cards from his cameras, put in new ones and change the batteries before taking Hector out. He headed out to the *chartreuse.*

Half an hour later, leaning forward in the saddle as Hector plodded up the slope, Bruno was wondering how difficult it would be to track down all the closed junk shops in Sarlat. He'd have to find out when Marcel had first launched his garage and restrict the search to those that had been open at the time. It would mean looking through old business directories and then trying to track down members of the family who had owned the shop and see if anybody remembered where the Bugatti radiator had come from. The prospect dismayed him, until he remembered that he could ask Gilles to do it. And then he thought, as he topped the rise onto the ridge that looked down on St. Denis, he had the evening with Martine to look forward to. He looked back to see that Balzac was still following along behind, running as fast as his short legs would allow. Bruno leaned forward and loosened the reins to let Hector know it was time to run.

For a time, at least, the ride drove all the other thoughts and concerns from his head. There was nothing but this moment, this speed, this wind in his face and this powerful, galloping creature that seemed almost to be a part of him. More than that, on horseback he felt himself to be much more a part of the physical world around him even as its trees flashed by sensed rather than seen.

As he slowed at the end of the ridge, the thought stayed with him. This sense that he felt of being connected to nature was at its most immediate and dramatic when he was riding, but it was also something he felt with his dog and even with his geese and chickens. Humans were meant to live with animals, he concluded, to know that humankind was not alone on this planet but shared it with other species in a state of mutual interdependence. People who lived in cities might know that intellectually, but could they ever truly feel it in the way he did in the woods with his horse and his dog? He turned in the saddle to watch Balzac catch up, and then unbidden Hector set off at a walk down the familiar bridle path that led to the ridge for the long canter back to the stables.

As Bruno finished rubbing down his horse, Gilles drove into the courtyard in Fabiola's old car, the Twingo that he'd started to use now that she had her new electric vehicle. They shook hands, and Gilles said, "The Perdigat farm is now a housing estate, a filling station and a couple of warehouses for supermarkets. It's right by the extension to the new autoroute. There's no trace of any old barns, and the farm and its contents were auctioned off fifty years ago. The next step is to check the old newspapers and try to find an announcement of the sale, which will give us the name of the auctioneers, and we can see if they have kept any records."

"There might be a shortcut," said Bruno, and pulled out his phone to call his counterpart, the municipal policeman of Terrasson, the nearest town to La Bachellerie. Grégoire was a pillar of the *département*'s tennis federation, and Bruno had met him often; his father had been the St. Denis policeman before him. They exchanged greetings, and Bruno explained he was trying to find out which company had auctioned the farm of Perdigat.

"Probably the Melvilles from Périgueux, they've always done most of the auctions around here," Grégoire replied. "But I'll ask my father, he might even remember it. The farm's partly built over now, of course. I'll call you back."

Gilles grinned. "You and your local knowledge, Bruno. I should have thought of that."

"I didn't know Grégoire's father was still alive, or I'd have gone straight to him," Bruno said, thinking that Grégoire was nearing sixty, close to retirement, so his father would be close to ninety. He'd certainly have been around at the time of the auction. He might even have known Félix's grandfather. If so, perhaps he could find a way of bringing the two men together.

"I have to go, Gilles, but there could be another clue," he said, and recounted how Annette had found the radiator at Marcel's garage and given it to Young.

"I'm disappointed that Young didn't tell me that himself," said Gilles. "We're supposed to be cooperating."

"Maybe he feels he's getting close to the car and the money it could bring him."

"We went through all that, remember? I'd better give him a call, and I'll count on you to call me back when you hear from Grégoire. Do you mind if I follow up with Marcel? His place is the big Citroën dealership, is that right?"

Bruno stopped at the gendarmerie to give Isabelle the data

cards from his cameras and got home not long after five. He fed his geese and chickens, got the fire going in the wood-burning stove and set the table for two. He was about to climb into the shower when Grégoire called him back to say his father remembered the sale. The auctioneer had indeed been Melville. The farm had been broken up into lots, and all the old farm equipment, mostly out of date, had been bought by a scrap-metal merchant and junk dealer in Sarlat named Bérégevoy.

"I don't think they're still in business, Bruno," Grégoire added.

"Thanks anyway," Bruno said. "You might also ask your dad if he remembers people called Boulier; they were *métayers* at Rastignac. One of them is in our *maison de retraite,* and he told me that he remembers seeing the château of Rastignac burning during the war. Your dad will certainly remember that. He's about your dad's age so they were probably at school together. He had a big brother, Henri, a Resistance fighter who died in the war. If your dad remembers the family, it might be nice to bring the two of them together to reminisce about old times."

"Good idea," said Grégoire. "I'll ask him. My father's always been interested in what happened at Rastignac, spent years talking to everyone in the area to try to establish whether the paintings had been stolen or burned in the fire. I'm sure he'd love to get together with someone who could talk about it with him. Old folks like to reminisce about their young days. Maybe one day someone will do the same for the two of us. Keep well, Bruno."

Bruno called Gilles to tell him about the Bérégevoy scrap-metal merchants and to commiserate. If the old tobacco barn at Perdigat had indeed been the last resting place of the chassis and engine of the legendary Bugatti, it had probably long since been melted down for scrap.

"It's not bad news as far as I'm concerned," Gilles replied. "Quite the opposite—it makes a good, haunting ending to my story. The most valuable car in the world, melted down and recycled, and some of its molecules are probably now speeding around in some of the family cars in France."

Bruno put his phone down and climbed into the shower that he'd built and tiled himself, thinking that someday he might invest in one of those grand multijet showers his friend Horst had installed. He shampooed his hair and was soaping himself down when he was suddenly aware of a shadow against the frosted glass of the sliding door. Then he heard a tap on the door and a woman's voice said, "Bruno?"

Was that Martine, arriving early, or was it another voice? With the shower running, he couldn't tell. Heaven forbid it was Isabelle making an unexpected visit. He slid open the door a crack and with relief saw it was Martine, smiling cheekily at him and swiftly unbuttoning her blouse to reveal a black bra. She began unzipping her jeans.

"I just showered at home before I came," she said. "But I think I'm in the mood for another." She reached behind her back to undo her bra. "I've brought the food, but I'm not hungry yet—at least, not for the food."

She climbed in to join him in the running water and put her arms around his neck. "You're already soapy," she said. "Why don't you soap me?"

22

For Bruno, it began as just another Saturday morning, rendered more piquant by the expectation of breakfast with Isabelle. This was the second, smaller market day of the week, and a few minutes before eight most of the stalls were already erected, and the early customers were moving purposefully from one to the next. Bruno had noticed that most of them shopped in the order in which they ate: first the olives stall and the organic bread, then the fish or the duck, then the fruit and vegetables and finally Stéphane's cheeses. Even those he knew to be apartment dwellers paused at the flower stall, the last one before the bridge, picking up seedlings of herbs for their balconies and window boxes. Bruno moved through the stalls, shaking hands and kissing cheeks, tasting a ripe fig and then a fat black olive.

"Not hot yet, come back later," Madame Vinh called to him from the glass-fronted stand where she kept the samosas and the *lumpia,* the prawn curries and *rendang* beef, for all of which the people of St. Denis had developed a taste. Takeout containers were stacked beside the vast cauldron of pho soup heating on the portable gas stove. It would be empty by noon. In the decade that Bruno had been the town policeman, the usual radishes and cucumbers had been joined by mangoes and papayas, heirloom tomatoes and pomelos. Sausage rolls and Cornish pasties now stood beside the quiche Lorraine. But the cheese and the charcuterie stalls were still the most thronged. The people of St. Denis were prepared to experiment and the stallholders were ready to adapt, but all of them always returned faithfully to the foie gras and smoked duck sausage, to the Brie de Meaux and Vacherin Mont d'Or, emblems of a nation that still liked to define itself by the way it ate.

Fauquet's café was crowded and the windows steamed up, people standing three deep at the bar and all the tables filled. This was no place for his dog. He tied Balzac's leash to a railing and then moved through the crowd, shaking hands until he caught Fauquet's eye and asked for coffee and croissants on the terrace. The café did not usually put the chairs and tables out into the open air until later, but Fauquet nodded and Bruno leaned across the counter to pick up a dishrag and the key that hung by the cash desk. He went outside to open the padlock to a discreet door into the storage area, pulled out two chairs and a small table. He put them at the far corner of the terrace, by the stone balustrade that overlooked the river, where he and Isabelle would be out of earshot of any other arrivals. He wiped the furniture clean with the rag, collected Balzac and took his seat. Once Isabelle arrived, the coffee and croissants had been served, and other regulars had liberated another half-dozen tables and lifted their faces to enjoy the gentle early morning sun.

"In Paris the cafés are installing heaters on the terraces," she said as he rose to greet her.

"It being Paris, they will probably be denouncing the perils of global warming while they cluster beneath the artificial warmth," he said and pointed up to the clear blue sky. "Here in the Périgord, we prefer solar power."

"My team has finally arrived and been issued its warrants

from the prefect, so at last we can get started," she said, sitting down to pet Balzac and tell him what a fine dog he was and how much she'd missed him.

"I hope you had a more interesting evening than I did," she said, looking up at Bruno. "I was staring at those images from your data cards until my brain flagged. It was always the same two Range Rovers coming and going, and so the high point was when a new vehicle turned up, until I realized it was you. The postman didn't even get out of his car, just pushed the supermarket flyers and catalogs into the box. And there was one courier delivery."

"Any result from the Bordeaux surveillance?"

"He had lunch with a junior professor of sociology whom we're now checking out, French but a Muslim convert and wearing her head scarf as if it were a veil. The guy from Toulouse whom he met at the station in Agen was interesting, a trade union rep at Airbus, already on the brigadier's watch list. They went to a kebab house to eat."

"These legalistic delays must be very frustrating for you," he said.

"They are, but that's the price Europe pays for human rights," she said wryly. "And since we French invented them, we've only got ourselves to blame. But the surveillance is only part of the operation. Mostly it's about tracking bank accounts and money trails, which is why we need the Americans, and that's going well."

"How much money are they moving through the vintage-car system?" he asked.

"They're being discreet, mostly cars in the very low six-figure range, nothing above two hundred thousand. But we think they're doing three or four at every auction, so the total is already close to five million."

"Do you know where the money is going?"

She shrugged. "Some of it, not all by any means. But we're building the map of local paymasters, giving the brigadier and his counterparts in other countries the names of people to watch. It's slow, but as the brigadier says, this is going to be a very long war."

"Do you want me to take your surveillance guys up to meet the farmer whose hut they'll be using?"

"That's the plan. We meet at the gendarmerie at eight-thirty and you can take them. The sooner they get started the better. Do you need me to come along and show our Eurojust credentials?"

"No, the farmer thinks it's a tax investigation. Eurojust will simply confuse him. His feud with Sylvestre is nominally over—they signed a deal for Oudinot to sell the land. But he still enjoys the thought of Sylvestre in tax trouble."

They made their way to Isabelle's temporary office in the gendarmerie just as two men in hunters' garb came into the building wearing rucksacks.

"Bruno, this is the team, Hanno and Friedrich. They've just been taking a preliminary look at the target building. And, guys, this is an old friend of mine, *chef de police* Bruno Courrèges, who runs this town. If you're very good and very lucky, you might get him to cook for you some evening."

"Are you the one who warned us about the geese?" Hanno asked, in serviceable French with a heavy Dutch accent. "Christ, I've never heard anything like it."

"There seemed to be two tribes of them, white geese and gray ones," said Friedrich, who was German. "They didn't seem to mix much. Is there any difference?"

"A lot," said Bruno, smiling as he explained. "The white ones get roasted to eat in wintertime, usually at Christmas, and the gray ones have the best livers, so we use them for foie gras."

"In Germany we eat them on the eve of St. Martin's Day, November eleventh," said Friedrich.

"Any excuse will do," Bruno replied, grinning. "How do you stuff them?"

"Pork sausage and apples."

"Guys," Isabelle chided, "if we can get back to business. Did you see a small hut near the target house? Bruno thinks he can get you installed there and the geese removed. Would that help?"

"Perfect, we should be able to get full audio there," said Hanno. "And we may be able to get into his computer."

"How would you do that?" Bruno asked.

"A pinhole camera to get the keystrokes for his password."

Isabelle rapped the table. "Okay, let's get started."

Well before nine, Bruno and the two technicians arrived at Oudinot's farm and declined the offer of coffee, only to learn that they had missed Martine. She had a few minutes earlier walked across to the *chartreuse* to thank Sylvestre for agreeing to the deal that would end the feud.

"Good," said Bruno. "That will provide a distraction while these men install their equipment in your hut."

Hanno and Friedrich, their surveillance gear in their rucksacks, followed in Bruno's footsteps as he crept carefully through the woodland and the undergrowth toward the hut. The area was littered with geese droppings, and the ammoniac stench inside the hut was daunting, even with the door open. The two technicians wrinkled their noses and glared their dismay at Bruno. He left them to it, heading back to Oudinot's farm where his van waited, when the phone at his waist began to vibrate. He pulled it out to look at the screen and smiled when he saw Martine was calling.

"Bonjour, *ma belle*," he said. "I'm missing you already."

"Bruno, stop. This is serious. It's Sylvestre. He's dead. I

couldn't find him anywhere although all the doors were open, and then I looked in the pool. He was facedown."

"*Merde.*" He gasped. "I'll be right there. Don't touch anything."

"I already pulled him out and tried to revive him."

"That's fine. I'm at your dad's place and I'm on the way."

He turned and crashed through the woods, skirting Oudinot's fence, and along the road to turn up the dirt path as he had on his first visit. Martine, her clothes drenched, was on her knees by the pool. The sliding glass arches that covered the pool had been partially opened. As he approached, Bruno saw a male body stretched out beside Martine. Nude except for bathing shorts, its eyes were open and glassy. He could detect no sign of injury. Draped on the rim of the pool lay a dark-colored, sodden bathrobe.

Bruno knelt down and put the back of his fingers on Sylvestre's neck. He was cold and had no pulse. The body was white except for the chest, which seemed bruised and red.

"You tried pumping his chest?" he asked.

"I came looking for him, found him in the pool, climbed in to haul him out and began pumping him. I was hopeful at first because a lot of water gushed from his mouth and nose, but that was all. Then I called you and started again."

"He's dead, sure enough." He helped her to her feet and hugged her. "It must have been a shock to find him this way. I'm sorry you had to see it."

"I'm fine, just sorry I came too late to be of any use. He must have drowned. Maybe he was drunk."

"Was the bathrobe there when you arrived?"

"No, he was wearing it or, rather, half wearing it, on one arm and shoulder. It came off when I was trying to get him out of the pool."

"You did well to get him out."

Bruno looked around. On the table were two tall glass vases, each with a burned-out candle inside. Beside them was a book, an ashtray, cigarettes and a lighter, two empty brandy glasses and an empty bottle of Drambuie, a Scottish liqueur that Bruno had drunk after one of Pamela's dinners. He rose to look more closely. A bath towel was draped over one of the chairs. At each end of the table was what looked like a metallic umbrella, an outdoor heater with a gas bottle in its base, designed for the heat to come out at the top and be reflected back down by the metal parasol. Each of the heaters was switched to ON. He slipped on some evidence gloves and rocked the gas cylinders. Each one was empty as if it had burned all night until the gas ran out.

The book was square, glossy and in English, with the photograph of a silver-blue Type 57 Atlantic on the cover, the one that he recalled was now in a California museum. The title was *Bugatti Yesterday and Today.* Beside the cigarettes on the table was a small leather pouch of the kind used for pipe tobacco. Bruno opened it and smelled marijuana. There were several stubbed-out joints in the ashtray alongside the cigarette butts. He put the ashtray, the glasses and bottle, the lighter and cigarette pack into separate evidence bags and called Fabiola to ask her to come up to certify a death. Then he called Isabelle.

"Bad news," he said. "One of your targets, Sylvestre, is dead."

"Putain," she said. "What happened?"

"He drowned in his pool sometime in the night. There are no visible injuries and nothing immediately suspicious. It looks like he was drunk and stoned."

"Maybe it was meant to look that way," she said. "Was it you who found him?"

"No, he was found by a neighbor, his cousin, less than half an hour ago. She got him out of the pool and tried to resuscitate him but no luck. Then she called me, and I got here maybe five minutes ago, no more."

"Is Freddy there?" she asked immediately.

"No immediate sign of him, but I'm about to take a good look around. Shall I bring Hanno and Friedrich here?"

"No, I'll do that when I arrive. I'll leave now."

"I already called a doctor."

"Merde," she said. "I wish you hadn't done that yet."

"No choice," he replied. "It's the law."

"See if you can find his phone or laptop anywhere and secure it, that's the priority now. And if you do find Freddy, hold him."

"What about J-J? Should I call him?"

"Not until I get there and see for myself. I'll probably want a full autopsy and forensic check. I'll ask the gendarmes here to send a team up to secure the grounds."

She sounded as if she were about to hang up, and he said quickly, "Don't forget your own laptop—the data cards, remember."

"Of course, thanks for reminding me," she said. "I remember that one of them covered part of the pool area, so it's a pity they're not infrared." She hung up.

"Sorry," he said to Martine. "Police commissioner."

She looked at him skeptically. "And who are Hanno and Friedrich?"

"Did your dad tell you about the surveillance operation?" She nodded. "They're the ones in the hut, installing the surveillance gear, which now won't be needed. Did you look in the lodge by the gate?"

"Yes, the door is open there, too."

"Do you mind staying here while I look around?"

"I'd rather come with you, and I need to get out of these wet clothes. Sylvestre isn't going anywhere."

"Call your mother and ask her to bring you a towel and some

fresh clothes. You can tell her what happened but that she is not to tell anyone else, okay? I'm sorry about this, but there's a lot more involved than I'm able to say."

"All this for a tax inspection?" she said, raising a cynical eyebrow. "I find that hard to believe."

Bruno shrugged. "When I can, I'll tell you the whole story, but it's likely that I don't know all of it."

"That was a woman's voice on the phone," she said. "All the police commissioners around here are men. I know that because I went to see them to talk about the plans for the rally."

"You're right. But she is a police commissioner, a Frenchwoman who used to work for the Police Nationale in Périgueux, but right now she's attached to Eurojust, and the surveillance is her operation. Now, excuse me, but I need to look around."

Martine looked at him, exasperated, then picked up her phone and began dialing. Bruno smiled apologetically and turned to head for the lodge where he had found Freddy on his last visit. Then he remembered something. He called the gendarmerie in St. Denis, and Sergeant Jules answered.

"Something very urgent, Jules," he said. "You know the big truck park in Le Buisson? I need you or someone to go there right away and secure the big van belonging to the guy from Alsace who had that old car at the parade. His name is Sylvestre Wémy, and there should be two cars inside, the one he showed off and a new electric car. Don't let anybody touch it until I get there or some of J-J's forensics people arrive."

"There's only me and Yveline here," Jules replied. "Just as Isabelle ran out the door she asked for the others to head up to Sylvestre's place to meet her there and be prepared to stay guarding it all day, but she didn't say why."

"You can tell Yveline that we found Sylvestre dead, drowned, and that Indian guy who was with him has disappeared. But I really need that truck of theirs to be secured if you have to do it yourself."

At the lodge where Freddy had stayed, the door was open, leading into a sparsely furnished sitting room with an armchair, a TV set and a rowing machine. He called out but heard no reply. Car magazines were scattered around the floor, and a driver's helmet was perched on top of the TV. The kitchen contained a machine to make espresso that looked complicated and expensive. The fridge contained bottles of mineral water, milk, apple juice and some yogurts. In the freezer compartment were ice cubes and two frozen pizzas. Upstairs were two bedrooms and a bathroom, soap and toothpaste on the sink, a towel that was still wet on the floor by the shower. Freddy had not been gone long. One bedroom was empty; the other contained an unmade bed, more car magazines and a handsome antique armoire that was empty. An adapter was still in the plug in the wall beside the bed, but whatever it recharged was gone.

Sylvestre's house was also deserted, but the bed in the main bedroom was made, the wardrobe was full of clothes, and the bathroom contained the usual range of toiletries. On top of the bed was a shirt, a sweater and trousers and on the floor beside it a pair of underpants, socks and shoes, as if he'd undressed in a hurry, perhaps before getting his bathrobe and going out to the pool. Bruno saw a wire snaking from an electric plug in the wall and disappearing beneath the underpants. He pushed the pants aside with his foot to reveal the charger for an iPhone, but the phone had gone. He put an evidence bag on top of it.

The bedside table was piled with books. The top one was titled *Bugatti 57: The Last French Bugatti.* It seemed to have more photos than text. Beneath it was a paperback that looked like a novel or a history book in English, *The Grand Prix Saboteurs* by Joe Saward. On the cover was a photo of a Bugatti like the one Sylvestre had brought to the vintage-car parade, with a swastika atop it. The long subtitle heralded the unknown story of the Grand Prix drivers who became wartime intelligence agents. At the bottom of the pile was a hardback, also in English, *A Different Danger: Three Champions at War* by Richard Armstrong.

Down in the kitchen everything was as he'd remembered it, except that the laptop was gone, and there was a single glass and an empty bottle of Chablis on the counter. He looked in the other rooms but failed to see the laptop anywhere. In the sitting room with its armchairs of leather and chrome was a large bookcase, almost filled with books on cars and issues of classic-car magazines, auction catalogs and invitations to more Concours d'Élégance. Bruno marveled at the scale of the subculture all this represented. Between the armchairs was a glass-and-chrome coffee table with several magazines on top, all of them from the Club Bugatti of France. The one on top was dated November 1996, and a bookmark had been inserted into its pages.

Bruno looked inside and skimmed an article by a woman named Stella Tayssedre, who had been Ettore Bugatti's secretary in Paris and a member of Benoist and Grover-Williams's Resistance network. She had been arrested by the Gestapo the same day as Benoist, along with her husband, and had been five months pregnant at the time. She was taken to the railway station at Compiègne along with Benoist and the others to board what she called "the train of death" to Germany. At the station, someone from the International Red Cross noticed her pregnancy and took her off the train. The Swedish consul subsequently managed to get her released, but her husband never returned.

Bruno closed the magazine, shaking his head at the thought of those grim times, but struck also by the breadth and depth of Sylvestre's research. Annette might have been irritated by her

English boyfriend's fixation on the lost Bugatti, but Sylvestre seemed just as obsessed.

The other two houses, one in each of the wings around the courtyard, were locked and the shutters closed. He walked back to the pool, where Martine and her mother, Odette, were standing by Sylvestre's body, Martine in dry clothes, jeans and a cotton sweater.

"Such a young man, it's so sad," said Odette. "What a terrible accident and such a shame that Martine had to be the one who found him."

He heard the sound of a car being driven fast, too fast for the road, and it went rushing past the entrance. It braked hard, reversed and then Isabelle climbed out, walking across and leaving the car door open and the engine running.

"Bonjour, mesdames," she said briskly. "I understand you live next door. You may return home. Thank you for your help, and we'll contact you as soon as we're done here. Just one question: did either of you see or hear anything in the course of last night?"

Martine and her mother shook their heads and left for Odette's car, parked in the driveway. Isabelle had to move her own car to let them out. When she got back, Bruno said, "Sylvestre's phone and laptop are both gone."

"What about cars?" she asked.

"That's Sylvestre's rented Range Rover in the courtyard. The one Freddy was using isn't here."

"Right." She pulled out her phone, dialed, introduced herself and said she wanted an emergency watch-and-detain order to go out to all airports, airlines and traffic police. She gave Freddy's name, two aliases that were new to Bruno and the license-plate number of his Range Rover.

"That was the brigadier," she said. "Now I have to try to get

Europol to move as fast." She dialed again and then said to him as she waited, "Could you bring Hanno and Friedrich here, please?" Then she turned back to her phone.

Bruno headed for the rear of the *chartreuse,* called out to identify himself, and Hanno poked his head around the door.

"Operation's over," Bruno said. "The target's dead, and Isabelle is here and sent me to get you."

"You're kidding," said Hanno, rolling his eyes. "At least we'll be out of this smell of duck shit."

"They're geese," said Bruno, and the two men started to repack their gear. Bruno pushed down the fence to let the two men come across and told them to follow him when they were ready and join him and Isabelle at the pool.

By the time Bruno got there, Fabiola had already arrived and was examining the body. Isabelle was still on her phone.

"Scratches on the back of his shoulders and some of his hair is pulled out at the back," said Fabiola.

"Could that have happened when Martine got him out of the pool?" he asked. "He's a lot heavier than her so she would have had a hard time."

"I doubt it, looks more like a struggle to me, as though somebody might have been holding his head underwater," she said. "We'll need to examine his fingernails, see if he scratched anybody. Could you bag his hands? And I'll want to know how much of that alcohol he had."

"That might not be all he had. There's an empty bottle of wine in the kitchen as well as that empty bottle of Drambuie out here. It's inside one of those evidence bags," said Bruno. "And he'd been smoking joints."

"Drunk and stoned, it wouldn't have been difficult to drown him." Fabiola turned to look at the surface of the pool. "Is that a bit of hair floating there?"

"There was a second glass with the Drambuie bottle. He may not have been drinking alone."

Isabelle joined them. "Are you saying it looks like murder by drowning?"

"I'm saying it could be, maybe even probably. There are signs of some kind of struggle. But if he was extremely drunk, he might have passed out in the pool and drowned that way."

"We're going to need J-J and the forensics team," Bruno said to Isabelle. "By the way, Sylvestre has a big van in a truck park near here, containing a vintage car and a fancy electric one. It looks like a traveling workshop inside. I've asked Sergeant Jules to secure it."

Isabelle nodded, dully. "Check on that, if you would. And see if there are any keys around here that might open it." She looked across at him, shaking her head. "If it hadn't been for those delays in getting the warrants—ah, there's no point crying over spilled milk. I'll call J-J now."

"I trust this means that J-J can now make public the murder inquiry into Monsieur Hugon," Bruno said.

"I suppose so," said Isabelle, as though it didn't much matter to her.

"In that case, do you mind if I look around for anything that might establish a link that could connect Hugon with Sylvestre and Freddy, perhaps papers or letters?" He wondered if he should tell her to pull herself together and act like the efficient, purposeful Isabelle he knew.

"Be my guest," she said. "You'll wear gloves, of course. Anything to do with finance or Dubai or Abu Dhabi, put it to one side."

She sighed deeply and looked at him. "This was the operation that was going to make my name and really put Eurojust on the map, penetrating the finance network, turning Sylvestre so he worked for me."

"I understand," he said. "I'm sorry it didn't work out as you hoped. But then you never want things to be too easy. And it's not as though you failed. You've mapped the network, traced some of the payment routes in Europe and the paymasters in the Gulf. And you've still got a shot at picking up Freddy."

"Dear Bruno, always looking for the positive in every disaster." She gave him a fond look and then braced herself. "And you're right. Time to gather what we can from the wreckage and start all over again."

23

The whole panoply of a murder investigation began to build around Bruno, forensics teams and photographers, uniformed police searching the grounds and detectives sifting through Sylvestre's Range Rover and all the contents of the houses. Bruno sat by the pool with his notebook out, skimming through it as he tried to work out what motive Freddy might have had to kill his partner and flee. Did he suspect that they were under surveillance and that Sylvestre might agree to work for the authorities to gain immunity from prosecution? Had Freddy learned that Sylvestre was taking money meant for the cause? Had he simply become too much of a risk? Might it have been personal, Freddy trying to take over Sylvestre's business? But in that case, would he not have prepared matters better? From the look of Freddy's place, he'd left in a hurry if not in a panic. And how could he take over Sylvestre's business ventures, unless Freddy was certain he could thumb his nose at a French extradition request?

Bruno could see no explanation that satisfied him. And Freddy had left all the books and journals behind that dealt with the lost Bugatti. Perhaps he had no interest in it, but it had been to Freddy that Hugon had mailed his research report or whatever it was. That reminded Bruno; he should ask J-J if his team had been able to break into Hugon's computer. The research report should be in there. And had Freddy and Sylvestre together killed Hugon or just one of them? There had been three coffee cups, Bruno remembered. And what was Sylvestre's second deal with the *notaire*? At least he could check that. He was about to ring Brosseil's office when he remembered there was someone who would need to know about the death. He called his friend Thomas in Alsace instead.

"I've got unpleasant news. Sylvestre was found dead this morning in his swimming pool."

"*Mon Dieu.* Was it an accident?" asked Thomas.

"We're not sure yet." Bruno explained the circumstances, said that the family feud had been settled and that two of Sylvestre's land deals were almost completed. "There's an autopsy later today, and I'll keep you informed."

"Thanks, I'd better tell the mayor. That's our richest citizen gone and the last of his line."

"Can you let me have the name of his lawyer, and find out if there's a will?" Bruno said, and then stopped. "Last of his line?"

"He was an only child and had no direct heirs. His father and grandfather were only sons."

"So who are the nearest relatives?" Bruno asked.

"None around here. I imagine it will be the ones he was having the feud with. They'll inherit a fortune."

"*Mon Dieu,*" said Bruno, his mind racing. "That's quite a motive. And it was his cousin Oudinot's daughter who found the body."

Martine had left him not long before eleven, he recalled. Fabiola was putting Sylvestre's death at somewhere between midnight and four in the morning; Sylvestre's immersion in the heated pool had made the usual body temperature tests meaningless.

But did she and her father know there were no other heirs to Sylvestre's estate?

"I'll call the lawyer and find out about a will, just as soon as I've seen the mayor. He'll probably want the body brought back here for a big funeral. It's quite an event in a town like this."

"I understand, and thanks, Thomas, and my love to Ingrid."

Rocked by the prospect that the woman he was sleeping with might be a murder suspect, Bruno tried to remember every meeting he'd had with Martine and Sylvestre, including that first time when the two cousins had been together at this very spot by the pool. There was nothing that suggested that Martine was anything but what she said, keen to help resolve the family feud, and a bit embarrassed by her father's hostility. Surely he now knew Martine well enough . . .

No, he didn't, he told himself. There had been only a few meetings, a lunch, some meals, two glorious evenings making love, a sense of mounting excitement that went beyond his attraction to her looks and brains and talent, the enjoyment he took in her presence, the pleasure he felt at the prospect of seeing her again. He liked her a lot, no, he more than liked her, and Bruno knew himself well enough to suspect that he was falling for her more and more deeply. And that would skew his judgment. Duty as well as decency required that he hand this over to J-J to investigate.

In the meantime, he had work to do. He called the *notaire*'s office, and after a short pause Brosseil came on the line.

"Bad news," he began. "Your new client, Sylvestre Wémy, is dead. Drowned in his pool last night. I'm at his place now. Those deals of his won't go through now, and I need to find out what they are. I know about Oudinot; it's the other one."

Brosseil stuttered something, dropped the phone and then said, "Sorry, it's a bit of a shock. At least the deposits are paid.

He did bank transfers for each of them from my office, so I'll get my fee, or some of it. The second deal was with Jérôme at the amusement park. Monsieur Wémy was planning to buy it, enlarge it and build it up. He said something about adding a car museum."

"The mayor will be sorry to hear that's fallen through," Bruno replied, recovering quickly from the surprise. "How much of a deposit did he put down? The usual ten percent?"

"No, fifty thousand to Oudinot, half the final price, and two hundred thousand to Jérôme, twenty percent. He paid extra because he wanted the deals wrapped up quickly before he went to China. I'd better get onto Oudinot and Jérôme."

"Oudinot already knows," Bruno said. "His daughter found the body, but don't pass that news around yet."

As he closed his phone, he wondered if someone other than Freddy had been involved in Sylvestre's death. The Oudinot family had a motive to loathe him in the past, but surely not once the land deal was agreed. Oudinot had been very pleased with the sale when Bruno had seen him. But then, he might expect to inherit. And Jérôme was looking at a million-euro payday if the sale of the amusement park had been completed. Could the lost Bugatti have been sufficient motive, perhaps for someone equally obsessed, like George Young? Certainly with all his books and hiring a researcher, Sylvestre had been far better organized in his search than Young's dependence on some old family memoir that hadn't taken him far. But that was hardly a motive for murder. And Young was aware of the legal complications of the vehicle's ownership if it was ever found. However much it might be worth, the finder would get only a fraction of an eventual sale price.

"I wish I could sit around a pool all day while others slave away," came J-J's booming voice.

"I'm thinking," said Bruno. "I'm trying to work out if anyone but Freddy might have had a motive."

"Start by asking yourself who else has fled the scene. That van you mentioned with Sylvestre's cars in it, did you find the key?"

"I found a key case in the kitchen with a lot of keys on it. I left it there in an evidence bag to be fingerprinted."

"That's done. Can you go down to wherever the van is parked with a forensics team, let them in and give them a hand? They've just arrived from Bergerac with Inspector Jofflin. You've worked with him before, and you've at least seen inside the van and know the cars."

"Okay, any interesting papers turned up yet?"

"Isabelle's handling that with her two guys, and she knows to keep a special eye out for anything that might have come from Hugon."

"What about Hugon's computer?"

"Yves can't get into it. We may have to send it to Bordeaux, maybe to Paris; they have machines that can run through millions of possible passwords in a few minutes. Given time, they'll break it."

"There's something you need to know," said Bruno. "The young woman who found the body, his cousin Martine. I'm involved with her, so I can't follow this up myself. But I've just learned from a friend in Alsace that Sylvestre has no other heirs. That means his estate will go to Martine and her parents, and there's been a long-standing and bitter family feud that I thought had been settled. Given Sylvestre's wealth, that's quite a motive, and I think you ought to pursue it, even though I've known the family for years, and I really don't think they are killers, least of all Martine. It would break my heart if I'm wrong."

J-J studied him in silence for a long moment. "Okay, Bruno, I'll look into it myself." His voice was quiet and sympathetic. "And thanks for telling me."

Bruno rose, went to get the keys, joined the team from Bergerac and headed for the truck garage at Le Buisson. Bruno did not know the security man on duty, but at the sight of Bruno's uniform and the police van that carried the forensic specialists, the guard opened the electronic gates to let them in. One of the keys opened the door. They pulled out the ramps, and Inspector Jofflin and Bruno donned their snowman suits and bootees and climbed in. From their van, two members of Jofflin's crew unloaded a portable generator, fired it up and connected two flood lamps to illuminate the two cars, ancient and modern, that dominated the van's interior. But that was not where Jofflin began his search. He looked at the racks of oils, lubricants and chemicals that lined one side of the van, each of them secured for travel with bungee cords. Then he looked at the workbench and the tools above it on their sturdy hooks. Beneath the workbench were several pieces of equipment. One by one, Jofflin pointed to a welding kit, a generator and something else that Bruno did not recognize.

"Three-dimensional printer, industrial size," said Jofflin. "All the race-car teams use them these days. They can design a new component or piece of bodywork over dinner, print it overnight and have it ready to test the next day. This one has DMLS, direct metal laser sintering."

"You mean they can print metal, not just plastics?" Bruno asked, thinking that Jofflin relished showing off his knowledge.

"Absolutely, that's the point. But this system can print both. Whoever designed this van really knew what they were doing. It's better equipped than most garages." He pointed to the van roof, where six curved steel girders, each anchored to the floor, rose up the walls and then curved in to meet at a fixture that held a hook and chain. "That's a heavy-duty engine hoist. They can lift out engines, print new parts and even electroplate them. Let me see . . ."

He looked along the cans of chemicals, muttering something

about permits. On a bookshelf above the workbench, Bruno saw a book-sized file marked "Permits" and asked Jofflin, "Is this what you're looking for?"

"That's it," said Jofflin and began leafing through. "Acids, hydroxides, metallic oxides, halogens, diisocyanates, it looks like all the approvals are here, even cyanide. That's for the electroplating."

Bruno's eyes widened. "You know J-J already has a cyanide-poisoning case, another murder. Could a specialist lab tell us whether the cyanide that was used in that killing came from the stuff they have here?"

"I don't know, but if the guys who drove this truck are possible suspects, you'd better tell J-J right away," Jofflin replied. "Meanwhile we'll inventory all this and check for fingerprints."

When Bruno called J-J to inform him of what had been found, J-J suggested that Jofflin call the Bordeaux lab directly to see if the batch of cyanide could be identified.

"In the meantime, Isabelle has come up with some papers from Sylvestre's house that look as if they're related to Hugon," J-J told Bruno, adding that it seemed to be a research report on the Bugatti. Even more interesting was a handwritten note of a phone conversation with Hugon, attached to it with a paper clip.

"I think Hugon was trying to blackmail Sylvestre," J-J said.

"How do you mean? What could he have on Sylvestre?"

"Information," said J-J. "At least, that's how I interpret the note."

It contained just a handful of words and figures: "Hugon," "Bugatti," "new lead," and then "bonus." Finally came the figure 5 followed by four zeros. After the figures had been scrawled, an exclamation point had been made so hard the pen had ripped the paper.

"Whoever wrote it was angry or maybe just excited," said J-J. "Maybe you should come back here and take a look."

"Sylvestre was rich," said Bruno. "Fifty thousand was like pocket change to him, but I suppose it could be a motive for murder. And we found no trace of fifty grand in Hugon's bank accounts."

"It certainly meant Sylvestre could no longer trust Hugon, and maybe Sylvestre wanted him silenced anyway," J-J replied. "Isabelle has people looking at Sylvestre's bank accounts as we speak. By the way, I went to the farm and talked to the Oudinots, and while they have only each other as alibis, they seemed genuinely stunned by his death. I think they're in the clear. Of course, I may be biased by the brioches Oudinot's wife served with the coffee. And that daughter of theirs is really something; you're a lucky man."

"Let's hope I'm still lucky after she's been grilled by you. I'll leave Jofflin and his guys to go over the truck, and I'll head back."

"One more thing—Isabelle has started to track Freddy. He took an early morning flight to Amsterdam from Bordeaux. It left just after six, so he must have set off from the house by four this morning at the latest. They're trying all the outbound flights from Amsterdam now but suspect he's using other ID."

"How did he buy the ticket?"

"At the airport with a platinum credit card, but he paid for a business-class return so was waved right through. He must have known they do extra checks on one-way tickets bought at the last minute."

When Bruno returned to the *chartreuse,* he found Philippe Delaron in the driveway, trying to take pictures of the house despite the two gendarmes standing stolidly in the way. Bruno brushed aside Philippe's questions and went looking for J-J. He was out of reach, closeted in Sylvestre's kitchen with Isabelle and the *procureur,* who had driven down from Périgueux to take charge of the inquiry. While Bruno had been at the truck garage, the forensic pathologist confirmed Fabiola's suspicion that Sylvestre had been held underwater until he drowned. That meant they were now dealing with two related murders. As he waited for J-J to be free, Bruno called Fabiola to tell her it looked like she'd been right about the cyanide.

She quickly changed the subject. "Gilles texted me to say he'd be back late. He's out at Rastignac again, seeing some local policeman who's a friend of yours," Fabiola told him. "He's gone with George Young in the E-type. They seem to be interested in junkyards all of a sudden."

"Have you told him about Sylvestre's death?" Bruno asked.

"Yes, I texted him back. Why, is it a secret? I assume he told Young, since they seem to be working together."

"Not a secret, it's just that we may need to talk to Young about his whereabouts last night. Since he knew Sylvestre, and they were rivals for the Bugatti, he's on the list of potential suspects."

"Annette won't like that."

"It's just routine; he's not a serious suspect. Anyway, since I assume they're sleeping together, she's his alibi."

"I'm not sure they are. She called me last night to complain about him being so obsessed with that old car he's hunting for," Fabiola said. "I told her I sympathized, since Gilles was also getting caught up in the thrill of the chase." Her voice dripped sarcasm, then became matter-of-fact. "I have a waiting room full of patients, so I may see you later with the horses. Bye, Bruno."

As Bruno put his phone away, Isabelle, J-J and the *procureur* came out of Sylvestre's house, and J-J waved him across to join them.

"It's me who wants to speak with you," said the *procureur*. "It's about this young man who nearly blinded a little girl. I've seen your recommendation, and I spoke to the mayor this morning on the drive down. I'll go along with the plan, but only on the condition that the parents sign a guarantee to enforce it. After all the fuss in the media about the case, I'm going to be criticized for being too soft, so the regimen is going to have to be really strict. And I don't want this kid to think he's getting away with something, so that means no phone for him and no computer. I'll e-mail you the text to print out, and I want it signed by both parents."

The *procureur* left, Isabelle had disappeared, and J-J led him into the kitchen and showed him the research report and the attached note. Bruno glanced at it and agreed; it was hard to put any other interpretation on it. Hugon was demanding more money for his new lead.

"Take a look at that document underneath," J-J said. "You know more about this business than I do. Let me know what you think, and then you'd better take care of whatever the *procureur* asked you to do. We've got more than enough manpower here."

The report was mainly a list of negatives. No Bugatti had been registered in the Dordogne or any neighboring *département* between 1939 and 1946, except for the Gironde, where most of the stock in the Alsace factory at Molsheim, which the German military had requisitioned, had been moved to a replacement factory on rue Alfred Danat in Bordeaux. There was nothing in the Vichy archives that suggested the car had been authorized to enter the Vichy zone. And there was no indication of any insurance policy being taken out on a car with the relevant chassis number after 1940.

Hugon had researched the history of the four Bugatti Atlantics, and Bruno was surprised to learn that until little more than ten years ago it had been assumed there were only three. The two bought by the English customers, Lord Rothschild and R. B. Pope, were silver-blue and sapphire blue. All the known photos of the black Atlantic were assumed to feature the car bought by the Holzschuch family, the car that was wrecked by a train at a level crossing in 1955.

Then a sharp-eyed French historian, Jean-Pierre Cornu, realized that the photos of the black Atlantic were of two different cars with different headlamps and different bumpers. In the spring of 1937, there had been a Concours d'Élégance in Juan-les-Pins on March 31, and another at Nice the next week. Each featured a black Atlantic, but they were different cars. In the first photograph, from Juan-les-Pins, Madame Holzschuch stood next to the car. In the second, at Nice, Yvonne Williams, the wife of William Grover-Williams, was featured, and this was the photo that appeared in the Bugatti catalog for 1938. This was also the car that Williams had taken to 121 miles per hour on the outskirts of London at a road test during the British automobile show in 1937, and it had also become the first car to reach 200 kilometers per hour, 125 miles per hour, at the Montlhéry circuit south of Paris.

Then came the crux of the report. The researcher confirmed that Grover-Williams and his wife had been guests at the Château de Rastignac, the first real connection between the car and the Périgord. He had now found evidence that a black Bugatti Atlantic had been seen at the château in 1941 and had then been dismantled and hidden in a disused tobacco barn just a few miles away. And he was now close to learning what had happened to it.

The researcher had to be Hugon, although no name was listed on the title page. The report, which included copies of the photos described in the text, was dated the day before the date on the post office receipt that had been in Hugon's pocket. That in turn was five days before Hugon's death. Bruno began to scribble down in his notebook the timeline of events.

The report was bound to have excited Sylvestre and Freddy. Presumably it was a day or two later that they had received

Hugon's phone call, demanding another fifty thousand euros. At that point they must have decided to take up the invitation to the St. Denis vintage-car show. They could then have visited Hugon and either forced him to tell them what he knew or gave him a check and learned the Atlantic's fate. Then they killed him in a way that looked like a heart attack and tore up the check.

That made sense, but it left two big questions. The first was Freddy's role. Sylvestre was the one obsessed by the car. Why had the report been sent to Freddy? Possibly, Bruno thought, because Sylvestre wanted to cover his own trail, probably because he was so well known in Alsace that collecting a parcel of documents from a *poste restante* would provoke unwelcome curiosity. And why use a *poste restante* rather than Sylvestre's home address, unless Sylvestre had wanted to conceal his interest? The far-bigger question was, if Sylvestre had learned of the car's fate and its hiding place just before killing Hugon, why had he not gone to find it and reap all the fame and fortune that would go with the dramatic discovery?

Perhaps Hugon had not finally established the car's whereabouts. Maybe the car's location was known, but it had been cached somewhere Sylvestre could not obtain physical possession. Or perhaps he could not even see it to confirm its presence; somewhere like a junkyard, mused Bruno, buried under tons of scrap metal.

He went to share his thoughts with J-J and found him with Isabelle, who was looking exhausted and elated at the same time.

"We're onto him, your Freddy," she said, looking at Bruno. "You've got us all calling him that now. It was Sylvestre's iPhone that did it. Freddy forgot to turn it off. We picked it up in the Bordeaux airport, and then in Schiphol in Amsterdam, where he landed not long after seven. We then lost the signal when he took off on another plane at eight-thirty. That gave us five flights to choose from, and we monitored each destination. He arrived in Athens just before noon. He's still there, and we're trying to get the Greek police to pick him up. And we think we have the name and passport number he's now using."

"Unless he spent the flight downloading everything on Sylvestre's iPhone onto his own," said J-J. "Then he could have emptied the memory and tossed the phone into an Athens waste-basket, where it's still transmitting. Meanwhile Freddy's on a new flight to Abu Dhabi or somewhere."

"Thanks," she said, tiredly. "Just what I needed. But that's not all. Sylvestre's bank accounts have all been emptied. Freddy must have used Sylvestre's laptop to do it, programming it to order the transfers while he was on the phone to Amsterdam. He hit the SEND button just after eight, but at least we now have all the details of the accounts to which he sent the money, and now we're able to monitor them."

"How much did he get?" J-J asked.

"Just over a million. Sylvestre had loaded up one account to finance the new Shanghai venture."

"So your operation has been a success," said Bruno. "You've mapped their finance network."

She nodded and said, "It's like that old medical joke. You know the one, where the doctor comes out of the operating the-ater wearing his scrubs and mask and tells the patient's family that the operation was a success, but unfortunately the patient died."

Isabelle walked out with Bruno when he left. At first she said nothing, but once they were out of earshot of the others, she turned to him. "I just did you a favor. I took down your two cameras before the forensics team turned up because I didn't want them found. For both our sakes, I didn't want the *procureur* realizing that we'd started the surveillance before we were legally authorized to do so. I'll get them back to you, but I want to review the data cards first."

"You won't be able to use them as evidence."

"Agreed, but it might help me know what happened. I'll keep you posted."

24

Bruno went first to Oudinot's farm to make sure all was well there and to ask Martine if she might be free that evening. In the house he found only Odette, rolling pastry and listening to a call-in show on Périgord Bleu about gardening. He said he hoped J-J's questions had not been a strain. Odette continued her rolling, cocked her head at the radio and said, "Idiots."

"They're saying it's a good weekend to plant mâche, which shows how little they know," she said, looking at Bruno. "You use the lunar calendar, don't you? Have you seen what it says for today? No gardening of any kind."

Bruno nodded; he had seen it, and it had eased his guilt a little for neglecting his garden with all the extra work involved with Sylvestre and Félix and the time he was spending with Martine.

"And have you seen the horoscope today? Read what it says about Virgo, that's Martine's sign. Read it out."

Bruno picked up *Sud Ouest*, already turned to the horoscope page. It was something that always reminded him of that happy first summer with Isabelle; she always read out both his and hers. He read aloud: "This is not a good time for romance. Avoid any new amorous entanglements; they are doomed to fail and make you miserable. Stick with old friends and family and take lots of exercise."

He put the paper down, and Odette looked him in the eye. "I'm not a fool, Bruno. I know Martine is seeing you, and she seems very happy about it, but it's not going to last. She's never going to settle down here, whatever fantasies Fernand may have about his daughter coming home to breed grandchildren. She never will. She's a big-city girl now, able and ambitious, and that's fine by me. If you two go on with this affair, you'll both be unhappy. What's more, she's a Virgo, you're a Libra; it can never work."

"I think you're reading a lot into a newspaper horoscope, Odette," he replied, embarrassed.

"I know my daughter. Anyway, you're coming to dinner tomorrow night, and then she's off, back to London next week, which is for the best."

"Isn't she staying for the funeral? Do you know if it's going to be here or in Alsace?"

"I don't know. It would be a bit hypocritical of us to put on a great show of mourning. Still, family is family when all's said and done."

"I'll see you tomorrow evening, and thank you for the invitation. I'll just go and have a word with Fernand and Martine."

"You'll find them down with the newborn calf, but they'll probably be talking about Sylvestre's will and who's going to inherit. I hope it's not us. Fernand and I aren't the kind of people who know what to do with money. Martine's different."

In the barn, the calf was being licked clean by its mother and trying to stand, rear legs first, and tottering. Martine squeezed his hand as he greeted her with the *bise* on both cheeks, and then he shook hands with Fernand.

"So the *commissaire*'s interrogation wasn't too difficult for you?" Bruno asked.

"No, he was very polite, just wanted to know if we'd seen

or heard anything and if we'd all been together in the house all night," Fernand said. "Do you know anything about Sylvestre's will?"

"I spoke to the police in Alsace, and they are contacting Sylvestre's family lawyer. We should know on Monday. And the mayor of his village in Alsace may want to have the funeral there."

"It's quite a shock," said Martine. "We're all a little bit stunned by what's happened, so I think the three of us will just have a quiet evening together here."

Bruno understood her message: no lovemaking tonight. "Well, I'll look forward to seeing you at dinner tomorrow."

The calf had made it to its feet, and the mother stood and nudged it with her head to get under her belly and toward her teats. The calf licked around her udder but seemed unsure what to do next. Martine reached down and put a teat firmly into the calf's mouth and then began stroking its throat to start the sucking and swallowing reflex. Her father watched her proudly and said, "Still a country girl at heart, our Martine."

Bruno went back to pick up his van and drove to the supermarket. Simon was in his office, leafing through what looked like sales figures, when Bruno came in, closing the door behind him. He sat down and handed across the printout of the *procureur*'s draft. Bruno had used his own official notepaper, with the seal of St. Denis and the heading of the Police Municipale.

"If you want to keep your son out of jail, you and your wife need to sign this. Where is she?"

"She's taken Tristan to our cottage near Arcachon," Simon replied. "She thought he needed a break after the shock of the arrest and being handcuffed."

Bruno shook his head. "You never learn, do you? Here I am trying to save that son of yours from a juvenile detention center, and you send him off for a vacation at the beach. You're thinking of him as some kind of victim in all this when in reality he's the perpetrator."

"It wasn't my idea. In fact I was against it—"

"But you never argue with your wife," Bruno interrupted. "That's half the trouble. She spoils him, she lies for him, perjures herself for his sake. And you put up with it, Simon. I think you're rotten parents. You've certainly done a lousy job of raising your son."

"One mistake . . . ," Simon began.

"More than one. Let's not forget he also faces a charge of possessing illegal drugs in commercial quantities. I doubt it will take me more than twenty minutes to get a few affidavits from his classmates saying he's been dealing drugs in the *collège*."

"You say you can keep him out of detention?" Simon began to scan the document, frowning as he read it. "You're going to make us responsible for his behavior?"

"It's called being a parent."

"And what's this forestry business?"

"It's part of the tough regimen the *procureur* requires as the price for keeping Tristan out of jail. You can guess what's likely to become of him in there and what kind of life lies ahead of him when he gets out. This way, he has a chance of finishing his education and maybe even going on to university. It's his last chance, and you and your wife have to sign up for it or it won't happen."

"He won't like this—no phone, no computer, not to be out of our custody at any time when he's not working. It sounds like house arrest."

"It's punishment; Tristan is not supposed to like it. Maybe if you'd been enough of a father to punish him earlier he wouldn't be in this mess now."

"They won't be back from Arcachon until next week."

Bruno sighed heavily. "You just don't get it, do you, Simon? If they're not back here tonight with that signed document on the *procureur*'s desk by Monday morning, the Arcachon police will go to your beach house and arrest your son. They will then hold him in a police cell until we get around to sending a prison van to take Tristan directly to the detention center to await trial."

"Will it be enough if I sign?"

"No, I've told the *procureur* that your wife is more than half the trouble. And if she doesn't sign, then we still have the perjury charge hanging over her."

"Our lawyer says—"

"Bullshit. Call your lawyer if you want, and he'll tell you that charging her with perjury is a matter for the *procureur*'s discretion. I just spoke to him, and he's decided to go with my recommendation to keep Tristan out of jail even though he knows he's going to get a lot of flak for going soft on your son. If you spurn his offer, he'll throw the book at all of you, starting with your wife."

"You say this plan for Tristan is your suggestion?"

"It's a joint recommendation to the *procureur* from me, the head of the gendarmes and the magistrate in charge of juvenile justice. It's been endorsed by the mayor, who personally arranged this forestry work."

Simon signed the document in small neat handwriting and printed *"Lu et approuvé"* above it—"read and approved"—the legal requirement in France.

"I'll get them back tonight and somehow I'll get her to sign it."

"And you will hand deliver that document first thing Monday morning to the *procureur*'s office in Périgueux. And you'd better get a receipt from his office because the mayor and I will need to see it."

Bruno rose and left without another word. He headed to the *mairie,* still fuming at the thought of Tristan being rewarded with a trip to the beach, to report to the mayor on Sylvestre's death. It might be a Saturday afternoon, but the mayor would be at work on his endless project of writing the history of St. Denis if there were no official duties to be performed. Bruno also wanted to check his e-mails. As he scrolled through, his phone pinged with an incoming text. It was Gilles, asking for a meeting at the *maison de retraite* in twenty minutes. He texted back confirmation and went back to the e-mails. One was from Tristan's mother.

"I will never forgive you for that dirty trick you played on me nor for what you have done to my boy. I'm one of the people who pays your salary and I begrudge every penny of it. You're a disgrace to your uniform," he read. He sighed, and forwarded copies to the *procureur* and to Annette. Then he printed it out twice, added one to his file on Tristan and took the other to the mayor, who was at his desk, fountain pen in hand, his manuscript before him and several old books open around him. He looked up as Bruno entered and gave him a copy of the denunciation.

"One of your voters doesn't like me," he said.

"What was the dirty trick?"

"She swore that Tristan was at home with her when he threw the stone that hit the little girl. I got her to sign a formal statement to that effect. Yveline was present when it all happened."

"I don't think the *procureur* would bring a perjury charge against a mother lying to protect her son."

"I think he will if she tries to block the forestry job you arranged as too tough on her precious son. She's taken him off to their weekend cottage in Arcachon so the poor boy can recover from his ordeal. She's the problem, and her false statement is our leverage."

The mayor put down his pen, removed his spectacles and rubbed his eyes. "What a foolish woman. Human folly never changes," he said, sighing. "I'm just working on the saddest moment in the history of our town. Do you know that St. Denis and its convent were sacked and burned in 1577, during what we call the Wars of Religion? The troops were Protestant, but they were having a private war among themselves, between Galliot de La Tour, the lord of Limeuil, and his brother Jacques. We have a square called la place du Temple because they built a Protestant chapel after the town was burned. The chapel was itself demolished a hundred years later when Louis XIV revoked the rights given to Protestants under the Edict of Nantes."

"I sometimes wondered why the square was so named when there was no temple."

"Now you know. What do you want me to do with this?" he waved a copy of the e-mail from Tristan's mother.

"Nothing really. I just wanted you to know about it. I've told Simon to be sure that Tristan and his mother return from the beach today. I also wanted to tell you that we have the results of one autopsy that confirms Hugon was murdered with cyanide and another that says Sylvestre was deliberately drowned in his pool."

When Bruno left the mayor's office, he went to the retirement home and was there to greet Gilles when he arrived in Fabiola's old Twingo with an elderly man in the passenger seat.

"Bonjour, Bruno," said the passenger, grinning at him. "Grégoire sends his regards."

Bruno realized this must be Grégoire's father, Étienne, come to visit Félix's grandfather. He had white hair and a white mustache and was wearing dark glasses, a suit and a tie. Bruno had always been struck by the formal way so many elderly people chose to dress.

"Am I right to think you're coming to visit an old schoolmate?" he asked, shaking the elderly hand through the open car window.

"That's right. Gilles called the *maison de retraite* and got him on the phone. I've brought an old school photo to see if he can pick me out. I'm pretty sure I recognized him, but it's a lifetime since we were last together."

Gilles let Étienne out and went off to park. Bruno matched his pace to the elderly shuffle and steered Étienne to the right door, already open, with their host rising to greet them. His photo album was under his arm. It was crowded in the small room, but Bruno perched on the windowsill, and Gilles was offered the easy chair when he arrived but remained standing. The two old men sat side by side on the bed to look at the photos and reminisce.

"Can I bring you gentlemen some coffee or some tea, maybe a glass of wine?" Gilles asked.

They agreed that they would each like a *petit blanc*. Gesturing with his head for Bruno to follow, Gilles led the way out and across the road to pick up a bottle of chilled Bergerac Sec from the corner shop. They then borrowed some glasses from the kitchen of the *maison de retraite*.

"I'm sure that Étienne knows something about this junk shop, but he's not talking," Gilles confided as they went. "He just said he wanted to see his old friend and talk to him. He thought it might trigger some memories."

"How much have you told him?" Bruno asked.

"Everything about the car, nothing about Sylvestre."

"You know Sylvestre was found dead in his pool this morning."

"Yes, Fabiola sent me a text. Naturally, I told Young. He made some joke about giving a medal to whoever did it. What was it, heart attack or something?"

"We won't be sure until the autopsy," Bruno said quickly. If Fabiola had not told Gilles of her suspicions, that meant Young would also not know. "I thought you and Young were going together to see Étienne in the E-type."

"He called to ask if we could go separately. He wanted to get back to Annette, feeling guilty about neglecting her on a Saturday, one of her days off."

They took in the wine and glasses, the two old men pausing in what had been animated conversation over the photo album. Bruno had the feeling they were up to something.

"Funny how the old photos bring it all back," said Gilles as Bruno opened the wine and poured out four glasses.

"Maybe with young memories like yours," said Étienne, raising his glass. "*Santé.*"

"So were you two in the same class?"

"Same school, different class. Étienne's older, but we were on the same soccer team. And his big brother is in the photo with Henri." Félix's grandfather pointed to another of the young men with an armband and Sten gun. "They'd been at school together, too, chased the same girls."

"So what happened to the scrap merchant Bérégevoy?" Bruno asked.

"He died sometime in the early seventies, but he'd run down his stock by then," Étienne replied. "He had a place near the viaduct in Sarlat, and when they started cleaning the town up they changed the zoning and he was told to move. I don't remember where he went, if I ever knew. He had a daughter, but she moved away when she got married."

"Her name was Célestine," said Gilles. "I checked her out in Sarlat, where she worked at the *mairie* before getting married in 1961. I'm trying to trace her now. She might know what happened to the remaining stock."

"Sounds like a dead end to me," said Étienne, with a quick, sideways glance at his old schoolmate.

Bruno's phone vibrated, and he saw it was Thomas calling from Alsace. He went outside to answer it, to learn that Thomas had tracked down Sylvestre's lawyer, passed on the news of his death and asked about a will.

"He hadn't drawn one up, although the lawyer had advised Sylvestre to do so," Thomas went on. "He said he might have used another lawyer, maybe in Paris because of the scale of the family holdings, but he'd check in the registry of wills and get back to me on Monday. Any more news?"

"The autopsy has been done, and it was murder, but we're not releasing that news yet. Somebody held his head underwater, but he was very drunk and also stoned."

"*Putain,* that's going to cause a stir. Any suspects?"

"That Indian partner of his took the first early morning flight from Bordeaux and cleared out Sylvestre's bank accounts. He's the obvious suspect and Europol is trying to track his movements after he landed in Amsterdam. If they lose his trail, the *procureur* will announce that it's a murder inquiry, but that probably won't be until Monday morning. I'll let you know. Keep this to yourself, or it's bound to leak."

They hung up, and Bruno turned on the record function on his phone, held it up to his ear as if still talking and went back to join the others. He said some words of farewell as if to end a conversation and then asked if anyone wanted more wine. Étienne held up his glass, so Bruno poured out some more, in the process leaving his phone discreetly behind a potted plant on the windowsill.

"We'll leave the wine with you. Gilles and I have a couple of errands to take care of," he said and turned to Gilles. "Will you drive Étienne back?"

Gilles nodded, saying he'd be back in an hour or so. Bruno and Gilles left the two old men together. Once outside, Bruno asked his friend to collect the phone when he picked up Étienne, saying Bruno had forgotten it.

"My phone is recording because, now that they're alone, I think we might learn something," he said. "What are your plans for this evening?"

"Nothing particular. Fabiola wants to exercise Victoria, which reminds me: you know Pamela and Fabiola are going fifty-fifty on the Andalusian horse? They also want to move all the horses, your Hector included, to the riding school. Pamela reckons that Victoria will be placid enough for the children when they move on from ponies. That would mean leaving Hector alone in our stables, which doesn't seem like a good idea. And having Hector there would mean an extra adult horse for her customers."

Bruno raised his eyebrows. He had once thought of stabling Hector on his own property, but he didn't like the thought of leaving him alone. And police work meant he could not always be back in time to exercise the horse. Until now, he could count on Fabiola to take Hector out behind her on a long rein. It made sense to leave all the horses at Pamela's stables, but would it change his relationship with his horse if others were to ride Hector from time to time? He wouldn't even have owned a horse if Pamela had not organized all his friends to band together and buy Hector for his birthday. He owed her too much to refuse.

"It makes sense," Bruno said. "Fabiola and I could ride Victoria and Hector over to Pamela's place this evening while you drive Étienne back."

"Pamela is coming back here for dinner afterward," Gilles added. "Why not join us? I bought oysters in the market this morning, and Fabiola is making her fondue. We all know how much you like it."

"That sounds good, and I'll bring some wine," said Bruno. "Just don't forget to pick up my phone when you collect Étienne."

25

That Sunday morning in St. Denis, the church bell was summoning the faithful to mass, Father Sentout was donning his vestments, and the less religious citizens were thronging to Fauquet's to buy the special *gâteaux,* fit to grace a Sunday lunch en famille. Bruno, wearing civilian clothes, was sitting on the café terrace and feeding the heel of his croissant to Balzac. After checking on the chickens, they had taken Bruno's morning run through the woods together and then, feeling the need for some more exercise, Bruno had cleaned out the ashes from his wood-burning stove while Balzac sat patiently watching. The dog had followed to observe Bruno empty the ashes onto that part of his vegetable garden that still lay fallow. Then he had turned over the soil to dig the ashes in, thinking that did not count as the kind of gardening forbidden by the lunar calendar. He had changed his sheets and towels, filled his washing machine, showered, shaved and headed into town, singing along to Piaf's "La Vie en Rose" on the radio.

Once in town and alone on the terrace with his dog, Bruno turned on the playback feature of his phone and tried once again to make out the indistinct and mumbled words it had recorded between the two men in the retirement home once he and Gilles had left them. The previous evening, over Fabiola's fondue, he and Gilles along with Fabiola and Pamela had tried with only occasional success to follow the conversation. But some words had come over clearly. One of them had been "Bugatti," a second had been "millions," a third had been "park," and the fourth had been "Bérégevoy," the name of the junkyard owner who had bought the contents of the barn at Perdigat.

Bruno was almost sure of a few more phrases, but there were some loose ends to tie up first. He called Marcel, the owner of the garage where Annette had bought the Bugatti radiator. Marcel remembered the name of the junk shop where he had bought the radiator. It had been the closing-down sale of Bérégevoy's place when the owner died. Had anyone else asked about that recently? Bruno asked. Yes, Marcel replied, two people: the Englishman who was supposed to be driving with Annette and then, in a separate visit, a reporter from *Paris Match*.

Another of the recorded words that Bruno was sure of was "Félix." The previous evening when they had been listening, Pamela had said that there had been a phone call for Félix at the stables that afternoon. The boy had then asked to use the computer in her office when he'd finished work.

"I was checking e-mails before coming over here, and there was a window that he must have left open on the computer. I remember it had a photo of an old car, which didn't interest me so I closed it," Pamela had said. She said she would look up the history function on her browser; Gilles had written down the steps she should take.

Bruno ordered a second cup of coffee and called her. Pamela reported that Félix had looked up websites about Bugatti, the Type 57 Atlantic, and the latest Concours d'Élégance at Villa d'Este in Italy, which had been won by Ralph Lauren's car. Félix had then looked at a YouTube video of that same *concours,* which carried the headline in English "Ralph Lauren's $40 million Bugatti Atlantic."

One did not need fluency in English to understand that, thought Bruno, thanking Pamela and then listening once again to the voices of the two men talking. But he heard only odd words or snatches of phrases. At one point Étienne had said "Rome," which baffled Bruno. He listened to that section again, and shortly before the reference to the Italian capital he was almost sure he heard the words *Naud qui l'a acheté.* Who or what was *"Naud"* and what had he bought? Bruno gave up and put the phone down. Perhaps if he gave it to J-J's forensics experts they could find a way to enhance the recording.

"Bonjour, Bruno," came a voice, and Bruno looked up, surprised to see his colleague Grégoire, Étienne's son. He invited him to sit down, share a coffee and recommended the quality of the croissants. Then as Grégoire made friends with Balzac, Bruno asked what brought him to St. Denis.

"My dad," came the reply. "He's always been religious and he said this morning he wanted to hear mass with his old school friend. He asked me to drive him over so here I am."

"Not religious yourself?" Bruno asked.

"Not really, just marriages and funerals, but it's a nice day for a drive, and it's not a day for gardening, so I was happy to agree. My wife's with them in the church now."

"Lunar calendar," said Bruno, smiling. "We're gardening by the same rules."

"They always worked for my dad, and his garden's still a sight to behold," Grégoire said. "Dad told me he'd often wanted to visit the amusement park here in St. Denis, so we'll go there after church. Then I thought we might make a day of it, go out for lunch and then drive home the long way up the Dordogne Valley and back through Sarlat."

Grégoire's coffee came, and then Balzac jumped to his feet

and looked across the square giving a little yelp of welcome before trotting across to welcome Isabelle. She dropped to one knee to greet the basset hound, struggling to manage her shoulder bag, a plastic bag and a large manila envelope as Balzac tried to clamber onto her lap. Bruno called to Fauquet, standing in the door to enjoy the sun on his face, for another croissant and coffee.

"Bonjour, Bruno," said Isabelle, offering each cheek for his *bise*. He introduced Grégoire, told her that he was also a cop and that the coffee and croissant were on their way.

"I remember you," said Grégoire. "You used to work for J-J in Périgueux. I think you were Inspector Perrault back then."

"And you were the municipal cop in Terrasson," she declared. "I remember you as well, that bank robbery that turned out to be an inside job. The guy went down for five years."

"A good case," said Grégoire. "I haven't seen you for ages, but J-J always said you'd be the one to succeed him."

Isabelle shook her head. "I transferred out. I'm with Eurojust these days, up in The Hague."

"So you're here on holiday, visiting old haunts?"

Bruno was sure Grégoire was simply making conversation, but Isabelle clammed up, saying simply, "Old haunts, old friends." She fell silent and devoted her attention to her croissant. Grégoire took the hint and rose to his feet, muttering something about the sermon being over by now.

"Mission complete?" Bruno asked Isabelle once Grégoire had gone.

"Pretty much, but we have a lot of follow-up to do on the banks they used," she said. "And there's going to be a legal row over whether we can confiscate his cars and garage as proceeds of a criminal enterprise. That's pretty much all that's left. Sylvestre was running out of money. Most of his Alsace properties were mortgaged up to the hilt."

"What about Freddy?"

"They lost him in Athens, found his phone dumped in a trash bin at the airport. The police showed his photo at all the check-in desks, and one of the attendants thought she checked him into a flight for Beirut, but she wasn't sure. We've got the numbers of the credit cards he used to buy tickets, so we're monitoring them, and we're asking the Emirates police to seal off the Abu Dhabi showroom.

"We've sworn out a murder warrant for him, but I'm not altogether sure Freddy was Sylvestre's killer," she went on. She finished the remainder of her coffee and handed Bruno the manila envelope and the plastic bag. "Your two cameras are in there, and I printed out some of the better stills from the data card."

She led Bruno through the photos. There was no sign of Freddy until he drove off in the middle of the night in his Range Rover. The timer on the print said he left at ten to four. But another car had come to the *chartreuse* after midnight. The image was too vague for the driver to be identifiable, but then the next print showed two people sitting by the pool. One of them was Sylvestre in a dark dressing gown. The other one had his back to the cameras. The image wasn't helped by the flaring on the film from the open-air heaters that Bruno remembered. It could be Freddy, it could even be a woman with short hair and wearing slacks, or it could be someone else altogether.

"It's clear that this other person and Sylvestre were drinking and smoking for over two hours," Isabelle said. She turned over the next still, which showed Sylvestre standing by the pool and the other person rising from a chair. The person was wearing what looked like jeans and a sweater. The next image showed Sylvestre being pushed into the pool, his unidentified companion following right behind.

"I've never watched a murder in process before this," said Bruno, shaken by what he was seeing but fascinated. "Could we enhance some of the images?"

"I tried, and I've got very good enhancement software on my computer. This is as good as you'll get."

The cameras couldn't see into the pool, and the next movement that was triggered was of the second person climbing out, still fully dressed, still with his or her back to the cameras.

"Here's your killer, standing right beneath one of the heaters and drying himself with a towel from the chair," she said. "Because of the flare we can't see the face, and then he covers his head with the towel and disappears. I say 'he' because his clothes are wet, and there's no sign of female breasts. The next thing we see is Freddy leaving in his car and that's all."

"I couldn't identify anyone from that," said Bruno.

"You may not need to. And if you take my advice, you won't use the prints in interrogation or when it comes to trial. Any decent lawyer would see through your little story about wildlife photography and argue the evidence was illegally obtained. If you have a suspect, don't let him know that you have the prints but use what the images tell you. You know when the killer arrived, what he did, when he left, and you have a car. It's a Peugeot, but it wasn't driven far enough onto the property for us to pick up a license number. If you can't leverage all that into a confession, you're in the wrong business. Above all you have the towel. I made sure it was bagged, and the forensics guys should be able to get some of the murderer's DNA from it."

She leaned forward and kissed him on the lips. "Good-bye, Bruno. Good luck," she said, giving Balzac a final caress. She headed back across the square to her rental car.

Bruno watched her go, called for the bill and began looking again through the prints, hoping against hope that something in the stance or dress of the killer might trigger something. Bruno was almost certain it was a man, but could it be Martine? She was tall enough, but there was no way she could ever have concealed her lovely breasts. It could be Freddy, but the skin of the arms seemed too pale. Who else might it be? Bruno looked again at the photos, pondering.

After a moment wrestling with his conscience, he called Fabiola and said, "I need you to do me a very big favor, but if you feel you can't do it, just tell me. I wouldn't ask if it wasn't really important."

"Tell me what it is," she said, and he explained. He could hear the reluctance in her voice when she replied that she'd think about it and call him back. Bruno put the photos back in their envelope and the envelope into the bag with the cameras and then glanced across the square where people were coming up the rue de Paris from the church.

As the crowd reached the crossroads, the numbers thinned, and Bruno saw the two old men. Félix was beside them and an elderly woman followed, whom Bruno did not know. Grégoire appeared in his car and greeted them all. The old men and the woman, presumably Grégoire's wife, climbed into the car, and Félix went to his bicycle, parked in the rack outside the *mairie,* and unlocked a chain from around the rear wheel. He cycled off, following the car.

Then Bruno recognized three more people, dressed for church, coming across the square toward him. It was Simon, his wife and Tristan. They came onto the terrace of the café and stood awkwardly before him. He rose saying "Bonjour, *monsieur-dame.*"

"As you can see, I got them back from the beach," said Simon. "And I heard from the mayor, so my wife has something to say to you."

She squared her shoulders, fixed her eyes at some point a little above Bruno's head and said quickly, without drawing breath, "I want to apologize for writing you that e-mail. I was very upset and not myself. And now that I know you are doing everything you can to prevent Tristan from being sent to prison, I want to thank you."

She stopped, dropped her eyes to look him in the face and nodded. Then she nudged her son, who kept his eyes on the ground. She nudged him again, and in a strained voice Tristan said, "Thank you, Bruno, for giving me this chance. I'll try not to let you down."

Mother and son then both turned to look challengingly at Simon, as if they had been given some grueling but unwelcome test and had managed, despite themselves, to pass it. Simon ignored them and stepped forward to hold out his hand. Bruno shook it.

"Thanks, Bruno. That document will be in the *procureur's* hands tomorrow morning."

He led his family back to his Mercedes, opening the passenger door for his wife. Bruno watched them leave, wondering what art of persuasion or force of character Simon had deployed for the apologies to be delivered. Or perhaps it was something the mayor might have said to Simon.

"It's a good job that family didn't try coming in my café," said Fauquet, coming out to clear away the coffee cups. "I wouldn't have served them, not after what that boy did. I never liked his mother anyway, stuck-up old bitch. Thinks she's the lady of the manor just because her old man manages a supermarket. It's just a big shop, when all's said and done."

"You've never liked him since he opened the bakery department in the supermarket and took some of your business away," said Bruno.

"You'd have to be pretty hard up to eat that frozen muck they reheat and sell as fresh bread, and don't even get me started about those mass-produced things they call cakes.

"They say it's not even his son," Fauquet went on. "Simon had just arrived in town as one of the undermanagers, and Amandine was working as a cashier. She'd been going out with a man from the butchery department who looked a lot like Tristan. He left town, and before you could turn around she was going out with Simon and married him a couple of months later. It was all before your time, Bruno. And then Simon was promoted to manager, and she started putting on airs. But some of us have long memories. Arnaud, his name was, Arnaud Messager. I wonder what happened to him?"

Something clicked in Bruno's mind. That phrase on the recording that had eluded him, the "Naud" who had bought something. It could have been Arnaud.

He reached for his wallet to pay Fauquet, who looked at him in surprise and said, "Losing your head? You already paid me once." Then he handed Bruno a large brown paper bag, big enough to hold a dozen baguettes. "Stale bread for your chickens," he said. "No charge, just give me a few eggs if you get any extra this week."

"Thanks, Fauquet," said Bruno. "Do you know of anyone else around here called Arnaud, apart from the guy you were just talking about?"

"Nobody who's still alive," said Fauquet. "There was a man who used to sell cheese in the market before Stéphane, but he wasn't from St. Denis. I think he was from Belvès. And there was Jérôme's dad, who started the amusement park, but he's been dead for over thirty years."

"Park," thought Bruno. And "Rome," that could be for "Jérôme." And Grégoire had said the two old men wanted to visit the amusement park. Bruno slapped a fist into his other hand and turned to kiss an astonished Fauquet on both cheeks.

"If I'm right, my friend, I'll get you a lot more than half-a-dozen eggs. You might just have solved a murder case!"

He used his key to get into the *mairie,* closed on Sundays, and went to his office to drop off the plastic bag. He then went into the registry to check the cadastre, the giant map that listed each house and property lot in the commune. He looked up the section that included the amusement park and then compared that with the tax records. He called the mayor and then Gilles.

"I think we're getting to the endgame for your story on the Bugatti," he told Gilles. "Can you meet me at the amusement park just as soon as you can? Call Young and see if he wants to join you. I finally worked out what the old boys were saying on my phone."

"On my way," Gilles replied, and with Balzac at his heels, Bruno walked over the bridge and turned right at the bank to go down the rue de la Paix toward the amusement park.

Bruno recognized Félix's bike, chained to the cycle rack outside the entrance to the park. He pulled out his wallet to buy a ticket, handed over a ten-euro note and asked the cashier if Jérôme was available.

"He's in the back," said the cashier, handing back a two-euro coin and calling for his boss. "But no dogs allowed."

"Bruno's an exception," said Jérôme, coming out to shake Bruno's hand. "What can I do for you?"

"You know your sale has fallen through?" Bruno began. "Sylvestre was found dead in his pool yesterday."

"I know, it was on the radio. Still, I get to keep the deposit, the *notaire* says, even if his heirs don't want to conclude the sale. That will give me enough to go ahead with the expansion."

"Remember you told me about your father's idea to expand the park with a museum of local life here in the nineteenth century? You said something about re-creating an old village and farm. How far did your dad get with the project?"

"I was still a boy at the time, but I have the plans he drew up and, with just a few modifications, that's what I'll be using."

"Did he buy anything that he planned to use, like old school desks, blackboards, farm equipment?"

"He bought a classroom full of those old double desks where

two kids sat side by side. And he got some old farm gear, plows and reapers, all horse drawn, a threshing drum, stuff like that. He bought a job lot from some junkyard that was going out of business. If the mayor gives me the go-ahead I'll look through it and see what can be salvaged."

"Where do you keep it?"

"In the old barn just beyond the windmill. Nothing's been moved since my dad put it there."

"Do you mind if I take a look around with my dog? I paid the entrance fee."

"You didn't have to do that, Bruno. And sure, take your dog. It's too late in the season for me to be busy."

"When the mayor turns up, tell him to look for me near the windmill."

Bruno strolled past the carousel and skirted around the line of parents and children waiting to buy *barbe à papa,* the tendrils of spun sugar on a stick that would turn their faces pink and ruin their teeth. He could hear the pop of air rifles at the shooting range and glanced across to see Grégoire taking aim, his wife at his side. Bruno could smell the aroma of frying sausages. He nodded and waved regretfully in return to a greeting and an invitation to join a group at the beer tent. Nobody was dancing on the stretch of bare ground, but three musicians were dutifully playing bal musette songs from the years before the war, or maybe even before the Great War.

He strolled on, through the water garden with its copy of a Japanese bridge and the benches in discreet corners beneath the fronds of the willow trees where courting couples could go after a successful navigation of the Tunnel of Love, or when the young lady had been suitably terrified by the Ghost Train.

Ahead of him stood the windmill on its slight mound and beside it stood the two old men, looking across the fence to the old barn where Jérôme's father had stored his junk. Bruno ducked back into the willows and knelt down to stroke Balzac into silence until he heard footsteps and a quiet, familiar voice saying his name. He beckoned the mayor to join him and put his finger to his lips.

"Did you check the cadastre and the tax files?" Bruno whispered.

"It's definitely town land, and no taxes have been paid for more than thirty years. I wasn't even mayor then. It must have been forgotten."

After a moment, a small figure emerged from the old barn and began running across the open ground toward the windmill. As he neared the fence, Bruno saw it was Félix and heard him call out, "Grandpa, I think we found it." He waved a flashlight in one hand and a small notebook in the other and then ducked beneath the fence and hugged his grandfather.

"I found the plate on the chassis and cleaned it. It's Bugatti, serial number 57453SC," Félix said. "But that's all there is, the chassis, the engine and the axles."

Bruno pushed through the willow fronds, the mayor behind him, watching the stunned faces of the two old men and returning a cheerful greeting from Félix.

"That's all you need," Bruno said. "That's enough for it to count as a restoration. Only the transmission is missing, and we might even find it with the rest of the junk. Bonjour, messieurs, and my congratulations."

"On behalf of St. Denis, my friends, let me thank you for your efforts," said the mayor. "But since this land and barn belong to the town, and we are claiming the contents in lieu of thirty years of unpaid rent and taxes, I'll have to ask you not to trespass again, young man. This time, of course, we'll let it go."

"Merde," said Étienne and then looked over Bruno's shoulder to where Gilles was pushing through the willows.

"Success, sort of," said Bruno. "What's left of the Bugatti is in the barn over there. Shall we go and see? And don't look too crestfallen, messieurs. St. Denis is a generous town, and I'm sure there'll be some suitable finder's fee for you to share."

They set off across the field, Bruno and Félix holding up the wire fence and helping the old men to get through before helping them across the uneven ground. The wooden doors of the barn were closed with a rusted chain and padlock that hadn't seen a key for decades.

"Come around here," said Félix and led them to the far side of the barn where a plank had been pulled away and then clumsily replaced. He pushed the plank aside and squeezed inside.

"I'll never get through there, pull another plank away," said the mayor and Bruno heaved the rotten wood aside.

"Careful," said Félix, shining the flashlight at Bruno's feet, illuminating a tangled maze of rusted machinery, plows, desks and rotted wooden shafts of farm carts. "I had to pick my way through, and some of it's still pretty sharp."

The mayor and the two old men stood at the gap, peering inside as Bruno and Gilles carefully picked their way through. Each of them pulled out his phone and started taking photos of the tangle and finally of the plate on the long chassis with that magic name BUGATTI.

"Lost for seventy years," said Gilles. "I never believed we could find it." And at that point, two phones began to ring, one immediately after the other. The mayor pulled out his phone and Gilles followed suit.

Bruno heard the mayor say, "Yveline, yes, we'll need gendarmes right away," while Gilles had a finger in one ear to cut the background noise and was loudly telling someone, probably George Young, where to find the barn.

Bruno picked his way out to the open air, and his phone began to vibrate at his waist. He saw that Fabiola was calling him back and hit the button to accept the call.

"I did as you asked, but it wasn't easy, and I feel bad about it. I don't even know if we'll still be talking after this, so I hope it's worth it," she said, her voice colder than ice. "And the answer is no, not last night and not for the last three nights." The phone cut off at her end.

The mayor came up and suggested that Bruno try to break the padlock, saying, "It's town property and I authorize you to open it."

"Shall we call in Delaron to take some photos?" Bruno asked. "We can tell him to hold the story until we have the car secured, and it would be good to have everything properly recorded."

The mayor nodded and pulled out his phone. Bruno sent Félix trotting back to ask Jérôme for a crowbar or a heavy screwdriver and invite him to join them.

"But don't tell him what you found," he called after the boy's disappearing back. Félix crossed another figure on the way, ducking though the fence and approaching them.

"So you finally found it, here in this barn," said Young, once he arrived. He shook hands with Gilles and Bruno and then looked curiously at the two old men. "Congratulations," he added, his tone sounding forced. "Was it kept here all along?"

"For about thirty years," said Gilles. "It was the former owner of the amusement park who bought Bérégevoy's junk and brought it here, planning to open some kind of old farm museum. He died before he could look through it, and the plan fell through. So here it all stayed."

"So in the end Sylvestre never knew where it was?" Young asked.

"I think he did," said Bruno. "He'd signed a contract with Jérôme, the current owner, to buy the whole park. Sylvestre assumed that would include this field and barn and all the contents. He was wrong. It belongs to the town. Jérôme's father was apparently a good friend of a former mayor, who said he could use the barn for a nominal rent and taxes. They signed an agreement to that effect, which is still in the town files, but neither rent nor taxes were ever paid."

Félix returned with Jérôme, carrying a crowbar. The mayor explained everything all over again as Jérôme's face first lit up with hope and excitement and then fell into gloom.

"Cheer up, Jérôme," the mayor went on. "I'm going to support your plan to enlarge the park and build the nineteenth-century village you told Bruno about. I think it will be a splendid addition to the town and bring in lots more tourists than your falling guillotine ever did. We'll even let you have this land and the barn and almost all the contents, once we've removed the Bugatti."

The siren of a gendarme van could be heard coming closer, and then they saw it at the far side of the field, on an unpaved road that skirted a campground. The van stopped, disgorged four gendarmes, and then Yveline climbed down from the driver's seat. They all ducked through the fence and headed toward the barn.

"Good," said the mayor. "They can help us move some of this junk so we can see the Bugatti properly, and then they can secure the barn. Bruno, break that padlock."

Bruno took the crowbar and levered free one of the clasps holding the chain, and Gilles helped him swing open the tall wooden doors, the rusted hinges groaning in protest after decades of disuse. With daylight streaming in, the contents of the barn seemed less of a jumble, even though the haze of ancient dust their entry had stirred up still hung in the stifling air. Most of the school desks were piled, quite neatly, by the entrance. Behind them were three antique farm carts.

Bruno left the mayor to deal with the gendarmes, and he and

Jérôme squeezed past the desks and clambered onto a cart. Reapers were stacked against the rear wall, and plows had been piled against the side of the barn through which Félix had first made his entry.

"Is that an oil drum?" Bruno asked, pointing to a large cylindrical object that was resting on the Bugatti's chassis.

"No, it's an old threshing drum," Jérôme replied. "And I think that's a twine baler beside it. They stopped using wire to hold the bales when they found animals swallowing little strips of it with the hay."

Gilles and Young clambered up onto the next cart to look down in silence at the object of their search. Young moved gingerly forward, lowered himself down and picked his way to the chassis, bending down to examine the vital plate.

"Five, seven, four, five, three followed by an *S* for *Surbaissée*, the lowered chassis, and a *C* for the supercharger," he said very quietly, as though to himself. "The most beautiful car in the world."

A gendarme's face appeared in the gap in the side of the barn, and Yveline was clambering up onto the third cart.

"I'm glad you're here," said Bruno, and then turned to look down at Young, still kneeling in reverence beside the chassis.

"While you're down there, would you mind telling me where you were the night before last, Friday night?"

Young looked up at him, startled. "What? Friday night, I was having dinner with Annette?"

"And after dinner?"

"None of your business."

"I'm afraid it is. This is important. Where were you from midnight until four in the morning?"

"I was with Annette."

"That's not true. You haven't slept with her for the past three nights."

Young's eyes flickered toward Yveline, and he swallowed. "It's true that we weren't together last night; we had a bit of a row over dinner."

"I'm not asking about last night. It's the night before that interests me, the night Sylvestre was murdered."

"Murdered? The radio said he drowned in his pool."

"He did. You pushed him in when he was drunk, jumped in after him and drowned him, and then you woke Freddy, told him the police were already after him and they'd be sure to blame him for Sylvestre's death."

Young gave a mocking laugh. "This is all a fantasy. You're making it up."

"No, I'm not," said Bruno. "You got to the *chartreuse* around midnight, and you sat beside the pool with Sylvestre, under those outdoor heaters. You were drinking Drambuie, him a lot more than you. And he was smoking joints. He was celebrating because he'd beaten you. He knew where the Bugatti was, and he'd just signed a contract with the owner of this amusement park to buy the place along with all its contents.

"He had one of his Bugatti books there on the table with him and, knowing Sylvestre, he probably started to gloat about how smart and rich he was and to mock you for having failed. You sat there, taking his taunts, getting angrier and angrier, trying to hold it in. When he went to the pool something inside of you snapped. You pushed him, jumped in after him and held his head underwater until he drowned."

"You have no evidence for this outlandish story," Young said.

"Yes, we do. And now we'll take you to the gendarmerie to test your DNA, and I'm pretty sure we'll match it to the traces on the Drambuie glass."

"Not so," Young shouted, triumphantly, shaking his head.

"You were about to admit everything by saying that you cleaned it before you left. I know. And I doubt whether we'll find any traces of you on the joints. That was Sylvestre's little vice, not yours. You don't even smoke. But you forgot one important thing."

"What do you mean? I admit nothing."

"You forgot the towel on which you dried your hair when you came out of the pool after killing him. That's what will convict you. Too bad, while you're in prison the Bugatti will be restored and looking magnificent."

Epilogue

For dinner with the Oudinots, Bruno had thought of taking a bottle of champagne to celebrate the finding of the Bugatti and the closing of the two murder cases. But since the family had been shaken up by events, he decided against it and instead took a bottle of Château de Tiregand from his cellar. It went perfectly with the veal escalopes that Odette had prepared with *morilles* mushrooms that she and her daughter had picked in the woods that day. The first course had been *oeufs mimosa* from goose eggs, for which Martine had made the mayonnaise. And when Bruno had arrived, she had insisted on champagne anyway to toast the end of the family feud.

"You didn't garden today, did you?" Odette had asked by way of greeting. He confessed to digging in some ashes, which she said might bend the lunar rules but probably wouldn't break them.

"I wouldn't get your hopes up," he had replied when Fernand had asked if there was any news yet about Sylvestre's will. He told them about the mortgaged properties in Alsace and the state's determination to seize what was left as criminal proceeds. "Hard to say what's going to happen to the *chartreuse,* but you'll keep your deposit money."

Young was in a police cell in Périgueux, and the British consul in Bordeaux was arranging a lawyer. Annette had arrived at Fabiola's house in tears. Gilles was writing up his story for the *Paris Match* website, with a longer story with photos for the next printed issue. Delaron was preparing his version for tomorrow's *Sud Ouest.* The chassis was now stored securely in the gendarmerie car park, along with the missing transmission, which had been found beneath an old plow.

"So what happens to the Bugatti now?" Martine asked.

"That's up to the mayor and the council," Bruno said. Possession might be nine-tenths of the law, but the commune could not afford a long legal battle with the Bugatti heirs and other potential claimants, he explained. And St. Denis certainly could not afford to pay for the restoration, which was certain to cost millions. Full restoration would mean re-creating the special bodywork, which of course could not be welded because the special alloy Bugatti used contained magnesium. It might not even be legal to re-create it because of the fire risk.

"The mayor is thinking of making a deal with the state, donating the car in return for a very handsome finder's fee and then putting it on display at the national auto museum as one of the greatest cars ever made, and made in France," Bruno said.

There would be a lot of people hoping for a share in that finder's fee, he thought: Étienne, Félix, Jérôme, Gilles and perhaps even Madame Hugon.

"But I don't know whether that idea will last," Bruno went on. "Not after the voters open their copies of *Sud Ouest* tomorrow and learn that it's worth forty million."

"Mon Dieu," said Fernand. "I had no idea any car could be so valuable. Why, for that amount of money we could scrap all the taxes in St. Denis for years and years to come."

Bruno exchanged a glance with Martine and said, "See what I mean about the reaction of the voters?"

He let his eyes linger on her. She was wearing a simple dress of dark blue, her arms bare, and a thin gold chain around her throat that carried a St. Christopher medal. He smiled to himself at the memory of how closely he'd been able to examine it and wondered whether he'd ever be fortunate enough to get so close again. Something of his thoughts must have been clear in his eyes, since she gave him a brilliant smile.

"Sadly, I've got to fly back to London tomorrow for at least a few weeks to find more sponsors for the electric-car rally," she said. "But then I'll be back to find out what happens to the *chartreuse* and Sylvestre's estate."

"So it's au revoir rather than farewell," Bruno said, raising his glass. Ah well, he thought, life would go on. He'd be dining with his friends at Pamela's house the following evening, the now-ritual Monday dinner, and hoping that Fabiola had forgiven him for getting her to ask Annette that crucial question about sleeping with Young.

"If the *chartreuse* somehow comes back to us, I told Dad I'd like to take over the small lodge house since I'll be back here a lot organizing the rally, and it would be good to have a permanent place here of my own." She raised an eyebrow at him as if expecting some reaction.

"In that case, you had better set two conditions," said Bruno. "Your dad will have to let you fix the driveway—"

"And he'll keep the geese back on this side of the hill," Odette interrupted. "You can leave that to me."

Acknowledgments

This tale began with my elder daughter, Kate, a motor-sports journalist who specializes in Formula 1 races and their history. Knowing my interest in the French Resistance during World War II, she asked if I knew the story of William Grover-Williams and Robert Benoist. They were two legendary drivers of the prewar years and close friends. During World War II they together ran a Resistance network in occupied France, arranging arms drops from Britain and carrying out a number of sabotage operations, principally against the Citroën factories. They were betrayed, arrested and killed, Benoist in Buchenwald and Grover-Williams in Sachsenhausen. My daughter then told me of the lost Bugatti, a Type 57 Atlantic, one of four ever built and the only one whose fate remains unknown. She then showed me a photograph of Yvonne Grover-Williams standing beside it in 1937, and another photo of Ralph Lauren's Atlantic. These images of this sensationally elegant automobile took my breath away and, at that moment, this novel came into my head and refused to leave.

I have taken a few liberties with the facts as they are known, suggesting that Grover-Williams was in France in 1941. He was parachuted in the following year. The incident of the downed RAF pilot is invented, but the PAT escape network was real and steered some six hundred airmen and other escapees over the mountains into Spain. Save for the presence of the Bugatti, the burning of Château de Rastignac in March 1944 is as described here. It has happily been rebuilt, to display once again its uncanny resemblance to the White House in Washington. Other than the sad fact that the fate of the lost Bugatti remains unknown (like the fate of the paintings stored at Rastignac), everything else is as faithful to the history of that glorious car as I could make it. I was greatly helped by a genial New York–based Bugatti enthusiast and historian, Walter Jamieson, who was extremely generous with his time and his library, and I am very grateful to him.

The amusement park is my invention, but Jérôme's plan to replace Joan of Arc and Marie Antoinette with a nineteenth-century French village owes a lot to the charmingly re-created village of Le Bournat in Le Bugue, on the banks of the Vézère River. It has an old schoolroom and parish church, a windmill and bakery, functioning workshops for the blacksmith and the knife maker and much more. On Wednesday evenings in summer it offers feasts, with vast joints of ham suspended and roasted over cinders, which are strongly recommended. Of the *marchés nocturnes,* I cannot speak too highly. They have added a wonderful new dimension to the attractions of the Périgord as a great tourist destination. Our family has been attending them since they began in the village of Audrix on Saturdays, which was when my wife first wrote about the culinary charms of these evening events in *Gourmet* magazine. Beaumont-du-Périgord has another excellent night market on Mondays, and now the big towns are offering their own.

All the Bruno books are indebted to my friends and neighbors in the Périgord and the lovely landscape they nurture. It has fertile soil, wonderful food, excellent wines, a temperate climate and more history packed into its borders than anywhere else on earth. It is a very special place, filled with enchantments. As Henry Miller wrote in *The Colossus of Maroussi:*

I believe that this great peaceful region of France will always be a sacred spot for man and that when the cities have killed off the poets this will be the refuge and the cradle of the poets to come. I repeat, it was most important for me to have seen the Dordogne: it gives me hope for the future of the race, for the future of the earth itself. France may one day exist no more, but the Dordogne will live on just as dreams live on and nourish the souls of men.

My profound thanks go to my family, who were the first to read this book, with special gratitude to Kate for giving me the idea and to our basset hound, Benson, on whom I practice dialogue during our walks. I am also very grateful to Jane and Caroline Wood in Britain, to Jonathan Segal in New York, and Anna von Planta in Zurich for their matchless editing skills.

The Bruno, Chief of Police Series

BRUNO, CHIEF OF POLICE

Meet Benoît Courrèges, aka Bruno, a policeman in a small village in the South of France. He's a former soldier who has embraced the pleasures and slow rhythms of country life. He lives in a restored shepherd's cottage, shops at the local market, and distills his own *vin de noix*. He has a gun but never wears it; he has the power to arrest but never uses it. Most of his policework involves helping local farmers—his friends and neighbors—to avoid paying EU inspectors' fines. But then the murder of an elderly North African who fought in the French army changes all that. Now Bruno must balance his beloved routines with an investigation that opens wounds from the dark years of Nazi occupation, and he soon discovers that even his seemingly perfect corner of *la belle France* is not exempt from his country's past.

Mystery

THE DARK VINEYARD

When a bevy of winemakers descend on St. Denis, competing for its land and spurring resentment among the villagers, the idyllic town—where Bruno Courrèges is the only policeman—finds itself the center of an intense drama, with suspicious fires at the agricultural research station that is working on genetically-modified crops. Two young men—Max, an environmentalist who hopes to make organic wine, and Fernando, the heir to an American wine fortune—become rivals for the affections of Jacqueline, a flirtatious, newly arrived Québécoise student of wine. Events grow ever darker, culminating in two suspicious deaths, and Bruno finds that the problems of the present are never far from those of the past.

Mystery

Something dangerous is afoot in St. Denis; in the space of a few weeks, the normally sleepy village sees attacks on Vietnamese vendors, arson at a local Asian restaurant, and subpar truffles from China smuggled into outgoing shipments at a nearby market. All of it threatens the Dordogne's truffle trade, worth millions of dollars each year, and all of it spells trouble for Bruno Courrèges, master chef, devoted oenophile, and beloved chief of police. When one of his hunting partners, a noted truffle expert, is murdered, Bruno's investigation into the murky events unfolding around St. Denis becomes infinitely more complicated. Because his friend wasn't just a connoisseur of French delicacies, he was a former high-profile intelligence agent—and someone wanted him dead.

Mystery

THE CROWDED GRAVE

It's spring in the idyllic village of St. Denis, and for Chief of Police Bruno Courrèges that means lamb stews, bottles of his beloved Pomerol, morning walks with his hound, Gigi, and a new string of regional crimes and international capers. When a local archaeological team searching for Neanderthal remains turns up a corpse with a watch on its wrist and a bullet in its head, it's up to Bruno to solve the case. But the task will not be easy, not with a meddlesome new magistrate, a series of attacks by animal rights activists on local foie gras producers, and a summit between France and Spain approaching—not to mention two beautiful, brilliant women vying for Bruno's affections.

Mystery

THE DEVIL'S CAVE

It's spring again in St. Denis. The village choir is preparing for its Easter concert, the wildflowers are blooming, and among the lazy whorls of the river a dead woman is found floating in a boat. This means another case for Bruno, the town's cherished chief of police. With the discovery of sinister markings and black candles near the body, it seems to Bruno that the occult might be involved. And as questions mount—most notably about a troubling real estate proposal in the region and the sudden reappearance of an elderly countess—Bruno and his colleagues are drawn ever closer to a climactic showdown in the Gouffre de Colombac: the place locals call the Devil's Cave.

Mystery

THE RESISTANCE MAN

It's summer in St. Denis for chief of police Bruno Courrèges, and that means a new season of cases. This time there are three weighing on his mind. First, there's the evidence that a veteran of the French Resistance is connected to a notorious train robbery; then, the burglary of a former British spymaster's estate; and, finally, the murder of an antiques dealer whose lover is conveniently on the lam. As Bruno investigates, it becomes clear that they are connected—however, figuring out how will take every skill he possesses. Add in juggling the complex affections of two powerful women, maneuvering village politics, and managing his irrepressible puppy, Balzac, and Bruno has his hands full once again.

Mystery

ALSO AVAILABLE
The Children Return
The Patriarch

VINTAGE BOOKS
Available wherever books are sold.
www.vintagebooks.com